To recapture the dream

Clive Hopkins

Published by New Generation Publishing in 2020

First Edition

ISBN 978-1-80031-575-4

www.newgeneration-publishing.com

New Generation Publishing

BY THE SAME AUTHOR

SEA STORIES

Challenger's War
China Sea Challenger
Challenger's Way

CRIME FICTION

An Appropriate Death
Remembrance Day
Sister Dear Sister Dead
Dead of Night

ABOUT THE AUTHOR

Born in London, Clive Hopkins served 10 years in the Royal Navy's 'small ships' before emmigrating to Canada where he worked for the Ontario provincial government. Returning to the UK, Clive joined IPC Industrial Press and has published a trilogy of naval faction novels featuring HMS Challenger and a series of crime fiction novels featuring DI 'Dibs' Beacon.

PROLOGUE

1948

Thinking back, Alice supposed she shouldn't have been surprised that he had left her; the real surprise was the cable announcing his impending return and, although unstated, his desire to see her again. He must want to see her, to start again; why, otherwise, would he have told her he was coming?

She had read, folded, unfolded, reread and refolded the cable a hundred times both before and since sending her reply. She hadn't needed to reply; she could have ignored it, refused to acknowledge his existence let alone any right he might think he had to come back into her life. He had left her, gone off to Canada without a word since, though she had to admit he had sent the child a doll.

She had done it all wrong; she knew that. She had loved him and should have kept herself only for him but she knew that that could not have been the way of it; not once it had started, not during the war; things had been different then.

Sure, her first act of unfaithfulness had been an act of charity, a kindness to a frightened boy in a man's uniform but she had to accept that, the second time it had been a way of comforting a desperately unhappy grown man, a grown man far from home and family and told not to come home.

How long had it been since the day they had fought so bitterly? Since the day she had told him in the heat of the argument he could leave if he wanted to, that she didn't need him. Now he was back, not actually back in Chatham, not actually back with her, not yet but soon; tomorrow perhaps.

Welcome home she had said in her reply to his cable but he didn't know where home was. He didn't know that she had since bought the hotel that they had dreamed of. She supposed home to him would be her father's pub, their home when he had gone. She tried to cast her mind back to then, to there, to what they had meant to each other before he had heard about the others.

He hadn't understood then but perhaps he now could; there had never been anyone else. Frank was the man she had wanted then and she had never loved another. She wondered if he could say the same, that there had never been anyone else?

She discarded the thought. Frank was a man; a man that women felt drawn to, a good man, a kind man. Frank was the man she had wanted then that, in truth, she still wanted. Incredibly, she could feel herself beginning to feel the way she had felt then, in nineteen forty three; waiting, waiting for him to come home from the sea as he was now. She looked again at the oval picture frame in which she had pasted their two photos; yes, she would wait for him.

CHAPTER ONE

1943

Alice put down the single broadsheet newspaper and poured a second cup of tea, sweetened it with the half spoonful of sugar the ration would allow and finished the slice of toast remaining on her plate.

'This is the BBC Home Service, Good Morning. Here is the eight o-clock news and this is Alva Liddell reading it.' The unusually up-beat voice on the hitherto un-listened-to wireless, broke through Alice's depression.

'The following telegram, addressed to the Prime Minister, has been received from General Sir Harold Alexander, Commanding the Allied Army Group in North Africa; "Sir. It is my duty to report that the Tunisian Campaign is over. All enemy resistance has ceased. We are masters of the North African shores" '

'The Prime Minister has stated that, with this new victory, the Axis' adventure in North Africa has been crushed and consigned to history; three hundred and twenty thousand German and Italian prisoners will take no further part in the war.' Alice glanced again at the discarded newspaper; the headline underlined how unfair the war was!

- 'COAL MINERS STRIKE FOR £5 MINIMUM' -

Soldiers like those in North Africa and sailors like her fiancé Frank, she knew, would be very happy to receive a £5 minimum wage; she knew also that they couldn't go on strike in the middle of a war. Although Frank's destroyer ran on furnace fuel oil not coal, she decided not to mention this depressing piece of home news when she wrote her weekly letter.

Any one who went on strike for more money at a time like this would be well advised not to show themselves in a military town like Chatham! There had already been fights between sailors and the well paid dockyard workers who didn't have to risk their lives at sea. Most of these had been caused by the suspicion amongst the sailors that the Docky's sons and cousins, nephews and best friend's relatives would all find well paid, relatively safe work in the dockyard, well out of harm's way in the deep shelters during air raids. It didn't have to be true, depression was widespread after four years of war.

Whilst Chatham, like all the other naval ports, was a regular target for the bombers, they were now used to it. She tried to imagine what it must be like for the soldiers in north Africa; for sailors like her Frank, defending the convoys against U-boats. The convoys that brought the sugar she had just spooned into her second cup of tea, the tea itself and probably the wheat from which her toasted bread had been made; even the marmalade was a luxury, there had been no fresh oranges in England for years. She prayed that God would protect Frank and all the other young men, and damned the miners to hell.

She would never tell Frank that she had seen grown men, three striped, twelve years service sailors, sitting crying quietly in the bar downstairs, oblivious of their surroundings. After the last war, her father had told her, they'd called it shell shock. The kindest thing to do was to ignore them, pretend that you hadn't seen them and, when they had had their cry, make sure that they had a pint of Best close at hand; no charge Jack.

It had been on one such occasion that Alice had offered comfort to the young sailor sitting alone in the corner of the saloon bar sobbing quietly into the jumpered arm cushioning his head on the marble topped table. She had sat down beside him and given him a cuddle; one thing had led to another.

In what everyone still regarded as the real world, he had been a junior clerk in a solicitor's office but had joined up as soon as he was old enough. As a trained operator, a TO, in wireless telegraphy, he would spend his war shut away below decks with no idea what was going on above or below him. Just conscious of the noises of gunfire, bombs and depth charges exploding and of his barely controlled fear of torpedoes speeding through the depths of the ocean to tear the bottom out of his ship; he didn't want to die.

He was not even nineteen years old and too scared to tell anybody how scared he was. What had been boyish good looks had been engraved with deep worry lines, his once bright blue eyes now lacklustre supported dark shadowed bags; Alice had done what came naturally to a woman. He never came back but she hoped he was still alive somewhere.

Since then, she had helped another, given comfort for an hour or two between long periods of the fear and uncertainty she could barely imagine. She felt that Frank would understand but hoped that he never found out.

After the war, when they had bought the hotel upon which they had set their hearts, the peace would bring back the commercial travellers, a regular trade which could be relied upon providing she gave them what they wanted; good food, a clean warm bed and a pleasant atmosphere. Most of them were married men and all they wanted was somewhere clean and comfortable to stay. The money was to be made from a regular clientele, not high prices and empty rooms.

With Frank's marriage allowance coming in regularly after they were wed, together with her earnings from working at her father's pub, it would be possible to buy a suitable property. It was simply a matter of timing. To buy just before the war ended and prices shot up. As soon as the war was over Frank would buy himself out of the service and they would live happily ever after; it never crossed her mind that Frank might not marry her.

The News Reader's voice interrupted her thoughts again. 'Russian Government sources have announced that the German Sixth Army is now in full retreat before advancing Soviet forces.' Perhaps, it will all be over soon; she hoped so.

Frank, though uncomfortable, was happy; he had made a decision, he had made up his mind, he knew what he wanted. What he wanted was Alice and not just in the carnal sense, though of course in that way too. Tall for a girl and genuinely blonde, her deep blue eyes had held his since the moment they had met; there was no doubt in his mind; he wanted, he needed Alice.

She had told him of her plan to buy a small commercial hotel when the war was over, when the peace came and everything returned to normal but, whilst his subconscious warmly imagined his future with Alice, his eyes ranged constantly over the twenty eight ships spread out across the dark grey sea. Across this whitecap-flecked monotone, the ships of the convoy huddled together as if for mutual warmth and protection from the elements.

November is not a good month for sailoring in the north Atlantic, indeed, few months are and, although still early in the evening, this far north, the sky was as dark a grey as the sea below it. In every ship, men like Frank waited, poised like sprinters on their blocks, watching. They watched the sky for signs of enemy aircraft and the sea for the tell-tale, feathered wake of a U-boat, its snorkel allowing it to breath fresh air whilst remaining hidden, out of sight just below the surface.

His conscious brain heard the Officer of the Watch ask the Plot if they had anything on radar and their negative reply but in his subconscious he held Alice in his arms, extracting real warmth and strength from the unreal embrace.

All this was now routine. In the four years that Britain had been at war, Frank and tens of thousands like him had learned to exist on two levels at the same time. The present, very conscious level, required for self-preservation and that other level, the level on which normality continued, making the war bearable, making the war worthwhile.

The pitch and roll combined into a screw-like motion that made life onboard hell. Below decks, water dripped down through the forced air ventilation system, spray and rain, windblown into the ventilator intakes on the upper decks, adding to the dampness of the mess decks already full of discarded wet oilskins, wet duffle coats and exhausted sailors. On the open bridge above them, Frank adjusted the towel wrapped round his throat and tucked inside his oilskin to prevent the rain running down his neck.

'Not much of a day, is it Bunts?'

The Officer of the Watch, the ship's only Sub Lieutenant, had completed his latest sweep of the horizon and all between it and his ship with the Barr and Stroud binoculars.

'No Sir. But, with any sort of luck, the subs will decide to stay down and not bother us.'

As a Leading Signalman, Frank was known as Bunts by everyone; a nickname derived from his having control of the bunting, the flags used for signalling when in company with other ships. Strictly speaking, the OOW should have addressed him as Leading Signalman if he expected to be addressed as Sir but that was for the real officers, not these wartime specials.

'Have to keep a good look out though, eh?'

'That's one of the few things you can rely on Sir. It's a hell of a long swim home from here.'

'You can say that again. Not something I fancy at all You're not married are you Bunts?'

Such intimate conversations between the officer of the watch and the close standing signalman were nowadays quite common.

'Not yet Sir. Got a girl lined up for next time I get back to Chatham though. Her Dad's a publican; thought I'd retire and help him drink the profits when this lot's over.'

'I don't think my wife would settle for anything that simple, worse luck. Hope everything works out OK for you.'

'So do I Sir; don't fancy doing this for the rest of my life.'

'Thought you were a long service man Bunts, a regular.'

'A man can change his mind, Sir.'

'Very wise.'

'Aircraft green five O, angle of sight six O.'

The lookout's cry directed every eye to that bearing and the action stations klaxon, its bright red painted button punched by the OOW, brought the Captain up from his sea cabin just below the bridge.

'Where away Sub?'

'Green five five Sir, tracking left to right. I think it's one of ours Sir, looks like a Wellington but it's too far away to be sure.'

'Very good. Stay at action stations 'til you're sure, then stand 'em down. I'll be in my cabin. Oh, and Sub, find out why Radar didn't get it first.'

On this outward, westbound leg of the convoy, most of the merchant ships were empty, riding high and capable of rapid manoeuvre; unlike the eastbound convoy they would meet and bring back. Eastbound, all the ships would be fully laden.

The aircraft flew steadily down the starboard side of the convoy, keeping well out of range of the escorts' gunners. This was no place to be shot down by accident.

'Confirmed Wellington Sir. Brylcream boys having a day at the seaside.'

'Thank you lookout, keep it simple eh?' The OOW bent over the voice pipe to the captain's cabin and opened the weather lid. Confirmed Wellington Sir.'

'OK Sub, revert to defence stations status.'

Most of the old merchant ships that had, in 1939, started the war carrying food and munitions from America - many of them worked out long before the war had even started – had since been sunk by either the Germans or the weather. At least now, most of the ships in convoy were either reliable if middle-aged or new and capable of steaming a few thousand miles without major breakdown. That was no reason for the seaman lookout to relax or the radar or asdic operators to sleep on the job though the constant ping-ping from the asdic sonar loudspeaker was almost soporific. It was when it changed to ping-pong that all hell would break loose. The returning echo warned of a U-boat's presence close to the convoy.

In the bunting store, a four foot high stowage space under the steering platform in the wheelhouse immediately in front of and below the ship's open bridge, Yeoman of Signals Scrumpy Higgins lay curled up and miserable.

At forty two, Scrumpy was by naval standards an old man whose stomach had long since given up all hope of recovery from the effects of large quantities of cider ashore and unending turbulence at sea; if some idiot hadn't started this war, he would have been retired by now, comfortable, ashore. If his messmates knew just how ill he was, some fool would report it to the Captain who would be duty bound to send him to see the medical officer and the MO would be equally duty bound to send him ashore. Scrumpy didn't want to be sent ashore.

What would he do ashore? Teach bloody WRNS how to take jobs from real sailormen? Scrumpy had joined the navy at the height of the depression, when jobs were few and far between, there was no way he was going to teach little girls to take men's jobs away from them, not even in wartime.

Here, in the warm dry store, he could hear the orders from the bridge to the helmsman and the pinging of the asdic. At the first hint of an echo, the change of tone would wake him and he would be on the bridge in less than two minutes. Should he be so soundly asleep that he didn't hear the first pong of the contact, he knew that the quartermaster on the wheel would stamp hard on the platform a few inches above his head, loud enough to wake the dead.

He took a sip from the bottle of illegally hoarded neat rum kept for such moments as this. All was quiet on the bridge, they hadn't had a U-boat contact in days and his stomach was giving him hell. What he needed was the anaesthetised sleep available only from his bottle. It was six o-clock. On the bridge the First Dog watchmen were being relieved and replaced by the men with the Last Dog watch who would stay at their posts until eight. He didn't want any supper, he would stay where he was.

Ashore, Alice unlocked the door of the Public and Saloon bars ready for the evening's trade; she wondered where Frank was, whether he was safe.

It was already dark outside but no streetlight had shed light on The Brook since Mr Chamberlain had announced that, once again, England was at war with Germany and the blackout imposed.

At intervals along the road, the glow of a drawn-on cigarette advertised the position of one of the girls waiting hopefully for a client generous enough to invite her into the warmth of one of the many pubs for a drink. Some would be lucky, for others it would be just one more night's work. The Brook served well as the town's red light district; the servicemen knew where it was, police knew where it was, the girls enjoyed the safety of numbers and the rest of the town could retain its reputation of almost peacetime respectability.

Looking between the merchant ships under their protection, Frank saw movement on the port side of the escort screen.

'Cheviot leaving the screen, Sir.'

'Thank you Bye. Now I wonder where she's off to?'

'No doubt the screen commander will tell us if he wants us to know, Sir.'

'The question was rhetorical Bye, it required no answer.'

'The answer was facetious, Sir, not intended to be taken seriously.'

Whilst happy to acknowledge the OOW's seniority in rank, officers had, occasionally, to be reminded that they were not superior beings.

Unable to signal directly to all the ships in the screen at once, the Screen Commander was advising the Commodore of the Convoy in the old luxury liner now serving as a troopship and in centre of the convoy. Simultaneously, the signal lamps on the Commodore's port and starboard wing bridges relayed Capt D's message to all concerned.

'Cheviot has reported life raft to port, Sir. She's being detached to investigate.'

'I thought all this peace and quiet was too good to be true.' The OOW leant over the voice pipe, lifting the weather lid. 'Captain Sir.'

Scrumpy Higgins appeared on the bridge followed closely by the Captain. They too had heard the Cheviot's siren as she turned away from the screen.

'OK Sub, I heard the report carry on.'

The screen closed up around the convoy, filling in the gap left by Cheviot and resumed their briefly disturbed progress westward.

On Cheviot, stopped now and wallowing in the heavy sea, all eyes were on the sea boat, the twenty seven foot, double ended whaler sent away to recover what appeared to be dead bodies on a life raft. There was no way to tell how long they had been in the water but, as there had been no sinking reported in this sector in the last few days, they could have been drifting for some time. In Cheviot, the watchers preferred not to think such thoughts.

In the boat, the Cox'n swore. 'Keep your fucking minds on the job and your eyes in the boat, it's no good all looking in different directions and trying to pull together at the same time. Two minutes and we'll be inboard. I reckon the First Lieutenant will have broken out a tot for us after a job like this.'

The whaler was lifted and swung inboard. Cheviot turned back towards the convoy to resume her position in the screen. On the bridge, Leading Signalman Dicky Bird was flashing the report of their findings by signal lamp to the Screen Commander whilst, below deck, the Sick Berth Attendant was trying to establish the identities of the recovered bodies. At least, if they could be given a name, they could become people again; they could be buried at sea with due respect and their families advised.

Comus too reverted to routine. The captain left instructions to be called should the need arise, Scrumpy returned to his hidehole and Frank Bye returned to the bridge from the flag deck below to which he had been ordered by the Yeoman in case flag signals should be required.

Soon it would be night and there would be less to see. He almost wished there could be some action but wiped the thought from his mind immediately. Action meant danger and he had every reason to avoid danger now that he had decided to ask Alice to marry him.

Above and ahead of the convoy the Wellington continued its square search pattern that would cover the maximum possible area of sea on either side of the approaching eastbound and fully laden convoy's course. Further to the east, in the UK, it was already night and Alice slept. It had been a busy night in the pub, there seemed to be more sailors about than usual.

The air raid siren woke her. She didn't know how long it had been sounding but her mother was shaking her by the shoulder. 'Come on Alice Love. Your father has gone down to put the kettle on.'

In the pub's cellar, her father had erected the low, table-shaped, steel mesh sided Morrison air raid shelter but they would only crawl into that if the bombs got very close. She hated being confined in there.

It had given quite a lot of innocent amusement to the neighbours when the lorry had come from the second hand shop in Rochester and the men had opened the double trap-door hatch outside the pub and, using the rails normally used to guide the brewery's barrels, slid the two big easy chairs and the sofa down into the space prepared below.

There had been plenty of comments about sitting out the war surrounded by barrels of best bitter but her father had also installed a small stove and laid in a supply of food. If the Germans bombed his pub, he and his could survive down there in some comfort until the heavy gang dug them out.

Alice wasn't afraid; worried of course but not afraid. The bombers were unlikely to be aiming for The Sailor's Return. The dockyard was over a mile away on the other side of the hill and she had noticed, everybody had, that the bomber's routine was to approach the target from the north; having swung round over Sittingbourne and Hoo. This way, they were already on their way home when they dropped their heavy load of bombs. Lightened, they could accelerate and climb quickly away from the target and its massed anti-aircraft guns.

Wrapped in her dressing gown, Alice snuggled into the warmth of the old sofa, her mind drifting to Frank and wondering if he was safe. Her father and mother, well wrapped in the blankets kept down there for such occasions, relaxed in the two big easy chairs. These were old but they were comfortable; they must have come from some big house that had been bombed and been salvaged by the owners or, if they had already been evacuated, liberated by someone else and sold to the second hand shop. The shop probably had scouts who located and arranged the purchase of such furniture, there was a steady demand for it from the Council for less fortunate victims of the bombing; those left with nothing.

She pictured Frank on his ship. For a moment, in her imagination, she saw the ship floating on a deep blue sea and bathed in warm sunshine, like the pictures of luxury liners she had seen in the pre-war magazines or even the navy's recruiting posters. The ground beneath her trembled as a stick of bombs missed the dockyard and exploded closer to the pub; dust, displaced, fell from the heavy wooden beams above her. She wrapped her dressing gown tighter around her to stop the shiver that gripped her. She hated the cellar, most of all she hated the war.

CHAPTER TWO

Frank threw himself on to the open boarding platform at the rear of the double-decker bus pulling away from the dockyard gate and, unable to see any landmarks in the blackout, counted the stops up the Dock Road hill and down into the town. He needn't have bothered, almost half of the passengers squeezed into the bus's two decks got off at the Town Hall where the weekly dance was being held in the ornate ballroom. Frank let the others push past him, making a beeline for the steps into the dry of the Town Hall; his immediate target was not the Town Hall but the Sailor's Return at the other end of The Brook.

A well used shortcut from the Town Hall bus stop to the two cinemas in the High Street, The Brook, a road famous for its pubs and prostitutes, was dark but he didn't need to see where he was going, To his left, as he walked, the unlit King's and Queen's Streets led up from The Brook's northern side towards the Great Lines recreation ground and the old War Memorial, widely asserted to list those who had caught a dose from The Brook's prostitutes during the last war. At the far end, on the corner with Slickets Hill, was the Sailor's Return and Alice. Head down, to keep the light rain out of his eyes, he hurried unglancing past the already positioned working girls sheltering in the dark doorways. He ignored them. Every military town had such a street.

In the months since last seeing Alice their only contact had been letters but, following the delivery of the latest convoy to Greenock, his ship's return to Chatham to be fitted with the latest radar equipment had allowed home leave for those with homes to go to. As an ex-Barnardo's boy, Frank had regarded the navy as home but, from the moment he had met Alice, the Sailor's Return had become his regular home ashore.

Within the three Medway towns, between Rochester bridge in the west and Gillingham railway station in the east, hundreds of pubs made a good living and an attractive barmaid like Alice had her choice of sailors from the ships in the dockyard, from HMS Pembroke the naval barracks or from it's nearby signal school.

There were also hundreds of Royal Marines and even more Royal Engineers from local barracks' if she wished to spread her net a little wider but Chatham was a sailor's town and the Sailor's Return was, for obvious reasons, a sailor's pub. Very few soldiers ventured into it a second time.

Amongst the sailors using the Return, her choice had been limited only by the faithfulness of the married men, the small but, in wartime, inflated number who were of the opposite persuasion and the Admiralty's apparently manic desire to keep sailors at sea. There must, she supposed, be some who didn't go into the available pubs but she had never met one.

He pushed his way through the crowd of drinkers already in the bar and caught Alice's eye. She leaned across the bar and kissed him full on the lips like they did in the American films.

'You got back then, I was worried about you.'

Her smile told him all he wanted to know; she loved him.

'Had someone to come back to, didn't I!'

He knew this conversation was stilted but romantic repartee had not featured largely in his adequate but all male education. In his childhood, any sign of gentleness would have been interpreted as weakness and exploited by his mates. Barnardo's boys were tough and able to hold their own in any situation involving other men but, with women, he knew he lacked sophistication.

'I'll be ready in a minute, Mum's just having her tea.'

16

She put a pint of best in front of him and moved up the bar to serve a crowd that had just come in. This was a busy time and she wished her mother would hurry up.

She had been looking forward to this evening for a week, ever since his entirely illegal telephone call to say that his ship was back, and knew exactly what she was going to say and what she was going to do now that he was back. By the time Frank Bye left the pub in the morning, she had every intention of being officially engaged; whatever Frank Bye might think about it.

She glanced at him; he was looking at her. It wasn't the first time she had been the subject of that look but Frank was different. Frank was a nice man, a gentle man, she knew all there was to know about him and she was sure Frank was the man she wanted.

In the months that they had been writing to each other, they had told each other all about their childhoods, their ambitions for the future and their likes and dislikes. He had told her about the Barnardo's home and the hard times; how he had then passed through HMS Ganges as a Boy Seaman Second Class. He had told her about the ships he had been in after joining the Andrew as sailors called the navy, and he had told her how he envied the married men who had a home to go to and a wife who cared about them when they were away.

She had told him about her Mum and Dad and the pub and that she too hoped to find someone who would be kind to her and gentle and would love her as she would love him. A man who would share her ambition to own a small hotel when the war was over and who would help her run it; a not too strenuous life and quite a good living if properly organised. She glanced at the clock behind her. Seven thirty. Where the hell was her mother!

'I'll put a bottle in your bed, I'll be locking the door at ten thirty, home or not.'

They both knew that this was meaningless as Alice had her own key but it had somehow become a standing joke between them, ever since Alice had been young enough and biddable enough to take orders from her mother.

She fetched her coat from the lobby behind the bar and ducked under the bar flap to join Frank

'Right, let's be having you lad.'

They linked arms and ignored the comments from passing sailors as they walked back along The Brook to the Town Hall. Frank felt ten feet tall. He knew what the other men thought and he didn't care. He knew that Alice was his girl, not some whore he had picked up. He drew her closer to him as if to protect her and she responded.

'I feel safe when I'm with you.'

The seven-piece dance band, the members of which were clearly too old to serve, played with enthusiasm but after two or three dances Frank took Alice to the adjacent lounge and found a table.

The Town Hall had not awarded itself a licence for the sale of alcohol, perhaps fearing the possible consequences of combining alcohol with sailors, and the coffee smelled awful; Frank collected two cups of tea and a small plate of sandwiches from the serving table He saw a tall, dark haired sailor talking to Alice, who glanced up when she said something. Seeing Frank he smiled and moved away.

Not the least surprised nor concerned that someone had tried to chat up Alice whilst he was busy elsewhere, Frank would have done the same thing had the positions been reversed. At a dance, all girls were fair game until they wore a ring, then they were out of bounds; unless of course they gave you the come on. In that event, it was every man for himself.

Some girls wore a ring to discourage unwanted approaches, it didn't necessarily mean that they were engaged or married. In wartime Chatham, there were always at least five fit, young men for every available girl and the ring at least put off the faint hearted; sorted the men from the boys.

On stage, in the ballroom, a girl had been singing to the men that they'd never know just how much she loved them, they'd never know just how much she cared, it was the latest song and Frank wished he could say things like that. The band slid seamlessly from the end of You'll Never Know into American Patrol - from Vera Lynn to Glenn Miller.

'Do you like Glenn Miller?'

Frank followed her out on to the floor. He knew who Glenn Miller was, of course, but had no strong feelings about him or indeed any other dance band. He had to admit though that the Yankee bands, Miller, Dorsey and the others did sound bigger and better than ours. But that's the Yanks, they just had to be bigger and better than everyone else. He wondered idly whether they could fight as well as they played; he suspected that they were going to find out pretty soon now.

'You're not with me' Alice said, 'what are you thinking about?'

'Sorry.'

Frank wasn't a very good dancer but he could manage the waltz, quickstep and the slow foxtrot which was all that was necessary to chat up a girl at a dance and, anyway, it was unmanly to dance too well, all your mates would take the mick. He led her into a spin turn at the corner of the floor and they swept diagonally across the floor in a fishtail, a step she had taught him on his last leave. 'I've got five days leave, then I've got to report back aboard.'

She knew that that meant more Atlantic convoys or, worse perhaps, the Archangel run, dodging U-boats and enemy aircraft in freezing weather all the way to Russia. Taking them the arms and ammunition that we needed ourselves and which the Russians would, as like as not, use against us when this war with Germany was over.

All this good old Uncle Joe Stalin nonsense was all very well for those as believed it and it helped to keep the bolshie factory shop stewards up to speed but, Frank had told her, he had listened to enough communist party speeches to know that whilst we were on their side in this war they were not on ours. They were fighting their own war for their own reasons and were not bothered if a few thousand English Jack Tars died in their cause without knowing what it was. He had seen the writing on the wall at the beginning of the war.

He believed that, when the Berlin-based National Socialist and Workers Party and the Moscow-based Union of Soviet Socialist Republics signed a non-aggression pact, the communist led British miners had promptly gone on strike, thus denying industry the power needed by the munitions factories supplying the Capitalist's war. They had only buckled down to work when Germany had later attacked glorious Mother Russia; the non-aggression pact notwithstanding.

Frank had told her, he wasn't a political animal but he had learned about real life as a Barnardo's boy and he could tell the difference between the so-called Socialist democracy and the real thing.

The Yanks gave him a pain in the arse with all their boasting and their better pay, even their uniforms were made of better material than his, but at least they were on our side. Been a bit late joining in as usual but once in they were now working like hell to get it finished. Alice could see that his heart wasn't in the dance. 'Take me home sweetheart.'

CHAPTER THREE

Alice opened the side door, the entrance to their private rooms upstairs and led Frank to the parlour on the first floor, above the bar. Whatever the state of affairs downstairs, what with the shortages of almost everything, there was no serious shortage up here; she took his coat and pointed to the comfortable- looking, over-stuffed sofa.

'What's your heart's desire?' Alice opened her father's drinks cabinet. 'You name it, I've probably got it. Dad likes to keep a good bar up here.'

Frank spotted a single malt amongst the bottles. He'd fancied drinking that ever since he had read about it in some book, the main character had always ordered a single malt.

'I'll have a single malt.'

Alice wasn't at all sure that her father was going to like his special malt being drunk by Frank but she had to jolly him out of his mood of depression if the evening was going to progress as intended.

She handed him the glass and switched on the electric wall fire.

'I'll put a record on to listen to, I've got the latest Bing Crosby.'

The gramophone up here was much better than any Frank had seen before. He had had one once and had had to wind it up but this was electric and in a very nice wooden cabinet like a piece of good furniture. Bing Crosby was going on about the folks that lived on the hill and Frank put his arm round Alice, drawing her closer.

'He's right, you know. We're Jack and Jill now but it would be nice to grow into Darby and Joan together.'

Alice's heart missed a beat. She had been convinced that she would have to ask him to marry her and here he was, pushing the boat out himself and, for him, very romantically too.

'Are you asking me to marry you?

Frank appeared to think about it for a moment.

'Yes. That is, if you'll have me. I know we haven't known each other for all that long but, in wartime, a week is a long time and we've been going together for nearly nine months. I've been away most of it, I know but we've been writing to each other and going out when I've got back to Chatham. What'll your Dad say?'

'He'll probably insist that you pay for that malt. That's for visitors, not family.'

They were only about a third of the way through the kiss when her mother came up from the bar below. Frank made to break off but Alice held him even tighter.

'Sorry I intruded. I was going to get a sandwich for your Dad. Is there anything I can get for you?'

'Frank's asked me to marry him.'

'You'd better tell your Dad. He may have something to say about that. I reckon if he'd wanted a son, he'd have swapped you for a boy long ago.'

'That means she approves' Alice told Frank 'and, if Mum approves, Dad approves; there's none of this democracy nonsense in this house.'

Frank wondered if he should take that as a warning but the moment passed and the warm feeling remained; I'm engaged to be married he told himself, and I only came ashore for a quick drink. This wasn't strictly true of course but it would be a good put down line for when he told his mates; it would stop them taking the Mickey.

'I've got to get permission from the CO' he said, remembering that in the navy you have to get permission for everything. 'Still, I'm twenty two years old, we've known each other for nine months and you ain't pregnant. That should prove that we are sober, respectable people, even if I'm not completely sober at this moment.'

Alice chose not to ask which King's Regulation or Admiralty Instruction required him to ask his Captain's permission to marry her. The navy was like that, KR's and AI's controlled everything. They would get married on his next home leave and that would be that.

It wouldn't do to rush these things. She would have the Banns called and she would march Frank Bye down the aisle of Saint James' in his number one uniform with his gold badges showing his rank and branch. Leading Signalman Bye, Service number C/JX 836366 would do her very well as a husband and she would give him everything that he wanted from a wife; starting tonight.

Downstairs, her Dad had closed the bar, ushered out all the last drinkers and locked the doors. He had washed the last few glasses in the sink under the bar and stood them on the towel to drain. He switched off the bar lights and turned to the stairs.

'Arthur. Your daughter says she's going to get married.'

Alice's mother had a way with words.

'She'll have to wait 'til tomorrow, I'm too tired to give her away to anybody tonight.'

Alice, listening through the open parlour door smiled. There would be no argument from Dad.

If the truth were known, he would probably be glad to get her off his back. Unmarried daughters in their twenties were not a thing to be encouraged. He'd do all he could to expedite the match.

Alice's mother called to Frank from the kitchen. 'You had better start calling me Sylvia; after you're wed, you can call me Mum and do as you're told like the rest of the family.'

'We'll take our supper upstairs', Arthur said, poking his head round the door; 'leave you two down here to talk.'

He hadn't congratulated Frank, nor for that matter Alice, but Frank understood. Lots of people were diffident about talking about really important things. Approval had been given and Frank knew that, henceforth, he was part of the family.

After the wedding, Arthur would call him Son, probably just the once but that would make the relationship formal. He looked across at Alice standing by the drinks cabinet, refilling his glass. She looked pleased and happy and that was good enough for him, they were as good as wed.

The record had finished long ago and Alice put on another. They sat on the sofa looking at each other.

'I love you very much, it's just that I'm not very good at saying it.'

She took his hand in hers. 'I'll teach you how to say all sorts of things that a girl likes to hear.'

In the background, Bing Crosby sang again, ignored by them both. Frank hadn't expected his proposal to be accepted as readily as it had been and he was unprepared for the assumption by Alice that he would be staying the night with her. Not just with her but in her bed. Hell! He hadn't thought to bring the necessary ashore with him, he would have to be careful and withdraw; he didn't want to get her pregnant now, not now that they were to be married; plenty of time for that when the war was over.

The needle spiralled noisily into the centre of the record, demanding their attention, forcing Alice to climb out of their embrace and to attend to it before it did any damage. Needles were in short supply, particularly metal ones, she didn't like the more muted sound produced by the fibre needles now available. She shut the lid and switched off the machine, she had heard her parents' door close some time before. 'Come on, we can go up now.'

With the ceiling light out, he pulled back one of the blackout curtains. Above the rooftops, he could see the stars and hoped that there wouldn't be a raid tonight. What was he doing? Thinking about bombers and air raids!

Lying beside Alice, her head cradled against his shoulder, he could still see the stars. Somehow, it was less urgent now. Not like all those other times when, having got to bed, it seemed necessary to rush into coitus before the girl changed her mind or, worse, before he lost his nerve and, with it, his ability.

'Penny for them.'

'Not worth a penny really. I was just thinking that now that I'm here in bed with you, something I've dreamed about hundreds of times, I don't want to rush at it like some drunken matelot in a brothel, I want it to take a long time.'

'So do I. Here, give me your hand.' She guided his hand inside her nightdress and over her breast. 'Now, gently, tease me a little, just lightly, that's right. Now rest a moment, make me want you to do it again then do it again a little more urgently but still gently; don't hurt me, that's right love, tease and squeeze, be gentle with me, lead me rather than drive me.'

He kissed her lips, his tongue moistening them and forcing its way through to meet hers coming from the other direction. He felt her arch her back pushing her breasts towards him. He felt himself hardening. Her hand found him and guided him towards her.

'I think you're going to be a good lover once we get used to each other and I'm going to teach you to be good for me.'

'I'm going to like that.'

Another four days of this would be the happiest four days of his life. If her father would spare her, they would just enjoy being together. Before the war, there had been a paddle steamer plying between Chatham and Southend in Essex but not now, of course. The Medway Queen had gone of to Dunkirk in nineteen forty and had remained in military service as a minesweeper ever since; pity, he wanted to take Alice somewhere special. They could discuss it in the morning; there must be somewhere to go, even now in the middle of a war.

As he drifted off to sleep, he was sure they'd think of somewhere to go,

CHAPTER FOUR

HMS Comus, together with the other ships that would form the convoy escort group, lay to the buoys in the centre of Lough Foyle. All had refuelled on entry from the big oil tanker moored in midstream where she was accessible to the warships and as far as possible from the town of Londonderry. Should she be bombed and explode, only minimal damage would be done ashore.

There could be no doubt that the Germans knew she was there and that the Foyle was used as a base for the anti-U-boat and mine sweeping flotillas of the British and one or two other navies.

On shore, one side of the Lough was in British Ulster and the other in neutral Eire; a country divided in its loyalties. The vast majority were anti-Nazi but enough to worry the Admiralty were sufficiently anti-British to present a possible source of trouble; certainly a source of intelligence to the enemy.

Onboard the moored ships, armed sentries patrolled the upper decks twenty-four/seven. All small boats seen were challenged and, if they drew too near, the duty watch of seamen would be called, ready to repel a boarding party or to ensure that limpet mines could not be attached to the ship's hull. The order to open fire on any boat suspected of ill-intent could be given by the Officer of the Watch without reference to higher authority.

Alongside the wharf, a little Hunt class destroyer was being repaired. For major damage she would have gone to Belfast but, for superficial damage from air attack, this was a more convenient base; and a hundred miles nearer her north Atlantic patrol area.

Alongside the wharf also, three trawlers converted for minesweeping, lay, their ship's companies taking a well-earned rest from the constant day-in day-out drudgery of sweeping and re-sweeping the narrow channels used by the convoys from America and elsewhere. Their patch was southwards from the north channel, between the Mull of Kintyre and the Fair Head, to and into the Firth of Clyde. Further south, past the Mull of Galloway, the Isle of Man and into the Mersey; the safe channel was maintained by sweepers based in Belfast Lough .

North from the Mull of Kintyre, past Islay and the Mull of Oa, and out into the deeper water too deep for moored mines, the little trawlers from Londonderry maintained a daily sweeping schedule finding and killing the floating mines sown by German aircraft and submarines every night.

Comus, Constance, Cheviot and Cossack swung to their buoys, ammunition lighters alongside, replenishing the little expended in defence of the last convoy. So little had been used, indeed, that it was more a matter of routine than of necessity. Further up the Lough, Cheerful, Chequers and Chancy waited their turn.

Relatively new, Cossack was the latest member of the flotilla, a replacement for the Tribal Class ship that had famously captured the Altmark but subsequently been lost. She was the new, and better equipped, leader of the Flotilla. These ships were the outcome of three years of anti-aircraft and anti-U-boat warfare experience translated into steel plates and electronics.

Two thousand five hundred and fifty tons fully equipped for sea, she was fitted with three 4.5 inch guns as main armament and seven 40mm anti-aircraft guns; four 21 inch torpedo tubes completed her armament just in case she was required to take on a German surface warship.

Unlike older destroyers, she had no depth charges aft but carried a multi-barrelled mortar where X-gun had been in the original design. Called, for no known reason, the Squid, this fired its projectiles forward over the top of the ship to land in front of her. In this way, the ship did not have to run over the enemy submarine's position to attack, she could pinpoint its position using the asdic anti-submarine indicating system then turn towards and fire. Canted slightly to starboard when fired, the projectiles missed their own ship's bridge by what seemed like a hair's breadth to those standing underneath.

Capable of over thirty knots, this class of ship served a multi-purpose role but, under present conditions, had a short life expectancy. Comfort had not been a major consideration in the design and shore leave was therefore uppermost in everyone's mind when in harbour.

'Libertymen to muster on the upper deck.'

Preceded by the Bosun's mate's pipe call, the broadcast over the ship's P A system spurred those going ashore to greater haste. Caps were straightened, white lanyards adjusted to show outside the narrow black silk scarf worn under the collar and through the bowed tapes in the front of the uniform jumper. All this clobber had reputedly had some use in the days of sail but served no possible purpose now. Even in wartime, the more anchor-faced of the Petty Officers and above could refuse leave to any sailor not properly dressed according to KR's and AI's. Frank heaved a sigh of relief, the OOD was one of the wavy line sailors of the RNVR. More interested in surviving the war and returning to civvy street than in King's Regulations and Admiralty Instructions.

Arriving ashore, the overloaded liberty boat, an MFV which in peacetime had been a motorised fishing vessel and, in wartime, served the fleet as a stores carrier, a mail boat and for any other duties that could be devised, bumped alongside the steps leading down from the wharf. Forty five libertymen, each with his own idea of what to do with his shore leave, stormed up the steps.

'Last boat back is midnight. Miss that and you're adrift and in the rattle.' The PO in charge of the MFV grinned at them, disappearing quickly along the wharf towards town, 'and don't try swimming it, the Irish crocodiles like the taste of English sailormen.'

Frank Bye, Mike Morse, known as Micky Mouse of course, Stripey Hodge and young Dick A'hern, one of the sparkers, knew where they were going. Having been into Londonderry before, they knew that such action as there was likely to be would be at Rosie's Kitchen, a pub not far from the docks and a firm favourite with sailors. By halfway through the evening, Rosie would be as drunk as most of her customers and standing on a table in the bar singing 'On the banks of the FFFFoyle', spittle spraying over anyone fool enough or drunk enough to be within range.

They elbowed their way into the Public and up to the end of the bar furthest from Rosie who was already in full voice. Londonderry was a good place for pubs and drinkers, war or no war. The quantity of the booze of all kinds, which washed over the border from the neutral Republic, was sufficient to maintain cordial relations between all present with no hint of shortage or rationing. Not like at home.

Young Dick, Trained Operator Wireless Telegraphy and all of eighteen years old, drained his first pint like an old sweat. Frank and Stripey, so called for his single good conduct stripe, took all of three or four seconds longer, ready for the second as soon as they could catch the eye of the girl behind the bar.

She was said to be Rosie's daughter but, if she was, Rosie had been an early starter; the barmaid was forty if she was a day; though heavily camouflaged by Max Factor. Rosie herself was one of those women who could be any age, one of those women who appeared to have stopped the ageing process somewhere about middle age and marked time since. She was reported to know enough names and addresses of accommodating young ladies to keep the entire British Grand Fleet in harbour for a month but, the boys weren't interested; tonight they were going on to the Corinthian Ballroom in town for a dance.

With two pints inside them, Frank and the others caught a bus into town. Away from the docks,

Londonderry was really a very nice town with a history of staunch patriotism and a proud record of defiance against the efforts of the Catholic minority to unite the six counties of Ulster with the Republic.

None of the visiting sailors knew or cared about the rights or wrongs of the Irish partition in '26, none of them had been born then. All they knew was that they had been warned to be on their guard against gangs of IRA sympathisers who would happily reduce their number if it would hurt the English. There were certain areas of Londonderry, referred to by the Catholic inhabitants as Free Derry, where it was better if sailors didn't go.

Luckily, the Corinthian wasn't in such an area and was a popular resort for those not determined to get as drunk as possible as quickly as possible. There, they could get drunk slowly and, with anything like reasonable luck, find a girl too.

CHAPTER FIVE

She was beautiful. Long dark hair, a waist half the size of her bust and hips, she was not dancing. Dick saw her first and left Frank and Stripey standing at the side of the dance floor.

'May I have this dance?'

The band were playing a tango and Dick hadn't the faintest idea how to do it but he considered this only a minor disadvantage. She wouldn't discover that he couldn't tango until after he had her in the middle of the floor and the chances were, once on the floor, she would stay there until at least the end of that tune. With any luck, it would be something that he did know how to do next and he could keep her on the floor and to himself.

'Are you a proddy?'

'Am I a what?'

'Are you a protestant?'

For the life of him, Dick couldn't imagine what that had to do with anything but admitted to being C of E, though not very often. This was not the usual chat up line Dick was accustomed to in England and he tried to steer the conversation into more regular territory.

'This is the first time I've been in Londonderry,' he lied,' are there many dance halls like this here?'

Dick swerved to avoid what he took to be another couple but which turned out to be a mirrored pillar in the middle of the floor.

'Sorry about that, thought it was two other people.'

'You'll get used to that. What's your name?'

The music stopped and Dick realised that he had got away with it. She had not complained about his inability to dance the tango. He dawdled as he led her off the floor, hoping that the music would start again before they reached the table at which she had been sitting but the band were walking off stage for their break.

'May I buy you a drink?'

'I don't drink alcohol but I'd like a cup of tea and a cake if you're flush with money.'

Dick caught Frank's eye and winked as she sat down at the table and he went to the bar in search of tea. Ah well, she was going to be cheap anyway. Perhaps tonight was going to be his lucky night, and sober too; he found two cakes and carried the tea to the table.

'I wish I was based here in Londonderry, maybe we could see each other regularly then.'

'I don't go steady with anyone and, certainly not a sailor. My Da would kill me!'

The band returned to the stage and announced the next dance as a foxtrot, they danced every dance after that. At ten, the bandleader announced the last waltz and Dick led her out on to the floor. With luck, he thought, she would let him take her home and there just might be somewhere to stop on the way, some nice deserted spot where they could get to know each other better.

'May I take you home?'

'You can walk me to my bus, if you like.'

'I'd like to go all the way with you.'

There, that should be plain enough for any one, she couldn't not understand that.

'But there'll be no bus back if you do.'

'I'll walk back. I don't have to be back onboard until midnight.'

'Well, it isn't far and you look like a fit young man.'

Bingo! He had struck gold tonight. Nothing could have been clearer than that. He was on to a winner. One he could boast about back onboard as the others had seen her with him and would confirm that she had been a real beauty.

The crowded bus stopped at the end of a long, dark road of small, terraced houses. The blackout was complete and she pulled a small torch from her handbag.

Half way down the road, his eyes were becoming more accustomed to the dark and he saw the alleyway between the terraces before she led him into it. Here the darkness was complete, total, except for the small circle of light made by her torch. She tipped it upwards, into his eyes.

He didn't hear a thing. He hadn't heard even one footstep since they had entered the alleyway but whoever hit him was right behind him; close enough to draw blood with the first blow.

'Get the fucking proddy's wallet' a man's voice said. 'we don't want to kill the Brit for nothing, do we?'

'Don't kill him, he's too young to die for a few quid.'

'Then take his fucking money and his ID and get going.'

'We'll leave the fool his boots and his life to thank God for.'

'Fuck that, those boots are good leather, I can get a few quid for them.'

It was light when he woke up, only just but light enough for him to see that he was lying in a pool of his own blood and that it had dried and stuck his hair to the pavement. He tried to raise his head and instantly regretted the manoeuvre. God, it hurt. In fact, just about every part of him hurt, they had done a magnificent job on him, he had been kicked comprehensively.

Footsteps stopped at the end of the alley.

'Hey you! What are you doing?'

The voice was rough, a beer drinker's voice but not unkind.

'God almighty,' it said, 'you're in one hell of a state. I'll get help.'

Dick could hear him knocking at the door of the house to the right of the alleyway's entrance.

'There's a poor benighted Englishman in the alley with his head all kicked in. I think he needs an ambulance if not a hearse.'

Footsteps gathered round him; shoes, female shoes, and a couple of pairs of working men's boots. The boots moved to either end of his aching body and lifted him.

'God but someone did a fine job on him.'

'That's the trouble with the blackout. Anyone could be lurking down an alley in the dark. What would a British sailor be doing down an alley in this part of Derry in the middle of the night anyway?'

'Well whatever he was doing down here last night, he has two problems this morning. Not only is the poor soul an Englishman, he's a very poorly Englishman with no boots.'

This raised a laugh and even Dick thought that, in almost any other circumstances, he could have enjoyed the joke. This morning however, he was in no condition for humorous banter. The settee was soft and the newspaper under his head kept his blood from the upholstery.

'Get Mrs Hearsey from number nineteen,' the owner of the settee said, 'she used to be a nurse and will be able to clean him up a bit. We can't have the poor soul dripping blood all over County Londonderry.'

The doctor at the military hospital had had him cleaned up, stitched up and stood up.

'Can't have you littering up my hospital.'

The military police had been summoned and waited outside in the 15cwt truck; no ambulance this trip. Kicked head or not, he was absent without leave and that was a crime.

'In the back, Jack.'

The instruction was clearly an order and Regulating Petty Officers are unaccustomed to having their orders questioned. Just my luck, he thought, get my head kicked in last night and get put in the rattle this morning. Whilst getting put in the rattle after a good run ashore was an occupational hazard accepted by sailors in every navy, getting yourself half kicked to death was definitely overdoing it.

A run ashore was supposed to be a pleasurable experience but he was going to regret this run ashore for some time. Not to mention the pain in his ribs, his kidneys and almost everywhere else, his head had a fire burning inside it. The symbol of Ulster was the red hand he remembered; now he knew why.

Delivered to the wharf and on to the MFV, Dick nursed his wounds quietly. The escort took his duties less than enthusiastically this morning. It had been a hard night and he was in no mood to be mucked about by some sprog sailor but, from the look of him, this one had had a highly professional working over.

'Drunk?'

'No such luck. If I'd been drunk, I probably wouldn't feel so bad. Took some girl home and got done over in an alley. Took my money and my paybook ID. even took my boots. I'll know her when I see her again.'

'Don't even think about it son, you wouldn't live to tell the tale, it's one of their less appealing local customs. Chat up some poor gormless sailorman, take him down a dark alley and lift his paybook, wallet and boots. The boots they sell, the money they spend and the paybook they give to the IRA who will use it to send one of their sabotage specialists into the dockyard in Belfast where he can do some patriotic damage.'

Not a bad bloke, Dick thought, for a cop. Military Police, all military police whether navy, army or even the other lot, were selected on the basis of being natural born bastards but, for a natural born bastard, this bloke seemed decent enough

At the gangway, he climbed aboard. 'You were lucky last night, son. Next time they'll bloody kill you.'

The MFV pulled away, heading back to the wharf. The quartermaster looked at him without pity.

'OK, get below and dressed in the rig of the day. You're on OOD's report at 1100.'

The flotilla formed line ahead, following Cossack out of the Lough. In a couple of hours they would meet and form a screen around a convoy out of Liverpool and escort it halfway to America. Mostly empty ships again, going to collect more war materials but valuable, even empty.

In Chatham, the Return was full of sailors, there seemed to be more sailors in Chatham than for a long time. The barracks was full to overflowing and something was obviously pending; something which would require a lot of sailors.

Alice wondered what it could be but didn't ask; she had seen the posters everywhere advising 'Be like Dad, keep Mum' and 'Careless talk costs lives'. She knew better than to ask anyone in the pub what was up but something was, that was clear.

At sea, Frank settled into the sea routine of sleeping, eating and keeping his watch on the bridge. In his mind, however, Alice kept him company; from now on, she would always be there with him and, he liked that idea.

CHAPTER SIX

Many of the American soldiers had found their way into local towns like Chatham. The trouble with the Yanks, Alice had heard said often enough in the bar, was that they had too much money; it wasn't fair but the girls had already noticed that many of them came from small country towns in the middle of nowhere and, oh boy, were they naive! If they wanted something, they would pay the asking price without a murmur.

All the girls knew that these boy-men had been told by their officers that, when they arrived in England, they must not cause trouble, must not boast about how much better it was in the good old US of A, must not take the mick out of the British servicemen in their poor quality, ill-fitting uniforms and with little money in their pockets. They had been told to remember that the Brits had been fighting the Nazis since 1939 and that it had been a long, hard war for them until they, the Americans came to their rescue.

They had been told to respect the local women whose husbands and boyfriends were away fighting and, like all good soldiers, they had said 'Yes Sir' and promptly forgotten the instructions. In the real world, women were women and it was every man for him self.

In Houston, Tex's father owned a service station and auto rental business that had been doing pretty well when Tex left but he had heard from his mother that the old fool had volunteered for the army. Silly old fool, he was too old to fight anyone; God, he had been in the last war! He wouldn't last through basic training, he would be sent home to look after the family business until Tex could get back to take over.

There was money to be made in auto rentals. The war had done wonders for the US economy and the demand for oil had made Texas the richest state in the Union as well as the biggest. After the war, there would be fortunes to be made by a man with big ideas and Tex had big ideas but, until he could get back to the good old US of A, he would just have to do what came naturally.

Cars here were cheap and, if he could get a supply of gas, he knew that he could rent them out to American soldiers who were not used to catching rare and unreliable buses or walking miles into town. Sure, the army laid on trucks but Tex knew that a fleet of taxis was a sure fire money spinner. Might just make a nice nest egg for when he got home. If he could find a supply of gasoline, there was a fortune to be made out of this little old war, just as long as you didn't get personally involved in the fighting and, he had met the girl who could make it all come true.

Actually, he had met her father who owned a local bar into which he had wandered unknowingly when in town. He didn't understand this sailor or soldier only pub nonsense, to him, money was money, take it and don't ask questions. He would talk to her about getting a couple of autos. She had seemed like a sensible, business-like girl and, if the scheme they had discussed worked, he would cut her in for a few pounds; not a lot but enough to ensure continuity of supply and a couple of unquestioning drivers.

At sea, as far as Frank could see, there was no discernable line where the sky met the sea. The driving rain totally obscured the horizon and dark grey clouds mimicked the colour of the sea perfectly. Comus was suspended between the two, totally unable to counter the effects of either whilst suffering from the effects of both.

To starboard, the sea marched endlessly across liquid hills and dales within which other ships appeared and disappeared as they lifted and fell on the swell that had come all the way from America. Out there, below the unseen horizon and unknown to the convoy, a merchant ship lay without power and totally at the mercy of the sea. Torpedoed and holed, with her number one hold flooded, the old three-island steamer Port Isaacs lay broached to between the heaving seas. The Chief Engineer hoped to be able to restart the main engines soon but the movement of the helpless ship made his endeavours more difficult than they would otherwise have been.

Down by the head, the screw stood idle above the water. Any attempt to restart the engines must wait until the ship could be trimmed and the screw lowered back into the water. Below, the pumps were trying to lower the water level in number one hold whilst flooding number four. With luck, and if the dividing bulkheads held, the Port Isaacs could be trimmed sufficiently to bring her screw back into the water and allow her to creep home to lick her wounds and deliver her much needed cargo.

On the open bridge of the destroyer, Frank Bye's binoculars were almost useless as the horizontally driven train and spray wetted the lenses. The captain, cocooned within his oilskins, sat in the high chair just aft of the binnacle from which position he had a good all-round view and was not in the way of the Officer of the Watch.

Normally, when the captain was on the bridge, Yeoman Higgins would have been there also but the captain himself had directed Scrumpy to go below. There was no point in his standing there getting soaked and tired when there was most unlikely to be any requirement for his specialist skills. Leading Signalman Bye could work watch and watch with him, ensuring that both were rested and alert when required.

Scrumpy had been pleased enough to go below into the dry but had made it quite clear to Frank that this wouldn't have been allowed by a professional, a proper Captain RN. If the captain was on the bridge, the Yeoman was on the bridge; that was the way it was done in the real navy.

'Bloody week-end sailors.'

A signal light flashed from the escort Screen Commander in Cossack. Frank abandoned his binoculars and squinted into the wind to read it.

Cheerful was being detached from the starboard side of the screen to search for the Port Isaacs, reported stopped and making water somewhere to the north of the convoy's present position.

It was standard practice for a lone U-boat to shadow a convoy, out of range of the escort's asdic and fall upon any merchant ship unfortunate enough to have trouble keeping up. Convoys moved at the best possible speed of the slowest vessel but it was by no means unknown for old, overworked and poorly maintained ships to fall by the wayside. If possible an escort would be detailed to stand by her until the problems could be rectified but this was not always possible. In this event, the one had been abandoned to save the many.

The thought crossed Frank's mind that, on the whole, he would rather be in Chatham with Alice, he said a silent prayer that trouble would not find them this trip.

Like all sailors, Frank believed in God though, like most sailors, he didn't believe in the church. Like all sailors however, he believed that a short, carefully worded prayer was never wasted.

In his mind, Alice stood like a lighthouse, her welcoming light offering comfort and the assurance of safety. One day, secure with Alice, he would be able to look back on these years with a mixture of joy and sorrow even, perhaps, a little pride. His joy at finding Alice though complete would be leavened by the memories of so many friends, friends of friends and the countless, unknown dead men who had helped win the war but would never see the peace.

He dragged his attention back to the present, putting behind him all thoughts of death; thoughts of death must not be allowed to take possession of even the smallest, darkest corner of his mind or all would be lost.

'Quartermaster.'

'Sir.'

The captain leaned over the voice pipe so that his voice wasn't blown away.

'Have your Mate organise some kye for the bridge staff, will you.'

'Aye aye, Sir.'

Lt. Cdr. Horton closed the lid on the voice pipe to prevent the rain finding its way down into the wheelhouse.

'Oh, good idea Sir.'

'Yes Sub and you should have thought of it first.'

'Oh, Sir. Yes Sir.'

'I'm going below Sub.'

'Yes Sir. Very good Sir.'

The kye arrived and the day faded into dusk.

'You're deep in thought Bunts.'

The OOW felt like talking and, as the signalman, Frank was now the only man on the bridge who could be talked to without interfering with his concentration.

'Thinking about after the war, Sir.'

'We should live so long. Still, I suppose one has to make some sort of plans.'

'Yes Sir. Had what you might call a better offer.'

The OOW knew better than to enquire too closely into a rating's private affairs but more interesting than just standing here on the bridge watching everything and seeing nothing.

'Good for you.'

'Going into the hotel business Sir. After I get married that is, of course.'

'Sounds like a good idea but do you know anything about the hotel business? It's not something you can just decide to do without some training I imagine. Like everything else I suspect, you have to have some sort of qualifications for it though, come to think of it, after some of the hotels I've stayed in, one has to wonder.'

'My wife to be is already in the business, Sir. We should be alright. She's a bright girl; must be if she's going to marry me, eh Sir.'

'I think I'll pass on that one Bye, if you don't mind.'

Frank smiled behind his binoculars as he did another sweep. Dead cagey these young officers, not prepared to commit themselves even in idle banter. The awkward silence was broken by Frank's seeing a shrouded light

41

flashing from Cossack. He read the faint blue light signalling from the Screen Commander.

'Signal from Captain D, Sir. Cheerful has found the Port Isaacs and is standing by her until daylight. Port Isaacs will proceed independently. Cheerful will return to the screen. ETA 1140z'

'Thank you''

'Captain Sir.' this down the voicepipe.

'Yes Sub?'

'Cheerful has found the Port Isaacs but she seems to be alright and will proceed independently in the morning. Cheerful will return to the screen, ETA 1140z.'

'Thank you Sub.'

In his sea cabin, little more than a bunk in a box, Lt. Cdr. Horton switched off the light again and closed his eyes. He wanted to apologise to the young Sub Lieutenant for being sharp with him about the kye but, of course, it wasn't possible. Captains do not apologise to Sub Lieutenants, not in the Royal Navy. He reached out in the dark and found the framed photograph of his wife, turned and looked at her in the dark.

'I promise you, Dot, I'll come home to you and, when this war's over I'll never leave you again.'

He heard her voice as he had when he had left her in London three months ago.

'Take care Darling, don't do anything silly, will you?'

Silly? God, he was going to be the least silly ship's captain in the whole of nautical history. He felt the ship turn on to the next leg of the zig zag course but nothing after that. With luck, he would sleep until morning.

CHAPTER SEVEN

Mrs Lt. Cdr. Horton had gone home to her parents when it had become obvious that her husband would not be coming home very often. Their London flat had been let to a young Staff Officer with a nice safe job somewhere under London; he probably knew where her husband was though she didn't.

Whilst Dot Horton suffered the sympathy of her parents, the London flat entertained a succession of off duty WRNS and innumerable previously unemployable debs, working as drivers for an assortment of Admirals, Generals and other top brass. Dot suspected that there were two wars going on and her husband was involved in the wrong one.

Before the war, Edward Samuel 'Punny' Horton had successfully maintained and improved the accountancy business inherited from his father. He had thus been in a position to spend quite a lot of his time and money on his forty-five foot ketch, The Bottom Line.

Whilst he enjoyed that little joke, puns were his real hobby; making them, collecting them and keeping a record of every one he came upon; one day, he had told Dot, he was going to publish an anthology of puns. He was sure there would be a good market for such a publication; perhaps it would make him rich.

Sometimes, nowadays, he wondered what had happened to the world in which such nonsense was acceptable or even possible. Sitting swathed in oilskins on the bridge of Comus in the north Atlantic was not his idea of being a sailor. Still, his experience in The Bottom Line had led to his membership of the RNVR and that, in turn, to the award of his second gold ring quite soon after his call-up in '39.

Knowledge of small ships was particularly valued, he had been told when they drafted him to the minesweeper in Sheerness. What they had meant but would not say was that capital ships, the battlewagons, fleet carriers and the heavy and even the light cruisers were reserved for the regular navy officers with a structured career to follow, war or no war. Such professionals were not to be squandered on sweepers, boom defence vessels, corvettes and the like; they were far too valuable. These dirty, uncomfortable and usually very dangerous postings should be awarded to the HO's, the Hostilities Only's, both Wardroom and Lower Deck.

The first pong from the asdic, indicating an underwater contact, coincided with the onset of torrential rain; the sort of rain that invariably found its way between the towel inside his oilskin neckband and the short hairs on the back of his neck, cold, wet and likely to continue for some time.

'Contact bearing green four zero. Confirmed submarine.'

That was why they all saw the lifeboat.

'Check contact, surface target on that bearing.'

'Definitely submarine Sir. Quite close to the surface, shouldn't wonder if she is having a look at us, Sir.'

The Klaxon for action stations sounded throughout the ship.

'Starboard twenty, revs for twenty five knots.'

The officer of the watch looked at the Captain .

'She must be sitting just under the lifeboat.'

'Lookouts. Any signs of life in that boat? Yeoman, make to Captain D. Have confirmed echo, am attacking. Get the bearing from the OOW.'

'Three bodies in the boat Sir.'

The starboard lookout's face was ashen. In this situation, the destruction of the U-boat must take precedence over the safety of any men in the boat; the Captain had no choice. If the U-boat escaped it could attack and sink any number of ships, killing many more sailors than presently lay in the bottom of the lifeboat. They looked dead already; the Captain sincerely hoped that they were.

'Let's see if we can prise her loose from her camouflage. Officer of the Watch,' The use of the full and proper title made any argument impossible. 'Steer directly for the boat as if we are about to drop depth charges. With luck, our gallant U-boat commander doesn't know that we don't carry any.'

He took in the horrified expression on the face of the young Sub Lieutenant.

'Do it!'

Ah well, he had to learn sometime that war isn't a game. War is systemised extermination; the winner was the one still alive at the end.

'Just a touch on the wheel at the last possible moment, if you will, Sub. See if we can miss the boat by enough to avoid overturning it but close enough to make the U-boat think we are going to depth charge or ram him. If we can flush him out, we might just get him and pick up the men in the boat too.'

The remote possibility of avoiding the deaths of the men in the boat was reflected in the slight lessening of the strain shown on the face of the young Sub. He bent his head over the voice pipe to the wheelhouse.

'Coxswain.'

'Sir.'

'Can you see the lifeboat ahead?'

'Intermittently, Sir.'

'Well, Coxswain, there is a U-boat immediately underneath it and the Captain would rather like to scare the shit out of it. I shall be ordering a minor change of course at the last moment. I don't want to hit the boat but I must flush out the U-boat that's underneath. Do you understand?'

'Aye aye, Sir.'

The Coxswain looked through the narrow slot of glass in front of him. In the middle of it, the Kent Clear View Screen's rotating disc of glass threw the rain and spray off, giving him the best possible view ahead. Normally there would be no need for him to see where he was going, simply to steer the course given but, in occasional situations, the ability to see what he was doing could help a great deal.

To the side of him, the Able Seaman on the engine room telegraph had heard the Sub's instructions and he also fixed his eyes directly ahead as if, simply by multiplying the number of eyes looking, they could improve the chances of avoiding the boat.

There was little chance and they knew it. In this sea and at this speed, the whole idea was ridiculous but, at least, the Old Man was going to try not to run down the sailors in the boat. With the destroyer's sharp bow bearing directly down upon them the U-boat would have little chance of a hit from a torpedo launch. Almost certainly any torpedoes launched would pass down either side of the approaching ship, deflected by the bow's pressure wave and be wasted.

Punny Horton was alright. As officers went, he was one of the best; he didn't get his manoeuvres from any Admiralty book of instructions to seamen.

'Target breaking left and going down fast.

The report from the asdic plot came only just in time.

'Hard to port Coxswain.'

There was discernable relief in the Sub Lieutenant's voice as he gave the order.

'Midships. Meet her. Asdic, give me a bearing as soon as possible.'

'Wheel amidships Sir, steady on zero seven zero.'

'Target depth now fifty feet, bearing zero nine zero, tracking left, range eight hundred.'

'Thank you plot. Wheelhouse, steer one one zero.'

'Steer one one zero, Sir.'

'Standby Squid.'

The Captain's voice on the telephone to the quarterdeck sounded absolutely calm. You'd think it was a bleeding exercise the way the Old Man gives orders; the communications rating on the quarterdeck passed on the order.

'Full pattern squid, Fire!'

The projectiles hissed above and only slightly to starboard of the bridge. Everyone ducked, instinctively and purposelessly.

'Starboard ten.'

As the bow paid off to starboard, all eyes were on the patch of sea into which the squids had fallen.

'Midships.'

'Wheel amidships Sir.'

'Plot. Don't leave us in the dark up here, give me a range and bearing.'

'Target bearing three four zero, depth two fifty. Steering three five zero, speed eight knots; he's making a run for it, Sir.'

"Course for attack please Sub."

Sub Lieutenant Banes leant over the voice pipe to the wheelhouse.

'Looks like the chase is on, Coxswain. Port twenty, steer three four zero.'

He wasn't sure but he thought he heard 'Tally Ho' from below. He turned to the Captain.

'I hope the plot logged the position of that lifeboat.'

'If they didn't, I'll send the buggers off in the seaboat to find it.'

'Target bearing three four zero. Range one thousand, depth still two fifty and speed still eight knots.'

The report from the asdic plot could be heard by everyone on the bridge,

'Stand by Squid.'

On the afterdeck the Squid crew waited for the order.

'Target stopped. Depth three hundred and increasing, range six hundred and closing.'

'Ah. We have a live one this time. A good move on his part. He's testing us to see what weapons we have. He knows we can fire forwards and he wants to know if we can fire forwards and backwards at the same time; well, not this time we can't.'

'Keep an eye on him plot. I don't want him popping up and shooting me up the arse.'

'Messenger.'

The bridge messenger was beside him before he had completed the call.

'Tell the Gunnery Officer that we are going to have a party up here and he is invited. Ask him to send a few hand grenades down to the quarterdeck.'

'Target bearing one seven zero, depth one fifty and rising. Range one thousand.'

'So, it's pop up for a quick look time, is it? Stop engines. Keep on top of him Plot, we can't afford to lose him now. Half ahead starboard, half astern port. Coxswain, catch her as she swings, steer one seven zero."

He watched the bridge compass spin round as the opposing screws bit into the water performing what a shore-side dancing instructor might have described as a reverse turn.

'Stop port. Half ahead port. Revs for thirty knots please, Sub, I want to be on to him by the time he realises we aren't where he thought we were going to be.'

'Plot. Where the hell is he?'

'Target bearing one eight zero, range nine hundred, depth about thirty feet and tracking left. I think we fooled them Sir, we were through their arc of fire too quickly for them to get any fish away.'

'Thank you Plot. If you're wrong, you're sacked! Ah, Guns, kind of you to come up.' He welcomed the Ginnery Officer to the bridge. 'I want to convince a U-boat that we are armed with depth charges as well as the squids. Would it be asking too much to arm say half a dozen hand grenades, toss them all into a box and toss the box over the side without blowing a hole in us or killing the quarterdeck team?'

'Not quite as you describe it, Sir but I'll see what I can do.'

'If you will, Guns. I want to convince him that we've dropped at least one depth charge, albeit some distance from him and, thus explaining the small amount of bang we make.'

'If you can keep the party going for ten minutes or so, I can probably organise one or two quite impressive underwater bangs Sir. With luck Sir, he may mistake them for distant depth charges but he may choose to disbelieve us. Not to be trusted, these Germans, Sir.'

'He can't afford to ignore the possibility, Guns. This time, he's the one being hunted and I want him to feel insecure.'

'Very good Sir.'

'Target bearing one seven zero, range seven hundred, depth one fifty and increasing. Course now zero nine zero.'

'Thank you Plot. Stand by Squid. Port ten please Sub. We'll try and catch him on the turn.'

'Target bearing red one zero. Target dead ahead Sir.'

'Thank you Plot. Fire Squid.'

Again the swish of the projectiles passing over and to the side of them made them all duck.

'Good fall of shot, Sir.'

'Thank you Sub. Come on Guns. Midships.'

The OOW repeated the order down the voice pipe.

'Plot. What course do I want to intercept?'

'I think we got him Sir. Getting some funny noises, could be blowing tanks. Bearing two seven zero, range about three hundred, rising fast.'

'Gun's crews close up.'

The Captain pressed the transmit tit on the microphone for the Tannoy system. 'The submarine appears to be surfacing to starboard, fire as you bear.'

'Explosion noises from target Sir. Target depth now increasing rapidly, bearing two nine zero. Moving right and down.'

'Keep on her, Plot. He might be trying to convince us that he is dead. If he succeeds, and he ain't, we could be!'

'Lost contact Sir.'

'Christ, Plot, how did you manage that? Stop engines. Keep silence in the ship. I don't want that U-boat's hydrophones telling her where we are if we don't know where he is.'

'Now which is the cat and which the mouse?'

'Well Sub. We have one small advantage. Without engines but up here in the wind, we shall be blown slowly and, more importantly, silently southwards. He, on the other hand, will remain almost stationary so, the longer we wait the further apart we shall be. Plot. What was the last bearing and range of the target?'

'Lost him on two nine four at about four fifty yards, Sir.'

The Captain looked in that direction. He had no idea where the U-boat was but with the ship's head pointing the way it was, it might be worth a try.

'Stand by Squid.'

The ship's head paid off a little more before the wind. It must have been like this in the days of sail, he thought, his eye on the slowly turning compass disk in front of him.

'Fire Squid.'

'Plot, I want to know if so much as a sardine moves down there.'

The Squid's diamond pattern salvo had been spread as widely as possible in the hope that one could find a target or, at least, be close enough to make a U-boat Captain move and give away his position.

'Now we wait.'

Comus had by now slewed round before the wind and sea and was broached to, lying in the trough between waves and rolling heavily from side to side as the seas passed under her. As she rose to each succeeding swell, the wind threw itself against her, rolling her to port, as she slipped down into the next trough, the wind effect lessened and the sea rolled her the other way.

'Not a good time to serve lunch, eh Sub? You'd better tell the engine room what's going on.'

The Sub Lieutenant returned the telephone handset to its cradle.

'Chief says that he will be as quiet as a mouse but that, if asked, he would prefer to be the cat, Sir.'

The Captain's steward chose this moment to reappear bearing hot, sweet tea and a pile of sandwiches.

'Thought you might like these Sir. During the interval like.'

'If we drop a couple of hand grenades now, Sir, the U-boat might think we are dropping depth charges some distance away. It might add to the confusion.'

'Brilliant, Sub. Ask Guns how he's doing.'

The Sub reached for the telephone to the quarterdeck and spoke.

'Ready when you are, Sir. Guns says he has rigged up five separate bangers inside holed drums. All he has to do is pull the pins, throw the weighted drums over and pray a little.'

'We'll give him a few moments more, just to give us time to have drifted further away, then we can start the party. Ask Guns to start praying in about two minutes. Steward, you'd better remove the cup and plates. There may be quite a bit of activity up here when we start.'

The muffled explosions of five 'depth charges' sounded quite realistically as if they had been dropped about a mile away. Silence on the surface and below.

'The question is, Sub, where the hell is he? He can't be sitting on the bottom out here and, if he isn't, then why can't we find him? Plot, what do you think?'

'Could be a very lucky man, Sir and found a layer of colder water to hide under. If he can keep that between him and us, Sir, he can lie doggo for as long as he likes. 'Course, he doesn't know that unless he has read the asdic manufacturer's handbook.'

'I suspect that he saw it before you did Chief.'

On the weather deck, the Chef was passing round sandwiches and hot tea to the men closed up at action stations, he having abandoned his own for the moment with permission; this to the accompaniment of the usual ribald comments.

'What do you bet, now that I've got a sarnie in one hand and a mug of char in the other, the U-boat will surface right in front of my bloody gun?'

'No chance, Hookey. Chef's sent some down for them and all. Very fair and open handed man, our Chef.'

This raised enough of a laugh to relieve the tension they were all feeling.

'I hope he remembered to put rat poison in theirs.'

'I hope he remembered which was which.'

'Signal from Captain D, Sir'. Scrumpy Higgins passed the sheet to the Captain and stood beside the chair waiting for the answer he knew must come.

The Captain passed the sheet to the OOW.

'D wants to know what we're doing, Sub.'

'The term waiting comes to mind Sir.'

'Alas, Sub, mere Lieutenant Commanders do not send one word answers to Captains D. Not even amateur Lieutenant Commanders like me.

Yeoman. Make to Captain D. Am sitting on a U-boat who has closed down all systems and is keeping silence in the boat. I have done likewise. Would be grateful if you could fire a few squids to confuse the enemy as to my position.'

Scrumpy flashed the signal prompting an immediate reply. 'From D Sir. Continue sitting on nest for fifteen minutes. If no hatchlings by then, assume infertile and return to station. Lifeboat recovered by Cheerful.'

There was no way of knowing for certain whether the U-boat was lying doggo under a fortuitous layer of colder water and thus screened from Comus's silent hydrophone search or lying dead on the bottom as a result of the squid attack.

'Revs for twenty knots, please Sub., rejoin the screen. Yeoman, make to Cossack. Am rejoining the screen.'

'Stand down action stations?'

'Yes please Sub.'

CHAPTER EIGHT

Tex Barrat had worked out his plan.

'What we need is a supply of gasoline for the fleet of cabs, Sarge. I'll supply the automobiles, you supply the gas from those trucks to keep our fleet on the road and we'll both get rich enough to go home in style.'

The Sergeant Tex was talking to was well known to him. Always on the lookout for an easy Dollar and, as Tex had told him, there would be plenty of easy Dollars in this little operation. As Transportation Sergeant, Sam Houston, a fellow Texan, could sidetrack enough gasoline from the constantly moving trucks to keep these itty-bitty English autos on the road; God, they could do more than twenty miles to the gallon. The trucks he would be short loading only did between seven and nine; two or three miles short measure would never be noticed and, anyway, who was going to notice it if he didn't?

Tex waited for the Sergeant to work out the logistics of the proposed operation and to recognise the benefits. Sam was slow but not stupid.

'OK, you're on. You get hold of the fleet and I'll supply the gas. You can't bring 'em in here to fill 'em up but we'll arrange a quiet spot for tank to tank transfer.'

'I knew you'd like it, once you'd had time to think about it.'

'It'll cost you two Dollars a load, and I want it in good old US of A Dollars, none of this local Mickey Mouse money.'

'It's a deal, Serge.'

'It's not that easy,' Alice told him later. 'If one of your cars is stopped on the road and can't prove it's a registered taxi, the police will assume that it's running on stolen petrol. There's a war on, you know, and they take a dim view of people stealing petrol or buying stolen petrol.'

'There must be a way round that. How do I get them registered as taxis?'

'You can't but I can do better than that. I can probably arrange for you to become a partner in an established taxi company. You supply the passengers and the petrol and the company proves the cars are licensed to trade. All above board and legal as long as no one checks up on how the company manages to get so much petrol. How much money have you got?'

'As much as it takes.'

She had been making a cup of coffee from the supply he had brought her from the PX but put down the cup.

'I may know someone that can help. Leave it with me.'

'I knew you were a winner.'

'I'll speak to him next time I see him. Anyway, you'll need drivers and you can't hire drivers just like that now, there's a war on. And you can't use women, they wouldn't be safe so we'll have to hope that he knows a few men who want some evening work It's got to look legit.' She liked to use the American words she had learned when talking to Americans. 'And, we don't want to rush things or he'll put his price up.'

The film was just the kind Alice liked. None of this happy in adversity nonsense made by the English studios doing their bit for the war effort, this was Gone With The Wind; a real story about love and war. A war that nobody recognised as related in any way to air raids and, anyway, only foreigners were involved. With Tex's arm round her shoulder and sitting in the dark, Alice felt safe from recognition and, with luck, from air raids. Frank wouldn't mind her going to the pictures with the Yank as long as that was all she did with him.

There weren't so many air raids now. Even the dockyard seemed to live a charmed life with no bombs hitting for weeks. That was just as well, she thought, with all those extra little boats in there. Landing craft she had heard them called. It was just as well that Jerry didn't know they were there.

She had only just convinced Tex that the lack of ice cream and popcorn in the cinema was the result of the war, not further evidence that the Brits had no idea how to run a movie house. The idea of a pre-war cinema serving afternoon tea and cakes during the interval between the two films of a double feature afternoon show struck Tex as crazy.

'What you do, he told her, is turn up the heating during the last reel of the first film and sell ice creams during the interval; that way you make a lot of money. Then you turn the heat down during the second feature and save fuel. If the major feature is any good, no one will notice that it's getting colder. The trouble with you Brits is, you have no idea of business.'

Every time he told her that, she smiled inwardly and, in her mind's eye, counted the money he would be giving her. Unlike the English sailors, the American soldiers appeared to have more money than sense. And, they were happy to spend it all and return to the base broke.

In addition to the silk stockings he had got for her, he had brought her chocolate and fruits she hadn't seen since before the war. There was no doubt about these Yanks, when they sent an army overseas, the sent the USA with them. Then there was the money too: English soldiers were dying for less than half what these Yanks got every week, the taxi business would be a money spinner, she was sure.

Bob Timmins was more than a little worried about his taxis. They had been good enough before the war but, after four years of no spare parts, there were signs that they couldn't last until the war was over. He had already bought one Humber from a family that had put it up on blocks in '39 and hadn't used it since but good cars, suitable for use as taxis, were few and far between. When he could find them, the owners wanted silly amounts of money for them, prices he couldn't afford.

Alice had approached him one evening when he had been having a drink in the Return's private bar, a quiet place where the civvies could drink in peace. It was very small but at least there were no servicemen in there getting drunk and aggressive.

It was more of a private club for her father's friends than a pub and the beer was still at pre-war prices to friends.

'Well, tell your Yankee friend I might be interested but he'll have to stay in the background. He'll have to buy me out and buy all the cars then employ me to run things. It'll have to remain Timmins' Taxis for the authorities. We can discuss how much he pays me later, OK?' He was sure that the whole idea was the beer talking and that her friend Tex wouldn't even remember the conversation next time he saw her but, if there was a chance here to sell his old cars for a good price and make a lot of money as well, he was more than pleased to listen to anybody's ideas. And, he knew where he could lay his hands on a few larger cars, suitable for funerals and that sort of thing, weddings and all that. He could sell them to this Yank for twice what he paid for them.

'Where's he going to get the money from?'

'Don't worry. He can afford it.'

'Alright then. And if I get a good price from your Yankee friend, I'll see you alright, your father would have my guts else.'

She told Tex the following night.

'I should make a few quid out of this too. After all, I've helped you get the contacts you need.'

'Don't worry Princess. You just do as you're told and I'll see you alright. Don't worry. I have three thousand lazy GI's out there in that camp and they all want transport. We're going to make a fortune sweetheart, both of us. You tell your Mr Timmins he can still call it Timmins Taxis but, from here on in, I'll be calling the shots. You have him come and see me here next Tuesday so we can talk money, OK?'

Alice nodded.

CHAPTER NINE

Alice lay on her back, her eyes open, her bedroom curtains shielding her from the bright moonlight outside; a bombers moon.

It would be funny if, when Frank came home from the war they bought the hotel from old granny Levin. She'd been trying to sell it for some time but, in wartime, no one bought property so near the dockyard, a regular target for the air raids.

The Sheldon Hotel was one of those tall, narrow, converted houses boasting ten letting rooms plus an owner's flat in the basement. The dining room and lounge took up most of the ground floor, together with the kitchen, this nowadays providing only a breakfast for some of her regular guests. The one bathroom separated the two best letting rooms on the second floor where some of the original splendour remained.

Above these, the third floor bedrooms were much as they had been when the house had been the private residence of one of the senior dockyard managers, in the last century. The servants' rooms, with a new toilet in what had been a walk-in linen cupboard, were up under the roof; their dormer windows giving a fine view across the roofs of the houses sloping down towards the river and, beyond the dockyard, to the Hoo peninsular.

These were now occupied by Mrs Levin's only proper tenants, a family of white Russian refugees, the Litvaks, who minded their own business and chose not to understand most of what was said to them.

Long experience had convinced them that ignorance was the best defence against authority. If you clearly didn't understand the instructions, they eventually got bored with issuing them and left you in peace. The Litvaks wanted to be left in peace.

Their world, in Russia, no longer existed. First the Bolsheviks had taken it from the Litvaks then the Nazis had taken it from the Bolsheviks. The Litvaks hoped that the Bolsheviks and the Nazis continued slaughtering each other until none were left; perhaps then they could go home.

They were warm and relatively safe in their attic in Gillingham, England. The rationing ensured that there was food for the table and Mr Litvak taught music at the local school. One day, God willing, this terrible war would be over and real life could begin again; the way it used to be. They were old and they were tired but they wanted to go home to die.

Alice, in her own bed at home, thought about her new friend and potential business partner Tex; wondered where he was and with whom, it was none of her business

To the US Army, he was just a Private First Class but, to Tex, it was the First Class that counted. He had always seen himself as First Class, even at school when the white kids had beaten up on him and called him a nigger. At least the Brits didn't call you nigger. Sometimes they looked at you a bid queerly but they were always polite and seemed to be grateful that you were here, and on their side.

There had been a few remarks made by the English sailors when the Yanks scooped up all the good looking girls but that had been mainly Bloody Yanks with only the occasional Black Bastard thrown in. Nothing personal. He understood that, he would have said the same thing if the positions had been reversed.

Mrs Litvak heard the air raid siren before her husband and woke him.

'It's a raid, we must go down to the basement.'

Mrs Levin had had a reinforced shelter built in what had been the coal cellar, under the front steps and extending out under the pavement in front of the house.

The round, metal lid of the old coalhole in the pavement had been welded shut and the roof was supported from below by heavy wooden beams. They were safe in there from anything short of a direct hit.

'I'm a musician, an artiste, I should not have to live in a hole in the ground, a converted coal cellar my God, perhaps we should have stayed in Russia and let the Bolsheviks murder us.'

Mr Litvak always complained when woken by an air raid. It made not the slightest difference to the German pilots above but it made him feel better, as if he still had some say in the matter, that he could, if he wished, refuse to go down into the air raid shelter.

First he would refuse then, when persuaded by his wife that he owed it to her to stay alive as long as she did, he would complain about the number of stairs. It had always been the same. By the time the Litvaks arrived in the shelter there was little room left; all the best positions had been taken by earlier arrivals. The girls from the first floor usually got there first, with their clients.

The Litvaks didn't really approve of the girls from the first floor but accepted that everyone had a right to live their life as they chose. If the best these girls could do was prostitution, who were they, penniless but grateful refugees from Russia, to complain?

The Litvaks had pride. It was all they did have. They had survived the revolution and the German invasion and found both a home and work in England. Honest work but, perhaps, everyone was not as fortunate as they.

'Do be quiet. The noise you make! The Germans will hear you and bomb this house specially.'

Mrs Litvak always said that and always, Mr Litvak replied that no doubt the German spy who lived in the loft above them had already told the pilots that there were two old White Russian refugees hiding in the cellar of the Sheldon Hotel.

The first bomb of the stick missed the dockyard by a few feet and the fifth hit the Sheldon Hotel; coming in through the front of the house, directly into the Litvak's tiny flat. Finding little resistance in the roof slates and old timbers, the bomb crashed through two floors before exploding in Room One.

Most of the blast had exploded through the large bay window, taking the glass and most of the frame across the road and chipping the brickwork of the houses opposite; most of the rest went back up through the hole in the roof. The thin partition walls between the first floor rooms collapsed, spreading splintered plasterboard and four by two timbers across the four beds evacuated only moments before.

The ceiling of the rooms had collapsed bringing down the bath from above and with it, a continuous flow of water from the ruptured pipes. It was this that probably saved the house from the fire.

In the cellar, they waited for the noises of explosion and collapse to subside. The atmosphere, thick with dust from the floors above and coal dust from the cellar walls almost totally obscured the light from the single forty watt bulb hanging from the beam above their heads. At least the light remained on, swinging wildly.

'There! See what you've done!' Mrs Litvak chastised her husband. 'You must have upset the Germans with your constant complaints. Now we are homeless again.'

His arm round her shoulder Mr Litvak allowed her to cry quietly, now that the immediate danger had passed. At least they were not dead like the family they had left in Russia. 'Will it never end?'

He tried the door and found it blocked, debris from above having fallen down the stairs against the outside.

'So, we wait. The salvage crew will be here as soon as they can and they will dig us out. Why don't we listen for the sound of their footsteps on the pavement above and then, when we hear someone, all shout out together so they'll know we're down here?'

On the other side of the hill, in Chatham, Alice slept curled up on the old sofa in the cellar having relinquished her own bed when the siren sounded.

CHAPTER TEN

A noon sight had fixed their position as well as possible but it had been a fleeting sight of the sun between clouds. Their precise position was of little interest to the OOW in Comus, he did as he was told by the escort screen commander, Captain D, in Cossack; hopefully, Captain D, in Cossack knew where they were.

Comus' job was to keep station on Cheviot, ahead of her in the V-shaped screen that surrounded the front and sides of the convoy and to keep an efficient asdic watch for submarines; HMS Challenger, as tail end Charlie, brought up the rear and kept watch for U-boats so unsporting as to lurk behind the convoy, keeping station close behind the last ship of the centre line, and therefore be in a position to fall upon any merchant ship so unfortunate as to have engine trouble and to be left behind by the others. It would be appreciated also, it had been made clear at the pre-sailing conference, if a good lookout for enemy aircraft could be kept also.

Captain D, Captain Benjamin Ludlow-Smith, considered himself something of a wag. A regular officer, the war had come at a fortuitous moment promotion-wise. Somewhat behind most of his contemporaries in promotion due to one or two jolly, but misjudged japes as a Sub Lieutenant, Captain Benjamin Ludlow-Smith allowed himself the pleasure of repartee at the expense of his junior officers.

With four rings on his arm and, as Captain in command of a flotilla of destroyers, he could reasonably expect to finish the war safe from the effects of his pre-war misunderstandings with Commodore, now Vice Admiral Weatherby; God rot his socks.

All things considered, Captain Benjamin Ludlow-Smith was a happy man. Things were going moderately well for him. His flotilla had destroyed enough U-boats and shepherded enough merchant ships with few losses to warrant a feeling of professional security. Things seemed to be getting a bit slow recently but, hell, that was the fault of the damned Germans. If they didn't send the U-boats to sea, his sailors couldn't sink the blighters.

He had a good team commanding the ships in his flotilla, even if some of them were RNVR; good chaps, for all that, he thought. When the war was over, they would all go back to being whatever they had been before but he would still be a Captain RN, possibly the captain of a capital ship, a battlewagon or perhaps even one of the new fleet carriers. That would ensure that his peacetime future was secure, he would very probably retire as an admiral.

His mother had always seen him as an Admiral. Perhaps it was just as well that she hadn't lived to see his disappointment at being passed over for promotion so often after those youthful pranks.

He hadn't meant the other fellow to drown, damn it, they were just skylarking. It was an accident that the motorboat he had been driving had hit the other boat. Anyway, they were both drunk, it had been the other fellow's fault as much as his but the other fellow was dead so Sub. Lieutenant Benjamin Ludlow-Smith had to take all the blame.

Then, there was the little matter of paying to replace the motorboat which had caught fire in the collision. Perhaps Hitler had done him a considerable service by starting this war while he was still young enough to regain the promotions previously denied him.

In Comus, Frank Bye kept his head and eyes moving, keeping a good look out for either signals from the other ships or aircraft. Nowadays, aircraft sighted were usually friendly but, not always. Hitler still had some of those long range Condors that could search out a convoy, miles from home, and bomb and machinegun the ships below, while advising U-boat headquarters of the convoy's position.

The major difference now was that Coastal Command had been supplied with Liberator bombers by the Americans for long range U-boat detection and the British Sunderland flying boats, developed from the pre-war luxury airline machines, were fantastic; they could stay up for hours and hours searching for the tell-tale signs of a wolf-pack of German submarines waiting for or approaching the convoys.

The recent development of the so-called Woolworth carriers, a flat deck bolted to the top of a fast merchant ship hull, had also made a difference. Most of the major, troop carrying convoys now crossing the Atlantic had the benefit of air defence right through what had been called the mid-Atlantic gap; too far out for land based fighters from either the UK or America. Now, with carrier based fighters ready to defend the convoy from air attack and long range search and destroy aircraft hounding and killing the U-boats, there might just be a reasonable chance of not only winning this war but of him actually seeing it won. Frank wanted very much to survive the war, he wanted to get home to Alice.

That some U-boats were still lurking about in the ocean, waiting for the chance to despatch some poor Jack to a watery grave, was obvious from this morning's little escapade. The question was, did we get him or is he still down there somewhere listening to the sound of our engines and lining up for an attack?

Whilst keeping his head and eyes moving, keeping a good lookout, Frank's ears were tuned in to the ping of the asdic loud speaker at the side of the bridge. As the first 'ping' returned by an underwater target as a 'pong', the bridge would burst into life again. Frank hoped this wouldn't happen. At four o'clock, he would slide gratefully down the ladder into the mess for his tea and some sleep.

From six until eight, he would be on watch again but, then, providing there were no panics, he could sleep until midnight. The noises of the other men in the mess playing uckers or cards or the hundred and one things that people do would not prevent him sleeping. Sleeping was something sailors became very good at. Under any conditions, storm or calm, noise or quiet, wet or dry, Frank could put his head down and sleep; instantly and until required.

He had learned to sleep and wake without any preamble, like throwing a switch. No snuggling down and getting comfortable first or slowly rising to the surface of consciousness after being called. Frank, like every other sailor, slept instantly and woke instantly - to order.

The cloud was breaking up and bright sunshine broke through the gaps to make the world look a better place. The sea was still grey, but then the north Atlantic always was grey, you had to be a long way south to see blue seas. The wind was less and it had all the hallmarks of being a pleasant evening. The sea would calm down and the U-boats would come up into the darkness to recharge their batteries and to fix their position by the stars. Tomorrow, it would all begin again; if, that is, they were lucky enough to get through the night without any action.

Frank supposed that, for the planners ashore, this was all very exciting. Plotting the position of ships and aircraft, U-boats and convoys, escorts and survivors but, on the bridge of Comus, Frank was having great difficulty concentrating on the job in hand. What he wanted to think about was Alice. Alice and after the war. Alice and him after the war, when they had a couple of kids in their own home. She was a clever girl. Alice would see to it that the money she was earning and the money he sent home every week by allotment through the pay office would be saved and, when the time came, invested in the small hotel they had talked about.

She would know when to buy. When the end of the war was in sight and, before prices went up as they would when the war ended. When the war ended, there would be a severe housing shortage, what with the thousands of houses bombed to smithereens by the Germans, and prices would go up until the builders could build replacements.

The builders wouldn't be slow to realise that the slower they built, the higher the prices they could demand. Oh yes, they would all be making the right patriotic noises about building better homes for returning heroes but, human nature being what it is, they would find some reason for taking their time and maximising their profits.

Funny really, there was no sign of an end to the war yet. Hitler still ruled Europe with the exception of Italy that had changed sides, and even there, the Germans were now fighting both the Allies and their own former allies the Italians. Still, we had thrown them out of Africa, things were beginning to go our way at last. The Americans and our chaps were even beginning to turn the tide against the Japs. Perhaps the corner had been turned at last. Perhaps Churchill was right, that we had passed the end of the beginning and that soon, the second front would be launched in Europe to mark the beginning of the end.

The Russians had survived the might of the German army and were fighting back, taking few prisoners, reportedly unable to see white flags against the snow. No one was going to check the weather reports to confirm that the snow existed. Not really fair, but you couldn't blame them if the newsreels had been true about what the Germans had done to them. They had, it was claimed, tried to destroy Russia completely rather than just capture it; no quarter was being given by either side.

It was April, nearly May and, with luck, he would get some leave when they got back to Greenock or Londonderry or wherever they were sent this time. It would be nice to go home to Chatham, to Alice. Strange how she meant so much to him now, how she involved in every thought and plan he made.

He had been on his own since his parents had died when he was eight and he had gone to the Dr Barnardo's home in Clapham. Now, he was half of a couple, Frank and Alice, Mr and Mrs Bye; or he would be when he got back to Chatham and married her. Soon, please God, soon.

Mrs Litvak heard the air raid siren before her husband and woke him from the fitful sleep he was managing in the dust filled shelter.

'It's the all clear.'

It was just then the weakened top floor fell into the third floor and that into the second, leaving a gaping hole between the two adjoining houses and showering dust and debris over the street outside. In the coal cellar, the light went out.

In the street, the ARP crew desperately dug away the loose debris to uncover the mains supply valve for the water and gas supplies. They could smell gas already and it only needed a small spark to ignite it and blow them all to hell and back.

Happily for those in the coal cellar, the gas was lighter than air and didn't collect in the cellar. Above them, the ARP crew decided that what they didn't know wouldn't worry them and dug on. The air holes in the coalhole cover were cleared again and the voice told them that there was no chance of digging them out from above so they would dig through to them from the cellar of the house next door.

Mrs Levin found the candles kept down there for just such a situation and lit one. She also lit the primus stove and the small kettle was already beginning to sing; she put two heaped spoonfuls of tea into the pot. The hell with rationing!

She had secreted a small supply of tea, sugar, biscuits and even a couple of tins of Spam down here for just such an emergency and, she was glad that she had. It would be some time before they would be able to knock through the wall from next door. They built houses properly in those days and that wall would not come down easily.

'Who's down there with you, Mrs Levin?'

Mrs Levin called up the names of those in the cellar, which, she suspected, would be used to notify next of kin if anything went wrong with the rescue.

'Should we start digging from this side?'

'No, leave it to us experts.'

The raid had been short and, largely ineffective. A few bombs had hit the dockyard but only one landing craft had been sunk at its moorings and a few others damaged but nothing that couldn't be fixed in a matter of hours. Most of the bombs had missed the dockyard altogether, falling along a straight path up the hill as the bombers had made their turn over Hoo and released their bombs on the way home; gaining height and speed as they shed their loads. The bombs had fallen more or less straight up Khyber Road, missing the barracks, hitting the signal school and continuing along Church Road where one had landed on the Sheldon Hotel. The last few had fallen astride the railway line from Gillingham to Rainham, causing more mess than damage amongst the allotments.

One of the bombers had crashed, probably due to the guns in the dockyard but possibly to those on the Hoo peninsular, there was always great competition between the two Ack Ack batteries. As the gunnery instructor had told any number of trainees since 1940, 'You don't shoot at the bleeding aircraft. You puts a great pile of rubbish into the air in front of 'im and 'ope he runs into something.'

This, perfectly sound principle at sea had one obvious drawback when applied ashore. What went up had to come down and it was the shrapnel from our own shells that did more damage to roofs and windows than the German bombs. However, one of the bombers had certainly crashed and it would be unsporting to blame the gunners for the collateral damage. On being hit, the bomber had veered to port and had come down on the salt marshes on the other side of the river.

Before the war, Mrs Levin's Sheldon Hotel had provided good, clean accommodation and reasonable comfort to a regular clientele of commercial travellers visiting the Medway towns in pursuit of orders for their employers. Most of these personable young men were now, no doubt, in one of the Services many, by now, possibly dead.

Sitting in the cellar, surrounded by the last guests it would ever accommodate, Mrs Levin wondered what she was to do once the salvage team dug them out. Still, she was alive and, as long as the Germans didn't bomb the bank, life would go on.

Unknown to Mrs Levin, Frank was of much the same opinion. With a little bit of luck, it would all come right in the end for Alice and him. When the war was over, he would buy himself out of the navy and they would settle down to run an hotel. He reckoned a hotel was a good, safe business.

CHAPTER ELEVEN

It wasn't the lookout that saw the aircraft. The OOW punched the action stations alarm, grabbed the microphone for the Tannoy system and shouted into it.

'Enemy aircraft bearing green four zero, elevation zero, closing fast. Fire when you bear.'

By the time he had lifted the lid of the voice pipe to the captain's cabin to report, the captain was on the bridge.

'Sorry about that, Sir. One moment there was nobody there and the next there was.'

The starboard lookout reported that the aircraft was gaining height as it approached the ship. The forward starboard Bofors gun spotted the target and opened fire; forty millimetre shells arcing away towards it, forcing the pilot to lose height again to avoid the incoming flack. At the last possible moment, the Condor bomber lifted sufficiently to fly over the ship, dropping down again immediately to what was effectively zero feet and heading towards the oil tanker in the centre of the convoy.

The portside Bofors dared not open fire for fear of hitting the tanker and, within seconds, the German had raked the tanker with machine gun fire and passed over it towards the destroyers on the opposite side of the screen. Unable to fire for fear of hitting the tanker, Cheerful and Cherub had to allow the Condor to pass over them before they could attack it with anything heavier than the Lewis guns on the bridge.

'An interesting manoeuvre. Rather more brave than useful, I would have thought, couldn't drop anything from that height.'

The captain watched the tiny dot in the sky that had been the aircraft disappear. The Focke-wolf Condor 200, having despatched the deep sea tug sent to the assistance of the crippled merchant ship to the north of the convoy had dropped to zero feet and made a rapid but stealthy approach. With no bombs left, the aircraft still had the ability to cause considerable damage with its heavy machineguns. The experienced pilot had judged it perfectly. Surprise got him past the Comus and, fear of hitting their own tanker had prevented any serious attempt at opposition to his stratagem until he had been over and past the other side of the convoy screen, luck had been with him.

On the tanker, their opinion was less sanguine. At the range achieved, it had been impossible for the aircraft's gunner to miss the bridge house. Heavy calibre shells had shattered the glass windows killing the Helmsman, the Telegraphsman and the Captain who had been bent over the chart table behind them. Momentarily out of control, the tanker slewed to port as the dying Helmsman fell, dragging the wheel round. Her Officer of the Watch had been spared without a scratch and, grabbing the spinning wheel, he put the ship back on to its proper course though, now somewhat out of station. The lookout on the starboard wing of the tanker's bridge was dead and the bridge messenger lay in a pool of blood beside the Captain. The OOW called to the port lookout.

'Get yourself in here and take the wheel.'

'Signal from D, Sir. You seem to have left the door open that time, please see to it that no more intruders gain access.'

In Comus, Frank handed the flimsy to the Captain who screwed it up and tossed it into the air. The wind caught it and carried it over the side before dropping it into the water. Typical RN, he thought.

'There would seem to be a problem Sir. What was the Condor doing over there?'

'That's a thought Sub. Bye, make to Captain D. Should I investigate to starboard for target of aircraft prior to its interest in us?'

A moment later the reply was forthcoming.

'Aircraft reported earlier this a.m. was friendly. Your intruder approached from different bearing. Remain on station.'

'But that's not possible, Sir.'

'Sub. In this navy, if Captain D says it was another aircraft, it was another aircraft. If Captain D says it was one of ours, then it was one of ours; perhaps we have a few Condor's on loan from Hitler. If you don't agree, you may write it up in your memoirs after the war or, in your case, you being a Regular, it would probably be better if you waited until after you've retired. Meanwhile, if the lookout fails to see any more approaching aircraft, you have my permission to keel haul him. Where's the Yeoman?'

'I've sent one of the signalmen to find out what the problem is, Sir. '

Scrumpy was where he spent most of his time, in the bunting store under the steering platform in the wheelhouse. Unable to get any response from him the signalman had gone to find the Sick Berth Attendant.

He didn't want to drop Scrumpy into trouble by simply reporting that he was unconscious in the flag store though, it was a miracle that the smell of rum hadn't wafted up to the bridge through the wheelhouse voice pipe.

The SBA had Scrumpy carried down to the sick bay and put into the bunk. Everyone knew about Scrumpy, for all his efforts to keep his condition a secret and, the SBA was not about to report to the Captain that his yeoman of signals was blind drunk.

'Tell Frank I have Scrumpy down here and that he's unconscious. Tell him that I'm doing what I can until we can get the MO transferred, I think his ulcer's perforated'

There was little chance of the MO being transferred at sea for Scrumpy's ulcer but, by the time the request had been made and refused and instructions given to the SBA on the best course of treatment, Scrumpy would be awake and very nearly sober. It was up to Scrumpy to get himself out of this mess as best he could. Looking at him, the

SBA had a lot of sympathy. The old man lying on the bunk had no business being at sea and, with anything like reasonable luck, he would be drafted ashore at the end of this trip; whether he wanted it or not.

As expected, the request was refused and no more was said about Scrumpy's condition other than that the SBA should report on his condition in 24 hours. If the Yeoman's condition had not improved, he would be transferred to Cossack where the MO could have a look at him; a possibility not considered agreeable by the SBA nor by Scrumpy when told. Under no circumstances could the MO be allowed to examine Scrumpy until they got back to England and he was sober.

'It would seem that you're on your own for a while, Bye. Who can work watch and watch with you until the Yeoman's fit enough?'

Frank hesitated for only a moment before answering the captain's question. 'Signalman Hastings is competent, Sir and I'm sure the Yeoman will be fit for duty very soon. You can't keep a good man down, Sir.'

Captain Horton gave Frank a suspicious look but chose not to question the opinion proffered. Captain Horton was not a professional commanding officer, he being what the professional RN's called a temporary gentleman, but he knew what Scrumpy's problem was as did everyone else in Comus; Scrumpy would be put ashore on return to the UK, like it or not.

The bricks dividing the coal cellar of the Sheldon Hotel from that of the house next door proved to be made of good quality materials and resisted the attack of the salvage team for more than two hours before finally collapsing releasing a cloud of dust into Mrs Levin's bed space.

'OK, everyone out. Make sure there's nothing left behind that could cause a fire. Put out those candles please Mrs Levin, there's gas about.'

As they trooped out into the early morning sunlight, they could see that the Sheldon Hotel would offer them no more hospitality. The whole front had collapsed, together with most of the upper floors that had concertina'd down from the roof.

Cups of tea, hot and sweet, the traditional British standby for such occasions were handed round. Mrs Levin's flat in the basement was undamaged except for the water damage caused earlier but they wouldn't let her go in in case the rest of the house collapsed into it whilst she was inside; the salvage crew would recover her things later, after it had been shored up. The Litvaks were once again without anything. No home and no possessions.

The Chief Warden called them all together.

'Go down to St. James' church hall. There's blankets and hot food there. Report to the WRVS and they will organise temporary accommodation, clothes, etc. He looked at Tex in his uniform. You, Yank, had better report to your CO and let him sort you out; OK?'

In the five days that followed, much of consequence happened. Tex insisted on being sent to see the MO If there was any way to avoid being sent to France when the invasion started, Tex was going to find it and use it.

The Litvaks, once again homeless and without any possessions of any kind, were found temporary accommodation in a house requisitioned by the local Council from an absent owner. The WRVS fount them clothes, food and such important items as toothbrushes. Replacement food and clothes coupons were issued.

June blew in more like March. Gales and foul weather swept through the English Channel. Through the last week of May and into the beginning of June, the Admiralty had concentrated every available minesweeper into the Channel, together with destroyer escorts to protect them as far as possible from attack by aircraft or the fast, deadly E-boats.

Sweeping in a regular and fixed pattern, the sweepers had no means of avoiding attack and depended totally upon others for their protection. The big fleet sweepers had four inch main armament for'ard of the bridge and a couple of 40mm Bofors for anti-aircraft protection but, unable to manoeuvre without falling prey to the mines they were trying to sweep, they presented sitting targets to attacking aircraft. Every day, and at night also, the sweepers ploughed furrows in the Channel.

The big fleet boats at the head of the line followed by the converted trawlers towing their paravane floats, each paravane slightly outboard of the one ahead, sweeping an ever widening channel through the German minefields.

Whenever weather conditions permitted German aircraft and E-boats would lay new mines in the swept channels. In foul weather, the E-boats were safely tied up in harbour and the aircraft grounded; the Royal Navy were winning more points than they lost.

Every inlet and creek from The Wash to Falmouth was full of ungainly boxlike landing craft. For months, armies, some real and some existing only in the form of masses of signals designed to confuse the listening enemy, had been assembling ready for the invasion without which the war could not be ended.

Constant, heavy bombing of Germany and selected targets in the rest of Europe by the RAF and the USAF had caused havoc on the ground but could not win the war. In England, soldiers in mud coloured and frequently mud covered uniforms showing the badges of regiments from England, Scotland and Wales, almost every country in the Empire and Commonwealth, Americans, Poles, Czechs, Dutch and French, Christians, Jews, Moslems, Hindus and innumerable others were joined together in one purpose, to smash for ever the German army occupying Europe from Russia to the borders of collaborating Spain. Warfare had never seen anything even remotely like the army gathered in southern England; it was trained, it was ready, it was better armed than any army in history and it was impatient.

At sea, in mid-Atlantic, the convoy Escort Commander, Captain D, hoisted a signal for all ships. It had started. 'The Allies have landed in France.'

The handover of the westbound convoy to the American ships escorting the eastbound went without a hitch and, course reversed, Comus headed back towards England and Frank towards Alice and a wedding.

CHAPTER TWELVE

The church even had flowers, though Frank had no idea where they had come from; some friend of Alice's dad, he guessed. His father in law to be's circle of friends also included the man acting as usher at the door, separating and directing the guests to either the Bride's or Bridegroom's side of the church. Frank wondered idly why it made a difference but accepted that that was the way it was done at church weddings; a bit like the Andrew really, a procedure for everything and, no doubt, somewhere there would be the ecclesiastical equivalent of Kings Regulations and Admiralty Instructions which had to be followed by every church in the land.

He was glad he had invited a few of his shipmates as he had no family to support him but he noticed that the usher was using his head and sending a few of the bride's supporters who weren't actually family over to the groom's side to fill the pews.

He had asked Scrumpy Higgins to be his best man and the Yeoman was doing him proud. Sober and in his Number One uniform, Scrumpy looked every inch the professional sailor. His uniform brushed until the mohair shone, the gold badges on his arms wiped with vinegar to remove any tarnish that might have accumulated whilst the suit had been stowed in his locker in the PO's mess and the stiffness of his collar would have made it unwearable under any other circumstances.

Frank's uniform was no less smart. Gold badges showed him to be a Leading Signalman, the single fouled anchor above his one good conduct stripe on his left arm and the crossed hand flags with star above and below on the other glistened in the sunlight coming through the windows. His new blue collar had been bleached to a colour suitable for a man who had been at sea for many years and his lanyard had been blancoed white to emphasise the contrast against the narrow black silk scarf against which it rested.

He had been up since six, ironing his new uniform, pressing into the trouser legs the seven horizontal creases said to represent the seven seas. Scrumpy had stayed overnight at the pub to ensure that he would be on hand when required in the morning and, more importantly, that he would be sober when he had to stand up for Frank in the church.

The wedding arrangements had been made by Alice's mum and she would not have her daughter's big day ruined by any sailor-like behaviour by Scrumpy Higgins nor, for that matter, anyone else!

The church was cool even though it was July but Frank was sweating. He had been measured for his new uniform by the man at Unifit's, the naval tailors in Station Road and he had managed to persuade them to finish it in three days so that he could get married looking smart.

The tailor had smiled at the obvious eagerness with which Frank viewed the prospect of his life sentence; he had been married for thirty years and had regretted almost every one of them. A word in the right ear at the factory however had ensured that the uniform had been completed in time; Frank found the note in the trouser pocket when he tried it on, 'Good luck sailor, God bless you.'

The clear, mature, feminine handwriting and the writer's good wishes had somehow made him feel that perhaps, if she had been alive, his mother would have approved and he felt a warmness towards the unknown writer.

The organist's notes accompanied Alice down the aisle and Frank watched her, awestruck by her beauty in the white wedding dress which clearly owed nothing to clothes rationing and the coupons issued by the government. The dress was of the purest white satin, full busted and long sleeved. The skirt, full, was decorated with flowers appliquéd by a loving hand long before the war had made such frippery unfashionable.

Alice's mother watched her daughter and brushed aside a tear as she saw in, her mind's eye, herself wearing the same dress all those years ago. How long was it? She knew exactly, she had been pregnant with Alice at the time but the dress had covered that and she had never told anyone, not even the man she had married. She saw the look on Alice's face and suspected that the dress might be today covering her first grandchild.

The couple stood, spotlighted by a beam of multi-coloured sunlight, the service complete. 'You may kiss your bride.' They marched down the aisle together into a new life as a married couple, as husband and wife, for ever, until death did them part; Frank hoped that wouldn't be too soon.

Granting them leave, the Captain had joked that getting married was a good idea, he himself would have married many times had his wife not insisted on him remaining faithful. He had granted leave to Scrumpy Higgins too with the quiet injunction that he should stay sober until after the wedding.

He had also made it clear that their leave ended in four days. No ifs or buts, no special pleading for compassionate leave would be accepted. Back on board in four days or he personally would ensure that they both spent the rest of the war in the detention quarters attached to Chatham barracks.

Scrumpy had suggested that that at least would ensure that they both survived the present hostilities. Lieutenant Commander Horton admitted to having a vested interest in getting this war finished as quickly as possible and no excuses would he accepted for delaying his return to his wife and civvy street. 'Was that clearly understood?'

They had both grinned and promised that they would be back in time to win the war for him and had left the Captain's Requestmen's table with every intention of doing just that; the Captain seemed to have forgotten his earlier decision to transfer Scrumpy out of the ship and into barracks where his disability could be dealt with and Scrumpy wasn't about to remind him.

The air raid siren sounded whilst Alice was upstairs changing out of her wedding dress and Frank left the others in the bar downstairs. Alice's father had declared the bar open house until the beer ran out, having wisely put aside a supply for that evening's normal trade. The brewery was paying for his daughter's reception but what they didn't know wasn't going to hurt them.

Alice stood, looking at herself in the mirror above the dressing table, wondering if it showed yet. Her wedding dress lay on the bed and she stood there in her petticoat, tidying the hair she had disturbed taking off the dress. Frank saw her and whistled.

She saw him in the mirror. 'Hallo sailor. Want a good time?'

Frank closed the door. Downstairs, the guests were celebrating and one or two had glanced out of the door at the sky to see if they could see any raiders. Nowadays, they tended to come in one's, sneaking in under the coastal radar, in the hope of doing some damage and getting out again before the gunners could get a bead on them. Seeing none, the wedding guests had returned to the bar, the war could wait; if the Germans came, they'd buy them a pint!

Scrumpy didn't know any of Alice's family, except her husband, he joked to himself and had decided that his part of the festivities was over and he could safely push off. He headed up the hill towards the NAFFI club; the walk would do him good. Upstairs, Frank and Alice ignored both the guests and the unseen German bombers.

He helped her undress, lingering, admiring each perfect part of her as it was exposed, seeing her as if for the first time, for the first time as Mrs Frank Bye. He touched her, gently at first then more urgently; downstairs was forgotten, the war was forgotten, nothing existed, neither time nor place, only this moment and the two of them.

It was funny he thought that he could hear their breathing so loudly, he wondered for a moment whether those downstairs could also hear it, it was so loud. Louder and louder, it intruded upon his consciousness until, even in his state of arousal, he realised that it wasn't their breathing he could hear, that had become so intrusive. He raised his head, dragging his wits away and recognised the sound of the asynchronous motors of the German bomber as it skimmed low over the pub, missing chimney pots by a few feet, to impact with a massive explosion half way up the hill on the road to Gillingham.

The crashing plane missed the hospital and the evacuated school but the patients in the first and the children in the shelters of the second both heard and felt the blast as the aircraft's fuel tanks exploded. Its empty bomb racks meant that the explosion was less severe than it might otherwise have been but Scrumpy, walking up the hill, died instantly. The locals rushed to the scene in the hope that they could be of some help to someone, anyone, even the crew of the bomber if any had survived.

Unmissed by the wedding reception at the Sailor's Return, Scrumpy joined all those other sailormen in heaven. In bed, above the reception, Frank Bye entered that other heaven.

Book Two

1945

CHAPTER THIRTEEN

The new Yeoman, Charlie Peters, had been competent and sober and quickly accepted as a popular member of Comus' Petty Officer's mess; Scrumpy Higgins was never mentioned, he had been one of them and then he wasn't, it was the navy's way. Frank had liked the new man who had wanted to recommend him for promotion but who had accepted that, if Frank wanted out of the navy, that was his right.

Personally, he had had his doubts about Frank's prospects. Too easy he thought; what did Frank know about hotels? As a Barnardo's boy and a sailor, Frank had never stayed in an hotel. Aggie Western's hostels and the Navy House in Chatham but not a proper hotel, Yeoman Peters had had his doubts and put forward his recommendation for Frank's promotion anyway.

'Just in case it all goes wrong mate,' he had told Frank;' it might help if you want to come back'

In the mess, it was generally agreed that it was up to the pongoes, the soldiers, now. The navy had done its bit, it had escorted the American and Canadian armies across the Atlantic, it had escorted the thousands of merchant ships full of food for the civvies and ammunition for the soldiers, it had exhausted itself ensuring that when, at last, the time had come, the soldiers could be landed on the beaches of France.

Frank was tired; the whole navy was tired. The ships were tired, worn out but, at last, the pressure was lessening, there were fewer and fewer U-boats at sea and the German long-range aircraft had long-since lost their French airfields to the advancing allied armies. Convoys now crossed the Atlantic like a bus service, eastwards to Europe full of war materials, food and now, even the occasional luxury. Westwards, holds empty but cabin and other accommodation given over to the repatriation of wounded to homes many had thought never to see again.

When it came, victory in Europe would be celebrated with a fervour only those who had faced death and escaped it could bring to such a festival. The war wasn't over yet perhaps but this was truly the beginning of the end.

For Frank, the end came when his request for discharge from the service by purchase was granted. The Japanese had succumbed to two atom bombs dropped by the Americans and the war was over. The new Government and the Admiralty, as in years past, were quick to discharge the Hostilities Only men who had made victory possible and to decommission ships into the strategic reserve.

Whilst awaiting their discharge into civvy street, thousands of these sailors were employed on those ships, cocooning their guns against the weather just in case the Ruskies decided to play up rough and they had to be recommissioned in a hurry. The more politically aware suspected that the Russians had their eye on the occupation of the whole of Europe and, if push came to shove, these old ships would have to be dragged out of their retirement very quickly indeed. Many were so old and tired that no amount of cocooning could make their preservation worthwhile however and these were left to rust until the scrap merchants came for them.

Frank felt odd, sleeping in Alice's room every night although he had slept there before. Now it was his room too, shared also with their tiny daughter Virginia until they found their hotel; Alice's efforts to find a suitable property before the war's end having been unsuccessful. The baby's cot had been put in the most draught-free corner, away from the window but it made the room appear very crowded. Every day that they weren't working downstairs in the bar or, in Frank's case in the cellar he having taken over the cellarage duties from Alice's father, they walked all over the Medway towns of Rochester, Chatham, and Gillingham looking at prospects. Hotels that might, just might for the right price, be available. Too old, too run down to be worth buying, the wrong location, the right location but the wrong price. It seemed to go on for ever although, Frank had to admit, it was only seven months since he had come ashore. There's got to be one somewhere, he kept telling Alice but she kept saying no to every one they inspected.

'It's no good buying the wrong one Love. We've only got a little money and we don't want to spend all of it up front when we know that there will be all sorts of refitting and renovations to do to make what we buy into what we want, an hotel that will attract a regular, well paid clientele that will ensure our future.'

She was right, of course but Frank was keen to get out of the pub, away from her parents and into a place of their own. He liked her parents but he was eager to get started on their own, in their own hotel, making money for themselves rather than for the brewery.

'Come on, there's another street on the other side of the station that might have something suitable. There must be one somewhere that has all the things we want!'

'Do you think we're being too choosey?'

'No Love. You're right, it has to be in the right place and in the right condition or we'll spend the first ten years rebuilding the damned thing. It's just that I want us to be together, just the three of us, working together.'

'I know Love and we will be soon, I'm sure we'll find what we want soon. '

'Well, we had better chop chop or the prices will have gone up too far for us to buy the place we want.'

The street on the other side of Chatham station had received a series of bombs meant for the railway line and nothing worth looking at had survived. Perhaps someone with all sorts of money could do something with these buildings but it wasn't going to be them. Probably, the Council would buy up the whole street and redevelop with the blocks of flats they were building all over the town.

'Come on lover, let's go home. I'm cold and I want a bath before we open this evening. Mum and Dad are going to the Chamber of Commerce meeting this evening and we're in charge on our own. At least that shows that they trust us not to make a mess of things.'

They held hands as they walked back to the Sailor's Return. 'Don't worry Love, we'll find something soon.'

He tightened his hold of her hand. ''course we will.'

The pub was warm and the bar friendly. Frank had lit a fire in the grate and talk was of the coming Christmas, the first peacetime Christmas since nineteen thirty eight. God what had happened since then; the world was not the same anymore, even the people had changed. It had been different during the war but now that peace had been declared, the wartime attitude of sharing and helping each other had gone. Sometimes, he wondered whether it had all been worthwhile. All those brave men dead, all those promises by the post-war Government that things would be better now that we had defeated fascism and elected a socialist government and what had they got?

Food rationing was even worse than during the war damn it, this government had put bread on ration; even the Germans hadn't forced the wartime government into that! Fuel was even shorter than during the war and all their talk of freedom had resulted in the continued direction of labour by a government unwilling to relinquish any of the emergency powers its predecessor had taken during the worst days of the war.

Frank knew many of the ex-service men he spoke to were disappointed, unhappy that the peace was not as advertised, many things were actually worse! Oh sure, nobody was being bombed now and nobody was being shot at as they scrambled through hedges in France but if that was the case, how come that now that they were all civvies again, other things were worse, not better.

Standing on the Strand at Gillingham, just downstream from Chatham, the other side of the dockyard, Frank could see the reserve fleet ships, moored fore and aft to buoys in midstream, dark, abandoned, no longer alive but haunted by the men who had fought them and died in them. Frank wondered whether, in a few years time when the civvies had full bellies again, anyone would remember them. Sometimes he went down there, just to look at the ships and would see others sitting on the park benches or just standing on the sea wall, looking at the ships; they would remember.

'It doesn't do to think about it. It's over, done, the ships will soon be scrapped just like us.' Frank recognised the speaker.

'That's going a bit far, isn't it?'

'I don't think so, I've had it with this country. I'm off I can tell you, me and two of me mates, we're taking our wives and kids to Australia where they appreciate a man who has a trade and young'ns; not like here.'

'Have you ever been to Aussie? Where are you going? It's a big country.'

'Don't have to worry about that mate. The Aussie Government is arranging everything, the passage on the ship, accommodation in a family hostel till we find our own place and a job all lined up. I tell you, mate, it's a darn site better deal than this lot gave us ex-servicemen.'

'Then I wish you luck mate maybe it's a good idea but I don't think that's for me. Too much like the Andrew if someone is telling you where to go and what to do. Still, good luck.' Frank left him standing there.

The pub had reverted to its peacetime occupation of providing a haven for those few, older sailors who chose to make it their run ashore, the youngsters who called in on their way to the cinema or dancehall and to those friends of Alice's dad who had been regulars before and throughout the war.

Chatter in the bar regularly returned to the war years but as if they had been years ago rather than just a matter of months. Stories started with, do you remember and ended with everybody laughing, desperate to convince themselves that it had all been in another lifetime, a previous incarnation.

Stories were told about the girls who had made The Brook, with its many pubs, the most popular street in Chatham, though of course that didn't include the Sailor's Return. One of Arthur's old friends spoke up from his seat beside the fire.

'Do you remember that big blonde girl, used to use the Beefeater pub down the other end of the street, she reckoned she could handle twenty soldiers in an evening?'

'Yeah, but only five sailors, eh Frank? Good thing you knew about Alice's Yank and his taxi's, eh Frank?' The laugh at the end of the remark was designed to ensure that Frank knew they were only joking; Alice was Frank's wife, Alice was Arthur's daughter and Alice was in the other bar, Alice, it was always emphasised, wasn't like that.

Arthur glared angrily at the speaker. 'Now then, Eddie, you know there was nothing like that here. Even if Alice's Yank was giving her a lot of money, we all know it was her share of the takings from the taxi's.'

'Course it was, Arthur. Everybody knows that'

Arthur had winked at Frank. 'True enough lad, they made a lot of money out of those old taxis but everyone knew that was all there was to it, eh John?' he turned for support to the man sitting at the end of the bar nursing his pint who grinned.

'God, it was the talk of the town, everyone thought it was a brilliant idea, just so long as nobody asked where they got their petrol. No questions, no pack drill, eh?

What the authorities didn't know wouldn't hurt 'em. Anyway, everyone knew he got the petrol from his mates in the American army so it was none of our business and it certainly meant that more Yanks came into town and spent their money. I reckon they provided a public service, Alice and her Yank, should've been given a bloody medal by the Town Hall.'

Frank laughed with the others but the phrase kept coming up in their stories; Alice and her Yank. He was sure there had been nothing between them, Alice and her Yank, she had told him all about Tex and the taxis but he wished they would stop talking about them as if they had been a couple. It was almost as if they had been married or something; it was beginning to get under his skin.

Tomorrow they would find the hotel they were looking for and they could leave the pub and all her father's cronies to talk amongst themselves about their war. He had had enough of the war, all he wanted was Alice, Virginia and a place of their own.

Christmas, the first Christmas since the war was terrible. Everyone tried very hard to make it jolly but the meat ration had been cut again and coal was being directed to the power stations and factories where it was needed to power the export drive; homes would have to make do. The Minister of Fuel and Power had issued so many demands for economy that he had become the subject of newspaper cartoons in which someone was shown stealing a lump of coal from a dump under a notice stating 'Beware: your Shinwell find you out,' a play on the Minister's name

Their search for a suitable property for their hotel was being frustrated also by the local authority's disinclination to derequisition properties they had taken over during the war. They should have given them back to the owners when these owners, if they had survived the war, returned to claim them but the new breed of lefty bureaucrats had no intention of returning these now valuable buildings without a fight through the courts. Many of the owners, unable to afford that, had given up without a fight and had become council tenants in their own homes; hoping that, in time, they would be returned to them or that they would receive compensation; perhaps after the next election.

The pub was closed on Christmas day and they all gathered in the upstairs parlour for the Christmas dinner Sylvia and Alice had prepared. A liberal application of spirits to both the meat gravy and to the Christmas pudding that followed ensured that Christmas day afternoon was spent in an alcoholic haze.

'You know what's in the cocktail cabinet there, Frank, get Alice and Sylvia whatever they want and yourself too, of course. I'll have a large single malt, if you've left me any that is.'

'Would you have let me marry Alice if you'd known I liked single malt whisky?'

'No I bloody wouldn't! But I have to admit, you've made yourself useful around here so I suppose I shouldn't complain. Now, if you could just see your way to removing both my daughter and yourself into your hotel, Sylvia and me could get back to being the happy young couple we used to be before Alice was born.'

'Don't be silly Arthur, you're not man enough for that any more.'

'Just you give me the chance my fine young Sylvia and I'll show you I'm man enough for you!'

'Oh well, if it's only man enough for me you're aiming for, you might just make it. I'm not the girl I used to be.'

'Mum! You're embarrassing me. '

'Then I shouldn't be, my girl. How do you think you came into this world? Spontaneous combustion? Virgin birth? No my girl, you were the result of some good old fashioned sex and it's about time you let us get back to it'

'What now? This minute?'

'Well, perhaps not this minute but soon Alice, soon.'

'Mum! That's enough, you're drunk.'

Frank saw that Arthur was already asleep in his chair and hoped that Sylvia wouldn't be too far behind him. This conversation was getting out of hand and he didn't like being referred to as if he wasn't there.

He thought about it, quietly sipping his drink, waiting for Sylvia to fall asleep so that he could talk to Alice about the constant irritation downstairs in the bar, of references to Alice and her Yank. He knew there had been other men before they had met, of course there had but he was now just drunk enough to broach the subject with Alice. He needed to know.

'Let's go for a walk Love. I'm too full and I don't want to just sit here and go to sleep like some old codger.'

'You're embarrassed! God, you're even blushing. Come on then, let's go and get some exercise.'

They walked down to the Town Hall and crossed the road to walk along the river frontage. Now that the war was over the barbed wire had been removed and the promenade tidied up a little.

'I want us to find a place of our own, I don't like living with your folks.'

She looked at him. 'Why? I thought you were happy there and, God knows, it's free which is a major advantage if we're trying to save every penny.'

"I don't know. There's just something about being so close to your mum and dad. I lie there at night wondering if they can hear us making love; they're just the other side of that wall. And, I don't like some of the talk in the bar when your father's there. It's as if they all know something that I don't know but nobody's going to tell me, I have to work it out from what they're saying.'

'Talk about what?'

'Talk about you and that Yank and other things.'

'But you know all about Tex, I told you didn't I.'

'Sometimes I wonder if I know all about everything.'

'Don't be silly sweetheart, of course you know everything. We'll find our hotel soon, I'm sure we will.'

CHAPTER FOURTEEN

The stranger in the bar wore a navy tie and blue blazer with grey trousers and black toecap-less shoes; every inch the typical ex sailor and almost certainly now a rep for some company wishing to sell something to the pub. He sat, waiting for an opportunity to speak to Frank privately which seemed a little odd as, usually, reps were not backward in coming forward when they had something to sell.

Frank mentioned it to Arthur who said he should deal with him as it would be good practice for when they had their hotel. Frank wondered if he detected in Arthur's voice some doubt whether the hotel would ever materialise but let it go. He wondered sometimes whether Alice's mum and dad were only too happy for them to go on running two of the bars and doing the cellaring, leaving Arthur to hold court in the private with his friends and Sylvia to spend most of her time upstairs goo-gooing at the baby.

'May we speak privately?'

'I don't see why that should be necessary, what are you selling?'

'Well, how can I put this,' the man's voice was so quiet that Frank could barely hear him, 'I just thought that you might be interested in a supply of Cognac. Directly imported from France, you might say and therefore a little cheaper that your usual supplier, if he has any that is of course.'

The brewery was responsible for the supply of all the drinks sold in its pubs and Frank guessed that the speaker would know that. 'I think you had better speak to the boss.'

Frank caught Arthur's eye and, leaving his conversation in the private bar, he came into the saloon and stood beside Frank.

'Problem?'

'I think this gentleman would like to make you an offer you can't afford to refuse, on the other hand, I suspect that you may choose to anyway. I'll leave you to discuss it.'

He moved away down the bar but remained within earshot just in case the stranger became threatening in any way.

'So, what's this offer then?'

The man looked round the bar, satisfying himself that no-one could hear their discussion.

'I am in a position to offer you a regular supply of imported Brandy, top quality and at a very reasonable price. I just wondered if you would be interested, I'm speaking to a number of publicans in the town and was sure that you wouldn't want to be left out.'

'I'm afraid you have picked the wrong pub, Son. The brewery supplies all our spirits so I'm not in a position to take advantage of what is, I'm sure, a very generous offer. Close the door on your way out, there's a good lad.'

The man shrugged his shoulders and left, giving Frank a look of sympathy.

'What do you reckon? Stolen or smuggled?' Frank moved back to talk to Arthur.

'Probably. Anyway, I want no part of it. I'm at the wrong time of life to get involved in defrauding the brewery. Still, he's the third in a matter of months so they must be selling it to someone locally or they wouldn't bother coming in here. I'm going to have my lunch, keep an eye on the private as well, will you? There's only old Bob in there and he's famous for nursing one pint for an entire lunchtime session.'

'OK. I'll manage, it's not busy here either. I'll give an eye to Alice in the public every so often, just in case she needs anything.'

'Good lad. Don't know what I'd do without you.'

Frank suddenly realised that he had seen the stranger before. He was one of the small group of ex matelots who gathered at the Gillingham Strand. Frank hadn't recognised him at once because he had never seen him dressed up before. Usually, he was in old trousers and a jersey and Frank had assumed that he had a boat there and was working on it.

Realisation dawned. He did have a boat. The proffered Cognac was probably smuggled, not stolen. He wasn't sure that would make any difference to Arthur but it did explain why the man had come to this pub; he had recognised Frank and had chanced his luck. Perhaps he'd learn more next time he went down to the Strand.

In the Public bar, Alice was talking to an elderly man. The man looked up and looked away when he saw it was Frank.

'Problem?' Frank asked. 'Can I help?'

'No, no problem Love. This is Mr Timmins. You remember me telling you about Mr Tilling, Timmin's Taxis.'

'Yeah, of course. How do you do Mr Timmins. I'm surprised we haven't met before.'

'Been away for a while lad. Thought I'd like to see a bit of the world once I'd sold the business. Been to the States you know, thought I'd like to see if it was really as good as all them Yanks said it was.'

'Is it?'

'Better son, better. Fantastic place. None of this crazy rationing or any of that direction of labour crap. Now that really is the land of the free and the home of the brave. You should try it son, take Alice and bugger off to America, this place's finished.

'This lot'll wreck it before the next election and they'll never be able to put it back together again; like humpty bloody dumpty if you ask me. Still, I'm off back there at the end of the month, just thought I'd pop in and see that Alice was alright, happy, that she had what she wanted.'

He offered Frank a cigarette, an American cigarette. 'Give it some thought, son. England's finished.' He smiled at Alice, winking one eye and left the bar.

'What was that all about?'

A knock on the bar in the Saloon called him away before Alice could answer and he served the customer with half a pint of brown ale. At this rate, they were not going to make a fortune this lunchtime so he left the drinker to his half and returned to Alice.

'Not what you'd call busy, is it'.

'No. I reckon old man Timmins might have something. Still, I don't want to go to America, I want our own place here. It'll pick up once rationing ends and everything gets back to normal, you'll see.'

'How long can the brewery hold out running pubs like this with no business worth bothering with? Do you reckon we'll find our hotel before they decide to close the pub, knock it down and build council flats on the site?'

'They won't do that Love.'

Frank wasn't sure about that but that was her father's problem. His problem was that he had seen Alice secrete a small package under the bar when he had come in and disturbed her discussion with old man Timmins.

'What's this?' He asked, picking it up.

'Mr Timmins gave it to me. Don't know what it is, he said it was a present from America. Just a little something he brought back.'

'Just a little something from your Yank?'

'Well, to be honest, yes it is but I didn't know it was coming and I don't even care if you throw it away without opening it.'

'No, I think we should open it. It's the least we can do after he carried it all that way.'

He stripped the paper from the packet and opened it. Inside, a gold eternity ring set with red and white stones was secured by a rubber band to a note. 'Thanks for everything Honey. Give me a call if you ever get to Texas.'

'I don't imagine he sent that for old time's sake in the taxi business!'

By the time he closed the door of the saloon bar, he had made up his mind. He went upstairs and packed a suitcase with his clothes, throwing in a toothbrush and his razor.

'What are you doing?' Alice stood in the doorway.

'I can't compete with Yanks who send you diamond and ruby rings, certainly not eternity rings! So now tell me again that there was nothing between you two but a couple of clapped out taxis! Is that what all the jokes in the bar have been about? No wonder you had two thousand Pounds in the bank! How much did you charge him?'

'There was nothing between us, I wouldn't do that to you.'

'I don't believe you I reckon that all the time I was at sea, all the time I was writing to you, telling you how much I loved you and wanted you, you were bedding this Yank, making your pile before I came back. Well, you can keep his ring, and his money too. I don't want any of it and, if that's the kind of girl you are, I don't want you either.'

He threw the last of his things into the green canvas, leather cornered, pussers suitcase. He thought about Virginia; damn it the child was out with her grandma. Was she really his? She wasn't Tex's, she was white but had there been others, others that he didn't know about? He slammed shut the case, snapping the locks closed. 'Shit!'

The manager at the Navy House, the sailor ashore's hostel, took pity on him, the place wasn't full and Frank was obviously ex navy. Officially he wasn't entitled to a cabin there but what the hell? He was obviously upset about something and, in Chatham these days that usually meant domestic troubles. The pussers suitcase confirmed it for him.

'OK mate but just the one night, alright?'

'Cheers. You're a pall.'

The tiny cabin was warm and the bed clean. During the night, the inevitable tap on the door woke Frank but he ignored it and the tapper moved on to try his luck at other doors.

It was the advertisement in the paper that Frank was reading that gave him the idea of emigrating. There had been a lot of talk about ex servicemen going to Australia but that didn't appeal to Frank. He had seen Perth in nineteen forty-five, just before his demobilisation and he had not been impressed.

Bit too wild west for him, he thought. Sydney was supposed to be a great city and Melbourne too but the catch with the cheap emigration to Aussie was that the Aussie government decided where you went and Frank had had enough of governments deciding what he was going to do and where.

He lit a cigarette and sipped his tea, folding the paper so that he could read it without it getting in the way of his cup. Canada. No cheap passages but they would accept young men prepared to work. No government direction about where they could go but, of course, he would have to go where the work was and that meant one of the cities initially.

Frank had met only two Canadians, sailors, in Glasgow a couple of years ago and had thought them less intimidating than the Yanks and, anyway, there was no way he was going to bloody America and there was nothing he wanted here.

He stubbed out his cigarette and finished his tea, pushing the cup away from him. Canada? Perhaps? It was certainly worthwhile ringing the telephone number given in the advertisement and asking questions. He didn't have to commit himself to anything, just ask a few questions.

What about Alice? What about the baby? Well? What about them? He would decide what to do about them when he had decided what he was going to do about himself.

He made the phone call, using the office telephone at the Navy House, the Manager let him use it saying that he would be doing his rounds for ten minutes and what he didn't see wouldn't worry him. He took the same attitude when Frank asked him if he could stay for a while. He could pay, he assured him; it was just that he didn't have anywhere else to stay at the moment.

'OK but stay out during the day. You can come in after six in the evening. I'll probably know how many cabins will be occupied by then and as long as yours isn't needed, you can stay for a few days, OK?'

'Fantastic mate. Cheers.'

'Oh, and, next time I knock on your door, open the bloody thing eh?'

The few days turned into a couple of months. He went back to the pub but Arthur advised him that Alice didn't want to see him. Personally, he liked Frank but Alice was his daughter and, if she said no, then no it was. 'Sorry son.' At the end of the second month, Frank gave up trying.

CHAPTER FIFTEEN

Greenock hadn't changed since those last days of the war when the river had been full of convoy escorts, transports, troopships, cruisers, minesweepers and all the other symbols of naval warfare; Greenock had looked grey and worn.

He had left the town in '45 with a travel warrant to Chatham barracks, HMS Pembroke, freedom and a new life with Alice planned in great detail. Now he was back. Greenock was still grey, dirty and war damaged, almost as if he hadn't been away at all.

At first, he hadn't wanted to believe what he had heard, stories about the American and, before that, English sailors. Frank had countered that, before meeting him, Alice had been free to go out with whoever she pleased; there were always stories about publican's daughters but once the dam burst, there were just too many stories from too many so called friends.

They had been happy. He had been discharged from the navy on to the emergency reserve and although they had been unable to find a small hotel for sale immediately, her father had helped him settle back into civvy street and given him work in the pub but the stories about Alice had persisted and then, the Yank had sent her that eternity ring!

Looking back, Frank knew that it had been the lack of any reasonable explanation for the two thousand Pounds in Alice's bank account that had chipped away at his confidence. So she had helped this Yank find a few old taxis and made some money from them but two thousand! That was one hell of a lot of money; five years wages if he had stayed in the navy. It was the two thousand pounds that had finally made Frank believe; then there was the ring.

He didn't like England the way it was but, with Alice, he had been sure that things would improve. He didn't like the direction of labour in peacetime, he didn't like the continued rationing and he didn't like the control of almost everything by the all-powerful state. This was not the England free and fair that he had fought for and worse, now it seemed that Alice wasn't the girl he had thought her to be. Even if only part of it was true, some of it must be and that made a difference.

It had been a bad afternoon. The baby, Virginia had been crying upstairs annoying Alice's mum who was looking after her whilst they both worked downstairs in the bars. Her parting comment still echoed round and round in his head.

'You were happy enough to plan the hotel, how did you suppose we were going to pay for it? From your wages as a sailor? Those taxis and the Yank will pay for it.'

The sheer impossibility of doing any such thing was obvious. Even then, angry as he was, Frank could only see the stupidity of it, he had stormed out and, when his attempt at return, he had been rebuffed. Sylvia had tried to help, so had Arthur but Alice had made it clear that if he couldn't trust her to tell him the truth, she could manage quite well without him. And here he was, back in Greenock.

The train had arrived an hour and a half late, the station hadn't been swept since he had left it two years ago, no one had taken down the fading wartime posters instructing everyone that careless talk costs lives and urging them to Be like Dad, keep Mum and, what was worse, he still loved Alice.

He couldn't just switch off his love, it was something that had grown slowly and, he imagined, it would only slowly die. He hoped it wouldn't take too long, he was miserable, lonely and, standing on the station platform unsure where to go, not at all sure that he had done the right thing.

It was too late now, nothing could be changed; he lodged his suitcase in the left luggage office and walked out into the street. Nobody bothered to ask him for his ticket. Nobody who didn't need to would be coming to Greenock.

CHAPTER SIXTEEN

The combination of the fading posters and the depressing state of Greenock in general were enough to send Frank in search of a drink. He also needed a bed for the night.

The big hotels that had been used before the war by the ocean liner passengers and, during the war by the admiralty as offices, remained closed and shuttered. The pre-war luxury trade had not returned with the peace and the admiralty had left for somewhere more entertaining but the dockside pubs were doing the same roaring trade that they always had.

The merchant navy sailors had had a hard war and were now back where they had been before. Signed on for the duration of the voyage and paid off as soon as they got back; even during the war it had been like that. One voyage contracts and, if the ship was sunk, a survivor's pay ended on the day of the sinking.

The few liners now using the port, now that peace had returned, put on a show of good conditions but these were almost entirely for the passengers. The seamen on deck, the stewards in the cabins and the firemen down below saw little improvement in their accommodation from before the war.

The White Star was a very ordinary pub by dockyard standards. Brightly lit and noisy with a more or less constant movement of men in and out; only the women, sitting in the comfortable, upholstered corner seats, were fixtures. From time to time one of these would get up, drape her coat about her and disappear out of the door with a customer; to reappear within ten minutes to finish the drink and continue her barely interrupted conversation.

They knew why they were there, the sailors knew why they were there, the publican knew why they were there and he knew also that, if the women weren't there, the sailors wouldn't be there and neither would he; everyday life in a dockside pub. Simple, traditional, straightforward and understood by all who passed that way.

Frank slipped through the door into the warm embrace of the bar. Here he would not be bothered by anyone and would be allowed to sit and drink his beer in as much misery as he chose. When he was ready to return to the land of the reasonably happy, that would be alright by them also. He could mind his own business and they would mind theirs but his entrance would not be missed. He ordered a pint, stood at the bar for a few minutes sipping it then drank the rest quickly and ordered another.

'Lord, you looked miserable when you came in. Look better now though so it can't have been that bad.'

She was about forty but could have been more or less depending upon how many drinks you'd had. She stood against the bar beside Frank trying to catch the eye of the barman, her empty glass held aloft.

'Port and lemon please Bill, there's a dear.'

Frank paid for her drink. She reminded him of the advertisement for KIWI boot polish showing a pair of old but shiny shoes above the caption, 'Well Worn but Worn Well.'

'Haven't seen you in here before. What ship?'

'Just passing through. Just came in out of the cold for a drink and to ask the landlord if he had a room to spare. Only arrived this afternoon and haven't fixed up anything yet. Got two days before I join my ship.'

'I've got a room. It'll cost you thirty bob.'

'That sum has a nice rounded sound to it. Shall we have another drink?'

Frank's wallet contained only just more than enough to pay his dues and his one suitcase had been left at the station, together with his immigration papers, passport and money; no point in inviting trouble. There were some real hard cases in towns like this. Many a simple sailorman had been relieved of their take home pay between the ship's gangway and the railway station but Frank knew the routine; never dress too smart, never flash money about and never, ever, start an argument in a dockside pub. They had two more drinks while they got to know each other.

The room was warm and dry and the bed, big enough for both of them and another when times were hard or if that was the client's fancy. She said he could have it to himself if he wished.

'My name's Betty Hunt, that's Hunt with a H, what's yours?'

'Thanks. They call me Goodbye but my name's Frank.'

He didn't tell her who they were and she didn't ask. Sailors often had funny names for each other, often based on the owner's proper name; Frank was happy for her to believe that he was just some sailorman passing through Greenock to sign on a ship that hadn't yet arrived.

Such seamen would have little money and would have with him only what he needed to get aboard. It was sailors coming back from the sea that would have their payoff money and even, perhaps a few presents for the family. Ships came into the Clyde from all over the world and the local fences had the means to redirect almost anything to a paying customer for cash.

Frank took a generous swig from the bottle she held out and stood up.

'Where's the head?'

'Second on the right across the landing.'

'Keep a couple of swigs of that for me. I'll be back in a minute.'

The chain didn't work first time and he tugged again, venting his anger at having thought of Alice. By the time he got back to Betty, he felt altogether better in every way. She had finished undressing and had slid under the bedclothes to keep warm and Frank followed her example, placing his clothes neatly on the chair. He then placed the chair against the door, its back wedged under the handle to prevent sudden, unexpected and unwelcome interruptions during the night.

You couldn't be too careful. That sleepy moment, after sexual satisfaction and a few drinks, was the ideal time for the arrival of the irate husband, boyfriend, pimp or whatever who would relieve you of what little you possessed before you could drag your senses back to planet earth. Betty didn't seem to be that type and they hadn't discussed money but there was no point in taking chances.

She watched what he was doing and grinned. 'You're not as green as you're cabbage looking, are you'

She made no objection to the arrangement and held up the bottle, there was one tot left.

'You said to save this.'

Frank could feel his blood coursing through his veins, could hear a rushing sound in his ears but pulled away from her.

The daylight showed through the window when they woke. It didn't exactly shine through, the sky was grey and overcast, waiting for rain and the window was so dirty that a tropical sun would have made little impression.

'Who the hell are you?'

'I came by to borrow a cup of sugar.'

'Oh, that's alright then, I thought there was a strange man in my bed.'

'There's nothing strange about me, love but I'll accept unusual if you want.'

'What I want is food.'

'If you make the outside look decent, I'll buy the inside some breakfast. There's bound to be a café round here somewhere, there always is.'

Bacon, eggs and toast and three cups of strong tea rebuilt the inner man.

'When's your ship due?'

'Tomorrow afternoon.'

'What are you going to do 'til then?'

'Thought I might go up to Glasgow this evening. Go to Barrowlands for a dance.'

'I knew you'd been here before. Only a local or a regular would know about Barrowlands. You want to take me?'

'Why not? It will save a whole lot of new introductions. You can act as my interpreter.'

'That's what I like about sailors, gallant. I'll meet you at the White Star at seven. I've got to go home and make sure my kid goes to school.'

'Who looks after your kid when you're working?'

'Mind your own business.'

'What are you going to do all day?'

'Help my mum mind her own business. I'll see you at seven.'

He took a long, deep drag at his cigarette, exhaling slowly. She left him sitting there. Not bad. She obviously didn't mind not working last night probably hopes that, when my ship returns, I'll look her up and let her earn some money; perhaps even bring her back a present. Last night had been a long-term investment; a rare experiment around here, he suspected.

Quite a girl. He bought another packet of cigarettes at the counter, noticing that they were 'recycled' duty-free's, then left, turning towards the station.

He collected his suitcase from the left luggage office and took it into the Gents. He changed his underclothes and shirt and took his suitcase back.

'This ain't a hotel.'

'You wouldn't like the class of clientele if it was.'

He wandered down towards the docks again. The ship would be in by now, he would be able to take a look at her. He had nothing better to do.

The old liner, a troopship during the war, was now employed transporting immigrants to Canada on a regular schedule. She had been repainted from the dark grey of her wartime livery but, somehow, she still looked tired, almost as if she was leaning against the wall for support.

She had seen better days, that much was clear. In her peacetime white and pale green paint, her funnel bright yellow with the big pale blue star emblazoned upon it and her white coated stewards busying themselves about the promenade deck folding and stacking deck chairs, she reminded Frank of an elderly lady down on her luck; what the newspaper ads called genteel poverty.

Fallen upon hard times he thought but desperately trying to keep up appearances. At least she looked seaworthy enough. She would get him to Canada and, probably many thousands more like him before being put down like an old horse no longer able to earn its keep.

CHAPTER SEVENTEEN

Their visit to Barrowlands had been a success, nothing much had changed since the war. There were more young men about out of uniform now than in those days but the atmosphere had been much the same; thick smoke, flashing lights and big band music, the kind of music you could dance to.

The effect of five Wee Macs on Frank and an equal number of port and lemons on Betty had been enough to dampen their ardour to the extent that sleep overtook them before passion was sufficiently aroused to act as an antidote. They had slept deeply, soundlessly and without interruption until, with the morning light filtering through the dirty window, Frank had stretched out to discover the empty space beside him. He glanced round the room.

Her clothes were gone, the chair was no longer wedged under the door handle and his wallet lay open and empty on the bedside table. A note lay beside it, held in place by three shillings in change.

'Sorry but good intentions don't pay the rent or feed the kid. This will buy your breakfast and a packet of fags to keep you going until you sign on this afternoon. I'll see you at the White Star when you get back. Thanks for a great night out, I owe you a free one, B.'

There had been only about two pounds in the wallet anyway; at least she had left him enough for some fags, some girls would have taken his clothes to the pawnshop as well.

The cabin was much as Frank had imagined it would be, an oversized cupboard with no window. Painted in bright colours only a year ago, it was still bright enough to pass muster. Two tiers of three bunks either side of the door left room in the middle for a tiny table. Not, Frank thought, top hotel standards but this would do him for a few days. Suitcases of earlier arrivals already reserved two of the bunks and Frank reserved his before going in search of a drink.

The promenade deck bar, refurbished to look much as it must have done before the war, was already full of young men celebrating their impending departure from England, a land of shortages and, in few days, they would celebrate with equal enthusiasm their arrival in Canada, a land of promise and plenty. No need for the endless anti U-boat zigzagging course corrections to which he had been accustomed when previously crossing the Atlantic, this would be a safe, pleasant and uneventful crossing taking just a few days; he might even enjoy it.

'How long before we sail?'

The questioner looked about sixteen and scared.

'Still time to jump ship and go home if you want to change your mind, son. Doubt if they'll give you a refund though.'

'Hell no. I've only just persuaded myself it was a good idea. If I even think about changing my mind now, I'll probably chicken out and go home to mum.'

'What would your mum think of that?'

'I don't know but I'm not going to give my dad the satisfaction of saying I told you so. He reckoned I wouldn't get as far as Glasgow, let alone Toronto. I don't think I could go home now even if I did jump ship.'

'You look a bit young for emigration lad, you got somewhere to go when we get there? Someone to look after you?'

'Yeah. My mum's sister married a Canadian during the war and I'm going to stay with them until I get something sorted out.'

'Then look at this way son. You probably have better immediate future prospects than most of these guys. I don't suppose more than one or two of them even know the name of a hotel in whatever town they're going to. I don't for one.'

The boy looked at Frank in awe.

'But how will you manage?'

'I'm a big lad, I'll be OK.'

'Buy you a drink?'

Frank looked at the lad. The steward would probably refuse to serve him.

'Better let me get it. What'll you have?'

'May I have a whisky?'

'You may have whatever you think you can drink son but, if it makes you ill, don't tell me about it.'

The boy almost choked to death. With the assistance of those closest patting him hard on the back and offering such advice as, bring it up, lad, it might be a gold watch, he recovered and, eyes streaming, attempted to smile.

'I didn't know it was like that!'

The visitors ashore bell rang and the stewards called on all not sailing to go ashore immediately.

'It's now or never lad.'

'I think I'll stay. Now that I've learned to drink I feel better.'

'What cabin are you in?'

'F13 but I haven't found it yet. Most of my things are in a trunk in the hold and I've only got this small case with me. I didn't know if it would be safe to leave it in the cabin.'

'Got anything worth stealing in there?'

'Only my clean underwear and shaving tackle. My money and passport have been lodged with the Purser's office. Mum said to make sure I did that first thing.'

'All your money?'

'No, I've got a few quid in my pocket for expenses onboard.'

'Then put your hand in your pocket, son; it's your round.'

Memories flooded back, memories of when he had been just a frightened kid like this lad and joining his first ship, not knowing what to do. God, it seemed a lifetime ago. In a way, he supposed, it was.

'You can stick with me if you like. You may need a friend.'

The lad looked relieved that someone else would make any difficult decisions. He stuck out his hand.

'My name's Peter Adams. '

'I'm Frank Bye.'

'You ever been on a ship before?'

'One or two but nothing like this.'

'What? Troopships, things like this?'

'No, warships, things like that.'

'Cor!'

'Nothing special. Just small ships, nothing like this. This is four or five times the size of anything I'm used to. Warm and dry and with waiter service, now that's what I call sailoring.'

In reality, there were many similarities between the Fairlight Head and a troopship. The passengers were mainly male, mostly young and mostly ex-service. The Purser was going to have his work cut out keeping this lot in order.

Transporting immigrants by the thousand was much the same as transporting troops but the civilian Purser lacked the authority of a Sergeant Major aboard a troopship. There was probably going to be quite a bit of trouble on this trip. Too many too fit young men with nothing to do and too much to drink; tailor made for trouble.

The PA system crackled into life and someone could be heard clearing his throat.

'Good afternoon, ladies and gentlemen. Welcome aboard Fairlight Head. We shall be sailing in ten minutes and those wishing to wave goodbye to their loved ones ashore should proceed to the port side promenade deck immediately. Welcome aboard and Bon Voyage.'

There was an audible click as the microphone was switched off and a general movement towards the double doors opening on to the promenade deck. Most of them seemed to have worked out which was the port side; been on a troopship, perhaps.

'You got anyone to wave to?'

'No.'

'Then this might be a good time for you to find your cabin. Most of them will be up on deck giving a fond last look to the UK.'

Cabin F13 was identical to Frank's though lower in the ship. Peter opened the door and saw that the lights were on inside. Suitcases reserved all but one of the bunks; Peter put his case on that.

Frank felt the ship vibrate as the main engines turned over. He didn't need to be on deck to know what was happening. The bow and stern lines would be released and hauled inboard. A tug would haul them off the wall, clear of the ships moored forward and aft of them and the ships own engines would then be put at slow and later half ahead until they were well clear and until they dropped the pilot. Next stop Quebec.

He finished his drink and walked over to the starboard side of the ship. On the other side of the river, he could just make out Helensburgh, at the mouth of the Gareloch. The loch was full of dark grey ships of all sorts and sizes. Cruisers, destroyers, frigates and even a fleet carrier could be seen in the middle of the loch where she had sufficient water. Further up the loch, he knew, there were groups of pensioned off corvettes, minesweepers and all manner of smaller ships. Many of them would be towed away for scrap quite soon, utterly exhausted. One or two, he knew, had actually survived from the previous war, though God only knew how. They would be the first to go, then the most heavily patched, followed in turn by the Woolworth carriers that would never be used again whatever happened. Frank wondered how many razor blades could be made from an entire navy.

He remained looking at them for some time, a genuine sadness sweeping over him as he thought of all the sailors that had sailed and fought them. How many had died? Did anyone, other than their loved ones, care? He doubted it.

The Fairlight Head gathered way quickly with the river and the ebbing tide pushing her towards the sea; as they passed Dunoon, the first lights of the evening could be seen ashore.

Soon, to starboard, the lights of Rothsay would show and, to port, those of Largs might be seen before being hidden by the island. Frank couldn't be sure, there had been no lights on his previous sailings from Greenock. The memories came back without being called, the number of times he had sailed from the Clyde. All those convoys; he thought of the friends he had sailed with and of those who had died.

'This is the last time, old friends.'

He whispered a sad farewell to all those who had sailed from here, hoped they would find whatever peace they were looking for.

Whatever Canada was like, he would be better off there than in England. As a final gesture of respect towards all those he had sailed with and who had not returned, he promised himself that he would look after the boy. He remembered Stripey Williams, the three-badge Signalman who had taken him under his wing, made him his winger when he joined his first ship.

'You be my winger,' he had said. 'You'll come to no harm with me, lad.'

BOOK THREE

1947

CHAPTER EIGHTEEN

Peter had found the bathroom and toilets, both clearly signposted from his cabin. He could feel the vibration of the ships engines through the deck and a feeling of uncertainty, fear, swept over him.

It had all seemed such a good idea at home. Just pack his bag and go to Canada. He could stay with Aunty Amy and her Canadian husband while he found a job and, once he had saved a little money, he could get himself a place of his own and be independent. No more yes Mum no Mum, no more school, no more waiting for pocket money each week from his stepfather; independent!

Frank seemed a nice enough bloke and friendly but, like Dad had said, you can't trust anybody you don't know. Keep your money safe and your hand on your ha'penny - whatever that meant.

His real father had been killed in the war and his Mum had married Fred to provide for him. Fred hadn't really taken to him but had been a good provider and hadn't been unkind to his Mum; perhaps with him out of the way, they would have fewer rows about money. With him gone, money wouldn't be so tight.

Well, he didn't have to worry about them now, it was Aunty Amy and Uncle John that he had to worry about, he'd never met either of them. Amy had agreed to take him in because he was her sister's boy. They knew no more about him than he knew about them; he hoped they would like him, he would try very hard to like them and give them the respect they deserved

On Deck, Frank wrapped his coat around him and looked out over the widening river. Cold, grey and oil streaked, it never changed. Once this must have been a clean, fast flowing river spilling the melting winter snows and the summer rains from the highlands into the sea. He tried to imagine it before man had started to build ships along its green banks, all shining and bright in the sunlight with fish and small boats playing catch as catch can.

The shipyards had attracted people to work in them and they had to build houses to live in and pubs to drink in; all the things with which man constantly spoiled the once beautiful places God had made. It was different in Canada, he had read, man had not yet had time to destroy it; perhaps there was still hope for Canada.

Over to port, he could see Gourock. They were well clear of Greenock now and he could feel the ship heal very slightly as she turned to head roughly south towards Ailsa Craig and the sea; he shook himself. Like Peter, he had felt almost afraid. For a moment he wondered whether he should have brought Alice and the child with him, perhaps in a new country they could have started again. He dismissed the thought immediately, too late now.

Throughout the ship, in bars and cabins, more than a thousand immigrants were, he imagined, clearing their minds of the past, making room for the future.

Peter found him once more sitting in the corner of the bar with a glass in his hand, he smiled at the boy.

'Found your cabin alright then?'

'Yes. The other bunks all had suitcases on them so I put mine on the only one that didn't. I hope that's OK.'

'That'll do, which one was left?'

'Bottom of three on the right as you go in, why?'

'Then have your head at the far end of the bunk when you turn in,'

'Why? It's made up with the pillow at the end nearest the door.'

'Because, young Sir, when some drunken nutter staggers back to the cabin with a skin full of booze and the ship's rolling a bit, he will turn to close the door and spew all over the nearest bunk. And, son, he will be facing your bunk at the time.'

Peter couldn't imagine such a situation, he had never seen a man drunk enough to vomit all over someone's bed but, if Frank said it could happen, who was he to ignore his advice. This was Frank's environment and he should know. He ordered a beer.

Sylvia and Francis Hurd faced each other over the 'tween bed table in Cabin C22. The cabin was quite large, with its own toilet and shower cubicle. Two neatly made up beds looked quite comfortable and small armchairs added to the almost homely appearance. C22 was on the port side, with a large square window to let in what daylight was available. Bedside lamps now added brightness to that given by the deckhead lamp. A third bed, more a cot really, had been squeezed into the cabin for Hazel; it cramped the available accommodation but was far safer, Sylvia had said, than putting Hazel up in the let-down bunk above the inboard bed. She could fall out of that, Sylvia had said.

At five years old, Hazel was a small, weak child with asthma. It was for Hazel that they were going to Canada; the dry climate of Alberta would they hoped be better for her. Sylvia had heard great things about Alberta, the wide prairie with the constant drying wind was, she thought, just what Hazel needed. She had seen pictures of big, healthy looking farmers and secretly admired these big, strong men who looked competent and happy. Her husband Francis never looked happy.

With her to push him, Francis had managed to get an offer of a job in Edmonton through the company he had worked for in Edinburgh. S.J. Srivenor & Son had imported grain from Alberta since the turn of the century and had a branch office in Edmonton which did their buying. Whilst Francis had been offered a job there he would, of course, lose the seniority he had accumulated in Edinburgh; he would have to start again as a clerk.

He was sorry to be leaving the security of Edinburgh and head office but he loved Hazel and, if she could grow up healthy in Alberta, then he, Francis Hurd, would accept any disadvantages that that might entail. He just wished that Sylvia wouldn't keep on about him having to establish himself in the new job and to recover the seniority he had lost. It had been largely her idea to go to Canada and it was unfair of her to keep pushing about getting quick promotion to restore the social position she had to give up for his daughter. God, they hadn't even reached Canada yet, hadn't even left the Clyde, and she was on about it again.

Ambition, that was what he had always lacked, she told him. He should have been the manager long ago but hadn't the push to reach the top. In Canada, she would just have to push him harder, especially now that he was starting again from the bottom.

Hazel lay in her cot, her eyes firmly closed against the light and her ears firmly closed against her parent's rowing. She was used to this but she didn't like it; she wheezed and choked, trying to catch her breath. Sylvia picked her up.

'Now see what's happened!'

She cuddled Hazel and reassured her softly.

'It'll be alright when we get to Alberta darling. We shall have a nice new house and there will be lots of new friends for you to play with. Once we are settled in, you can go to school and meet lots of other children and you will be someone special, because you have come all the way from Edinburgh in Scotland.'

Francis flinched. He doubted whether the Canadians would care where they had come from. Indeed, so he understood, the whole attitude of the Canadians was that it didn't matter where you came from, nor what you had been before you arrived. In Canada, everyone started equal and had to find their own level by working hard enough to get whatever it was that they wanted.

He was going to have his work cut out to get any sort of promotion and more money for the first couple of years. Until he knew as much about the local business as those already working there, he was at a serious disadvantage. He would have to learn all he could about this side of the trade; buying and shipping was altogether different from dealing with the paperwork created after the grain had been received in Scotland.

The cost of the cabin had been the cause of the latest discord. Sylvia had insisted on an outboard cabin on C deck, away from the common herd and all those uncouth ex-servicemen. They were, she had said, only going to avoid being called back if there was another war and she had heard that there would be one soon against the Russians.

She knew about such men. No honour, no morals and always drunk. She had seen them often enough in Edinburgh when the sailors from the Rosyth navy base had been staggering from pub to pub before ending up sleeping on the Waverly station, waiting for the first morning train. She had even been whistled after by some of them!

Francis' boarding instructions had told him that they were second sitting for dinner and, now that the first sitting had been called, he told Sylvia to change if she was going to; anything to change the subject.

CHAPTER NINETEEN

The lights were on in the cabin and two men were playing cards at the tiny table, they looked up.

'Want a game?'

'No thanks, my mummy always told me not to play cards with strange men.'

'Suit yourself.'

Frank opened his suitcase, took out his washing things and left the men playing their game. The water was hot and the shave made him feel better; he stood under the shower without drawing the curtain so that he could keep his eye on his clothes. The card game was still in progress when he got back to the cabin.

'My name's Frank Bye.'

The players glanced up at him but said nothing. The third man half smiled and said he was Joe Savage; he looked at Frank.

'Army?'

'Navy.'

'You know about ships then.'

'Some.'

'How rough will it get then? Will we all be sick?'

The dealer looked up from his hand. 'A right kill joy you're going to be if all you can think of is to ask are we going to sick. Can't you think of anything better?'

'It may not worry you but I've never been on a ship and I don't think I'm going to like it much, it's moving already!'

Frank adjusted his tie and stuffed his dirty shirt into his suitcase, there was obviously no chance of washing it onboard. If he hung it up to dry, it would almost certainly take wings and disappear.

'We should be alright this trip. It's too early for winter gales and this thing is about twelve thousand tons, should be like staying at the Ritz.'

'He's never done that neither.'

'I'm Sid and this is Len,' the dealer spoke through a cloud of smoke, 'now bugger off mate, we're busy.'

'You not eating?'

'You heard me mate, bugger off. If we'd wanted light conversation we'd have booked on A deck.'

'Suit yourself.'

Frank closed the door behind him, wondering if they could be trusted. What the Hell, he had nothing worth stealing in his case and what little there was in there was easily and cheaply replaceable. Dinner was more important and he was hungry.

When he got back from dinner they were still at it. The atmosphere was rank with cigarette smoke and beer that one or other had brought down from the bar. Frank was certain that the cabin steward wouldn't have served it to them.

'There was some kid down here asking for you. Told him you were out.'

'Cheers. I'll take a look, see if I can find him, don't wait up for me, I may be quite late.'

The English Pub bar was a change from the Promenade Bar that they had been in earlier; life here seemed to be largely involved with beer and darts, leagues and teams had already been arranged and two games were already in progress.

In the American Bar, the lights were brighter and the place seemed to have attracted the married couples and a few single girls. A juke-box belted out the latest trans-Atlantic record and one or two couples were dancing on the tiny floor. Funny how, in no time at all, people found their way towards their natural environment. The serious drinkers to the English Pub, the young boasters to the Promenade Bar and the more civilised to here, where they could sit in comfort, dance if they wanted to and talk if they could out shout the juke-box. When next he saw young Peter he would advise him to make this his base also; he would be safe here, unless some girl got him.

He spotted a table and caught the eye of a steward, ordered a Scotch, neat, and sat watching the other people. Fascinating things, people; no two alike yet somehow they managed to find kindred souls in the most unlikely places.

'May we join you?'

'Yes, of course.'

The couple sat down at Frank's table.

'Order me a gin and Italian.'

Frank caught the man's eye and smiled. Here was a woman who knew what she wanted and, Frank suspected, her husband was expected to provide it on demand. The man held out his hand.

'I'm Francis Hurd, this is my wife Sylvia.'

'Hallo, I'm Frank Bye.'

'Our daughter Hazel is asleep in our cabin on C Deck.'

Sylvia emphasised the deck letter for Frank's benefit but her attention was focused on her husband. She looked at Francis and then round the room, looking for a steward; why was he so useless? Francis was in luck. He spotted and attracted the attention of the steward before she did and ordered the drinks.

'Quite nice in here, isn't it? Rather like a decent hotel.'

The arrival of the drinks saved Frank from the need to answer her and she, glancing at the bill, didn't notice that he hadn't.

'God, what prices!'

She glared at the steward who looked at Francis and Frank, trying to decide which one she belonged to, though somehow, she didn't look as if she belonged to anybody. She had to be with one of them though; he focused on Francis, the strained look gave him away.

'Will there be anything else, Sir?'

Francis's expression was sufficient answer. Frank asked for another Scotch.

'There's no hurry.'

'Have you been to Canada before? We're going to Edmonton, that's in Alberta you know. My husband has been offered an important position there with a grain exporting company. The same company he worked for in Edinburgh, really. They've asked him to go out and take charge of their Edmonton office.'

Frank saw the pained expression on Francis's face and looked very impressed.

'How very lucky. I'm gong to Toronto but I haven't got a job to go to, I'll just have to find one when I get there.'

Sylvia looked at Francis but spoke to Frank.

'How very brave. I don't think my husband would do anything like that.'

'I'm sure he wouldn't, Frank agreed, I'm sure he wouldn't put you and your daughter into such jeopardy.'

He lifted his class to Francis, finishing his drink in wry salute. Sylvia smiled at him.

'No, no, of course not.'

Frank excused himself and drifted over to the Juke-box, he didn't want to get bogged down with those two. He looked around to see if there was anyone he could ask to dance.

He spotted two young girls sitting at a table close to the floor, suggesting that they might perhaps dance if asked. The fairer of the two gave Frank the once over as he approached.

'Would you dance with me?'

She stood up immediately.

'Normally, in this situation, I would ask if you came here often but, in the circumstances, it doesn't seem appropriate.'

She giggled. 'No, it isn't is it.'

'My name's Frank, what do they call you?'

'My name's Sarah and my friend is Judy, we're nurses. We're going out to work in a hospital in Canada.'

They danced, holding each other close as much from necessity as any desire for intimacy. The floor was crowded and couples were trying not to bump into each other; the slow foxtrot degenerated into a shuffle round the floor.

'Not the Hammersmith Palais, is it?'

Frank knew the Palais well.

'No but, even that gets crowded on a Saturday night.'

'I thought you'd know it,' Sarah said, 'we go on Sundays too. They have a Sunday Club but you have to be a member to get in. You have to wait a week to get in but, for ten bob, they'll back date the membership application and let you in anyway. It's only the Council that insists on the wait, the Manager told me once when I wanted to get a boy in with me. Said it was the Watch Committee but I don't know what that is.'

The music stopped and he escorted her back to her table.

'May I join you? I have a married couple at my table and it's all they can do to be civil to each other. Doesn't make for a happy atmosphere.'

'Why not. As long as you don't take that as an invitation to move into our cabin too.'

'Are you on your own in your cabin, then?'

'No, there are four of us. Two married women going out to join their husbands. They're quite nice but I'm sure they are afraid to enjoy themselves just in case their husbands find out.'

'You're lucky. I'm sharing with five others down in the bowels of the ship. Just six bunks, a suitcase rack and a smell of stale beer and cigarette smoke. Still, it's only for a few days, I've been in worse.'

Sarah introduced him to Judy who looked surprised that she had brought him back to their table. Clearly there had been no plan to acquire partners.

She looked him over. Not bad. He'd shaved, his fingernails were clean and he was sober; more than could be said for most of the single men onboard. Sarah told her that Frank knew the Palais.

'So do thousands of other people.'

'Well, I said he could come and sit with us anyway.'

Judy wasn't too pleased about this arrangement but accepted the situation. Frank sat down between them, that being the only unoccupied chair; the fourth chair being taken up by their jackets. He caught the eye of the steward who, quite unabashed by the change of table, brought him the Scotch he had ordered.

'Get a bit domestic over there did it?'

'You could say that.'

Frank turned to the girls. 'Can I get you something?'

They ordered what they wanted and the steward bustled off with a smirk on his face. Didn't take him long to get himself organised he thought, looking back at Frank.

Judy refused Frank's request for a dance but Sarah accepted. He led her back on to the floor.

'Judy got a problem?'

'She doesn't like men very much. Had some trouble in the past I believe.'

'Well, she won't have any trouble from me; this trip is strictly for laughs.' He thought of young Peter. 'I seem to have been elected chaperone to a sixteen year old kid, I'm on my best behaviour.'

'Boy or girl?'

'Boy. Only met him in the bar just before we sailed but he seemed so lost and helpless, I sort of adopted him. He's on his own and doesn't know anything about anything; he ain't safe on his own.'

'Where is he?'

'I've no idea at the moment but I'm sure that, if he gets into any trouble, he'll come looking for me. This isn't a very big ship, he should be able to find me if he needs me.'

In the morning they had dropped the Pilot and turned up through the North Channel. As he sat down for his breakfast, Frank felt the effect of the first of the Atlantic rollers; a long, heavy swell that had left the American coast days before and been driven across three thousand miles of ocean. He felt the ship lifting in response to the

124

on-coming sea, compared it with the remembered movement of a destroyer and was happy; this was going to be a doddle.

The salon was less than full, some of the passengers were already feeling a bit seasick, he spread himself out more comfortably, taking advantage of the extra space available. The steward watched and smiled.

'God help us if it gets rough, you seem alright though, Sir.'

'When I get sea sick, you may ask the Captain to change course for the Canaries; then I can be sick in the warm.'

The steward grinned. 'Navy?'

'Ex- very Ex-.'

'Me too. Captain's Steward on the KG five.'

'Bit of a come down, isn't it? This, I mean.'

'Maybe so mate but at least now I get home to the wife regular. She likes that.'

This short conversation ensured that Frank's plate, when it arrived, was piled high with bacon and eggs, fried bread and a mountain of mushrooms. He was going to be well fed this trip.

Across the salon, he saw the two girls. No sign of sickness there yet. Peter was nowhere to be seen, he would drop by the lad's cabin later, just to make sure; he waved to the girls who had found a table closer to the door.

When he found it, cabin F13 was a shambles. There was vomit on the floor, discarded clothes lying where they had been dropped the night before and three of the bunks contained what could have passed for dead bodies had their occupant's groaning not belied this first impression; there was no sign of Peter. Frank gave a moment's thought to the poor cabin steward who would have to sort this out. As he turned to go, the steward came down the passage and Frank nodded towards the door of F13.

'I wouldn't, if I were you. I'd leave this lot 'til last.'

'I would Love but most of them are like that. It'll get better in a day or two.'

The fresh air smelled good and tasted good. He found Peter on the boat deck. Up here, the wind was fresh and had blown the smell of vomit out of the boy's nose and he was beginning to feel better.

'Thought I might find you up here,' Frank greeted him. 'Best place for clearing the sinuses.'

Up here, a long way above the water, the movement of the ship was more pronounced. They were no longer heading straight into the oncoming sea and the movement had become more like the well remembered Atlantic corkscrew motion, the bow lifting to the sea then sliding off to port as the north west wind caught her; with a top hamper of five or six decks, she caught the wind easily and he decided that it might be a problem for some of the less sailor-like of the passengers. Peter looked at him, hoping for a little sympathy.

'What's it like in your cabin? I don't think I can go back to mine, it's awful.'

'It'll be better by tonight. Last night they had had too much to drink and weren't ready for the movement of the ship. By tonight, they'll all be jolly jack tars.'

'I don't believe that, I know I won't be.'

'You eaten?'

'No, couldn't face it.'

'Come on. We'll find you a sandwich and some coffee. You'll feel better on a full stomach.'

'Morning Frank, this your little friend?'

Sarah smiled at him from across the deck; Judy said nothing but acknowledged his arrival with Peter when they crossed over, taking advantage of a slight roll to speed up their steps.

'Morning girls, all is well?'

'Yes. Great ain't it? Is it going to be like this, like a roller coaster, all the way?'

'Probably. The hills might get a little steeper before we get all the way over but nothing too exciting. Girls, this is Peter, say "good morning" Peter.'

The girls said 'Good morning Peter.'

'Peter, these are Sarah and Judy. Say good morning, then we can all go and get some coffee.'

The girls declined the offer of coffee saying that they wanted to stay up here in the fresh air. Wasn't it just marvellous? Sarah said that, had she been a boy, she would definitely have been a sailor. Frank told her that it would have been much more fun for everybody if she hadn't been a boy. He heard Judy saying something about typical man as they descended the ladder to the promenade deck and the smell of fresh coffee coming from the bar.

The coffee tasted as good as it smelled, the ship was obviously victualled on the Canadian side of the Atlantic. Britain hadn't smelled coffee like that since the Yanks had gone home after the war, taking their black market coffee with them.

'What's your cabin like? Any chance of a swap do you think?'

'My cabin is a sea-going cupboard presently hiding five dead bodies.' 'It'll be OK tonight though when everyone has settled down, they can't stay dead for the whole trip.'

'I think I'll sleep up on deck tonight, in the fresh air.'

Frank grinned at him. 'You'll probably find it's quite crowded up there if it gets any rougher. You'll be alright, just wedge yourself into your bunk so that you don't roll around and you'll be fine.'

The girls joined them, trying to smooth their hair.

'It's blowing a gale out there.'

They sat and Sarah lit a cigarette, offering the pack to Frank and Peter.

Both declined.

'How are the wives doing? Do they still think it's worthwhile going out to meet their husbands or are they seasick too?'

127

Frank explained to Peter that the girls were sharing their cabin with two wives going out to join their husbands.

'They seem alright so far. I think one of them has a problem though; not been entirely true to her marriage vows I suspect.'

'Pregnant?'

'Can't be sure but could be. Certainly she's terrified that someone at home will write to her husband and tell him what's been going on.'

'Can't see why she should be true, Judy said, husbands never are.'

Frank picked up the point. 'You married?'

'No bloody fear but my father was and it never helped my mum. She found out eventually that he'd fucked his way across north Africa with the Eighth Army and then up through Italy and into Austria before finally catching a dose and spending the rest of the war in hospital. By the time he got out of the VD ward, it was VE day and they sent him home to his wife all cleaned up.'

The embarrassed silence that followed this statement was broken by the arrival of their coffee and Peter's breakfast sandwiches.

'It's not just the men, you know,' Frank said. 'Some of the wives were just the same.'

'Can we change the subject?' Sarah said. 'I hear there's a film on this afternoon, shall we go?'

The sandwiches had obviously made Peter feel better and he picked up the cue.

'What is it?'

'The Maltese Falcon, it's a detective story.'

Peter looked interested. 'I just love that Sydney Greenstreet's voice, he's the classic baddy isn't he? I like the way he always laughs when he speaks, just to show he's superior. I wish I could sound like that.'

'Being very fat helps,' Frank suggested, 'it gives the voice a fuller, richer timbre.'

Peter laughed. 'I wondered why I couldn't do it. I'll have to put on a little weight, about twenty stone should do it.'

'Not on coffee and sandwiches.' Sarah told him.

A shaft of sunlight struck through the window on to the table. Although low down, almost on the horizon, its appearance made everyone feel better. On the promenade deck, walker's steps got lighter and smiles peeked out from amongst the hung over black looks. By lunchtime, the sun would be high and down aft, over the Riviera Deck where the covered swimming pool was. It would allow some of the more hardy to try their luck at getting a light tan.

The pool would remain covered this trip but the rigid cover allowed a good open space for deck chairs and loungers; for those wanting fresh air and an escape from the constant music and voices in the bars and other public rooms. Few of the cabins offered anything as comfortable.

CHAPTER TWENTY

After three days of idleness Frank was bored, it had never before occurred to him to wonder what passengers did at sea. He had never been on a troopship with no duties and anyway, this was different; here he was a paying passenger, he was entitled to be waited upon by the stewards. A bit like being an officer in the Andrew he thought unkindly.

'Your Aunt married a Canadian I hear'. Sarah had decided that Peter needed bringing out of himself, he was much too shy for his own good. 'What does he do for a living?'

'He's in prison.' Peter paused for effect, he had rehearsed this speech in his mind many times. When he got out of the army, he got a job there through the Veteran's Office. It's a good job, no hassle and, as he's working for the Government so it's safe too. No money, he says but you can't get fired.

'He says most of the prisoners are harmless drunks who get sentenced to a few months to dry out then they go straight back on the booze as soon as they're released; get arrested again and come back in for a few more months. He says most of the clients are regulars, friends almost.'

Frank's mind wandered back to Chatham. He wondered if Alice would get her hotel and the regular clients she hoped for. He pushed the question to the back of his mind, it was none of his business now, he was on his way to Canada and a new life without her. The possibility of there being something doing with Sarah when they got to Toronto crossed his mind but he pushed that away also; he didn't need or want any entanglements.

Their, now regular, morning coffee finished, they went up on to the boat deck to catch what September sun there was and to stretch their legs with a brisk walk. Two seamen were working on the lifeboats on the starboard side, releasing and pulling back the covers and inspecting the inside of each boat. Satisfied by whatever they had seen, the covers were replaced.

'Checking for stowaways?'

The seamen looked at Frank, looked at the two girls and back at Frank.

'Where did you find those two?'

'Clinging to number three Carley float. Thought I'd better bring 'em inboard.'

'OK Jack but, if you find any more, let me know, eh?'

'Bloody typical of men!' Judy was clearly annoyed. 'Talk about us as if we weren't here!'

'It might be a good deal,' Sarah said, 'those two look better than the two we've got.'

Judy ignored her, walking ahead of them increasing her pace until she was almost running. Frank watched her go.

'She may not be happy but she's going to be super fit by the time we get there if she keeps that up. Too much like hard work for me.'

In their cabin, Francis and Sylvia were warring again and Hazel, trying to ignore them, played with her dolls. She undressed each one carefully and then dressed it again, cooing at it all the time, telling it what a lovely baby it was and that she loved it. Sylvia hit Francis across the face with a loud smack.

'You just don't care,' she screamed at him, 'you don't care what I think about anything.'

'Of course I do, of course I do. It's just that, in business, you must leave things to me. I know what I'm doing and I can't just push my way to the manager's job just like that. It takes time to get established and to earn the respect necessary to attract promotion. Then, if there's a vacancy, I might stand a chance of getting it; it's a matter of seniority and experience.'

'Of course you have seniority. You were sent out by Head Office in Edinburgh, that gives you seniority.'

'I haven't been sent out by Head Office in Edinburgh, they very kindly arranged for Edmonton to offer me a job if I came out. That's not the same thing at all. We've got to learn to fit into the new environment and not upset the locals by boasting about being sent out from Head Office. Anyway, strictly speaking, Edinburgh isn't Head Office, they are separate companies.'

Sylvia's snort broke into Hazel's train of thought and she looked at her mother. Looking down again at her dolls, she gave each one a cuddle and stroked its hair. If this went on much longer she would have one of her asthma attacks, she just knew she would, then they would stop rowing and pay some attention to her. She looked up at Sylvia.

'Look Mummy, Sally has her best dress on.'

'How very clever of her dear, now play quietly while Mummy and Daddy talk.'

Francis reached down and stroked Hazel's hair.

'Do you think your dollies would like to go for a walk up on deck?'

'Oh yes, they'd love that.'

'That's right, ignore me. You take the damned dollies for a walk up on deck and take Hazel with you; I'm going to lie down, I've got a headache.'

Damn Francis. He just wouldn't take the initiative, he wouldn't push himself forward when he should. God, at this rate, he would still be a junior clerk when he died. And, where would that leave her?

It just isn't fair. She had to do everything for this family. She lay down on the bed and closed her eyes.

I wonder what happened to that fellow at our table in the bar last night? He just seemed to disappear from the dance floor; she wished Frances would just disappear. She heard the water running in the shower in the next door cabin. She thought, that's a good idea, I'll take a shower, maybe that'll make me feel better.

She undressed and stood under the cascading water, turning the pressure up to full and feeling the needles of water stinging her skin. She lifted her breasts up towards the rose, taking the full pressure against them and feeling the skin tighten in response.

'Damn Francis! Damn, damn, damn him'

She turned off the water and dragged a towel from the rail. If he hadn't taken Hazel up on deck, they could have made love. She hadn't felt like making love for ages, maybe that was what she needed; she wondered why Francis never seemed to need it. She towelled herself gently, mopping up the dampness from her skin rather than rubbing it off. She would get dressed and go up for a coffee and talk to somebody, anybody, just so long as it wasn't Francis. She left a note on the table. Gone for a sailor.

'Hallo Darlin, on our own are we?'

Sylvia gave the speaker a look of utter loathing.

'I'm a respectable married woman and my husband is onboard with me.'

Now why did she say that, she wondered. Whilst true, it was hardly necessary. She looked at him, not her type at all.

'Suit yourself Darlin, just thought I'd make the offer.'

He turned back to the bar, the stool head squeaking as it turned. Sylvia sat at a table as far from the bar as she could get. There seemed to be no happy medium. Men were either like Francis or like that man at the bar. Why hadn't God taken some woman's advice when designing men? Perhaps, she thought, He should have made woman first.

The Steward took her order and winked at her.

'Don't take too much notice of him, nodding towards the bar, he's been there since I opened this morning. It takes some like that; cold sober, he wouldn't say boo to a goose, they don't mean any harm, Love.'

He adjusted the napkin across his forearm, an affectation he had obviously developed over a number of years of stewarding.

'I'll get your coffee, white isn't it?'

She wanted to say no, that she wanted it black and strong but she hated black coffee and she knew that she could never drink it if she did. She hated the way waiters always knew what she was going to order before she had even looked at the menu, she hated being so utterly predictable. Right now, she thought, she hated life altogether. It was so unfair and it was all Francis's fault.

'I hope he falls overboard!'

Unaware that she had spoken aloud, she looked round the room, smiling at a couple at the next table. They assumed that her fervent hope had been directed towards the drunk at the bar.

It had been a good day. His friendship with Peter and the girls had made the time pass pleasantly over the three days and they had become a group. Even Judy had calmed down and was beginning to relax; not always so on guard.

He explained his errand to the Chief Steward. Was it possible, he asked, to bring Peter, Sarah and Judy on to his table at dinner?

'It's very difficult, Sir. You understand, once everyone has found their seat, they like to go to the same one every time.'

A tightly folded pound note changed hands.

'I'll see what can be arranged, Sir. There's often some simple adjustment that can be made to accommodate special requests. Leave it with me Sir.'

Frank made his way back to the boat deck where he had left the others.

'Either we shall find ourselves all together at dinner or the Chief Steward has just gipped me out of a quid.'

He was certain that quite a few people had been to see the Chief Steward and made similar requests, now that they were beginning to sort themselves out into parties. On a good trip, Frank thought, the Chief Steward could make a couple of hundreds quid, no tax, no deductions. Not bad.

Peter looked at him in awe.

'I wouldn't know how to approach the Chief Steward to change the seating plan.'

'Neither did I at your age son. It comes with age and experience, like everything else, don't worry about it.'

Frank had never done it before either but he wasn't going to admit that in front of the girls. Anyway, he had seen enough pound notes change hands in the past to know that anything was possible if approached in the proper manner.

The weather was glorious. The sun bright, the wind not too strong and the sea about as calm as the north Atlantic ever was. It was chilly but if they got cold they could simply go down to one of the bars. On reflection, he thought, being a passenger had a lot to recommend it. It was a lot more comfortable than being a sea-going bunting tosser. Mind, he had always been lucky, luckier than some of his mates. He'd never been sunk, never been wounded and had managed to keep out of serious trouble; he had had a much better war than a lot of people. He dragged his mind back to the present.

'How about a drink before we eat?'

The cocktail bar was a small area just outside the entrance to the dining salon and they managed to find a table where they wouldn't be kicked when the crowd came down. The first sitting was already inside, wading through their brown Windsor soup, roast beef and Yorkshire pudding and trifle or fruit and custard to follow. After the limitations of wartime ashore and the even greater limitations imposed on the messdecks of His Majesty's Ships, even this choice-less menu sounded good.

'Let me pay for these, Sarah said. You're already a pound out to the Chief Steward.'

Frank saw no reason to object. After all, they were not together enough to warrant his paying for everything. Peter probably didn't have enough pocket money with him to play host to two grown women but the girls could afford to look after themselves or they wouldn't have come. Even so, he wouldn't take advantage of them.

'Why not? Mine's half a pint. Don't want to spoil my dinner.'

The girls ordered sherry for themselves and a beer for the boys. Frank noticed that she gave the steward a five Pound note. The steward looked at Sarah, looked at the note and back at Sarah, finally deciding to accept it.

'Last time I offered one of those,' Frank said catching her eye, they insisted that I write my name and address on it and then asked for some form of identification It's never occurred to me before but maybe that's why they make them so big with lots of plain white space; so that you can write on them.'

'Yes, but then, you look dishonest.'

'You look delicious so I might accept a menu from you but not a five Pound note.'

Peter had listened to this banter without understanding any of it.

'What's so special about a five Pound note?'

'That the average working bloke doesn't earn that much in a week so wouldn't have one unless it was come by dishonestly or it was a forgery.'

Peter looked somewhat put out by this intelligence.

'That's what my Dad gave me for the trip. He said I would need a few quid and gave me four of those.'

'Don't worry lad, you look honest. Anyway, the Purser will change them into spending type money for you as he's looking after your bankroll and all that.'

The steward brought the drinks over and placed them on the table, offering Sarah four Pound notes and some change on a saucer; she left a shilling on the saucer.

'Thank you Madam.'

The brightly lit boat deck was cold but the weather was still clear and the wind not too strong to allow them to get some after dinner exercise. The sea rose and fell rhythmically like silent, moonlit dunes marching across a limitless desert. The high clouds, broken, allowed the moonlight to be reflected off the wake following the ship as the miles fell away astern.

They could hear below them, in the American Bar, the juke-box playing a comedy number about there being nobody here but us chickens. It was no sillier than the one that had been popular a few years ago about mares eating oats, does eating oats and little lambs eating ivy. Sung quickly enough, it sounded like gibberish. Perhaps it was, there had been a need for happy, nonsense songs then. Songs for people to sing whilst sitting, crouched and frightened in air raid shelters, songs that didn't have to make sense, just so long as they raised a smile.

Frank had spent the entire war convinced that he would rather be at sea being shot at than sitting in an air raid shelter with no idea what was happening up above. At least, at sea, he had known what the danger was and could do something about it. Ashore, they had been unable to do anything but pray.

Stop thinking about the war, he told himself. It's over, done with and everyone is safe again, he had seen reports in the papers that more civilians had been killed in the war than soldiers, sailors and airmen and now they were suffering again.

He wanted to forget the war it was over he told himself again. Germany was destroyed. Although much of Europe was in ruins, normality was slowly returning; faster there than at home!

In post-war Britain rationing of everything was not only still in force but products such as bread and potatoes had been added to the rationed list, something even the full might of Germany had never been able to force upon them. Since the war, the meat ration had actually been halved and horse meat, whale meat and other improbable and, hitherto unheard of fishy products, offered in its place. What the hell was snook?

The uncorrected rumour was spread that, not only did the wicked, capitalist Americans want their war loan repaid, they were sending all that Marshal Aid to Europe to help rebuild Germany, France and all the other countries that had surrendered but not to us, their only real allies.

The better papers, what the Labour Government called the Tory Press, argued that this was not so, that the war loan repayments were being delayed and Marshal Aid was indeed being given to the British Government. They, instead of spending it to rebuild the British factories destroyed or worked to death by the war, were reportedly squandering it on nationalisation schemes. Subsidising the import of Virginia tobacco so that the working man, the labour Government's natural voters, could have his fag with his still war-quality pint of beer. They claimed this as a valid use of the money; Frank didn't know what was true,

Then had come the winter. The Thames was frozen over, the trains had stopped, the Smithfield meat porters in London went on strike and the docker's leaders had brought them out on strike also, thus ensuring that nothing could be imported to replace that being denied to the population by the strikers' actions.

Alright, that had finally been enough, even for this Government, and the army and the navy had been brought in to work the docks but not before even time itself stopped when Big Ben froze solid. There was no light, no heat, the factories were at a standstill for lack of power, the roads were blocked with snow and the railways closed down. As a result of the chaos created by the weather and their union leaders; millions of victorious Britain's workers were once more without work and, therefore, without pay. Communist bastards!

Frank shook himself like a dog trying to shake water from its coat. Forget it, he told himself, it's not your problem now, you're going to Canada, a land of plenty. First Alice had been unfaithful to him then the labour Government that they had all voted for had destroyed the country.

It was none of his business now, he was out of it. His boat had sailed, he was on his way to the new world to a new life.

'Come on,' he took Sarah's hand, 'it's dancing time.'

He led her down into the bar, warm and smoke filled, leaving Peter to escort Judy. He had to break what was becoming a habit, thinking of the past. The future was his and, unless he snapped out of this misery, it would be no better than the past and all this would have been wasted.

CHAPTER TWENTY-ONE

Seven days of almost perfect weather but now Frank watched the moisture condense on the cold steel of the exposed promenade deck, running down the paintwork to form puddles on the wooden planking. The looked-for first sighting of the north American continent was made impossible by the fog rolling down from the Newfoundland Banks and blanketing everything. It reminded him of other such days, he wondered if he would ever forget the navy and then, whether he would ever forget Alice? Alice. At least the baby was white so it couldn't be her Yank's bastard. Perhaps he had been hasty.

In a couple of days he would be in Toronto, in a new life; he would have other problems to worry about but, now that they were so nearly there, time seemed to drag.

A drink, chatting, even a visit to the cinema to see Sun Valley Serenade, an old movie featuring the Glenn Miller band. had reminded him of Alice and had seemed to take up only moments of an interminable day. The first signs of separation had already begun to appear in the so recently formed on-board relationships. The girls had begun to withdraw into themselves, Peter had kept repeating that his Aunt was to meet him at the station but that, as she hadn't seen a photograph of him since he was twelve, he wondered how she would recognise him.

Frank recognised the signs. Shipboard relationships wouldn't stand the pressure of shore-side. Ashore it would be different; ashore they were different people, no longer shipmates but today they had done their best to maintain their fading friendships.

The position, course and speed notice on the Purser's Office notice board told them that they would, by nightfall be into the Cabot Strait and, by the morning, past Anticosti Island and entering the St Lawrence River.

Immigration Officers would join the ship with the River Pilot and all passengers disembarking at Quebec should report to the library at 0830 for processing. For those carrying on to Montreal, a half-day tour of Quebec City had been arranged; bookings through the Purser, please.

Very few of the passengers were scheduled to disembark at Quebec and the Immigration Officers announced that they would start on processing the Montreal leavers. Frank told Peter to get his passport and immigration papers from the Purser and to meet him in the library. They might as well get it sorted this morning if they could, rather than leave it until tomorrow and have to stand in line for hours. They could then go ashore this afternoon and have a look at Quebec. From the ship, they would be able to see it as Wolfe had seen it; as a prize to be captured.

'Quebec is the only walled city in north America. The city's fortifications straddle a natural promontory overlooking the river and thus provide an almost perfect defence against attack from that quarter. The landward side walls are higher and thicker as was considered necessary.'

The girl's voice, Canadian with a strong French accent, was getting on Frank's nerves. He hadn't come all this way to be lectured by what sounded like a music hall French maid. The four of them had joined the half-day tour rather than stay onboard and, after half an hour or so, it had dawned on him what it was about Quebec that was bugging him; no war damage.

There were no vacant sites with piled high rubble. There were no signs anywhere of strain or undue wear and tear as there were still at home. He must remember, he told himself, home was now not England but Toronto. There were no static water tanks constructed in the flooded basements and cellars of bombed houses, the water green and turgid and still unused after two years of peace. Here, everything looked bright and clean, even the old buildings looked bright and fresh with new paint. With shining clean windows, some shops with still used unnecessary lights inside to illuminate the impossibly wide range of things for sale. Many of the immigrant tourists, particularly the younger ones, had never seen such wonders.

The guide's condescendingly anti-British attitude had upset Frank but, on reflection, it wasn't her fault. She had no conception of the destruction, confusion and fear that had engulfed Europe while she had sat at her school desk, learning how the perfidious Englishman Wolfe had outsmarted the gallant Frenchman Montcalm by sneaking up from below by an unexpected, indirect and undefended route instead of attacking at the Anse de Foulon as expected of a gentleman. That was history to her; the rest of the world was thousands of miles away and largely unknown.

Since the end of the European's war, in which many Canadians had died, the flood of immigrants had placed a heavy burden on Canada. At first, they had welcomed the poor, worn out refugees from the desolation that was Europe. They had seen it on newsreels at the movie houses, refugees arriving with nothing but a cardboard suitcase and a memory of a home that no longer existed. Now, many thought of these incomers as dirty D.P.'s. Displaced Persons the authorities had called them, and the Government should do something to stop them coming.

She had maintained her steady commentary as they drove back to the docks by a different route, her thoughts totally separate from her actions. She knew the commentary by heart, she had given it almost daily for two years during the summer and, now that she had left university, she worked for the tour company on a part-time, on-call, basis. Ships like this were one of the regular calls she received out of the regular tourist season, there seemed to be no end to the numbers flooding into her country. Sometimes, one of the tourists would interrupt her flow with a question that wouldn't have been necessary if they had been listening. One day, she would talk nonsense to them just to see if anyone noticed.

They all stepped down from the bus, most of the passengers avoiding eye contact with her, simply nodding as they passed her without offering a tip. Frank smiled at her and slipped her an American dollar bill, mimicking the American accent he had heard so often at home.

'I just lurve your accent honey. It's so cute, you sound almost like a real Frenchy.;

He had passed her and was mounting the gangway up the side of the ship by the time she realised that she had just been put down by a dirty DP.

The ship pulled away from the dock wall at precisely 1600 as advertised; two busy tugs pulled her out into the stream, away from the other dockside traffic and let her go. The Pilot gave them his usual farewell wave of thanks and looked at the captain.

'Half ahead, Captain, if you please. Once we've passed the buoy, we'll try for a steady ten knots whilst the daylight lasts and come down a bit for the dark hours. We don't want to arrive too early do we?'

None of this discussion was necessary, more a matter of politeness. The pilot had been taking ships both bigger and smaller than the Fairlight Head up and down the St Lawrence for nearly thirty years and the captain knew he had. He had, in fact, taken this ship up river on quite a few occasions in the past two years.

The last night onboard was always party night. Paper hats appeared on the dinner tables and the stewards were especially attentive, bringing drinks, second helpings, anything else requested; working hard to justify the hoped for tips.

Sarah and Judy had had their hair permed and were wearing dresses suitable for the occasion instead of the rather less ostentatious clothes they had worn until now.

Tonight, they wanted to make an impression, they wanted to be remembered. Frank looked them over appreciatively. He turned to Peter.

'I even fancy yours tonight.'

'You want to swap?'

'Not a chance. If there's anything going free tonight, it will be with Sarah, not your bird. Might be worth you trying it on just for the hell of it though, you never know your luck.'

'No thanks. I don't think I'll risk getting my head snapped off.'

'You're acting like a coward Sir.'

'I'm not acting!'

Peter had made great progress on the way over. The frightened small boy of Greenock was no more, he was glad he had met Frank and the girls.

Dinner went well. The girls were relaxed and inclined to drink one or two extra glasses of wine. Frank and Peter paid court and the atmosphere at their table was one of relaxed friendship. Across the room, Sylvia Hurd's voice rose above the general din.

'I want another drink! How dare you say I've had enough already?'

Francis tried to crawl into his collar, his face bright red. He signed to the steward.

'Give her whatever she wants.'

'What she wants or what she needs, Sir?'

She demanded champagne but had the presence of mind to specify non-vintage before the steward tried to inflate the bill. Until today, they had been with the first sitting at Dinner but, with some of the passengers having either disembarked at Quebec or staying in their cabins packing, there was only one sitting tonight. It was a bit crowded but it made for a party atmosphere and she knew just what sort of party she wanted tonight.

CHAPTER TWENTY-TWO

A stage had been set up at one end of the dining salon and the Chief Purser was asking for volunteers to entertain the other guests but it was obviously still much too early. Nowhere near enough had been drunk to overcome the Englishman's natural lack of enthusiasm for showing off in public.

'I'll bet you a quid that the first one up is a Taffy who thinks he can sing, either that or a Jock who thinks he's a comedian.'

'What's your speciality?'

Frank smiled at Judy. 'Nothing that they would let me do up there.'

'I thought all sailors did a turn.'

'Not that sort of turn, Love.'

Sarah blushed but Judy hadn't finished.

'I'll bet you a pound you daren't go up there and sing.'

'Hey, that's not fair, you know I can't sing.'

'Hard luck sailor. Its either you go up there and sing or you owe me a pound.'

Frank handed her a pound note and called the steward across.

'This young lady would like to order a round of drinks.'

Further aft but on the same deck, the day salon had been cleared of most of its furniture and the carpet rolled back to expose a large dance floor which unlike the postage stamp floor in the American Bar was of sprung maple, obviously a survival from the ship's pre-war luxury trade days. A five piece band embarked at Quebec were preparing for what they knew usually turned out to be a long evening.

The Bob Harris Band had come aboard to play for the one evening on the way to Montreal. There they would have the day off before playing again on the return trip down river. As their leader often told them, it may not be fame but it's regular and it's a living. Frank and the others found their way aft.

'That's better, a real dance floor.'

Peter asked Judy if she would dance with him.

'There's nobody else on the floor yet.'

'Does that mean you can't or that you think that I can't?'

'Can you?'

'Bronze medal.'

He swept her on to the floor for a waltz, his steps measured and precise. Judy, after a moment's hesitation, relaxed and let him lead, swinging and working the floor with unexpected ease and confidence.

'Do you think they'd mind if we joined them?'

Frank led Sarah on to the floor. At least this time it wasn't rolling from side to side or pitching up and down as it had at sea. The steps they managed were rather more pedestrian than Peter's and Judy's but good enough to encourage other couples to come on to the floor and actually dance.

'You just never know, do you? Fancy Peter being able to dance like that.'

'Sneaky, these modern kids. At his age, I wouldn't have dared do that.'

Frank avoided a couple dancing cheek to cheek with their eyes closed.

'You can't do it now,' Sarah told him.

After the customary three numbers from the band, they returned to the table.

'That's the hardest I've worked for years, Judy said I'd nearly forgotten how.'

One or two more dances were managed before the floor became too crowded for anything more than a Palais shuffle.

'Ah well,' Frank whispered into Sarah's ear, 'at least we can have a rest; we may want our energy later.'

He got no response but decided that that wasn't a definite no.

Montreal, although founded by the French in 1642 lacked the sense of theatre that made Quebec special but here, the transatlantic ships emptied themselves of passengers and freight. For Frank, that was one suitcase containing, the demob suit, as issued by a grateful British Government to all the men discharged from the services. He had chosen the pale grey chalk-stripe double breasted rather than the only alternative available on the day he had passed through Chatham Barracks on his way into civvy street; he couldn't see himself in Lovat tweed.

A few shirts, three ties, some socks, shoes and some underpants. He had had the case with him in the cabin throughout the trip but the steward had insisted on taking it ashore with the rest of the baggage. Frank gave him ten bob, a fortune but he reckoned the poor bloke would get nothing from his fellow inmates.

'If I ever decide to go back to sea,' he told him, 'I'm going to have your job.'

'You have to be in the union.'

'How do I get in the union?'

'You have to have a job.'

'How about all my time in the Andrew?'

'Don't count, mate; no union card, no job. No job, no union card.'

Frank recognised why it was that he was leaving England, why it was taking England so long to recover; he hoped it would be different in Canada.

His case was in the customs shed for him to claim. He lifted it on to the table in front of the customs officer, lid uppermost, showing his initials and the fouled anchor symbol denoting the Royal Navy.

'Anything to declare Jack?'

'Mafeking's been relieved.'

'That's all I need this morning, a comedian. Push off Jack, and good luck.'

The two girls and Peter took rather longer to find their trunks and cases but joined him on the railway station platform after making arrangements for them to be transported unaccompanied.

'You're travelling light.' Sarah looked at his case.

'With all my worldly goods I did this case endow. And, it's a hell of a lot cheaper than a wife.' He remembered the phrase from the wedding service.

Frank had reserved only a couchette in the day car but the others had reserved sleeping berths and they went their separate ways to get organised.

'See you in the Club Car when you've got yourselves sorted,' Frank told them.

Behind the bar, the advertisement said, 'Everybody likes the man with the White Owl Cigar - 10c.'

Frank wondered what they tasted like. He had never smoked a cigar so there were going to be all sorts of new experiences in Canada. He worked it out. There were four Dollars to the Pound so their Dollar was worth five bob. Ten percent of that was sixpence. He wondered what a sixpenny cigar would taste like and decided against trying one.

CHAPTER TWENTY-THREE

Toronto's Union Station had clearly been designed to impress any arriving immigrant. Frank said goodbye to the girls and watched the station empty while he waited with young Peter who, now that he was about to be abandoned by Frank, had lost some of the assurance he had acquired on the ship. A man and woman approached them, looking quizzical.

'Are you Peter? Peter Adams?'

'Er, yes. Are you uncle John?'

'Of course we are.' His aunt gave him a hug. 'Welcome to Canada, we expected you to be alone.'

Peter introduced Frank.

'Thanks for all your help on the way over. I hope we can meet again sometime, I owe you.'

Frank watched the three of them leave, Peter's cases and trunk ferried by a Red Cap to the street and lifted into the back of the big Ford station wagon.

The red crucifix at the top of the sign almost made Frank ignore it, he wasn't looking for the chapel but the legend below it caught his attention - Immigrant Assistance and Information.

The elderly man sat behind a large desk flanked by two comfortable looking easy chairs. He looked up as Frank entered, his eye ranging over him.

'Ex navy, English and single. How can I help you Jack?'

'Very good. How come you're so sure?'

'Suitcase is pusser's issue, you're male and you're on your own.'

Frank was impressed but suspected that the man had done the same routine many times before.

'I've just arrived. I need accommodation at a price I can afford and I need a job.'

'Sit down, let's see what we can do.'

Frank looked at the dog collar. His experience of dog collared, elderly gentlemen had not been unfailingly good.

'Have you any money at all?'

'Enough to afford a reasonable hotel for a few days. I've heard about immigrant hostels and have no intention of going anywhere near one if I can avoid it.'

The Padre picked up the telephone, dialled, spoke and returned the instrument to its cradle.

'You're booked in at the Ford hotel. It's a nice enough place where you won't be bothered. Now, a job. You're ex service, that's the most obvious demob suit I've ever seen, so we shouldn't have any problem there.'

'Yeah, Regular.'

'Good, that makes you a Veteran.'

Frank smiled at the idea of being thought a veteran at just twenty-five. The only veteran Frank had known was a first war destroyer forced back into service in the second. She had been old, worn out and of very little use and Frank didn't feel any of these things. Anyway, he'd had a friend on the old Veteran when she went down with all hands and he didn't want to be reminded.

'The Canadians are,' the Padre said,' a generous and well-meaning lot but are, on occasions, rather less than punctilious when it comes to detail.

'At the end of the war, the Federal Government decided that the Provincial Governments must provide employment for veterans; they were, of course, trying to prevent the chaos experienced after the first war but, in their enthusiasm, they forgot to specify who's army these veterans should have been in. You are therefore entitled to be found a job of some kind by the Veteran's Office in Parliament Buildings, here in Toronto; you, the Germans, the Russians, the Italians, anyone who can show that they were in some one's army, etc. It was obviously not the first time that he had given this little speech. I was at the

Flying Angel Club in Gib For most of the war, were you ever there?'

Frank admitted that he had been but that he'd probably been drunk at the time. Runs ashore were rare, not to be wasted sober and certainly not in the Flying Angle Club with its soft drinks, ping pong tables and Padres.

'What were you?'

'Killick Bunting.'

'Well, there ain't much call here for semaphore signallers but, if you'll take what's available until something better comes up, you'll get along just fine.

'Get yourself over to the Ford and get yourself sorted out, then you can push on to the Vet's Office in the morning; unless you want to go over there this afternoon, they work nine through five Let them have their lunch in peace though, if you want them on your side.'

'I'll go over this afternoon. Might as well get it all sorted out in one day if I can'

'My number's on that note. If I can help, give me a ring. We ex- matelots must stick together, eh?'

Frank went in search of the Ford hotel and some lunch. The Ford didn't have a dining room but there was a coffee shop in the lobby. He took a light lunch and a lot of coffee. He felt in need of something a little stronger but decided that going for a job interview smelling of booze would probably be a mistake.

Sitting behind the desk, one foot propped against an open draw and leaning back against the wall behind him, the interviewer had clearly lunched better than Frank. Frank could see that the man didn't much like his job.

'OK friend. What sort of job are you looking for? What did you do over 'ome?' The attempt at the English accent was a mistake.

'My last paid employment was killing people but I thought I might try something a little less positive.'

He met the eye of the man behind the desk, locked-on and won the contest.

151

'Yeah, right, OK.'

The man's foot came off the open draw and the chair tipped back on to an even keel.

'I'll try anything that's just about legal.' Frank told him.

'So? What do you want to do?'

'I've no idea. What's going? Do you have a list of jobs available?'

The foot went back on to the draw and the chair tipped back again.

'That's not what they usually say. Usually they want to do whatever they did in the old country.'

'By they, I assume you mean the Brits. Well, we've been through that bit already. I thought, you know, a new country, a new lifestyle; something different; all that stuff.'

'Yeah right.'

'Why don't you just read out your list and I'll tell you when to stop, OK?'

'Yeah, right. Er, do you want to work outdoors or inside?'

'I've done the outdoors bit, inside in the warm and dry might be nice.'

'You wouldn't like to join our navy, I suppose? Your seniority would count.'

'Thanks but no thanks.'

'Just thought I'd ask.'

Frank decided that he had better take charge of this interview or it would go nowhere.

'What were you? You must have been in something yourself.'

'Army, Private. Never got out of Canada.'

'You're lucky mate. I hardly ever got back to England.'

Rapport established they worked their way through the list; a damn funny way to run a country but, different times, different countries, different systems he guessed.

'This is different, how about this? They want a clerk/typist at the Reformatory.'

'Tell me more.'

'The pay's rubbish but, as a civil servant, you can't get fired. Much the same as this really, except I don't have to look after prisoners.'

'A Reformatory's for smally boys, yeah?'

'No. That's a Boys Home. Here, if a man gets sent down for up to two years, he goes to a reformatory. Two years or more and he goes to a penitentiary. Whether anybody has ever been reformed, I have no idea but that's the system, take it or leave it.'

'It sounds like the kind of place any of us could end up in.'

'Yeah. At the Reformatory, they got mainly drunks and a few petty larcenists with one or two auto theft thrown in to make up the numbers; nothing heavy, no danger to the staff. Quite a good little number if you can live on the money.'

'OK, so tell me, what is the money?'

'Two thousand the year. Take home's quite good though, you don't have to pay unemployment insurance and you get Blue Cross health insurance thrown in for free.'

Frank did his sums. Divide by four to Pounds, divide by fifty two for weeks.

'Ain't a lot, is it.' Mental arithmetic told him that it was about twice what he would have got in England!

'It gets better each year. If you keep your nose clean.'

'Ah well, my Mum always said I'd end up in jail. What's the next step?'

'I'll give you a letter to the Burser. I'll ring him and tell him you're coming for an interview. When do you want to go?'

'How about now?'

'I'll tell you one thing for nothing, friend, you're the first Brit we've had in here who's been that keen to work. Usually they want to be whatever they were over 'ome and want to be paid more for doing it badly. We keep on getting them sent back to us as lazy complainers.'

'If I decide to complain, I'll be sure to come and ask for you, OK?'

'You'll do alright here Buddy, you have the right attitude.'

Letters were typed and phone calls made. It struck Frank as quite amazing just how fast the Canadians could work if they chose to. In England, he would have been thrown out of the office for cheek and, even if he'd survived the interview, he would have had to wait days for the letter to be dictated, typed, checked and signed by somebody more senior than the interviewer.

'I spoke to the Burser. He said to warn you that he used to be a Royal Marine before he came here after the last war.'

'That's all I need! A bloody bootneck.'

The reformatory was on the outskirts of town, set in open ground not yet developed but a huge sign advertised a local auto dealer; Bob Tyler, Your Local Chevrolet Dealer – Keenest Prices – Best Trade Ins. If he was going to work out here, he'd need a car. Shortage of funds made this something of a problem but that was tomorrow's problem; today's was to get the job.

The office door was ajar, he knocked and entered clasping the large folder containing his immigration papers, service demobilisation papers, letter from the Veteran's Office, passport and various other bits of paper he had been told to take with him. The Burser, about fifty five, short grey hair brushed straight back bootneck fashion looked up and noticed the bulging folder.

'Brought your lunch?'

Frank liked him.

'Sit yourself down, tell me who you are, where you're from and what you've got that I might need.'

'Frank Bye Ex-RN and I need a job.'

'You'll do. No fancy claims, I like that. Did that fool in the Vet's Office tell you I'm ex-RM from the first war?'

'Yes but, if you don't tell anybody, I won't.'

'Can you clerk and type?'

'I can type. It's probably the only thing the Andrew taught me that has any practical use in civvy street. I can read and write so I can clerk.'

'Today's Thursday. Can you start Monday?'

'Yes Sir.'

'You don't call me Sir. My name's Fred MacDonald. You can call me Mr MacDonald until I call you Frank, OK?'

He threw the folder into his In Tray. 'I'll get to that later, let you have it back Monday. How about a cup of coffee?'

He flicked the switch on the intercom box on his desk.

'Can we have some coffee in here?'

'So, when did you arrive in Toronto and where are you living?'

'Got here this morning and I've taken a room at the Ford until I can find something cheaper.'

'Then we'd better get you out of there before you go bankrupt. How did you get on to us so quickly, or have you been in Canada some time?'

'No, I arrived this morning straight from the boat. I met the Padre at the station and he put me up to going to the Vet's Office and, from there, it was all down hill.'

'Don't push your luck Son. You haven't tried it yet.'

He flicked the intercom switch again. 'Have Paul come in here, will you.'

'Paul's wife works at the Y, the YMCA, she can probably find you a room closer to here and cheaper than the Ford. The nearest public transport is the streetcar stop two blocks down towards the lakeshore. I'll get Paul to run you around so that you can get your bearings.'

Paul came in. MacDonald introduced them.

'Frank's joining us on Monday, your old job. He's staying at the Ford so he needs a room nearer to here. Can Brenda help him out, do you think?'

'The only man allowed in her room is me but I'll ask her what she knows, have her look on the notice board at the Y.'

'Are you busy?'

'Always busy Sir, Mr MacDonald, Sir.'

'Well get unbusy for this afternoon. Take Frank here over to the Y and get him sorted out, OK?'

'What will Loretta say?'

'I'll tell Loretta. You sort out our new friend here.'

'Who's Loretta?'

'She, Frank, will be your boss Be nice to her and she'll be nice to you. I take it you have no objections to working for a woman?'

'If I'd known, I'd have asked for more money.'

'Get him out of here Paul. He's talking as if he's been here for ever already. Why do I always get the wise guys?'

CHAPTER TWENTY-FOUR

The Toronto Y was much the same as such places anywhere. The usual collection of rooms for reading, writing, coffee and table tennis plus, a gymnasium much better than any Frank had ever seen, the decoration was better too. Brenda had already checked if there was a spare room but as always, the club was full. She had also checked the notice board on which Rooms For Rent were advertised by house owners who wanted tenants that they felt they could trust; the sort of man who would be a member of the YMCA.

She came out from behind the counter-like reception desk. Frank had imagined a girl working in the Y would probably be a homely type but Brenda was a stunner. The introductions completed, they sat at a nearby table from which she could see her desk should anybody want her; Paul collected coffee from the machine.

'I've got three rooms which might be OK but they're going to want their rent up front for the first few weeks I expect. Until they are sure of you, you know.'

'What sort of money are we talking about?'

'About five a week, I imagine, why don't you drink your coffee then Paul can run you over to look at them,' Frank nodded. 'Been here long?'

'All day. Got here this morning, I'm fresh off the boat.'

'Didn't take you long to get yourself organised, did it?'

'Had nothing better to do. Was at a lose end, you might say.'

'Do you know anybody in Toronto?'

'Not a soul.'

'Then, we'd better get you membership here. It'll be somewhere to come rather than sitting in your room and you'll meet people here.' She sent Paul off to get a membership application form from behind her desk, are you married?'

'Not now.'

'I see. One of those marriages was it, the war and all that?' It wasn't really a question, more an acceptance of a very common situation. 'I'm sure you will soon find friends here.'

Paul also brought over a map of Toronto and they marked the locations of the three rooms from the For Rent cards.

'I'll draw in the streetcar routes as well, so that you can find your way better,' Brenda marked the major routes with red crayon. 'If it's any good, this room will be the easiest for getting to work.' She pointed to the one she meant. 'You'll get a streetcar direct from there to Long Branch and change there. Get off at the bottom of Vine, then it's a two block walk up to the reformatory. I guess you'll be getting a car soon, that's a hell of a walk in the snow.'

Paul had filled in the membership application form and Frank signed it and gave Brenda the two Dollars.

'Right. Shall we a-hunting go?'

Brenda, back behind her desk, watched them leave, wondering.

'You any good at navigation?'

'Only at sea where there's nothing to hit and nothing to confuse me but I'll do my best.' He spread the map over his knee.

Allowing for his lack of knowledge of one-way streets, Frank did quite well. The first room was awful. High under the roof of an old house with only a very small window for lighting, it had mauve, quilted wallpaper; it looked like a padded cell, they smiled, thanked the woman and left.

'That would have been awful,' Paul said. 'You'd have been certifiable within days of moving in with that wallpaper.'

158

The next, the one that Brenda had marked as the most convenient, proved to be not much better and the third was worse than the first. They returned to the Y for more coffee and a council of war with Brenda.

'What about Bob and Agnes,' Paul asked. 'Haven't they just built an apartment in their basement?'

Brenda nodded. 'I could ask but they will want more than five bucks a week for that, it's a two room apartment with shower and a kitchen.'

'God, girl, it's only a plasterboard division in their basement, they can't expect much for that. The windows are up at eye level, for starters.' Brenda went back to the telephone.

'What did you do before you came to Canada'

Frank decided to treat Paul's enquiry as a friendly approach. 'I was a sailor in The King's Navee. What about you? Have you always worked at the reformatory?'

'God no, I did a couple of years in the Air Force, guarding airfields mostly, then when the war ended, I decided that although the Government mayn't pay well, it does pay regular and that's important if you're thinking of getting married. The holidays are good too, you could do a lot worse. My old man was out of work more often than in it before the war so I decided that security was probably more comfortable than the alternative.'

Brenda came back, looking pleased.

'I think it may be alright. You can go over and take a look and, if you like it, she'll take ten Dollars a week but she wants it up front and I've had to guarantee that you will pay regular. It's only because you work with Paul that she is prepared to consider letting it to a single man and there'll be some house rules about visiting females I guess, she has two small children.' To Paul she said, 'Agnes was a bit worried about taking a single man with Bob doing shift work and being away some nights. I hope we're doing the right thing.'

'Where's your Christian charity?' Brenda smiled at her husband. 'You forget dear, I'm Jewish, I just work at the

Y.' Paul turned to Frank. 'If you let Brenda down, I will personally ensure that you regret it.'

'Fear not, good Sir, trouble I don't need and anyway, there's an old adage in England that a wise bird never fouls its own nest.'

It was agreed. He liked Agnes, she seemed a good sort, no side, plain speaking, he liked that, it kept life simple. He could move in tomorrow morning and Paul offered to help with the essentials. The apartment was furnished but lacked everything else.

'See you in the morning.'

Paul left him at his hotel and he watched the car pull away and join the homeward crawl that was already making its way out of the city centre towards the fast growing suburbs. In his room, he flopped on to the bed and slept the sleep of the exhausted.

He didn't know what woke him but a glance at his watch told him that he had been asleep for nearly three hours. He washed, shaved and went in search of a drink and something to eat in the American Bar, wondering idly why they called it that; funny place, this Canada.

'What's your pleasure Sir?'

'I need a large whiskey, no ice, no soda and you'd better put another measure on top of that, just to hold it down.'

'Been that kind of a day has it Sir?'

'You can say that again!'

The waitress went in search of the water of life.

CHAPTER TWENTY-FIVE

In the district known to Torontonians as downtown, Eaton's and Simpson's stores both had SALE posters in their windows but then, if one had, the other would have to. Old Cyrus Eaton had issued a mail order catalogue from his warehouse on the Toronto waterfront and, as Canada grew, so did Eaton's business. By 1939, Eaton's was the biggest department store in Toronto as well as remaining the biggest mail order house in Canada. The only effect of the war had been to limit competition.

There were no shortages here now. At home, there were shortages of everything but here, in Eaton's bargain basement, there were none. No rationing, no coupons, that had all gone with the outbreak of peace, here was peace and almost unimaginable plenty. Frank wondered what Alice would think if she could see this. Don't think of her, don't think of the past at all. He followed Paul.

Aisle after aisle of quality goods, no Utility mark labels on any of this, although it was all at bargain prices. Down here there was about an acre of ends of lines, returns from mail order sales, slight imperfects and every single piece of it better than anything Frank had ever owned.

They selected the essentials, arranged for same-day delivery and went in search of food.

''Have you been to England?'

'No, I was called up by the Air force just before it all ended and never got further than boot camp and guard duties at airfields three thousand five hundred miles from the nearest enemy. You could call it a nice quiet number.'

'Not to worry. The way the Ruskies are playing up, you may get your chance after all. I reckon it'll be someone else's turn then, I've done mine.'

'Aren't you on some kind of reserve?'

'Only in England. If I stay here, your Government might be able to call me up but then who'd look after your prisoners?'

They found the coffee shop and sat.

'You should have seen it last time. They turned it into a POW camp with the army providing the guards. All the civilian prisoners were sent somewhere else, probably into the army! Mind you, there weren't a lot of them.

'When the war ended, the army sent all their guards home to their farms or wherever and half of the POW's claimed that, as veterans, the Ontario Government had to find them jobs. No way were they going back to a clapped out Europe, ruined by five years of war.'

'Frankly, I don't blame them but I reckon it was a damned cheek. We've actually got three guards who were POW's and I wouldn't be surprised to find that some of the prisoners used to be guards. It's a crazy old world we live in.'

'Have you any other immigrants working there? The Vet's office seemed to think that, at the money you're offering, there wouldn't be a lot of volunteers.'

'Most of the guards and staff are. The natives prefer to get paid more in industry and commerce, things have really begun to look up since the war. There's money to be made out there if you're prepared to work hard enough.'

'Then, why aren't you out there grafting for it?'

'I told you. My old man was out of work most of his life and I prefer security. Anyway, most of the new companies and factories are American owned and, just as soon as the first hiccup comes, they'll close down the Canadian branches to preserve jobs at home; just like they did last time. But, when that happens, we'll be the ones who still have a job!'

'You reckon it will all go belly up then?'

'I reckon in another two maybe three years when Europe gets back on it's feet, demand will turn down if it doesn't peter out all together and then we return to bust!

Then the Yanks will go home and take their jobs with them.'

'Perhaps there'll be enough immigrants to tip the population balance in Canada's favour, I gather there have been thousands of 'em every year.'

'That's the trouble, we need the population but we don't want the immigrants, if you follow my drift. We don't mind guys like you, single, prepared to take any job going to pay your way, you'll fit in OK no problem, its the damned DP's. The ones from Europe who lay down and let the Germans roll right over them. After we'd rolled 'em back, they stood up and claimed that it was the Allies that had bombed and destroyed Europe so they should be allowed to come and live over here.'

Frank understood the problem and could sympathise but had no sensible solution to suggest, he decided that it was time to change the subject.

'What time do you think they'll deliver my gear?'

'It depends. They load the truck with the furthest away load on last so that they can get it off first and work their way back to base by half of four. They sign off at five and like to get their paperwork done before they clock off. Yours will probably be the last load; about half three, I should think, perhaps a little later.'

'I need some groceries.'

'Lakeshore at Long branch, there's some shops there. It's nearer to home and it's a penny or two cheaper than here in town, we'll go there directly.'

They finished their coffee and Paul paid the waitress, Frank noticed that he left a tip.

'That's the sort of thing which will mark me as an immigrant. Knowing whether to tip and, if so, how much. It's different everywhere and, if I'm going to blend into the background around here, pretend I've been here for ever, I'd better find out about the little things like that.'

'In that suit, there's no way you will blend into the background but it depends upon where you are. In a restaurant like that, ten percent is OK and welcomed as they don't pay too well. If you go up market, nightclubs and such, it depends who you're tipping. The hat-check girl or washroom attendant about a Dollar if you're showing off, fifty cents if you don't give a damn. Head waiters, a five Dollar bill will get you a decent table, more than that will mark you down as a mug. In a bar, you don't expect to tip unless you're waited on at table then you're back to about ten percent.

"Don't worry about it. Looking the way you do at the present, the waitress will probably slip you a few cents.'

He held up his hand to deflect the expected blow, smiling. 'There's nothing wrong with that suit but it obviously ain't local. We'll get you sorted out after payday. You can't expect to become one of us overnight.'

The drive out on Lakeshore Boulevard to Long branch, ran alongside High Park and Frank noticed St. Joseph's hospital as they passed. He wondered how the girls were getting on.

The streetcar tracks in the centre of the road meant that they had to stop every so often, if a streetcar stopped, to let the people reach the sidewalk and, at St. Joseph's, a lot of people got off, some of them in nurses uniforms.

Not the sort of uniforms he had seen in England but plain white dresses with white stockings and shoes; all very aseptic looking but not very practical and, anyway, worn for the ride on the streetcar, they couldn't have been very aseptic, ah well, different places, different customs.

'That's the Catholic hospital.'

'Do you have to be a Catholic to get treated there?'

'No, but I think you do to work there.'

Frank didn't think that Sarah and Judy were Catholics but he let the thought pass, it was none of his business.

'I know a couple of girls who have just come over to work there, met them on the boat.'

'Will they be living in the nurses hostel?'

'I've no idea, why?'

'It has something of a reputation. All the fellows know it and regard it as a sort of dating agency. All the men's clubs, the Y and all the others, always send invitations to the nurse's hostel if they organise a dance or a picnic in the summer. There's always a few unattached nurses looking for a safe date.'

Frank made a mental note.

'One of the House Mothers has been there for years and can be relied on to come to any dance or picnic or any party that's going. They call her Harley, after the motorbike, they reckon she's the best ride in town. Got enough fat on her to absorb all the bumps and, if you tell Brenda I told you that, I'll deny it.'

'She probably knows about her already, word gets around amongst the girls faster than it does amongst the men.'

'Yeah, you're probably right but she doesn't know that I know so keep your mouth shut, OK?'

They drove past the streetcar terminus at Long branch where, if you wanted to go further, you had to buy another ticket. This was as far as the central fare zone went. Paul explained it all and Frank understood about half of it.

On the other side of the boulevard they could see the lake, grey and with low waves running from west to east along the shore; it looked like it might be cold. About a mile further on, Paul pulled over and parked the car.

'Everybody out!'

The row of shops along both sides of the street looked a bit like a film set for a wild-west movie. The important looking, single story storefronts were backed by what looked like brick sheds; not very impressive but, no doubt, practical. About half way down the left hand side, a big neon sign identified Honest Ed's. A few doors along from that was a Loblaws supermarket. Food was bought and money changed hands. Frank looked at his change.

'I'm going to have to stop this working for a living business, I can't afford it!'

They stopped off at the Y for lunch with Brenda who found the whole thing amusing.

'You're supposed to do it the other way around, she told him. First you work, then you get paid, then, and only then, do you spend. It's an old fashioned system but it's been found to work in the past. I strongly recommend you try it.'

'I'd like to but it seems that I'm fated to do it all backwards. Roll on pay day, that's all I can say.'

The panel truck pulled up outside the house. Agnes had the door open and pointed to the covered front porch.

'Set it all down in there, we'll sort it out.'

'It's no bother Mam, we'll take it wherever you want it.'

'Thanks but no thanks. Just set it down right there. We'll manage.'

'Just sign here then Mam.'

As the truck pulled away, Paul came out from the kitchen, cup of coffee in hand.

'Do you want to give Bob and Frank a hand down the stairs with that lot,' Agnes asked him. 'The fewer people who know there's an apartment down stairs, the happier I shall be.'

Frank wondered how many of the houses in the street, or in Toronto for that matter, had apartments in their basements with none of the income being declared for tax but, as long as the Government collected enough taxes to pay his wages, Frank wasn't going to rock anybody's boat.

'How come you can just take a day off work, like this, to help me out?'

Paul put the coffee table in front of the settee. 'Officially I'm at work. Mac knows where I am if he needs me, no sweat. I can catch up on the work on Monday and we like to think that we all help each other out over here, that's how the west was won.'

'This ain't the west.'

'It's west of where you come from.'

'Now that you have a table to put it on, I'll give you this,' Agnes placed a huge bowl of fresh fruit on the coffee table. 'Just to say welcome to Canada.'

'That really is most kind of you, thank you very much indeed.'

'You'll want to get settled in so I'll leave you to get on with it. Why don't you come and have Sunday lunch with us upstairs? Nothing special, just meat and potatoes but it'll leave you free from cooking. Can you cook?'

'In the navy, we can do anything, we're not allowed to take our wives with us. I can cook, sew, darn, knit, wash, iron and clean house so you've no need to worry. I shan't burn down your house nor let it get too dirty. I will come to lunch on Sunday though and, thank you for inviting me.'

'That's a great deal more than Bob can do, or Paul either,' she left him to get on with organising his things. 'Oh, by the way,' she said from the top of the stairs 'I can't allow you to keep any pets down here; I'm sure you understand.'

The small windows were just above eye level but let in enough light during the day and, at night, it didn't matter were they were. It seemed a bit strange, looking out of the window at ground level, the grass of what they hoped would be a lawn would have to be kept short or it would act as a curtain. A bit like looking out through the scuttle in the for'ard lower messdeck of a destroyer; through them you could almost see the fishes swimming past at sea.

The apartment comprised a single, small bedroom, just big enough for a double bed, wardrobe and built-in vanity unit with draws under and a bedside table on which Agnes had put a small lamp with a pink shade. The lamp looked like the sort of present people receive and put in the loft until the giver visits and is then put on display for an hour or so. Come pay day, he would buy another lamp but, in the meantime, it had to be better than nothing.

In the lounge, a two-seater settee and one armchair in grey uncut moquette fabric filled half of the room, the coffee table and a bookcase completed the furnishings. A small mat, placed in front of the settee, slipped across the polished linoleum floor every time he trod on it; it would have to go as soon as possible, ideally before he broke his neck. He decided to leave it in- situ until the weekend, just in case Agnes came down for anything.

In the kitchen, a tall cupboard, an old but serviceable ice box, a sink with draining board attached, a table and two chairs provided all necessary facilities. In the corner beside the sink, an electric cooker showed all the hallmarks of having been upstairs and in regular use until very recently. No doubt, his rent was paying for its replacement.

From the kitchen, a door gave access to the remainder of the house's basement, much of which was equipped as a workroom for Bob. It also acted as a store for sacks of onions, potatoes and, on carefully erected shelves, apples and pears. Agnes was from the country and believed in putting by a little fresh fruit and vegetables for the winter. It was from this part of the basement also that another flight of steps led up from behind the huge boiler to the floor above and its own front door. The apartment was probably at the top of the range that Frank could afford and was clean, convenient and warm; he was happy with it.

The percolator provided a welcoming background sound and Frank flopped down on to the settee. In a few minutes he would drag himself out to the kitchen and pour himself a cup; if he stayed awake for long enough. Tomorrow he would go walk about in this new district and see what it was like. Tonight, just as soon as he had made his bed, he was going to sleep like the dead. He was glad to be free from the hotel and all the disadvantages that that entailed.

Sitting there, he thought momentarily about Alice, what she would think of the apartment; in the kitchen the coffee percolator plopped roughly in sync with his snores.

CHAPTER TWENTY-SIX

Monday. With directions from Agnes, Frank walked to work. At first glance, the car park appeared full of giant American cars but, down at the far end and, as if trying to hide, an old English Humber Hawk stood covered with dust. That it hadn't moved in yonks was obvious.

He reported to Mr MacDonald's secretary who called Paul. There being no answer on Paul's telephone, she told Frank to follow her, she would take him up to Mrs Vetchik's office; Mrs Vetchik was the office manager, his boss. He got the impression that the secretary didn't welcome newcomers. Her tone of voice was such that he half expected to be referred to as a dirty DP.

Mrs Vetchik however was another thing altogether. About forty, dark with one or two grey hairs hiding amongst the others and obviously pleased to see him. Frank liked the look of her. A full, open face, eyes that saw without staring and a generous mouth. She was smiling.

'Mac tells me you can type. How many fingers do you use?'

'All of them most of the time and most of them some of the time. I can knock up about sixty words per minute cold sober and, perhaps, a little more after a tot; I tend to lose accuracy after two tots.'

'Sixty will do nicely, thank you. We don't allow booze in this office.' She led the way down the long, narrow office, introducing him to everyone as they passed.

'This will be your desk, it should be loaded with paper, carbon sheets, etc., envelopes and pencils. Now, I understand that you know Paul already and I have arranged for him to take you through the job; it was his until he got himself promoted but, if he comes in late many more times, he might just get busted back to where he started. Why don't you get yourself a cup of coffee from the machine over there and make sure that you are comfortable here. If Paul isn't in by then, I'll take you through it myself.'

'Sorry Loretta, I overslept.' Paul slipped out of his coat and threw it casually over the back of the chair of the adjoining desk. Loretta smiled at him.

'That's alright Paul. Once more and you're in trouble.'

Paul hooked his chair over with his left foot and sat down beside Frank. 'Lovely girl but hard as nails. She smiles a lot but watch out for her bite.'

'I've met a few like that at sea. I learned always to wear a life preserver.'

'Right. First, take off your jacket. No-one wears a jacket in the office here; we leave the uniforms to the guys downstairs and on the gate.'

It took about an hour for Paul to take Frank through all aspects of the job. Primarily, just filling in forms with inmates' data, typing up standard letters to various agencies who needed to know that the inmate was inside and the occasional letter about the inmate to a priest or some agency to which he was calling for assistance. Once in a while, Paul told him, he would have to do a letter to the Court to accompany the inmate being returned to face further charges, nothing too serious; all the master letters were already on file.

Frank looked at the in tray and was far from surprised to find it full. No doubt, everyone had dumped their excess in his tray; new boy's perks. He started work on what must have two or three week's forms.

The office had been formed out of what must have been a row of small storerooms, little better than cupboards. The dividing walls had been taken down to form a long, shallow room with the desks lined up along the innermost wall and looking outwards through the windows over the car park.

Outside the nearest window to Frank, a tall silver birch tree stood, its leaves all gone. In the summer, it would provide a little shade against the sun that would shine in through all of the windows, right into the eyes of the people working at the desks; all except his. That could be an unexpected bonus come the summer but that was months away, first there was the winter to be overcome, walking to work was not a happy prospect when the snow came and he would have to do something about that quite soon. Paul came over.

'I just thought. I haven't shown you where the can is, he led the way out though the nearest door and down the corridor. This afternoon, I'll take you on a tour of the whole facility and introduce you to the guards. It'd be a pity if they stopped you coming in to work, wouldn't it. Did you bring any lunch? There's a canteen but most of us just bring sandwiches and eat at our desks.'

Frank admitted that, being unsure of the routine, he had made up some sandwiches and put them in his pocket. They now rested at the back of a desk draw.

By lunchtime, Frank had made considerable inroads into the pile of work that had been gathered up for him from all the other desks and he felt better, more at home, relaxed.

'Do you want to let me see what you've done?'

Loretta Vetchik's enquiry carried enough authority to make it clear that it was not a question. Frank collected his morning's work together and walked over to her desk.

She put the work to one side and took out her sandwich lunch.

'Do you like smoked ham?'

'With mustard?'

'With mustard.'

'I like smoked ham.'

'What would you have said if I'd told you there was no mustard?'

'I'd have said that I liked smoked ham.'

'Then what's with all the questions about mustard?'

'Just making polite conversation.'

'Well, don't get too smart too soon. There are some people here who don't like DP's. Watch your step downstairs until you get the feel of the place, OK?' She handed him a sandwich.

'How do you like your coffee? '

She smiled. 'Black, no sugar.'

He collected two cups of coffee from the machine and picked up his own sandwiches from his desk. He noticed Paul smile as he passed; he leant over.

'I think she likes me.'

'Don't bet on it.'

He put his sandwiches down on Loretta's desk.

'Shall we go Dutch?'

Paul introduced him to the Governor and his Deputy, another ex Royal Marine, Frank made a remark about bootnecks running the navy's detention centres and was informed in no uncertain manner that the Deputy Governor had been a bandsman and First Aider, not a policeman.

'I believe in reformation not incarceration.'

Paul got him out of the office as quickly as he could.

'You blew that one. No sense of humour, I should have warned you, you obviously have no fear of saying your piece.'

'Forget it, I'm accident prone.'

'What's all this about bootnecks anyway?'

'Well, for the last hundred and fifty years or more, the primary function of Royal Marines on navy ships has been to protect the officers from mutinous sailors. Of course, there hasn't been a mutiny since Fletcher Christian set Captain Bligh adrift in his own rowboat, but there's still a natural distrust between matelots and bootnecks. Nonsense of course but it provides a little innocent merriment amongst those who know what we're talking about.'

'I thought there had been a mutiny in the Royal Navy just before the war?'

'Not a proper one. Invergordon was more an industrial strike than a mutiny. Nobody tried to hang the Captains and Officers from their own yardarms or anything like that. No fun at all so I was told.'

They toured the buildings, Paul introducing him to the guards and then walked over to the workshops where the inmates made boots for the Canadian Army and the RCMP. From there, they went on to the farm where the care of a few cows and a sty of pigs occupied a great deal of inmates' time and, finally, down into the shale pit; the least popular work station amongst the inmates and the guards. Hot in the summer and cold in the winter, the pit was wet in between times.

The shale itself was shipped out to a refinery for oil extraction so the pit was used mainly as a punishment detail for inmates who pushed their luck too far with the guards and, similarly, for guards who managed to upset their Captain.

Half way down the side of the pit, nearest to the buildings and furthest from the lake, Frank saw what was clearly part of a beach, a sandy beach. Paul saw him looking at it.

'They reckon that the lake shore was here years ago but it has been drying out and the beach moving south for God knows how long.'

As the shale was well below the beach level, the lake shore mush have moved back and forth quite a few times both before and since the last ice age. Frank made a mental note to ask some questions about it.

One of the ways that he had passed his time at sea, when not on watch, was reading and he had found himself fascinated by archaeology and, from that, geology. Come the summer, he would take a closer look at the pit. He picked up a fragment of broken, blackened stone and showed it to Paul.

'That stone was used as an edge for a fire on the beach and, look, there are some fish bones here too. Someone camped here when this was the lake shore. Don't you find that interesting?'

Paul shrugged.

'Not really. Who cares that some Indian camped here thousands of years ago. He's hardly likely to jump and say boo!'

'This guy was here long before the Indians.'

'Then he's no danger to us!'

They climbed out of the pit.

'Who's is the old Humber over there?' Frank indicated the old black car at the far end of the car park.

'That's Mac's. It used to be a staff car when the British Air Force was based out at the airport. Mac picked it up for cheap when the war ended. Ran if for a year or two until he bought the big ford over there.'

'There weren't any new cars for a year or two after the war, it took the yanks some time to get back into full peacetime production and all the new ones could be sold in the US so we had to wait. They reckon that they're going to build an assembly plant here in Toronto to serve the Canadian market, that'll make for a few new jobs.'

'Does it go?'

'How the hell should I know, why?'

'I wondered if he would rent it to me until I can afford to buy one. I walked to work this morning but that's going to be doing it the hard way if the weather breaks.'

'You'd best ask him. He won't mind, it's doing him no good parked there.'

The office felt warm after the grand tour. Loretta handed Frank the work he had done before lunch.

'These seem OK. See if you can find the files they belong to and file them, OK? The file room's across the hall and up the stairs, another ex- cupboard.'

Each inmate, they preferred the term inmate to prisoner for some reason, had a file for each period spent in the reformatory. Most of them seemed to have quite a few files.

'What's taking you so long?'

Loretta had closed the door behind her.

'I was just working out the system. New file for each sentence, some of these guys appear to be regular clients.'

She took the last file from his hand and stuffed it back into the cabinet, closing the draw with a bang.

'You're the intelligent type. I prefer men with a few brains, most of the men working here are brawn. That's OK in its place but I like to talk before and after.'

Frank recognised the signals being sent but couldn't believe she meant the signals he was receiving.

'So do I but the atmosphere is also important too, don't you think?'

The shutters came down behind her eyes.

'I want all those forms completed today, before you go home. Check with me before you leave, OK?'

By the time he got back to his desk, Loretta was in conference with Cherry, one of the other clerks. He got stuck in to the pile of forms awaiting completion; Paul sidled over.

'What happened? You can't be that quick.'

'Nothing happened. What should have happened?'

'Meet me in the can in five minutes.'

He went back to his own desk and rearranged some papers for a few minutes then left the office without looking back. Frank waited a moment or two then collected up the forms he had completed and made for the filing room.

'What's all the fuss?'

Paul flushed the can to cover the sound of their voices. 'You were supposed to try to give it to her.'

'What? There in the filing room? Just like that?'

'Not really. She always follows a new male into the file room and offers it to him. You're supposed to try to get it, to take her, then she threatens to tell Mac and get you fired. It's her little way of showing who's boss. She's done that to every new man who's joined in years. What the hell did you say to get her back in the office so quick?'

'I told her that I like the atmosphere to be right as, I'm sure she does.'

'You, boy, could just be in serious trouble. I'd keep out of her way for a few days if I were you.'

'She wants me to check with her before leaving tonight.'

'OK but, tell her I'm giving you a ride home as you don't have a car. That might just get you off the hook.'

The sound of the flushing toilet covered the sound of his departure. By the time Frank got back to his desk, Paul was talking to Loretta about something and neither of them saw him come in and sit down.

CHAPTER TWENTY-SEVEN

It was Wednesday when Cherry followed him into the file room and closed the door.

'I hear you said no to Loretta.'

Frank did his best to misunderstand.

'I'm sorry? No about what to Loretta?'

'Come off it, the whole place knows. You're the first man to say no to Loretta in years and she's steaming mad about it; you a pansy or something?'

'Nope. I just get dizzy doing it standing up.'

'Well, you'd better find some other way to do it soon or this place won't be worth working in.'

He escaped to the safety of his desk. The Vet's Office hadn't warned him about this.

In the course of the rest of the week, Frank noticed that he was being watched. Every person he met looked him over as if trying to decide whether he was a pansy or not. You could never be sure with these Brits, he heard one guard tell another, they ain't like us.

In Paul's car on Friday evening Frank told him.

'I'm beginning to feel like a goldfish in a bowl. I seem to be under observation by the entire establishment; I'm even beginning to suspect that the inmates have heard about it too.'

'It's just that no one has said no to Loretta before and lived to tell the tale. She used to be Mac's secretary until her little hobby got too well known. He had to promote her out of his office or explain to his wife why he hadn't done so. Poor guy hadn't any choice. Out she had to go and, as no one was prepared to face an enquiry for wrongful dismissal, the only out was up. He had to create a whole new job for her; Office manager. Told her that, now that the office was getting bigger, with more staff, he had to have someone in charge that he could trust. You've got to hand it to the old boy, he did a good job on her. She never suspected a thing, she even offered him a little thank you present in his office but he had already arranged for the telephone to ring five minutes into the interview.'

'Well, I'm not sure I like being a seven day wonder. I hope it only lasts seven days.'

He was saved from further embarrassment by the breakout over the weekend.

By Monday morning, everybody had a new subject of conversation and, by the following Friday, payday, Frank was accepted as just one of the guys. A little different perhaps being a Brit but one of the guys.

'Mac wants to see you in his office.' Loretta's expression suggested that she knew why.

Mac's office looked as it always looked, like a work-free zone. He had the knack of keeping his paperwork in orderly packs; this was obviously a stress-free zone if not work-free. 'You wanted to see me?'

'Sit down Frank. I've asked you to come down so that I can explain what I've done. There's no need to tell anyone else about this you understand?' Frank nodded. 'I've arranged for you to be paid three week's money this month, although you've only worked for two, and three week's next month. That should make matters a little easier for you. Are you settling in OK?'

'Yes, I think so. Everyone has been most kind and helpful.'

'Yes. I heard about Loretta by the way; I think you can call me Mac from now on, I reckon you deserve that much recognition. What baffles me is why you're still here, she must be getting old or something. If you make it through to the end of next month, I reckon you should be safe. Have a good weekend.'

'Thanks. There is something I'd like to ask you about, if I may?'

'Shoot.'

'Your old Humber Hawk. I can't afford to buy a car yet but if you would rent that to me for a few months it would help me out. I'm cadging lifts from Paul at the moment but we've been late a couple of times and I don't want to upset Loretta at the moment.'

'Christ! I haven't used that in about eighteen months but, if you can get it to go, sure you can borrow it. Have it, be my guest, I don't need it and you might be able to trade it in on something useful later. Why don't you have a word with the Captain of the Guard and have a couple of the inmates fix it up some? This place is full of experts. They can get anything to start if they want to steal it.'

'Thanks. That's a good idea. I'm no expert on cars, didn't have a lot of them at sea as you'll remember. Is it OK if we work on it in the yard over the weekend?'

The weekend dawned bright and clear, crisp enough to make the prospect of physical work attractive. Frank walked to the main gate and checked in with the guard. Luckily it was one that he already knew.

'I'll probably be here all morning trying to get the brute to work.'

The old car had already been washed down and looked pretty good to him. The bodywork would repay a good polish but there was practically no rust to be seen anywhere other than one rear wing which had been hit at some time.

Frank put down the bag of rags and dusters he had borrowed from Agnes and went in search of a bucket to wash down the inside. The leather upholstery was in good condition but would clearly repay a little effort with soap and water plus a little wax to follow.

Back in the guardhouse, three men waited for him. The guard called them over.

'Meet Joe, Mike and Dave. The Chief thought you might like a little expert help. These three guys probably the best car strippers in the business and I really mean in the business. Just you give them the keys and come on in and have a cup of coffee. Can't have the staff working and the inmates standing around watching.'

The working party seemed happy enough to have something to do and set about the old car. Within minutes, the hood was off and Mike's head disappeared inside the engine compartment. Joe and Dave had the seats out and put to one side whilst the carpet was taken out and laid on the ground for cleaning.

'By the time those three have finished with it, the only thing you'll recognise is the number plate. It's out of date, by the way, you'll need a new one.'

'Do you want to tell me why I'm suddenly so popular? I only just got off the boat.'

'You ain't. That's the Burser's car and it never does any harm to do one of the bosses a favour.'

Mike came over and reported that the engine was probably OK but a new set of plugs would help. The battery needed to be put on charge or, possibly, replaced.

The guard nodded. 'Stick that one on charge over in the garage and ask the guard there if they have any plugs that would fit this old buggy.' He turned to Frank. 'I doubt if they'll have anything suitable for that but there's a service station down in Long Branch that specialises in British autos. They'll have anything you need. Ask Mike what type you need and you can use my wheels, it the old Olds over there.'

It was the first time Frank had driven a left hand drive car and the Oldsmobile was twice the size of anything he had driven in England but, with a great deal of luck, he found the gears without too much noise and grinding and shot through the main gate with a show of entirely false confidence.

Limey's Garage was, as reported, a specialist in English cars and had the required plugs. 'If you want it checked out properly, just bring it over. All our mechanics are UK trained immigrants so they know what they're doing, OK?'

Frank bought oil, an oil filter, an air filter, a new set of plug leads and a new condenser and points just to be on the safe side. It was as he drove back through the main gate that it dawned on him that he didn't have a driving licence.

The old Humber was up on four piles of bricks and without wheels. Joe and Dave had taken them over to the garage to check and inflate the tires. Mike, who was obviously the mechanic of the team and, equally obviously the headman, was drinking coffee in the guardhouse.

'I thought I'd better get these as well, just in case.'

Frank handed over his purchases and Mike examined them.

'You know about autos?'

'Not a lot.'

'I've never worked on anything like this before. Big, expensive American cars I know about, that's what we steal but this little buggy looks like it might be ok.'

'That little buggy,' Frank told him, 'is a big, expensive auto in England.'

'Ah yes but then England ain't very big, is it.'

'You been there?'

'Yeah. I was over for a while, helping out with your war.'

He drifted back over to the car, coffee mug in hand, his head disappeared inside the hood again. Frank turned to the guard.

'As prisons go, this seems a very democratic sort of place.'

'Yeah well, you see, this ain't what you might call a real prison is it? No real baddies here, they go to the Pen. We just get the drunks, the occasional druggy and the petty larcenists and layabouts. Mike is probably the nearest thing we have to a real criminal in here and he ain't exactly a violent type, just steals cars. Nothing serious, usually from visiting Americans'

'I hear this was a POW camp during the war.'

'Yeah, I was here then. It was a hoot. The army guards knew that the prisoners couldn't escape back to Germany so discipline was a bit slack. The guards called all the prisoners Kraut, whether they were German or not, and the prisoners called all the guards Yank, which none of them were; made for a bit off fun.'

'Which were you?'

'I was a Kraut. My name's Brauniger but I call myself Brown now. I was brought here as a prisoner in forty four and decided to stay. Now I'm a guard and Mike, who was a Canadian soldier, is the prisoner; life's one long game of chance, ain't it?' Frank agreed, life was certainly that.

By lunchtime, the old car looked almost new. Fully valeted, the inside smelled of new leather and polish. The outside gleamed and, with the hood replaced, the engine sounded like a well-oiled clock. The working party had returned to their block, packets of cigarettes stuffed inside their socks and Frank was considering the next move.

The Chevy powered through the gate, the driver giving Frank and the guard a wave.

'Oh shit! It's the Valkyrie.' Brown disappeared into the Guardhouse.

Loretta packed her car and came over. She looked over the old car and nodded appreciatively.

'Thought you might be interested in lunch. I've a basket in the trunk.'

'I'll have to wash up first, I'm covered in oil and rust.'

'There wasn't any rust on it the last time I was in it.'

Frank asked the guard if he could use the washroom.

'I'd better tell the boys to call you Sir, if you're going to keep this up.'

'Sorry?'

'You've only been here a few days and already you have the Burser's car and the Burser's mistress. I reckon you'll have his job by the end of the month.'

'The car's on loan.'

'How about the Valkyrie?'

CHAPTER TWENTY-EIGHT

Loretta let in the clutch.

'I thought we might go down by the lake. It's cool but fine, the view will be worth the few minutes drive and I don't suppose you've been down there yet anyway.'

She struck out westwards along Lakeshore Boulevard and in minutes the houses were left behind. This had been open country until recently but now, raw, open sites showed where the new houses were being built for the returned heroes. Expensive houses for the richer heroes and less expensive for the ordinary heroes. Every one, whatever its listed price, with a six months guarantee; the sign said so.

'Six months doesn't seem much of a guarantee on a house.'

'In this life, you're lucky to get a guarantee on anything. They'll probably stand for ever if they're looked after but giving a guarantee with a new house is a new idea here. It's supposed to make them more attractive to the buyer's wife! What guarantee do you get with a new house in England?'

'I've no idea. I don't think it has occurred to anyone that a house needed a guarantee. The place is full of houses that have stood for hundreds of years.'

'I've seen pictures of England. You live in little houses, all joined together with grass roofs. This must come as quite a surprise to you; that the ordinary people live in big, new, detached houses.'

'Where does your name Vetchik come from?'

'Czechoslovakia, but that was my father when he was a young man, why?'

'Because your knowledge of Europe, particularly England, is a couple of hundred years out of date. The thatched cottages you're talking about are now the homes of the very rich for weekends; they're the only ones who can afford the insurance premiums on thatched roofs and wooden beamed cottages. The rest of us, the ordinary people as you call us, live in modern houses or blocks of purpose-built flats with tiled or slate roofs and central heating. Now that the war is over, we ordinary people can afford to buy cars and go on holidays like you rich Canadians!'

Frank knew that this was not universally true but Loretta didn't and he wasn't going to be put down by her or, for that matter, anyone else. He may have decided to leave England for a better life in Canada but he wasn't going to let anyone badmouth England to him; he'd just spent five years fighting for it.

'Hey, I like you, you've got nerve. You're not afraid to speak up for yourself. That's good, you'll get on over here.'

She turned the Chevy through the gates into the picnic area beside the lake. The tables were made out of split logs, long benches made the same way had been placed down each side, ready for the picnickers to spread their food and enjoy the view. Here, under the trees, it was much colder and Loretta rolled the car down towards the shore where the sun could keep it warm.

'Get the basket out of the trunk, we'll eat in the car where it's warmer.'

Frank opened the lid of the boot and picked up the basket of food.

'God, what have you got in here? It weighs a ton!'

Loretta had moved into the back seat. From the back of the front bench seat, the shelf-like table was hung ready to receive the lunch.

'I like to picnic in a little style,' she said, waiving him into the seat beside her. 'We'll have the place to ourselves today, I imagine.'

Frank agreed that it was a bit cold for picnicking outside.

'Keep the beer out of sight, just in case'

She saw the puzzled look on his face. 'It's the law here. No drinking in public, the bottle must be invisible in case it causes the children to go astray! Actually, drinking in public is OK but there must be no evidence that it is alcoholic; lemonade is OK.

'We were dry until quite recently and, although we grownups are now allowed to drink, we have to buy our liquor from a Government liquor store and keep it wrapped and hidden until we get indoors so, you see, the land of the free is not as free as you thought.'

'I thought the land of the free and the home of the brave was the one on the other side of the lake.'

'Shut up and drink your beer.'

The food was good. The bread was fresh with a good crisp crust, the butter was firm and creamy but not quite salt enough for Frank's taste. Loretta had sliced the ham thick and had remembered to bring the mustard; an apple pie remained in the basket for afterwards, together with a lump of cheese.

The beer was German or perhaps a Czechoslovakian type lager brewed in the USA but had a bite to it and it went down well with the bread and ham.

'Welcome to your first Canadian picnic.'

'I'm amazed at how easy coming here has all been for me. I fall straight into a job, the boss lends me his car, a colleague finds me a flat and my manager takes me down to the lakeshore for a picnic and even provides the food and booze. Truly, there is a God and my old Chief Yeoman was right.'

'What's a Chief Yeoman and what was he right about?'

'He was my boss in the navy and he maintained that the good Lord looked after children, idiots and drunks and that, on that basis, I couldn't lose.'

'Which are you then?'

'Certainly the second, possibly still the first and, occasionally the third.'

'Well, you ain't going to be the third this afternoon, I want you sober. You're definitely not the second, we've already established that but, if you want to be the first then you will have to let me complete your education. I just hope you are a slow learner, that all.'

Her hand closed over his and guided it to her thigh. The skirt of her dress had ridden up as they had been sitting there and he could feel that there was nothing beneath it. She held his hand there for a moment then lifted it.

'Get rid of all this rubbish, put it back in the basket and put that back in the trunk. We'll have another beer later.' The guard had been right; she did like giving orders.

It didn't take long. Indeed it didn't take long enough. Long before Loretta was even on the verge he had spent all that had been saved since Alice. The silence in the back of the car was almost touchable in its intensity, he could actually feel her disappointment, her anger.

He felt it rise from her loins, still tight and thrusting forwards through her body, finally reaching her mouth.

'You useless bastard. You're not going to leave me like this!'

It took longer than he had ever thought possible. Time after time he thought Loretta was about to burst through that final barrier into the full flood of satisfaction only to draw back from the edge of success.

When it came, it came in a rush; relief for both of them. Frank felt himself matching her final thrusts with his own, experiencing a second, more intense satisfaction than before, his satisfaction matching hers in an agony of pleasure.

'So, you're not just a good talker then.'

Slowly, feeling came back into his legs and he had to push himself up on to the seat beside her.

'It's never been like that before. Maybe it's the Yankee beer.'

'It's a good tutor and you're a good student. I'm glad you refused me in the filing room. That was worth waiting for but don't you ever refuse me again, never!'

Monday morning. The guard stopped Paul's car and indicated that Frank should wind down his window. He lowered his head, close to Frank's.

'I don't know what you did to her on Saturday but the Valkyrie smiled at me this morning. Never been known before!'

'I don't remember Saturday. Wasn't I working on the old Humber?'

'No you f-ing weren't but if that's the way you want it told, that's OK with me.'

He went back to his guardhouse whistling and, without looking back, the door closed behind him.

'What was all that about?'

Frank met Paul's look. 'I've no idea. Loretta dropped by on Saturday with some bread and cheese when I was working on the Humber, that's all.'

'I doubt if that was all but, if that's your story, it's OK with me.' Paul gunned the motor and slid the car into its parking space. 'I just hope you know what you're doing.'

'The Royal Navy seldom knew what it was doing but it has survived since King Alfred defeated the Danes.'

'When the hell was that?'

'About 880 AD.'

'On your own head be it.'

Loretta wished them both good morning as they passed her desk.

'Frank, I want you to take over welfare from Gordon. All you have to do is process any inmate's requests that come up from the guards downstairs. Gordon will show you what to do.'

Loretta turned to Gordon and flashed him a smile that told him she had just done him a big favour and that he owed her. Gordon handed Frank a file.

'All you have to do is to make sure that any request for a family visit, medical request or request for a priest to visit is arranged. They are entitled to three family visits a month and they can see a priest or a doctor any time they want. We must ensure that they see either of these within twenty four hours or the Prisoner's Welfare people will be up here going bananas.

'He dropped the file on Frank's desk. There are two regular requesters who get all stroppy if they don't get what they want immediately but don't let them get to you, you'll soon get the hang of it.'

Gordon, and his wife Cherry, were also English immigrants but had been there almost two years and considered themselves natives. Like Frank, Gordon and Cherry had found the Reformatory via the Vet's Office and had settled down happy to spend the rest of their life clerking at the next desk to each other. Frank wondered if they had any plans to start a family but decided that it was none of his business anyway. He liked them both but didn't think that either was the type of person he would want to make a close friend; anyway, they were inseparable, you want one, you have to have both.

Over coffee, Frank mentioned to Gordon that there seemed to be only two native Canadians in the office; Loretta and Paul.

'Yeah, well, we use the Canadians to fill the cages downstairs and the Brits to do the hard jobs up here.'

The siren sounded outside the window, a sound like the all clear at home during the war.

'Oh shit! Someone's doing a bunk. Probably didn't like the breakfast this morning.'

Paul's comment served very well to inform Frank of the meaning of the siren and reassure him that there was nothing for him to worry about.

'You're the welfare officer,' he said grinning, 'you get to interview him when they bring him back Try to find out who or what upset him. Did some guard call him a naughty word perhaps?'

Loretta rang down to the guard's office.

'No sweat. It's just Bob Marley f-ing off again. When he gets tired of running he'll stop at a police station and let them bring him back again.'

Paul gave Frank the background. 'Bob Marley's a regular escaper, he never goes far or does anything while he's out. Just likes to prove that he can escape anytime he likes; guy's an Indian. Likes to demonstrate that the white man can't keep him locked up if he wants to go. There's no harm in him when he's sober but drunk, he can get a bit troublesome.

'What usually happens is that he gets a few drinks inside him, trots along to the local cop shop and starts a fight.

'They arrest him, check out his ID, find he's an escaped inmate and throw him into the tank to sober up. Next morning they bring him back here and we sign for him; no problem, good as gold.

'Everyone's happy with this arrangement. He's shown that he's one clever Indian and can escape from the white man's prison and we give him a few extra days on his sentence to show that he's one very naughty Indian. Honour is served all round.'

'But how does he escape?'

'No problem. He gets himself put on the shale pit detail. The pit is outside the main fence so he just waits for the guard to be looking the other way and buggers off. The guard notices he's missing, rings the Captain's office and reports it. The Captain sounds the siren and rings the local police who know to wait for him to show up; like I say, no problem.'

Frank digested this information, suspecting that it was not entirely true. Somehow, he didn't see an English prison taking so light a view of an escape but then, as they'd already told him this wasn't a real prison; funny lot, these Canadians.

As everyone else ignored the siren and continued with their work, Frank did the same. Under his calm exterior however, he was wondering what he would do when he had to interview the escapee on his return.

To the best of his knowledge, he had never met a Red Indian. He knew that they weren't red and he knew that they weren't Indian but his only knowledge of them had been drawn from the hundreds of American cowboy movies he'd watched as a boy in England. He had almost forgotten England.

Ah well, it was another little adventure. He'd get Marley's file later and swot up on his subject. One thing you could say for this job he thought, it wasn't humdrum.

CHAPTER TWENTY-NINE

At St. Joseph's hospital, Sarah and Judy waited to be interviewed by the Matron who had already done her homework from the girl's application forms filled out in the UK before they left. They already had the jobs, the interview was more a matter of introductions and job specification than anything else; crossing the T's and dotting the I's.

'You Sarah, will be working in the operating rooms and you, Judy will be working in the recovery rooms. Sister Mary will be your section boss, I'll take you down and introduce you.'

Like all other Senior Departmental Heads, Sister Mary was both a nursing sister and a nun. She welcomed the girls warmly enough but there was a certain reservation in her manner.

'Whilst you're here, I'll introduce you to the rest of the surgical team on duty this morning.' She turned to a young man with hair so blonde it could only have come from a bottle.

'Doctor Jacobs, let me introduce you to the two new members of our little team. This is Sarah and this is Judy.'

'Ah, new grist to the mill. Welcome to purgatory girls. Perhaps you can tell me why they always put the OR's in the basement?'

'Oh, Doctor Jacobs, it isn't fair to tease the new girls like that. You should know better.'

Her tone clearly indicated that young Doctor Jacobs was one of her favourites, one of her special naughty boys.

Sarah smiled at him and shook his hand. Judy offered the suggestion that perhaps it was so that the physicians could always look down on them.

'Where did you find this one Sister? She obviously doesn't approve of us stabbers and choppers.'

He smiled at Judy. His teeth, so perfectly matched and white that they appeared to be false, almost gleaming under the strong lights; it was obviously a well-rehearsed routine.

'I shall try to convert you if you come down here.'

'Well, you and Sister Mary can take turns. It should make life interesting.' Judy turned to meet another doctor who had just come into the room.

'Hallo, I'm Doctor Franklin. From the accent, you're obviously just over from the UK and clearly don't understand that you're supposed to swoon at Doctor Jacobs' good looks and repartee, not cut him down to size.'

'I'm sorry,' Judy smiled. 'Perhaps we could run through the script again from the top?'

Sister Mary pushed them gently towards the door. 'I think we should move on so that you can meet the other members of the OR team.'

She approved of nurses being immune to the Dr Jacobs's of this world but she was not sure that Judy was going to fit in without some difficulty; just a little too sure of herself.

Dr Franklin winked at Judy. 'Perhaps we shall meet in the cafeteria.'

'What do you think of Dr Jacobs?' Sarah asked later.

'Sheep in wolf's clothing '

The rest of the team on duty that morning had been pleasant and, by comparison with Jacobs, ordinary; the other nurses seemed genuinely pleased to meet them. They had obviously been listening through the swing doors of the OR to Judy's put down of Dr Jacobs and approved. The general atmosphere was friendly and efficient; Sarah and Judy both felt happy with their appointments to the OR team. It would be just like home.

For the rest of their shift, the two girls were introduced to faces that came and went through the department, were shown where everything was kept and taken up to the cafeteria for coffee.

The free and easy atmosphere of the OR permeated the entire hospital, unlike British hospitals where authority was based upon title and status, St Joseph's ran on more democratic lines. In the cafeteria, Sarah, Judy and one of their new friends Sally, were joined at their table by Dr Franklin.

'Thought I might meet up with you here. Welcome to the centre of the hospital's universe. Within these four walls are hatched more plots and schemes than you could shake a stick at. Take Sally here, she's been trying to attract the attention of that young doctor over there for weeks but he is presently immune to her wiles due to his being madly in love with the daughter of a very rich grocer. He, alas, knows nothing about groceries and she, nothing about surgery so they have only the one thing in common. This being so, Sally has only to wait until the fires of passion die down to attract his attention to her obviously superior intelligence. If, it's her intelligence she wishes to offer him, that is.'

Sally kicked him under the table.

'Do all the doctors use this cafeteria?'

'There is but the one, there's no class distinction here. I worked in an English hospital for a while during the war. Couldn't get on with all their ranks and titles and petty class distinctions, I thought medicine was about curing the sick but I saw precious little of it in England. Too busy insisting on being called by some title or other and leaving the nurses to do all the work. That reminds me, you will be pleased to hear that here, all doctors are called Doctor.

"There are no Mr's pretending that they are too grand to be called Doctor; we find that it is simpler that way. Our way, the patients know which ones are the doctors and which are not.'

'How do you know which is which?'

'Ah well, you see, we're old fashioned here, we use names. You'll soon get used to it, don't worry. Sally here will look after you, won't you Sal?'

'He's full of blarney,' she said, ignoring his use of the diminutive of her name. 'We all wear name badges so that everyone, including the patients, knows who is who and who they are talking to. It's no problem after the first day or so, you'll soon get used to it   We reckon that, as the patient is paying our wages, he is entitled to know who's who.'

Judy nodded. 'Democracy,' her eyebrows rose, 'now there's a novelty; it'll never catch one, you know.'

'It already did, here,' Sally snapped. 'We actually believe in it and work hard at it, we even fought a war to defend it!'

The silence hung over the table like a blanket.

'I'm sorry, that didn't come out the way I meant it. Didn't mean to criticise what you Brits did in the war, it must have been hell on earth. It's just that democracy is taken very seriously here, we believe that every individual is responsible for defending it, it's a personal thing.'

Judy touched her hand. 'It's Ok, it is to us too; it's just that we aren't accustomed to hearing anyone actually say it out loud. It doesn't mean we don't believe just as strongly as you.'

Sarah changed the subject.

'What's with this Dr Jacobs? His teeth may be real but that hair just can't be.'

Dr Franklin excused himself with the comment that he couldn't be seen chatting to the hired help. It would ruin his hopes of ever working in England again.

'Jacobs is our tame Jew,' Sally said. 'He thinks we don't know but everyone does. He's a brilliant surgeon but unsure of himself in other respects so he pretends to be a Catholic like the rest of us; I think Sister Mary is in love with him a little. It doesn't really matter, we have lots of non-Catholics working here.'

'Well, you just got two more.'

'No problem.'

For the rest of the day, they made themselves generally useful around the department. They would not become part of a surgical team until they knew everyone else in the department, knew where everything was kept and had convinced Sister Mary that they knew what they were doing. Sister Mary jealously guarded the safety of her patients and no one joined the team round the table until she was convinced absolutely that they could be relied upon.

In an emergency, Sister Mary preferred to have an all-Catholic team so that their prayer could intercede on behalf of the patient. She remained unconvinced that Protestant prayers would be received with the same degree of urgency.

It was not always possible, in an emergency, to ensure an all-Catholic team so she liked to be absolutely sure than any non-Catholics were the very best possible technical alternative. Her patients remained unconscious of this but would have been very grateful had they known. Sister Mary was a good woman and the world will always have a place for a good woman.

In the nurses hostel that night, Sarah and Judy exchanged thoughts.

'On balance, it should be OK, at least until we find our feet.'

By the weekend, they had become part of the hospital, knew their way around most of it and recognised the people they needed to know even when both were wearing masks in the OR; the badges helped, they had to admit.

Sally acted as guide and mentor, introducing them to all the other girls in the hostel and showing them around generally. Her parents and her home would be snowed in for much of the winter, she had told them so she would have to go up north and see them before the snow came.

'Mum and Dad are proud of me being a nurse but, like most country people, regard Toronto as a totally alien and wicked world. They even worry about me getting sick though, God knows, I'm in the right place for it. At least your arrival will give me something to tell them about in my next letter.

'Mum was born in Canada to Irish immigrant parents and regards the English as only one step higher than the devil himself. Dad is from Estonian stock a generation further back. He's never met an Englishman but I think he suspects Mum's opinion is, at best, slightly biased. I shall be told to use along spoon when supping with you two, English and protestant too!'

The notice on the board in the cafeteria announcing the First Winter Dance at the YMCA on the following Saturday night resulted in much good humoured rummaging in suitcases looking for suitable clothes, something not too obviously English.

Having never been to a dance in Canada, or at a YMCA for that matter, it was difficult to define just what constituted obviously English so the other girls were brought in on a consultancy basis.

Eventually, a suitable ensemble was identified for each of them though in fact both belonged to Sarah. Judy didn't really feel comfortable in a light dress with a hooped skirt.

'I look like something from one of those American movies, State Fair or one of the other country musicals. Not my scene but, when in Rome!'

She would conform until she felt secure enough to make her own decisions.

Mrs Backlaker, the Deputy Housemother at the hostel had laid on a bus to take the girls to the Y at seven thirty. A bit early, this allowed the girls time to get themselves prettied up when they arrived. She did like her girls to look like young ladies, especially at the First Winter Dance; their success at subsequent dances depended upon it.

As always, she would attend herself, later in the evening, just to ensure that the girls left alone and came home on the bus. It wouldn't do for any of them to go astray at the First Dance.

Mrs Backlaker didn't dance herself but she did like the young men who lived at the Y. So well mannered, so young, so strong; so out of town!

If asked, which she would never be, she would have to say that she preferred the country boys to the city boys. The latter had more conversation but, frequently, little else. Country boys, especially those from the farms, were more adept at recognising biological signals. She knew that 'her boys' called her Harley behind her back but she took it as a compliment that she was considered the best ride in town.

The gymnasium had been cleared of all its normal equipment and the floor polished for the dance. Tables and chairs had been moved in from the cafeteria that had been closed for the evening; a soda fountain and coffee bar had been set up in the gym for the dancers.

At the far end, an improvised stage lifted the five-piece band into view above the dancers. A standing mike had been provided for the vocalist, a young man living at the Y until he could get a room closer to the university, ideally one he could share with another student to save on the rent.

Whilst the nurses gathered round the inadequate mirrors in the rest room set aside for Ladies, the first few young men were gathering in the Gym, coffee in hand and listening to the band try out a few tunes before the dance proper started.

Inside the Ladies rest room, a great deal of giggling masked the general disinclination to be the first girl into the Gym. Judy saw Sarah hesitating with the others inside the door, no one wanting to be the one to open it.

'Come on, let's go and sort the men from the boys.' She led the other girls across the lobby and into the Gym. 'The Hammersmith Palais it ain't but let's not knock it 'til we've tried it, eh?' She smiled at a ginger haired youth who, unaccustomed to such forward behaviour, blushed to a bright pink that didn't go with his hair colouring. 'God, they're young! I know it's the Young Men's Christian Association but, do they have to be this young?'

'Shut up and sit down,' Sarah told her. 'You're scaring off the prospects.'

Judy glanced round the room. 'Prospects? By the look of most of them, they need mothering but, as I'm not interested anyway, I suppose they'll do.'

CHAPTER THIRTY

Robert, Edward Marley, the file said, Born Nippissing, Ontario, September 9, 1922. Etobicoke Indian.

First Offence, Toronto, March 11, 1942. Drunk and Disorderly plus assault with a deadly weapon, tomahawk purchased from local souvenir shop. Sentence: 3 months, Toronto Reformatory."

Clearly, the Bench had not taken this Deadly Weapon too seriously.

There followed a long list of subsequent arrests, imprisonments and rearrests at a rate of roughly two per year since. The file also included a report prepared by the prison authorities in 1942 stating that Robert, Edward Marley was indeed a Chief of the Etobicoke; a sub-tribe of the Algonquin group, Indian name, Little Horse. Parents respectable non-reservation Indians, father working for Toronto Cleansing Department; mother housewife and mother to two younger children, both girls.

There was also a report dated January 1943 to the effect that Robert, Edward Marley had volunteered for army service but had been rejected on the grounds of his being of Unsuitable Character. Frank wondered what was a suitable character for going half way across the world to kill people.

The Canadian army's D-Day landings, led by an Indian Chief in full regalia might have had an unnerving effect upon the German defenders. The Brits had been led by Scottish pipers; perhaps if the Canadians had been led ashore by a drunken Indian Chief waving a tomahawk, their casualties might have been considerably fewer than had actually been the case. Frank remembered that the Canadians had not been lucky in their choice of landing ground.

Robert Edward Marley's speciality appeared to be Drunk and Assault upon the Person. He had obviously decided against deadly weapons since his first incarceration. The person involved was invariably a young, white woman who's bottom had been pinched by what she had taken to be a life-sized wooden Indian standing outside a cigar store.

These offences appeared to take place in October and January, thus ensuring that the said Robert, Edward Marley had a warm and relatively comfortable home for the winter months. In the summer, Marley went north and caused no trouble to anyone.

Frank replaced the file and went back to processing the paperwork piled up on his desk. Someone had been stockpiling this for weeks but, at least, this way he would learn a lot very quickly.

The internal mail produced a note for Frank from the Guardroom that his car was ready, the battery had been OK after a long trickle charge; a PS enquired whether Frank knew that he needed to get himself a Canadian driving licence within six months. Until then, his English licence would serve. Frank decided that he wouldn't mention that he didn't have an English licence, it would only complicate matters.

Monday mornings never bothered Frank. After so many years at sea watch keeping, one day looked much the same as any other. Some turned out to be better than others but, on the whole, Frank enjoyed life.

After Dr. Barnardo's and boy's service in the navy, almost anything was a good life if it didn't involve getting up in the middle of the night, being shouted at or being shot at. Sure, once he had got promoted, he had been in a position to do the shouting but somehow, he'd never got the kick out of it that others seemed to enjoy.

There was a note on his desk. Robert, Edward Marley had been recaptured; actually he had reported to the police station on Bloor, cold and hungry and desirous of a bed and a hot meal. He would be up before the bench that morning and would, no doubt, be returned to the reformatory's questionable safe keeping that afternoon. Frank noticed that the word safekeeping had been underlined. He showed the note to Loretta.

'I suppose I'd better interview him as soon as he arrives?'

'Just don't believe a word he tells you. He loves to tell tall tales, particularly to ignorant immigrants like you who know nothing about anything.'

'So, now's my chance to learn, eh?'

'Just take anything he tells you with a large pinch of salt and check back with me before you do or agree to do anything, OK?'

By lunchtime, Frank had finished most of the work on his desk and retrieved Marley's file to read whilst eating his sandwiches.

Marley had never married. Frank wondered why. He never offended in the summer months. Frank wondered where he went and whether he always went to the same place and, if so, why.

He was clearly quite harmless, if you discounted the twice-yearly bottom pinching, obviously designed to get him a bed for the winter months.

'I'm quite looking forward to this,' he told Paul over coffee. 'This could be really interesting.'

'Yeah but, watch him. Remember, Indian speak with forked tongue; especially when talking to white man.'

'I seem to remember from the old cowboy movies that it was the white man who spoke with forked tongue.'

'Yeah, him too but, not in here. Do you want me to sit in with you?'

'No thanks. I'll press the panic button if it all gets hairy.'

Paul grinned. 'The last time anyone pressed that was when Loretta had someone trapped in there.'

'Now that's downright cowardly. Did anyone rush to his assistance?'

'No, they left me in there with her for twenty minutes before ringing to see if I needed any help!'

'What happened?'

'Nothing serious but I reckon I blew my promotion prospects for a year or more. Trouble is, with her reputation, no one would ever believe me. If Brenda ever finds out she'll kill her and, then me'

Loretta had seen the wagon come in through the gate. 'Do you want to go down and meet him at reception? He's just arrived.'

'No, I don't think so. I'll ring reception and have him taken to the interview room when he's finished checking in. It won't do him any harm to wait a while, he ain't going anywhere.'

Twenty five minutes later, Frank gathered up an armful of files and made for the door.

'What's all that?'

'This, Gordon, is bullshit.'

Ten years in His Majesty's Steamer service, otherwise known as the Royal Navy, had not been entirely wasted on Frank. The armful of papers, when carefully and slowly arranged on the desk in the interview room in front of the waiting Robert Edward Marley, would establish who was in charge of the interview, standard procedure for establishing authority. Frank explained this to Gordon

Loretta had listened to his explanation. 'You're one sneaky Limey.'

'Well, if you don't hold rank, you have to show gravitas!' To emphasise the point, he put on his jacket before going downstairs.

Marley had been waiting for about a quarter of an hour when Frank had himself shown into the interview room by a guard.

'Good afternoon, Mr Marley,' Frank began. 'My name is Bye.

We haven't met but I am in charge of inmate's welfare so, before we get down to business, have you any problem with anything?' Frank paused only long enough to draw a breath. 'I arranged this afternoon's little meeting so that we could get to know one another. I understand that you will be returning to your old accommodation block, do you have a problem with that?'

Without giving Marley an opportunity to answer the question, Frank went on. 'I've read your files and I have to admit that they don't tell me a great deal about you.' Frank shuffled a few of the papers, extracting one at random.

'You claim to be an Etobicoke Indian Chief. Do you want to elaborate on that?' He paused to see if Marley would rise to the bait.

'I am a Chief of the Etobicoke tribe, who says I ain't?'

Frank held up his hand to stem the flow.

'No one has said that you aren't but that's all there is on the file. There must be more to it than that. Is the fact relevant to your persistent offending? Is your record some sort of protest about your tribe having been dispossessed? As an Englishman, and a newcomer to your country you understand, I know very little about the history of this area. Perhaps you would like to talk about it if it's relevant.'

Frank again paused long enough to give Marley an opportunity to speak but not long enough to realise that he was ad-libbing.

'No, it ain't relevant. Well, not to the offence anyway.'

'Mr Marley, I spent ten years as a sailor and am less than bothered about your twice-yearly pinching of some girl's arse. I am interested however in why you say that the offence is irrelevant but that the offending is. Do you want to explain that?'

'What difference would it make?'

'To your sentence, none whatever but I'm sure you will appreciate that the easier you make my life the easier I can make yours.'

'What do you want to know?'

The contact had been established. From here on, it would be easy.

'Why don't we start at the beginning. You were, I see, born in Nippissing on the ninth of September nineteen twenty two, which makes you about the same age as me. Do you want to take it from there?'

Nearly an hour later, Frank had heard the full life story of Chief Little Horse, born on the reservation but moved to the city by the time he was five. He had, at first, liked the city but school came as a rude awakening.

The other boys called him a dirty Indian, the girls wouldn't talk to him at all and the teachers established their authority over the class by beating him as a warning to the others. The only lessons he had enjoyed were history. History, as written by the white man, tended to be one sided but did discover that the public library had a lot of much more interesting books about the early years.

He'd spent his summer holidays on the reservation with his grand parents who told him a lot of tales of which some might actually have been true. Clearly, history according to the Indians was just as one sided as that according to the whites.

He left school as soon as he was able and got a job working for the Cleansing Department like his dad but soon found that, even here, there were jobs which were the preserve of the white man and others, the meanest and dirtiest, reserved for the Indians.

Of course, the whites didn't call themselves that, they called themselves Canadians, the inference being that, if they were Canadians, then he wasn't. It was a constant irritation, leading to many fights and, eventually, the sack.

He had no clear recollection of what had caused the assault with a deadly weapon in 1942 but there had been so many attendances in court that he, now, didn't make any attempt to remember what they were for.

His father had disowned him and refused him shelter when he came out of prison and, it being May, he had gone north to see his grandparents and to try and find his Indian self.

He had done alright, survived, but it was clear that he wasn't either a real Indian or a Canadian. Since then, he had spent the summer months doing odd jobs around the woods and lakes for the tourist lodges and motels; they liked to show off their tame Indian. In the fall, he came south to Toronto, got himself arrested and settled down to spend the winter in jail. At least, in here, he got fed for free.

He knew, the magistrates knew that his assaults were more on the woman's dignity than on their persons and had, over the years, got used to sending him down for three months or until the spring weather would allow him to go north again, away from their jurisdiction.

It was an arrangement satisfactory to all concerned unless, of course, you included the women who's bottoms had been pinched; and nobody had ever asked them what they thought.

'Now, is there anybody you want told that you are back with us? Parents? Tribal Elders?'

'No. Nobody gives a shit where I am.'

'Is there anything you want to ask me before you go back to your block?'

'Yeah, can I still work down the pit?'

'Work details aren't my responsibility but, as that's where you absconded from, I doubt if they will send you back there for a while.'

'Hell, I only escape every so often to liven things up a little. Gets me status in the block; I don't need to go again for a while, everyone knows that'

'Then why do you want to work down the pit?

'It's full of fossils and things from long before you white men came to my country and I like to collect them. If you can get me put back down there, I'll show you what I've found; that's, if you're interested.'

'Have you noticed the old beach and the fire stones?'

'Hey! You into history?'

'Enough to know that those remains are from long before your ancestors came this far north. I'll have a word with the officer in charge of the work details but I can't hold out much promise of anything immediately, OK?'

'You're alright for a paleface.'

'You're alright for a pesky red Indian.'

'Peace?'

'Peace.'

Frank rang for an escort to take Marley back to his block.

Paul was waiting for him when he got back to the office, a cup of coffee in his outstretched hand.

'Where the hell have you been? You've been gone nearly an hour.'

'Fascinating. Have you ever talked to him? I mean, properly.'

'Christ no, why would I want to do that?'

'Cos, I think he is a lot brighter than he would like us to believe and quite an interesting character.'

'Don't bother with the Indian. You'll have enough trouble getting accepted in Canada without upsetting people by being too friendly with the Indians.'

'Surely nobody's worried about Indians nowadays? They're hardly going to rise up and throw you all out of their country, are they?'

'It's still a touchy subject, particularly with the first generation Canadians. They're not confident enough about their own position to risk being friendly with some dirty Indian. You, remember, are a dirty DP and they are dirty Indians. It's all part of the process of establishing your position in the pecking order. The old white families are at the top and everyone else falls into place below them based on how many generations have been born here. Indians confuse the issue, so they don't count for nothing!'

'Ah I see, a hierarchical structure in a classless society.'

'I don't mind you taking the piss here in the office, we've already decided that you're probably OK but I wouldn't recommend that you do it outside; this ain't the sophisticated society you're used to in London, England. Here, we're still a bit too provincial to be sure that you're kidding.'

The following day, Frank had a word with the Work Clerk.

'No chance! He sure took you for a soft-hearted immigrant. The Indian looks after the pigs until I decide he's going some place different. OK?'

'OK, no problem. I told him, I'd ask, that's all.'

'I heard you spent nearly all afternoon with him yesterday. It would be a mistake to let the others think he has a friend in the office, he being just an Indian. Could cause a lot of trouble for the guards and that would mean a lot of trouble for you, you get my drift?'

'It couldn't be clearer. I'll keep my distance. Thanks for the tip.'

'From what I hear, you're grinding Mac's woman as well as driving his old car. If I was you, I'd slow down a bit 'til you find out which way the wind blows around here. We don't take kindly to some limey remittance man coming over here and doing his own thing without so much as a by-your-leave.'

'Wish I was a remittance man. To be one of them you have to have rich parents and I don't, I don't have any parents at all! Don't worry, I'm just some poor limey immigrant trying to find his way around a new country and I'm grateful for your advice.'

'Hey! I'm an orphan too. You just feel free to ask my advice any time, OK?'

'Yeah, we orphans must stick together, eh?'

Back at the office, Frank told Paul what had happened.

'I did warn you. Now, leave it alone for a week or two then buy the Work Clerk a cup of coffee some lunch time, just to show there's no hard feelings.'

CHAPTER THIRTY-ONE

Agnes knocked on Frank's door at the top of the short staircase.

'Bob and I thought you might like to take Sunday lunch with us. It'll save you cooking and the kids were away last time you ate with us. It'll give you a chance to get to know them – and them you. You're quite a celebrity you know, you're the first real live Englishman they've met or, haven't yet met but will'

'Their Irish grandmother has been filling them with terrible stories about the English, how they started the potato famine in Ireland to kill all the Irish and things like that; I hope it's not true. Now they don't know whether to believe her and be afraid of you or meet you and risk finding out that grandma is telling them tall tales.'

'Should I wear a hat to hide the horns?'

'Only if you tuck the forked tail inside your pants too. Say about one o- clock?'

'I'll look forward to it, it should be an interesting event.'

He finished shaving and drank his coffee. Coffee, good coffee, here, now, was smooth tasting and left a happy feeling in the stomach and, it was cheap, unlike the stuff available at home. He put the meat back in the icebox. It hadn't had time to lose its chill and it would be OK for later in the week; perhaps, he would invite Loretta over for dinner one evening. A sort of return match, he would run the idea past Agnes at lunch, she could hardly object in front of the kids.

The lunch smelled and, eventually, looked much the same as Sunday lunch in England; roast meat with vegetables, with soup before and fruit and cream to follow; Agnes had obviously made an effort to make him feel at home. Had the cream been custard, with a thick creamy skin, he could have thought himself in heaven.

As soon as he arrived, Agnes offered him a Coke. 'Lunch will be ready in twenty minutes.'

'I'm sorry, I'm too early.'

'No. You can get to know the kids while I sort out the food. Bob, you can come and carve the meat, it will be easier than doing it at the table with an extra place set.'

'He's Robert, known as Robert to avoid confusion with Dad and I'm Sandra known as Sandy,' Sandy explained very grownuply. 'I'm the oldest, he's only ten!'

'But I'm a boy!'

Robert grabbed Frank's hand and shook it firmly.

'How do you do Robert, I'm sure we are going to be great friends. We men have got to stick together to keep these women in their proper place haven't we.'

Sandy refused to shake hands with him.

'We don't like the English. Grandma says they're all wicked and hate the Irish.'

'My Dad's name was Bye and he was English sure enough but my Mum's name was O'Ryan so I reckon I'm half Irish myself.'

'Why did she marry an Englishman?'

'Perhaps she loved him. I don't know, they both died when I was younger than you are now. After that, I lived in a home for kids with no parents until I went to sea.'

'How old were you when you went to sea?' Robert asked, 'I want to be a sailor.'

'Well, I was just fifteen years old but, if I were you, I'd wait a little longer than that   If you get a good education first, you could be the Captain instead of just a sailor.'

'I hate it here. She's bossy and always telling me what to do.'

'Well, that's life, I'm afraid but when you grow up, you will be a man and men always outrank women.'

'Don't let Agnes hear you telling them that, she'll kill you!'

Bob had come into the room with some steaming pots for the table. 'She's a great believer in all this equality of sexes nonsense. Just because they were allowed to do men's work during the war, they think they're equal.'

'I'll equal you if I come in there, Bob Stannard! And, I'll probably do it with a rolling pin.'

'There you are,' Bob said. 'Come on you kids, up to the table before your mother gets vicious.'

The food demanded serious attention for some time before Frank asked if, perhaps the kids might like to see the inside of the reformatory.

'I don't want to see the inside of a grotty prison,' Sandy said. 'It's full of nasty people who have been wicked.'

Robert was instantly enthusiastic. 'Who's in there?'

'Nobody very wicked, I'm afraid. They're very ordinary people who have been a little naughty; there's an Indian Chief though, he's interesting. They work in a boot and shoe factory or on the farm or, if they have been naughty, down in the shale pit. It's quite interesting really.'

Sandy turned up her nose. 'I hope they didn't make my shoes!'

'They make them for the army and the police so they actually make the boots that chase them, that's a nice twist, you've got to agree.'

'When?' Robert was keen.

'I'll ask the Governor for permission when I see him next week. Perhaps he'll let me take you in next weekend. Things are pretty quiet at weekends.'

'Boys are horrid! Fancy wanting to see a prison, Mum will never let you go in there.'

'Yes I will, why not? I just hope they keep you in there and never, never let you out. What do you think, Bob?'

'Sweetheart, if the boy wants to go, why not? It will certainly give him something to boast about at school. I don't suppose any of the other boys have ever been inside a prison. What will you show him, Frank?'

'I've no idea. I suppose I could show him the farm, the workshops and all that. There would be no one working at the weekend so he wouldn't actually meet any of the inmates, that wouldn't be possible.'

'Boys are awful. Fancy anyone wanting to see an old farm and a factory!' Sandy was disdainful as only young girls can be and Robert took no notice of her other than to stick his tongue out at her.

'I suppose I could take him down into the shale pit too. There's an old beach level showing where the lake came up to there long ago.'

'Hey! That's fantastic. I'll be the only one in my class that's ever seen inside a prison, maybe in the whole school!'

'Boys are yukky!'

'So are girls.'

'Shut up the pair of you. Remember, Frank isn't used to you. He might think you behave like this all the time.'

'You mean they don't?'

'He's got you there,' Bob laughed. 'Admit it Agnes, we've bred a couple of horrors.'

'It's Ok,' Frank said. 'In the home, we were required to be quiet and obedient at all times but it didn't always work out quite like that. Sometimes it turned out more like a riot than a discussion but, on the whole, we usually did as we were told just as, I imagine, these two do.'

'What was it like at sea, was it scary?'

'Sometimes but most of the time it was pretty ordinary. I've got some photos somewhere. If you like, I'll try and find them and show you sometime.'

'This afternoon?'

'No dear. Now don't make a nuisance of yourself.'

Agnes turned to Bob. 'If we've finished, I suggest that Sandy gives me a hand with the dishes while you two men entertain our guest.'

'Why do you live in our basement?'

Bob frowned at Robert.

'You shouldn't ask questions like that!'

'Why not?'

'Yes, why not? It's OK, I don't mind, it's a perfectly reasonable question if you're ten years old. I live in your basement because I need somewhere to live that's close to where I work and, until I can afford to buy my own house as your Mum and Dad have done Until then, the apartment your Dad built in the basement will do me very nicely.'

'You've got our old icebox down there, I saw it. We've got a new refrigerator.'

'The icebox will do well enough. It may not be as modern as your refrigerator but it keeps my food fresh and, as I don't have a lot of it, it will do me very nicely thank you.'

'I put it down there just temporarily, we'll get a fridge at the end of the month.' Bob sounded embarrassed.

'Don't worry about it, the icebox is fine. Actually, I'm glad you did put it down there. I've never seen one before so, as my old housemaster used to say, you learn a little something every day.'

'What did you have in England?'

'Nothing, Robert. I didn't have my own home in England. I lived in an hotel after I came out of the navy until I came over here.'

'What's a hotel?'

'That's enough questions,' Bob looked almost embarrassed, 'Why don't you go out and feed your rabbits in the yard?'

'Do you want to come and see my rabbits?'

'Out!'

Agnes handed Frank a cup of coffee. 'I'm sorry he's such a chatterbox, we just hope he'll grow out of it.'

'Don't give it a thought. When you're ten, the world is full of questions. I wish I'd had someone to ask when I was his age, I might have got on a whole lot better than I did. As it was, I had to wait until I joined the navy before anyone took the slightest notice of me.'

'You seem to have survived without too much damage,' Agnes said, 'I don't think I could have emigrated to a new country where I didn't know anyone; certainly not without a job to go to and somewhere to live.'

'That's not clever, it's not even brave, it's foolhardy but, if you're on your own, it's no big deal,' Frank had already picked up some of the local jargon, 'the most you can lose is time and I've got lots of that. I can always go back if it all turns nasty.'

'Do you think you'll go back?'

'No, I like the place, I like the people and the food's good. What more could any reasonable man ask?'

They enjoyed their coffee without interruption from Robert who had taken his rabbits from their cages and was playing with them on the stubby grass.

'He'll lose them if he's not careful,' Sandy said in her bossy voice. 'I've told him they'll run away if he lets them out.'

'I think Robert's right, you are a bossy boots' Frank told her. 'You're right of course, but if they run away, the rabbits will be happy enough and Robert will have learned a lesson; that's life'

He turned to Agnes. 'I must thank you for a most excellent lunch. I'll let you know what the Governor says but, as it seems to be a remarkably free and easy place, he'll probably agree.'

They walked him to his door. 'It was nice to have you for lunch, you certainly made an impression on Robert and, I think, Sandy likes you too or she wouldn't have argued. If she doesn't like someone, she usually just stays quiet. Let us know if there's anything you need or have a problem with; take advantage of our local knowledge.'

'You're very kind. I imagine you have no objection to my inviting someone over for dinner some evening? They would have to ring your doorbell, of course.'

'No, of course not. That's your apartment, you must do as you please down there. Just don't set fire to the place, it would be a little embarrassing if the Chief of the local Fire Department's house went up in smoke.'

Frank shut the door behind him and went down the few stairs to his own den. He would suggest dinner to Loretta for about Wednesday, it would give him time to get a few things in.

Outside the small, high window of the lounge Robert was crying. One of the rabbits had run off and Sandy was giving him a hard time.

'I told you! Now let that be a lesson to you.'

Agnes opened the kitchen window. 'Quiet you two, it's Sunday afternoon.'

On the whole, the dance at the Y had been a success but the girls both realised that Toronto's YMCA was a far cry from even the smallest of the London dancehalls. Here, girls were expected to sit quietly and wait for one of the boys to ask them if they would like to dance. There was no custom of two uninvited girls dancing together. Judy had been accused of being rude to one spotty faced youth by declining the honour and was not any too pleased.

Sarah shook her head.

'You always were a bit positive, even at home. Perhaps they aren't used to girls who speak their minds. Perhaps you should have had one dance with him, he wasn't that bad.' Sally, Francine and Naomi agreed. 'It's perfectly OK to decline a second invitation but it's not done to refuse the first.'

'How about that guy in the woolly jumper?' Sally pointed. 'Looks like something out of an old English movie about the Scottish highlands or somewhere like that.'

'Now that's really unkind,' Sarah laughed. 'He looks a bit like my brother actually.'

'Did any of you notice Harley's choice?' Naomi described a square with her hands; 'now there was a country boy, but big with it!'

'Who's Harley?'

The other girls all looked at Judy then burst out laughing.

'Mrs Backlaker, the Deputy Housemother. She's known throughout the length and breadth of Toronto as the most comfortable ride in town and, she's had almost every well-equipped country boy who's ever passed through the Y. Only one at a time, you understand but she's been here a long time, years, so she must have had hundreds.'

Naomi held her forearm vertically, with the fist clenched on top. 'She likes 'em big and thick, she doesn't reckon city boys.'

'Well, they're all talk, aren't they,' Sally said. 'I prefer a country boy with the brains to come to the city to a city boy who's all chat and no brains.'

'Yeah, but you're a yokel yourself so, you would, wouldn't you?'

'A little less of the yokel, if you please Naomi. We yokels are the people you city slickers make a living out of. If it wasn't for us yokels, you'd have to cheat and steal from each other.'

'We do, my dear, we do! Never mind, it was only the first dance of the winter, they'll have plenty more. You'll meet someone nice before Christmas, someone to party with and, when you do, you'll have to knit him a Peter Heater for a Christmas present.'

Judy guessed what a Peter Heater was from the ribald laughter that followed that advice.

'The fun of it,' Francine explained, 'is taking the measurements and arranging for one or two fittings. One fitting is no fun and, more than two would suggest that you weren't a very good knitter.'

'Or measurer,' Sally said.

'Or perhaps have a very poor memory,' suggested Judy.

'I always lose my notes,' Francine said, 'and have to do it again.'

'Are they colour coded,' Sarah asked. 'Say, red for hot, blue for cold, etc?'

Judy laughed. 'If they were, they would all be large and red to flatter the boys and to preserve the reputation of the knitters.'

Sally smiled. 'If I meet a nice boy, I'll knit him a small blue one so that none of you lot try to steal him away from me. Then, I'll secretly make him one out of one of my Dad's mink.'

'Whatever you do,' Naomi warned her,' remember to take out its teeth before you give it to him. You know men can't stand the sight of blood.'

The group broke up. Judy joined Sarah in the landing kitchen, an overgrown cupboard fitted with a single hot plate stove and a saucepan for boiling milk, or if the girls felt ambitious, scrambling eggs.

'Do you want to bring your coffee back to my room? We could chat.'

Sarah sat on Judy's bed, cross-legged, clasping her coffee mug in both hands.

Sarah wasn't happy. 'I don't think I'm going to like it much here, It's so different, so provincial.'

Judy took Sarah's coffee mug from her, placing it on the bedside table. 'It'll be alright, trust me. I'll make it good for you.' She squeezed Sarah's hand.

CHAPTER THIRTY-TWO

'What would a ten year old want, looking round a prison?' The Governor regarded Frank as if he was some sort of lunatic for even suggesting such a thing.

'We can't have him wandering round the cellblocks, poking his nose between the bars, the Prisoners' Welfare people would be down here like a dose of salts!'

'There aren't any bars and I thought I might show him round the farm and the workshops when nobody is actually working. Down the pit too, if I can, he might be interested in seeing the beach level they've uncovered as a sort of history lesson.'

'Have a word with Captain Singleton. If the Captain of the Guard says you can, I guess its OK with me. Mind you, I think it's the silliest idea I've ever heard and, if the kid has nightmares, don't tell me!'

'Thanks.'

Captain Singleton looked at Frank for a full minute without speaking.

'You are joking. Tell me you're joking, please!'

'The Governor says its OK with him.'

'Leave it with me. I'll have a word with the Governor and come back to you on this.'

By Thursday evening, when Frank and Loretta were sitting over dinner and more than half a bottle of wine had been drunk, the idea seemed even sillier than it had on Monday morning

'You're quite mad, you know that? You have no idea what you've started. Singleton is going mad, the Governor has decided that, just maybe, it's a good public relations exercise and referred it to the PR Department at Parliament Buildings for approval, and this lamb is overdone for my taste!'

'Sorry about that. At sea, we reckon that all meat should be overcooked to ensure that it's quite dead, all the way through. The ship's cold room sometimes wasn't as cold as it might have been and there was always a slight risk of the butcher walking in and meeting the meat walking out.'

'Ugh! Why didn't they fix it?'

'Oh they always had some lame excuse or other like, don't you know there's a war on or, can't get the parts you know, it's the war. Always some lame excuse or other.'

'I think you're kidding me.'

'I wish I was. Well, just a little perhaps but the middle of the Atlantic ocean is a damned silly place to be in a war and haute cuisine tended to get pushed to the bottom of the priorities list.'

'Were you ever shipwrecked?'

'I don't think they call it shipwrecked nowadays but, no. I was always very lucky.'

'Pour me another glass of that plonk and you might just get lucky again. I'll say this for you Europeans, if you were a Canadian, that bottle would be beer or, if lucky, whiskey; your average Cannuck isn't in to wine, he can't make it in his basement.'

'Course he can, all you need is a lot of fruit, almost any kind of fruit will do but I had to get Bob to buy this for me, I don't have a liquor licence yet. What sort of a God forsaken country is this where you have to get a licence from the government to buy a bottle of wine from a Government owned liquor store? What are they afraid of, for God's sake?'

'We tend to be more into moonshine and home made beer than grape juice. We like to blow our heads off when we drink. The taste is not a major consideration.'

'Well, we Europeans prefer to make our guests feel relaxed and happy rather than out of their skulls so, we'll finish this bottle then see what develops. How are you at washing dishes?'

'I always get water everywhere, make a hell of a mess. I'll have to take all my clothes off or I'll have nothing dry to go home in.'

He refilled her glass.

'Are you trying to get me drunk?'

'I didn't think it was necessary.'

'It ain't and it can be downright dangerous, I might lose some of my more ladylike inhibitions.'

'Not down here, you don't. These walls are only plasterboard and I should hate to get thrown out for making too much noise; not just keeping the kids awake but completing their education at the same time. Try this, it's a south American coffee liqueur.'

'OK smart arse, how do you drink it? Like a shot of booze or like a glass of wine?'

'Take a little into your mouth and hold it there, caressing it with your tongue, letting the heat creep through the sweetness then, slowly allow it to trickle down your throat and let it build up a fire in your stomach. You'll get a wonderful, warm glow in your heart.'

'You're a smooth talking bastard for a sailor. Why Sir, I do believe you're trying to seduce me! It's not that I object, you understand, it's just that I'm not used to it. With most of the men I've known, the question is do I take my knickers off before or after dinner?'

'Never before, my dear. Terribly uncivilised unless of course you intend eating in bed. I suppose you could put them back on while you eat and take them off again afterwards but it does seem to be a lot of fuss over very little.'

'I don't know many men who can do encores.'

'Well, we've established that I'm no good at auditions. Cold blooded sex is like butchering meat, too clinical to enjoy. Pleasure should be courted, built up to slowly then enjoyed with no thought for the morrow other than perhaps, that it might then be repeated.'

'Shut up and take your clothes off.'

'Are we going to do the dishes?'

'The only dish that's going to get done around here is me. Where the hell is the bathroom?'

'You're an uncouth colonial but even that has its attractions.'

'Bring the strawberries with you. I shall feed you one at a time for a long time and, where you'll be eating them from, you won't need any cream.'

Loretta lay on the bed, the blankets in a pile on the floor where she had thrown them. Frank lay beside her, his hand cradling a breast. The stains from the strawberry juice gave his face a wild look. Loretta forced a strawberry from between her lips between his, her tongue pushing it back, back into his throat, making him gag. Her hand felt the small spasm caused by his gagging; she brought her hand up to his lips and wiped them.

'I've relented, you may have cream after all.'

'Thank you.'

'You're welcome.'

'I'm glad I came to Canada.'

'I'm glad you came to Canada.'

'I want a cup of coffee.'

'So do I.'

She rolled over on to her side, releasing him. 'It's your house, you make the coffee.'

She held the cup between her upturned hands, breathing in the heavily scented steam, her eyes closed.

'Is this bliss, do you think, post-prandial or post-nuptial?'

'It must be post-prandial, we ain't married. Now shut up and drink your coffee!'

The bedclothes remained on the floor and the dishes in the sink long after Loretta had said goodnight to Agnes who just happened to be passing the basement door when she left.

'A Canadian girl, someone you work with?'

'Yes Agnes, she's someone I work with. Goodnight Agnes.'

'I'm glad you've found a friend already. Somebody who can show you how things are done around here.'

'I'm glad too. Goodnight Agnes.'

'It's OK. You can bring him this weekend. Saturday a.m.' Singleton regarded Frank as a source of trouble. 'I don't pretend that I approve of this but the Boss has checked it out with the Public Relations people and they, God damn them, think it's a great idea! They think we should invite parties of school kids!'

'Get him here at about ten o clock. I'll arrange for an escort and, for God's sake, keep him out of trouble. Don't let him hurt himself down the pit or anything, OK?'

Frank decided that a simple thank you would be best.

'Thanks, I'll take good care of him. His mother will skin me else!'

Loretta advised him to keep out of Singleton's way for a few days. 'We have a good thing going here and we don't need some damned limey immigrant fouling it all up for us. Just keep out of his way so he can't have a go at you about it. I hope you're not getting too close to his mother.'

'Singleton's?

'He didn't have one.'

CHAPTER THIRTY-THREE

On Thursday evening, three weeks later, Bob was waiting for Frank to get home.

'Glad I caught you. I think you might have started something you can't or won't want to finish with this prison visit you arranged for Robert.'

'Why so?'

'It seems that Robert told his friends at school about it and the teacher told him to write an essay about it so that he could read it out to the class. Mrs Downey, that's his teacher, was so impressed with it that she showed it to the Head Master. Now, I've had a note from him asking if I can arrange for a whole posse of kids to be shown round your history pit. Seems he thinks it would be a good way to illustrate the lessons about extending and receding ice caps, glacial moraines and all that stuff. I admit I don't even know what he's talking about but I understand that you do.'

'Not a lot. I picked up a little about it reading books at sea. At sea, you'll read anything that has words or, even better, pictures in it. There used to be posters pasted up in village halls and places like that; a picture of a sailor with the caption, 'What's the use of a pair of navy blue eyes if he has nothing to read?' I don't think anyone checked what books were donated, they just sent them to the first ship they heard the name of.

'A lot of places adopted a particular ship and sent all sorts of goodies. Books, socks, scarves, even letters addressed to Dear Jack. I'm sure they meant well but a lot of it was useless. Still, that's life. As that guy Parkinson says, ninety percent of everything is rubbish.'

'But can you arrange it?'

'God knows. I'll mention it to the Boss but I suspect he will refer the Head Master to downtown. It's a safe bet that

I can't arrange it. I'll see him today and let you know. If I don't come home tonight, he's probably had me shot.'

The Governor didn't shoot him but it is quite possible that the idea did occur to him.

'Oh shit! I was afraid something like this might happen, once we open the gates to one lot, who knows where it will all end?' Frank wisely remained silent. 'There's no way I'm going to tell the Head Master to write to Head Office at Parliament Buildings. No. Don't even tell them where Head Office is, let them find out for themselves. Perhaps if we make it difficult enough, they won't bother. Meanwhile, if I were you, I wouldn't mention this to anyone here, anyone!

'If we're going to get involved in taking day trippers down that damned pit, I want the idea to come from Head Office. Do I make myself clear?'

'I savvy Chief. Not a word.'

'I should have known better than to hire a bloody sailor. I'll tell Mac so too!'

Just to prove that there is a God, it snowed that weekend. All work in the pit was stopped. About three weeks later, Frank was sent for.

The Governor sat at his desk, Captain Singleton, Mac and the Chaplain occupied the only other chairs.

'Come in Frank. See if you can find a seat somewhere. It seems that as a result of your little expedition down the pit with your young friend, Head Office has decided that it might be a good idea if we organised conducted tours down there for groups of school children and their teachers. If there's anything I like less than school kids, it's teachers!'

'I don't know what the hell you told that kid but he sure as hell impressed his teacher and now the Head Teacher has written to Head Office asking if he can take all the other kids down there. Something to do with the last ice age or something; what in hell did you tell that kid?'

'I only showed him the beach level we had uncovered and told him that the lake must have come all the way up here many years ago if it was a beach. I probably told him something about the sand and gravel bed being laid down by the glacier in the ice age. You know, kids are always interested in that sort of thing.'

'Well, so are the big kids in the Public Relations Department downtown and they have decided that we have a national heritage here which should be saved and shown to the public. They are of the opinion that this will improve the Department of Correction's image with the general public.'

'I said it would all come to a no good end,' Singleton offered. 'I said so at the time, didn't I say so?' He turned to the Governor for confirmation.

'Yes. You did and I agreed with you at the time too but that was then and now is now. The reason you are invited to this little party Frank is that the PR boys have decided that there should be someone here to take charge of these marauding hoards of school kids and teachers and it has been decided unanimously that you're the man for the job!'

Frank nodded but kept silent. He was on thin ice and he thought it best to let the Boss do the talking.

'Liaise with Captain Singleton here and with the PR people downtown and get something organised for the spring. At least we have time to work out a way to do it without the teachers getting mixed up with the inmates and being marched off to the accommodation blocks though, God knows, that might just be a good idea, it might discourage others.'

Frank left the meting. There had been a group of new entries delivered and he had a great pile of registration forms, welfare request forms, special notice forms and other bumf in his in tray.

'When you've finished that lot,' Loretta told him, 'I want a breakdown of all inmates' hobbies and interests, legal ones that is, their educational standard and qualifications, OK?'

'Right.'

'And, when you've done that, I want a breakdown of all their religious beliefs. Not just Christian, Jewish, etc. I want every damn free church and sect listed.'

'Yeah OK What's this all for?'

'Some idiot in the Public Relations Department downtown has just discovered that we exist. He wants to know all about the reformatory, the inmates, the staff and what we are doing to reform them!'

'Who the staff?'

'Don't smart arse me. Just get it done. I want a draft report on my desk by the weekend.'

'Yes Sir, Madam, Sir, it shall be as you order.'

Loretta turned back to her work. 'I knew you were going to be trouble.'

Outside the window, Frank could see that the tree had lost its last leaf, blown away on the stiff wind cutting down from the north. The sky had that green tint associated with impending snow. He started on the pile of induction forms, remembering to make a special note of race, religion, hobbies and qualifications. By lunchtime it was obvious that this was going to be a major operation, requiring some pre-compilation planning. Paul put a cup of coffee on top of the pile.

'Who's been a naughty boy then? Who isn't teacher's pet today?'

Frank smiled. 'I do seem to be knee deep in it today.'

'The way I see it, you're up to your chin and sinking fast. Not to worry though, I'm sure you'll think of something to put her in a good mood by tomorrow morning; for all our sakes. She can be a regular Pegasus when she wants to.'

'Pegasus?'

'An old nag that flies into the air at the least provocation.'

Frank stuffed the remains of his sandwich into his mouth and reached for a Gestetner waxed stencil master, rolling it into his typewriter. He divided the sheet into columns about an inch wide, leaving the left hand margin at about two and a half inches. Into this, he typed the names of all the inmates.

Eleven hundred and four entries later, he rolled off ten copies from each master; heading the lists Hobbies, Religions, Education and Race and, stuffing the remainder into a file for future use if required, started making lists.

He spent the afternoon completing entries in the file room, eventually looking at his watch.

'Christ! It's seven o clock! I'm for home', he waved goodnight to the guard on the gate as he left.

'You don't get brownie points for working on your own time here,' the guard called after him.

He plugged in the kettle and reached for the ringing phone.

'Why don't you come over here for dinner?' It was Loretta, 'I've got a couple of chops under the grill.' He switched off the kettle.

'I'll say this for you,' Loretta said handing him a beer, 'you're a worker when you have to be. How are you doing with this list thing?'

'I've broken the back of it but we have a small snag.'

'Problem?'

'Yes. The files don't have all the information we need. No one asked the right questions.'

'No one wanted to know, then!'

'We'll have to do a survey. Get all the inmates to fill in a questionnaire. Will they co-operate?'

'Give the blank forms to Singleton to issue. He likes issuing ultimatums.'

'He must have been a right pain in the neck in the army.'

'He never was. He was here throughout the war on the civilian staff. He only got made Captain a year or two ago.'

'Ah, that explains why he's always toughest and most military when he's talking to ex-servicemen. Afraid someone will twig that he isn't all that he would have us believe him to be.'

'Few of us are quite what we would have others believe us to be. Take you, for example. You would like us all to believe that you're a big, strong ex-sailorman, afraid of no one and nothing, capable of taking on the world single-handed. But you ain't! You're just as afraid as the rest of us.

"If you were the macho-man you pretend to be, you would have kicked me out of the car for giving you orders when we went down to the lakeshore for our picnic. But you didn't, did you? You were happy to be told what to do and how to do it. It relieved you of the responsibility for satisfying me and you liked it that way. Well, now you know what you're on for dessert tonight, you set the table while I get the chops. Oh, and open me another beer too!'

Frank took a bottle from the fridge and put it on the table in front of Loretta's chair. He placed a condom beside it and let himself out of her apartment.

CHAPTER THIRTY-FOUR

The atmosphere in the office was one of strain. A nervous silence greeted Frank.

'She's been asking if you were here yet.'

'Thanks Gordon, I'll see her when she gets back. Where is she?'

'Down with the Boss.'

Paul looked across at him and half smiled. 'What have you been up to then?'

'Absolutely nothing.'

'Ah, so that's it,' Paul's smile spread across his face, 'I don't think she is a happy little girl this morning.'

'It's her age.'

'I wouldn't tell her that if I were you.'

'I wouldn't dream of it.'

He went into the file room to continue abstracting information from the files then remembered what Loretta had said the night before. The questionnaire was easy to prepare and, by the time she returned, he was standing by the duplicating machine, watching copies fall into the tray.

'That machine is quite capable of looking after itself, there's no need for you to stand there watching it work. If you've nothing better to do, I'll find you something!'

He put the prepared memo to Captain Singleton in front of her. 'Do you want to sign this?'

She read it through and signed it. 'Make sure he knows that I want it back by Thursday morning and, I want all the forms back, not just most of them! The trouble with people around here is that they're basically incompetent.'

Frank said nothing. Winked slowly and turned away.

Singleton, of course, complained about the pressure of work and his inability to guarantee that the questionnaire would be returned by Thursday morning, knowing perfectly well that he would make sure that it was. He wouldn't risk being thought anything but ultra efficient.

There were bound to be a few who refused to complete the form, saying that they would rather go to jail than infringe their right to privacy. He knew too that they would fall into line eventually having demonstrated their position as hard men to the other inmates.

No one really wanted to upset the Captain of the Guard. Life was pretty easy and no one wanted to be sent to the penitentiary for the balance of their sentence, there were some genuine hard men in there.

Frank kept his head down over his desk for the rest of the morning, giving Loretta no opportunity to meet his eye. At lunchtime, he went down to his car in the hope of getting a little privacy.

Sitting there, reading a magazine article on geology and glaciation, Frank didn't hear the Governor until he reached the car.

'Swatting up, I see. I gather Loretta has given you another project too.'

'I get the feeling that I'm not her favourite person just at the moment but its no problem, I'll survive. The survey might produce some useful data but God alone knows what the PR department will do with it. Have you any idea what's in their mind?'

'Not a clue. To be honest, I think they're just hoping something will turn up, something interesting. To be honest, I didn't really know there was a Public Relations Department until you started this Send your Kid To Prison Plan. Frankly, I'm not best pleased with having the spotlight turned on us like this. If we're not careful, some smart politician will start asking questions and offering advice and, then, the shit will really fly.

'Everybody will start asking questions and offering advice and the rest of us will have to take up defensive positions to protect ourselves from the bullshit.

'As long as no one knew that there was a reformatory here or, at least, never gave the place a thought, we were perfectly safe and had a quiet life. I had hoped to make it through to pension without trouble.'

'How about we follow the good old service tradition of answering the last order first? That way, the more questions they ask, the fewer we ever get to answer.'

'I'll go along with that but don't you ever try to pull any of that old service shit on me, OK?'

'OK Chief. Sorry I got you into all this. It seemed like a good idea at the time and a good way to repay some of the kindness of Agnes and Bob.'

'Yeah, I know, the road to hell is paved with good intent and all that. By the way, what have you done to upset Loretta?'

'I suspect it's more a sin of omission that one of commission.'

'Well, get her off of my back! She was down in my office this morning going on about bloody incompetent immigrants.'

Frank filled two mugs with coffee at the machine and put one down in front of Loretta. 'Peace?'

'Not until those chops are eaten.'

'Tonight?'

'Seven o-clock.'

'It'll be a pleasure.'

'It had better be!'

Loretta had cut up the chops and made a pork casserole that, in spite of the precooked meat, tasted very good. There were no bottle of beer in sight and he thought it best not mention it. It was past two when he got home and Agnes was asleep in the lounge, the door open. He closed his door quietly and crept down the stairs, hoping they wouldn't creak. Tomorrow, Bob would be back from the conference.

The results of the questionnaire had been gathered and the report completed. The Governor, MacDonald, Loretta, Captain Singleton and Frank were sitting in the

Governor's office. Mac leaned against the hot radiator, his pipe in his hand, unlit. He didn't smoke it in anyone else's office but he always carried it about with him: Loretta called it his comforter.

'OK, what do we have?'

'We know the race, religion, academic qualifications and major hobbies of all the inmates, in addition to all the information we have had for years. The question is,' Loretta said, 'what are we to do with it?'

Mac smiled at her. 'Frank and I have had a chat about that and Captain Singleton agrees with us that we sit on the answers until someone actually asks a specific question. You won't have come upon it Loretta but, in the services there is a rule that says you must always obey the last order first. The last order was to obtain this information, no one has actually asked us to supply it. There is another useful service dictum that states that you never volunteer for anything so, we sit on this until someone asks a specific question and then we answer just that question and, only that question. OK?'

'I take it that we are hoping that no one will ever get round to asking any specific questions.'

'That's it. With any luck, with Christmas coming up and all that, they will forget that they ever asked us to prepare this data. Just so long as nobody reminds them, we can all relax and carry on as before.'

Mac stepped away from the radiator, pointing his pipe at Frank. 'And, the next time some idiot suggests bringing his landlady's kids to see a ten thousand year old beach, the answer is definitely NO, is that clear?'

'What happens in the spring, when the question of school visits come up again?' Loretta liked her T's crossed and her I's dotted.

'We'll leave that until it comes up. Frank here is in charge of school visits but, until someone actually wants to come, we do and say absolutely nothing.'

The meeting broke up. Captain Singleton returned to his office closed the door and breathed a sigh of relief. He hadn't been required to decide anything and, by the look of it, he wouldn't be. This new guy Frank had his head on the block if anything went wrong with anything and he could always be fired.

The Governor watched them close the door behind them. Right, that's that. Any problems arising had either been shelved or transferred to Loretta's department. She, in turn, could always fire Frank if it all went bad.

Frank followed Loretta up the stairs. At the top, outside the office door, she turned to him. 'You know your head is on the block for this one?'

At lunchtime, she dropped a note on his desk. Five minutes later he entered the file room; she closed the door behind him. 'How about we go away for a long weekend?'

'Where to?'

'Who cares?'

'I do.'

'OK. It's not too cold yet, not much real snow. We could go up to Manatoulin Island, there's a nice motel there; all log cabins and big wood burning stoves. What do you say?

'Sounds very Canadian.'

'I'll take that as a yes.'

'I've got a couple of days holiday owing to me already, shall we go on Friday and come back Tuesday? I can always tell them I'm going sight seeing while it's still possible; that I want to see some of their wonderful country.'

'You say that and someone will probably hit you. You would sound like one of those stupid American tourists who come over the Rainbow Bridge at Niagra and expect to see snow on the Canadian side. If you really want to upset an Ontario Canadian, either call him an American or ask stupid American questions. They think that Canada is the land of perpetual snow with red-coated Mounties stationed every few hundred yards. Singing!'

Frank returned to his desk whistling the theme from Rose Marie whilst Loretta found a couple of files to take back to her desk. She filled out both leave requests forms and took them down to the Bursar's office.

'I haven't any boots suitable for snow walking.' Frank told her when they met at the coffee machine later.

'What size do you take?'

'English size seven.'

'What's that in Canadian?'

'No idea, haven't bought any shoes since I got here.'

She looked down at his feet. 'I may have some that will fit you. Not mine, of course, some that seem to have been left behind by someone. You can try them on at dinner tonight.'

'I didn't realise I was coming to dinner tonight.'

'You've got to try your boots on, haven't you?'

Frank knew when he had been out manoeuvred; anyway, it solved the problem of what to have for dinner.

He arrived at Loretta's apartment carrying a small case in which he had packed just about everything he had that was warm; luckily, he had kept his seaman's jersey, its oiled goat's wool would keep out almost anything.

The unplanned dinner was made by emptying Loretta's fridge of bacon, German style smoked sausage, eggs and the inevitable beans with bread. 'Have a look in the wardrobe, there are all sorts of things in there.'

A couple of suits, a pair of slacks, shirts, underwear, socks, even a couple of quite awful ties; a heavy lumberjack style coat struck Frank as the only thing suitable for the coming weekend. He tried it on, a bit big but definitely wearable.

'Don't tell me, you're a secret cross dresser.'

'I am not! You're not the first man in my life you know.'

'I imagine I mustn't wear any of this to the office?'

'It's no secret that Mac and I had something going, he used to keep a few things here.'

'This coat is great and the leather German sea boots will do nicely with a couple of pairs of thick socks in them.'

'Take whatever you want, I'll dump the rest sometime.'

She brought the coffee in and sat down on the settee. 'We'll throw your case in the back of my car in the morning, then we can shoot off straight from work.'

'Are you driving then?'

'How much snow and slush driving experience have you had in England?'

'Not a lot. Slush is really all we ever get but the answer's none really.'

'So, I'm driving!'

They left the office a little after three, under a greying sky. From Toronto, they took the main drag through Brampton and Orangeville, heading up towards Owen Sound. From there on, Loretta told him, the size and quality of the road deteriorated but remained black top; a heavily used road in the summer by tourists but almost unused in winter.

The place names mirrored the nationalities of those that had opened up the territory. English, Scottish and French mainly with one or two Indian names left over. From Owen Sound, their route would take them along the Bruce peninsula and on to Tobermory; the ferry would pass Fitzwilliam Island on its way to South Baymouth on the main island. All the names sounded familiar to Frank.

'There's a hell of a lot of Scotsmen been here before us!'

Frank read the map he had taken from the glove compartment under the car's dashboard. With little other traffic on the road, driving was easy and the little snow that there was had been swept aside into grey slush by the heavy trucks. Once past Owen Sound, there was no evidence of other traffic at all. The snow lay white on the road, undisturbed but so thinly laid that it presented no problems.

'It looks like a giant Christmas card.'

'You wait 'til the snow's properly lying. Christmas cards aren't in it! Up here, it can white out in a matter of minutes, no trace of where the road is until you hit a tree; then you know you've missed it!'

The Christmas card effect was spoiled by the onset of rain. Rain blown almost horizontally by the strong wind. The snow on the trees disappeared almost instantly, cascading down onto the fast thawing ground covering.

Night driving in these conditions was no fun but with not even a village between them and Tobermory, there was nothing to do but drive. The regular sweep back and forth of the windshield wipers, squeaking on the alternate sweeps, mesmerised them then jolted them awake for mile after mile.

Since leaving the office, the old Chevy had gobbled up miles. Once past the attentions of local police in each of the towns they had passed through, Loretta had opened up the speed to a steady seventy; slowing only when the onset of rain had made this dangerous.

They had stopped for food and coffee at the roadside diner at Wiarton, the last sign of civilisation they had seen but Loretta was beginning to feel the effect of having driven almost three hundred miles. She had hoped to make it to the Sound by eleven but it was clear that anything before midnight would be a miracle.

'It's pretty straight and clear from here, in spite of the rain. You English must be used to rain so it's your turn to take a lesson in long distance driving.' She pulled in to the side of the road and Frank opened his door, the strength of the wind surprised him. He had been able to feel the occasional effect of the wind against the car's body but had not realised just how strong it had become.

'Just remember to stay in the middle of the road unless you see something coming towards you. Anything trying to overtake in this will flash his lights at you so you don't have to worry about that. Oh, and, for God's sake, remember to pull over to the right not the left, if someone does come towards us, OK?'

Frank wiped his face with his handkerchief, put the wetted cotton over the heater outlet by his foot, let in the clutch and pulled away. 'There you are, smooth as a baby's bum!'

The wind had been noticeable all through the drive but now, on the narrow peninsula, its real strength was obvious. Gusting against the port bow of the big car, Frank was forced to make constant corrections to avoid being blown off the road altogether. Once this became instinctive, he increased the speed again but decided that about fifty was as fast as was safe.

The road bore to the left after a while and he was driving almost head into the wind which made it much easier to keep to a line down the centre of the road. The headlights cut a hole through the rain just far enough ahead for him to feel safe at that speed but it was almost half past twelve when he pulled into the parking lot of the Tobermory Motel. The lights were out and all signs of life absent.

'Stay in the car, I'll go and try to knock up someone in the office.'

Judging his run to coincide with a momentary lull in the wind, Frank ran to the office and hammered on the door. 'Hallo inside there. Hallo inside.'

It took three or four hammerings on the door to cause a reaction within but, eventually, a light switched on and a voice demanded identification.

'Who's out there on a God forsaken night like this?'

'Cash customers.'

The door bolts were pulled back. 'What time do you call this? No decent, honest body would be out at this time of night.'

The accent was pure Scots, no Canadian overlay at all.

'Never mind the old country morality, let us in, its peeing down out here and blowing a gale.'

'My God! It's an Englishman. Are you lost, Laddie?'

'Not yet!'

'Run yourself over to cabin number two, I'll meet you there with the key. Bloody English tourists, they ought to know better than to be out in this weather.'

Loretta ran from the car to the open cabin door whilst Frank got soaked bringing in the cases from the trunk.

'You can sign in in the morning, good night to you.'

The man gone, they heard a door slam then all was quiet except for the wind through the trees.

The cabin was warm and dry. The twin beds, divided by a locker type cupboard, looked comfortable and a pile of blankets showed that the Scotsman was a good host, if somewhat short of temper in the middle of the night.

'Find me a towel amongst that pile on the bed will you', Loretta said. 'I'm going to take a shower; I'm bushed, we should have stopped earlier.'

Frank handed her a towel as she stepped out from under the spray of hot water, her skin was pink and looked warm; he drew her to him and kissed her. 'Get yourself under that while I sort out what we need' she told him.

Warm, dry and feeling civilised again, Frank saw that Loretta was already in bed, she opened one eye and smiled up at him.

'I've got what we need.'

Her hand came up out of the bed clasping a small but serviceable sized bottle of whisky. 'Do you need a glass or will you join me on the bottle?'

Two snorts from the bottle and fifteen minutes in the warm bed cleared Frank's mind of anything except sleep; Loretta was already asleep.

He looked at her lying there, untroubled and comfortable. Funny how young she looked asleep, she must be all of forty-five, asleep she looked about twenty. He liked what he saw and tried to remind himself to tell her so in the morning. As he slid down into sleep it occurred to him that when he was her age, she would be drawing her pension. 'What the hell,' he told himself, ' I've always preferred older women.'

The morning was bright and clear but still windy. The sleep had been deep and untroubled and both felt refreshed and ready for food. Indeed, food was paramount amongst their considerations. A wash and a shave, mass cleaning of teeth and combing of hair and they ventured forth.

The Scotsman was clearly in a better humour this morning and the smell of coffee hit them as they opened the cabin door. They followed the smell to the small diner beside the office.

'It'll be bacon and eggs will it?'

He had filled the toaster with four slices of bread as they came to the door, the griddle was hot and he cracked four eggs on to it beside the bacon already sizzling.

'Do we get a choice?'

'Yep. That or nothing.'

Frank turned to Loretta. 'I fancy some bacon and eggs, coffee and toast sweetheart, how about you?'

'That sounds about right to me,' Loretta sat down on one of the stools in front of the counter and smiled at the Scotsman. 'He's learning fast.'

'So, it's an international gathering is it?' Loretta's obviously Canadian accent had made him look round at them. 'It's a strange time for tourists to be here and, if you're running from the police, you're on the wrong road; this one ends two miles ahead.'

Loretta pulled her wallet from her bag, extracted a pasteboard card and held it out to him.

'I am the police, well auxiliary anyway, and if we don't get our breakfast in five minutes flat, I'll send you down for twenty years. We're starving.'

He examined the card and handed it back. 'They'll be sending girl Mounties up here next!'

He shovelled bacon and eggs on to two plates, caught the toast as it popped out of the machine and put it down in front of them. 'Ketchup?'

'God no, What do you think we are, Americans?'

'Get a lot of them up here. They like to go abroad for their vacations. God, on a fine day, you can see America from here but they think they're abroad and they're good for the local economy.'

Breakfast and two cups of strong coffee later, Loretta asked him the obvious question.

'When does the ferry said for South Baymouth?'

'Not today, hen. too rough. Tomorrow maybe but I doubt it, these northwest gales play havoc with the lake. In a hurry are we?'

'This is just a weekend trip. I'd hoped we could get across to the island so that I could show this Englishman a little bit of what little remains of real Canada.'

'You won't make it this weekend hen, and if you did, you like as not wouldn't get back.'

'What now?' Frank asked. 'It's your trip.'

'I guess we'll just have to drift back. We'll go by Sarnia, have a look at Uncle Tom's Cabin perhaps.'

'I thought that was a book!'

'Ignoramus!'

Loretta asked if they could have something put up for lunch, in case they got stuck somewhere.

'There's not a lot about the place really. We're closed but I'll put you up something.'

They packed the few things they had used and threw the cases back into the trunk. 'Go and pay the man,' Loretta told him, 'and see what he's found for us to eat.'

CHAPTER THIRTY-FIVE

Already the fine morning was closing down on them, low clouds skimming over the lake, cutting out the sun. Back in the car with Loretta driving again, Frank said, 'I don't know what he has given us for our lunch but it cost two Dollars.'

'Don't worry, it'll be well worth it. These guys are very good to travellers when they're not being swamped by them and, anyway, he obviously liked to hear your English accent; probably made him feel quite at home.'

She turned left onto the road and speeded up, trying to outrun the weather. The greenish tint of the clouds rushing past them suggested that these were not to be the bringers of more rain but of snow and, from the look of them, lots of it. The peninsula was no place to get stranded in a blizzard, there might not be another vehicle along for days; particularly, if the weather closed right in. The Scotsman would probably ring the police and tell them that they were on the road, just in case.

The wind helped their flight south but, by the time they reached Wiarton, snow was falling heavily. 'Coffee stop.'

Loretta pulled off the road into the diner they had stopped at on the way up.

'Good morning.' The girl behind the counter smiled at them, 'I hope you're going south. The road north will be blocked by tonight, I reckon.'

'Yes, we drove up last night but the ferry isn't running over to the island so we reckoned to drift back down towards Sarnia and Dresden, then back to Toronto from there.'

'My Dad says this snow is going to settle and drift. Might be better if you head back to Toronto directly when you've finished your coffee. That road down the coast can get blocked in a hundred places between here and Sarnia if it really snows and the ploughs won't be out 'til Monday if you're lucky.'

'I can think of worse things,' Loretta winked at the girl, nodding towards Frank.

'Suit yourself. The back of a car is OK with me on a warm summer's night but, in my opinion, under ten feet of snow it's definitely a no-no.'

Frank broke out the map. 'She might just be right.'

'Well, I ain't going home this side of Monday so that's that!'

They looked at the map, stretched out on the counter between their coffee cups.

'We'll go to Kitchener, then back along the lake shore from Hamilton. We'll find somewhere to stay down there, somewhere.'

Frank folded the map and drank his coffee. 'OK, it's your party.'

Driving back along the same road that they had driven north on the night before was boring but, with a stop in a drive-in picnic area for lunch, he had to admit that it looked different in daylight. The road more or less followed the rail track or, perhaps, it was the other way around. In either case, it ensured that the driving was easy and Frank drove as far as Fergus. There, Loretta slid across the bench seat, pushing Frank out of the car. He ran round to the other side and got in to her warm seat.

She swung the car off the main road on to what looked like an English country road, going off to the right. Immediately, the black top surface disappeared and they were running on gravel track.

'And, where are you going to my pretty maid?'

'It's a shortcut. We can get to Kitchener through Waterloo. I thought I'd confuse your European history.'

'In this weather, you may well confuse more than my sense of history, how far is it?'

'About thirty miles, I guess but it's a very pretty route.'

'In this weather, everything looks white. Are you sure it's worth the risk?'

'Chicken!'

'The word you're looking for is coward but, if you're game, include me in.'

By the time they reached Waterloo, Frank had pushed the car back on to the road twice and hammered the collapsed offside front wing off the wheel using a large rock. It hadn't improved the paintwork any but it had kept them mobile.

'I thought you said you had better drive because I hadn't much experience of driving on snow and slush!'

'Stop moaning and think yourself lucky you have seen so much off-track Canada on your first weekend out of the city!'

'If, by off-track, you mean about three million identical trees interspersed with snow filled ditches and a female lunatic driving a beat up old car down an invisible track then, I am indeed blessed. Pull in at that service station, I'll see if I can get a bulb for the offside front light, it seems to have given up trying.'

'Trouble?' The boy was looking at the crumpled offside front wing.

'Nothing we can't handle. Some fool put a tree right in front of the car.'

'Where was that?'

'Somewhere between here and Fergus.'

'Hey!' The boy's eyebrows lifted. 'you're English ain't ya?' He transferred the gum to the other cheek and Frank thought he was going to spit but he didn't.

'Yeah, but the driver ain't!'

'I wouldn't go that way in this weather. OK when the snow is hard but not now.'

'Yeah, we kinda worked that out for ourselves.'

The boy found the bulb and fitted it while Frank talked to Loretta.

'Got to encourage local enterprise.'

The boy pocketed the dollar bill and retreated into the warmth of the office chewing as Loretta pulled away.

On the main road to Kitchener, the conditions were much better. Other, almost constant traffic kept the road clear of slush, spraying it over the settling snow on either side of the tarmac. Once there, Loretta pulled off the road again.

'History lesson begins here.' She led him into the diner. 'You order the coffee, I'm going to the can.'

The girl was quick and smiled as she took Frank's money. 'Is that an English accent?'

'Yes.'

'Thought so. Don't get a lot of foreigners in here this late in the year. Mostly summer they come by.'

'Yes, I imagine they do. Bit cold for tourists now, eh?'

The girl was undecided whether to keep up the conversation when she saw Loretta coming out of the rest room. She decided that it would be a waste and wandered off down to the other end of the long counter. Loretta, noticing the look and hurried departure of the girl, picked up her coffee.

'Let's sit over there.'

They sat at a table by a window and, for a moment, watched the snow swirling about in the uncertain wind created by the passing traffic.

'Right, history. By Canadian standards, Kitchener is an old town. It used to be called Sand Hills for what was then a perfectly obvious reason. With the coming of a lot of immigrants from Germany at the beginning of the century, they changed the name to Berlin;' Frank's attention was attracted by the siren of a passing police car spraying all and sundry with slush as it powered up the centre of the road, it's lights flashing.

'That carried on happily until about midway through the first war with being German being less fashionable; they held a town meeting and decided to demonstrate their Canadianess and allegiance to the British Commonwealth and all that by changing the name to something famously

243

British, hence Kitchener. An example of patriotism and cowardice combining to solve their problem.' She took a sip of her coffee.

'It sounds a bit far fetched to me but, if you say so, I'll take your word for it. We British were at war with France off and on for a thousand years but the south of England is full of villages with French names; it never occurred to anyone to change them. Mind you, our pronunciation is so bad that I doubt if the locals knew that they were French names!'

'But, England was conquered by William of Normandy wasn't it? So you're all really French anyway.'

'I wouldn't try out that argument in England if I were you. Anyway, William wasn't French, he was Norman, descended from the Norsemen or Vikings and so was the King of England at the time so it was just a little family quarrel.'

'Well, if you're going to stay here, you will have to learn a little Canadian history. We're very proud of it. We Canadians all came out here because we wanted to, not like the Aussies, because we were sent! Isn't that why you came?'

'Not really, I came over because I heard you were here.'

'Smooth talking bastard, pay for the coffee!'

'I paid already.'

Back on the road she asked him, 'Just why did you come over?'

'It's a long story but, in brief, I didn't settle too well when I came out of the navy so I thought why not? There was nothing I wanted there so I came here to see what it was like.'

'That's not all of it, is it? I can tell you've been married. I can always tell the married ones, they don't push so hard, they take their time and allow things to develop at their own speed rather than trying to bring a relationship to a head too quickly.'

'I thought it was you that picked me up! I was just standing there, minding my own business when, suddenly, I found I was knee deep in a relationship with you. Very good that, knee deep, in view of our first occasion.'

'Watch it buster or you'll be knee deep in the snow with nowhere to go.'

'Yes. I used to be married but when I came home the hero, I found that she'd been on the game for years. The way I heard it, everybody had had her; most of the Navy, two thirds of the Marines and the entire U.S. Seventh Army Transport Division. Somehow it didn't seem the same after that. That's not entirely fair but you know how these stories spread.'

'Any kids?'

'One.'

'Yours?'

'How the hell do I know?'

'Does it look like you?'

'Well, it's white.'

'But what do you think?'

'Yeah, she could be but I'll never know for sure.'

'Do you send money home to her?'

'No. Her mother is quite capable of supporting her. Probably better than I can. Anyway, they don't know where I am. I'll probably get divorced some time, I can't prove her adultery but I'm not in any hurry to get married again. Does that worry you?'

'God no! I was married once too. It didn't work out. He couldn't tell the difference between a marriage bed and all-in wrestling. One day he hit me too hard and I let him have it with the iron I was using at the time. They saved his life but he's in a nursing home now; doesn't know what day it is. Doesn't even know his name.

'I send him money to the home but he'll never get better. He's in there for life but I've never got round to trying to divorce him either. Doubt if I could, anyway, too many questions to answer.'

They drove on in silence, each digesting what the other had said.

'You should send money for the kid.'

'Yeah.'

She had obviously forgotten about Uncle Tom's Cabin and Canadian history, they were travelling east, back towards Toronto. It was still snowing, though this was no problem on the main road. Elsewhere, the first real snow of the winter was settling and the wind was drifting it high against the sides of houses and trees. The silence between them felt right, not oppressive but comfortable, as if they saw no reason to talk; just being together was enough. They stopped once, for groceries and gas, about fifty miles from Toronto.

'No one at the office knows about my husband. I want your solemn oath that you won't spread the word, I shouldn't have told you.' Her eyes searched his, looking for a sign, some reassurance. It was the first time she had looked vulnerable.

'As far as I'm concerned, you're as single as I am. It's none of my business and, certainly, none of theirs.'

Loretta kissed him on the cheek; he closed his eyes as the car swerved dangerously across the road.

'If you kill us both, it won't matter whether either of us is married!'

In almost ten years, she hadn't cried about it. At first, she had been only too pleased that she no longer had to live with him, being beaten up whenever he had a beer or two inside him. The judge had put her on probation; he had understood. After a while, she had wondered how he was and had made enquiries at the nursing home. He was happy enough, she had been told, he had no recollection of events of even the previous day; he lived in the present. He was physically fit enough and he would almost certainly live to a ripe old age. 'Did she wish to come and see him?'

It was obvious that the nuns did not approve of her and were defensive about their patient. After that first time, she had never gone to see him again. It wouldn't have been fair on either of them. Once, before the alcohol had got to him, he had been a fine, attractive young man. She had loved him and wanted him. Perhaps it was something she had done which had made him take that one extra drink, the one that pushed him over the edge into dependency.

She had seen many like him since then. There was a drying out clinic at the reformatory. Sometimes, she remembered, she had seen them brought in in straight jackets, desperately trying to fight back against the dragon that threatened to devour them; one day, she would pluck up the courage to go and see him again. She wiped a tear from her cheek with the back of her hand.

'You should send money for the kid.'

Frank looked at her. It had been half an hour since she had said anything to him. He reached out a finger, scooping up a tear before it fell and transferred it to his lips, tasting it.

'You're more of an old salt than I am.'

She stared straight ahead, her eyes on the road, saying nothing.

CHAPTER THIRTY-SIX

It was still only Saturday, Toronto would be full of shoppers. This evening, couples would be going to cinemas or restaurants, doing those things requiring a basis of two.

Loretta heard the music from the other room and wondered who had turned on the radio, then remembered that Frank was there.

'Find some records, she called, we don't want some fool telling us that it's snowing in downtown Toronto and that we should all go home before the roads get snowed in.'

She had grilled the lamb chops and, by cutting the potatoes into very small cubes and the cabbage into strips, cooking time had been reduced to acceptable proportions.

'Come and eat!'

'That smells like food.'

'Sunday breakfast early. This way we can stay in bed 'til tomorrow afternoon.'

He watched her as she ate, almost able to read the memories passing behind the eyes as she fed the food into her mouth. Clearly, the talk about wives and husbands had had an effect on her. The hard shell had been broken and he could see the woman inside. He let her drift, paying little attention to the meal or, indeed, him. Given time, she would arrive at a plateau upon which she could settle; upon which she could re-establish her defences. When she had found it, she would be back in this world, with him.

Whilst she got the coffee, he glanced at the newspaper they had bought with the groceries. Unusually, winter had come early in England. A pre-Christmas snowfall had resulted in the unprepared government being criticised in the UK Press; the Globe and Mail had picked up the story for the benefit of the many British immigrants in Toronto.

He threw the paper onto the side table; he might read it tomorrow.

The coffee seemed to be the catalyst; he smiled at her.

'Welcome home.'

'Where have I been?'

'I don't know but wherever it was, I wasn't there and you weren't here'.

'Sorry. This evening seems to have gotten out of hand. I'm usually more in control than this.'

'There was this other girl here while you were away. Nice girl, softer than you but very like you in other ways. Probably it was your kid sister.'

'No. Dad gave up when Mum had me. He wanted a son very badly.'

'Well, I'm glad he was disappointed. I'm not into boys but I like you as a girl.'

'I like you too. No, don't smile, I really like you; like you as a person. Sure I wanted you as a lover but I think I would like to have you as a friend as well. Do you reckon we could manage that? It ain't easy, I've tried in the past and one thing always seems to get in the way of the other.'

'Perhaps you were trying too hard? The secret of a good, lasting relationship is to just let it run its course; don't push, just accept whatever happens. Think of it as they would have in the old days. As God wills it, so shall it be.'

'I've never thought of you as religious.'

'I believe in God the way all sailors do. Not the God of cathedrals and Archbishops and all that but the God who can be anything or anyone he wants to be at the time he meets you. He decides what it is and all you have to do is take his word for it.'

'That's very profound, I'm not sure I understand.'

'That's the point you see. Your God and my God may or may not be the same. Everyman's relationship with his God is his own business, a private relationship based on his own experience; not what some bureaucrat in a frock and dog collar tells him it is.

'When you've been at sea for a while, particularly in wartime you realise that, when necessary, you can have a quiet, private word with God and sort out the problems between you.   You don't need a lot of other people mumbling and singing, standing up and kneeling down by numbers and being told what to say and think by some bloke in a frock.'

'But didn't Christ say that wherever two or more people are gathered together in my name, that is God's house or something?   Anyway, it's probably blasphemous to suggest that you can have a personal relationship with God.'

'That wasn't Christ. That was some guy who translated the bible into Greek or Latin from the original Arabic or something like that. He had a vested interest in organising gatherings,   building   churches,   appointing   Bishops, Archbishops,   Popes,   Cardinals   and   all   the   other bureaucrats who make a very good living out of other people's belief in God.'

'I seem to have hit a nerve.'

'No, not really.   Perhaps I'm really an anarchist at heart. I don't like being organised, belonging to an organised group.'

'There's nothing wrong with your heart, of that I'm sure.'

The stack of records Frank had put on the autochange had run out and Loretta put some more on, selecting dance music rather than vocals.

'Move that Chesterfield,' she told him, 'then we can dance.'

Frank turned off the main light, leaving only the small table lamp to give atmosphere to the room.   He took Loretta in his arms and moved in time with the music. In the confined space, it was impossible to do more than move gently backwards and forwards, swaying like long grass in a gentle breeze.

'Do you come here often?'

'Shut up, kiss me and take me to bed.'

CHAPTER THIRTY-SEVEN

'Will Frank come back?' Alice's mother asked, a quizzical expression on her face. Clearly she thought it an important question; maybe it was, it's being nearly Christmas.

'How the hell do I know. I don't even know where he is.'

'Do you want him back?'

Alice was silent for a moment. 'Yes, I think I do but it's not up to me is it? It's up to him, he's the one that's pushed off. He knows where we are if he decides he wants us There's nothing I can do.'

'I liked Frank.'

'So did I Mum, that's why I married him.'

'Maybe he'll come back when he's got over his anger. You did him a great wrong going with other men.'

'It would have been alright after a few years, it wouldn't have mattered what other people said, not once we were settled and established in our own home. Anyway, there were only two. That child sailor I found crying in the public bar and the Chief, who was married and hadn't seen his wife in two years. She'd told him not to bother coming home; the poor soul was suicidal. I helped them, that's all.'

'Well, the cat's out of the bag now anyway, everybody knows or thinks they know all about you and your men. Perhaps when he's had time to think it over, he'll want you back anyway. Whatever they say.'

'Perhaps.'

'What'll you tell the child when she asks where her Daddy is at Christmas?'

'I don't know Mum. Why, suddenly, all the questions?'

'Your father and I were discussing it last night. We will have to retire in a year or two, three or four maybe at most. What will you do then? Get a job in someone else's pub? You won't like working for other people, you know.'

'Why will you have to retire?'

'Well, we don't own this pub, you know, we manage it for the brewery. They will want to put someone younger in, one of these days.'

Alice knew she was right. She had seen the signs herself of modernising. The sailors now were all youngsters, as many of them visiting the milk bars in the High Street as coming into the pubs. Times were certainly changing now that the war was over.

The pubs had been packed to the doors during the war, whatever the quality of the beer served, now they were almost empty except on Saturday nights. The drinkers nowadays were two, maybe three pints a night men, saving their money or sending it home to their wives. The almost carefree days of the war, when no one knew whether they would still be alive next payday, were gone. Now that all the danger had gone out of life, all the fun seemed to have gone out of the pubs.

'Maybe he'll come back at Christmas.'

'Maybe.'

Alice didn't think it likely. If he hadn't come back by now, he must have established himself somewhere else, perhaps with someone else. It was months since he had left. Not a word, nothing. She wondered where he was, what he was doing, who he was with and whether he ever thought about her. There was nobody, no man, in her life. She had made no attempt to replace Frank, she didn't need anyone anyway, she had Virginia. Maybe Frank would come back, one day. She went down stairs to make sure all was ready for opening time.

She heard Virginia chattering to her grandma in the parlour. She would just have to carry on saving every penny, hoping that, by the time she did have to leave The Return, she would have enough to buy a small hotel but the price being asked was higher every time she went to view a prospect. Another year, maybe, it all depended on what became available and how much they wanted for it. Perhaps she could borrow from the bank, she didn't like the idea. Borrowed money had to be repaid whether the hotel was making money or not. She would ask her Dad what he thought.

It was opening time. She unlocked the doors and looked out into the street. In the old days, during the war, there would have been someone into the bar almost as soon as it was opened. Now, the street was deserted, even the girls had gone.

It was early yet. Business would pick up later but at this rate, The Return was in as much danger of closing as some of the others; they would be lucky to last three or four years before the Brewery decided that enough was enough and there were too many pubs in Chatham. She had to admit it, there were too many pubs in Chatham for the modern, peacetime navy.

'I've opened up,' she called up the stairs, 'not a soul in sight!"

'Alright, I'll be down shortly.'

It was her mother that called. Her father seemed to take less and less interest in the day-to-day running of the pub now that business was so slack. He would be down later, when the regulars began to drift in after they had had their tea.

The dockyard workers he had known since he was a boy and those of the regular sailors who happened to be in Chatham at the moment, business wasn't that bad. Better than pre-war but not a patch on the war years. The brewers must have made a fortune during the war.

They too had been lucky. The war had brought more money into Chatham, and therefore into The Return in four or five years than her father could have made in a lifetime at pre-war rates. Prices had edged up, profits also; profits rather than better prices, actually and his wages from the brewery had followed them upwards though, not at the same rate.

He was not dissatisfied, he would be able to retire soon, once Alice got herself sorted out. Pity about Frank, he had liked Frank. Silly bitch, fancy thinking she could keep a secret like that in a place like Chatham; half the women in the town had been on the game and the other half knew which were which and were happy to tell tales.

He poured himself a single malt and sat, looking into the fire. 'Silly bitch!'

'Who?'

'Sorry love, forgot you were there. Alice of course, what are we going to do with her?'

'Something will come up. Perhaps she'll find the hotel she's looking for at a price she can afford.'

'Perhaps pigs will fly?'

'Perhaps, if we ask around, you know, let the trade know that we might be interested if anyone hears of anything suitable.'

'Well, some of those hotels up by Gillingham station have lost a lot of business since the war. Maybe one of them might be suitable. I'll drop a hint or two in the Rep's ears. Perhaps some of them call on them too, you never know, something might come of it.'

Downstairs, in the bar, the first customer of the evening had arrived. 'Hallo Alice, your Dad not down yet then?'

Alice called up the stairs.

'Dad, Uncle Tony's here, asking for you.'

'Tell him he's got to pay like everyone else!'

Uncle Tony smiled at her and shouted up the stairs. 'I heard that, you tight old bugger.'

CHAPTER THIRTY-EIGHT

Christmas in Toronto was something totally outside Frank's experience. Loretta took him on a tour of the uptown suburbs where every house stood in its own grounds. Almost every snow-covered roof was adorned with a brightly painted and fairy-lighted cut out of Santa, a sack over his shoulder and climbing into an oversized chimney.

Below, on the virgin white lawns, equally brightly painted cut outs of sleighs and reindeer stood, waiting for Santa's return. In the trees, fairy lights switched themselves on and off, creating a flickering wonderland. He had never seen anything even remotely like this, not even before the war; this was a new world, one totally unimagined by the boy brought up in a children's home in Clapham.

Barnardo's had been good to Frank. He had been fed, clothed and educated better than he would have been had his parents lived. He had needed for nothing but then, no one at the home could ever have imagined this; not even the housemasters, nor would they ever.

In the front gardens, cut outs of elves sat poised over half completed toys, hammers in hand; some even had spectacles balanced on the end of the nose and bright knitted, woolly pointed hats drooping over their ears.

Every house had something. Even the smallest had dressed a giant Christmas tree in lights and placed a huge, twinkling star on the roof. The messages 'Merry Christmas One and All', 'Noel' and 'Happy Xmas' stood proudly from the ridge of almost every roof. Even the Country Club, surrounded by its tennis courts, had an illuminated sign on its roof big enough to be seen from the road. 'God Bless Ye Merry Gentlemen' flashed on and off rhythmically, the neon tubes flashing in time with the Christmas carol broadcast from the holly-covered loudspeakers by the big twin gates. Frank stared, dumbstruck.

Loretta drove them into High Park. Every road through the park and every path through the snow covered trees was laced with fairy lights suspended from chains connecting the lamp posts which he hadn't noticed the last time he had been there. People, mostly couples, were strolling through this fairyland, hand in hand. Children ran back and forth ooing and ahing, pointing first to one thing then to another. Frank drew Loretta to him, tears running down his cheeks, he kissed her, 'Happy Christmas.'

'Happy Christmas lover. It's at times like this that you wish you had a kid to give presents to doesn't it. Oh God I'm sorry, I forgot Forgive me, I shouldn't have said that.'

'Perhaps I should send her something. After all, it wasn't her fault.'

He took Loretta's hand in his and they skipped down the path like a pair of five year olds.

'I may grow up next year, would you like that?'

She waved a stiffened finger under his nose, 'Don't you dare! There's enough bloody grown-ups in the world already.'

The box wrapped, on the outside with stout brown paper and within with Christmas paper, came as a surprise in Chatham. The Canadian stamps above the address meant nothing to Alice and the postmark was too blurred to make out; she helped Virginia undo the wrapper and open the box. The card said 'Happy Christmas'.

The doll said Mama as they lifted it out of the box and the dress of fine silk fell around its legs to hang perfectly. The bodice emphasised the delicate colouring of the doll's cheeks, neck and hands; each finger perfectly formed and with its nail painted in pink to match the lipstick. Virginia burst into tears, clasping the doll to her.

'May I keep her, Mummy?'

Alice gave them both a cuddle, 'Of course you may, Darling. It's a present from Canada for you.'

'Who's Canada?'

'I don't know, darling. Perhaps that's a special name for daddy.'

'Where is Daddy?'

'I don't know darling but now you have a lovely dolly to remind you of him; what shall we call her?'

'Daddy.'

'You can't call a little girl doll Daddy, darling.'

'I want to.'

'Let's call her Canada. That could be a little girl's name.'

'I want to call her Daddy!'

Alice knew her daughter well enough not to argue further. If she wanted to call the doll Daddy then, Daddy it would be.

'Run down and show it to Grandma and Grandpa sweetheart, tell them she's a present from Canada.'

Outside Frank's office window, the tree bore a blanket of snow. The seasonal rush of new inmates resulting from over enthusiastic Christmas and New Year celebrations had been received and processed. Frank was not busy.

His first Christmas in Canada had been an entirely new experience. The rooftop decorations, the fairy-lighted trees in the park and in so many gardens, the parties around Christmas trees and, even, a barbecue on the lakeshore with everyone dressed up as Father Christmas. A giant bonfire had been lit on the beach, potatoes baked, sausages grilled on the sharpened ends of sticks and innumerable thermos flasks of what purported to be cold tea had been passed round, adding to the general good nature of the event.

Now, in January, the sky outside the office window was leaden, the snow lay deep with more to come and the branches of the trees stood out in stark contrast; white snow on the top of each branch, dark wood below.

Frank shuddered involuntarily. The temperature inside the building was much higher than it would have been in an English office but the view through the window made him feel cold. He thought about England, of Chatham, of Alice and of Virginia. Had he been right to send the doll? He hadn't given any indication of where he was living but Alice now knew that he was in Canada. Did he care?

Perhaps he shouldn't have sent it. He should have left the door from the past closed. He had, until now, been able to empty his mind of all things English, concentrating on becoming a Canadian but, by sending the doll, he had cracked open that door, had allowed England and Alice to re-enter his mind, to infect his thinking; to join him in Canada.

'Shit!' He shouldn't have sent it. It was an acknowledgement that the past extended into the present and, God help him, into the future.

The office was quiet, everyone concentrating on their work as a means of avoiding yet another re-examination of the holidays. Post-Christmas remorse, he thought, that's what's wrong with us all; the next sunny day would dispel the gloom and everyone would start thinking about spring. It would all be alright in a day or two, he would feel better when the sun came out.

He forced his mind round to the organisation of school visits to the pit. Safety, that was the major problem, mustn't let the little darlings get into any trouble down there. There ought to be a giant diagram, showing what the beach area would have been like when the pre-Indians had laid the fire and cooked their fish. Perhaps they should dig out and expose more of the beach so that the kids could see enough of it to understand the diagram?

It would have to show the beach surrounded by trees, exclusively pine at that time he suspected, and have adjacent panels showing the wildlife that would have inhabited the pine forest; animals, birds, the types of fish that would have been in the lake, etc., other panels should explain and illustrate the pre-Indian way of life, the types of shelter the people would have built, the type of boat they might have had, who knew the answers?

Perhaps he could discuss it with the Department of Archaeology at the University. Perhaps they should, together, produce a short booklet or leaflet for the schools sending children; something the teachers could base a lesson on so that the kids would have some idea what they were coming to see and what it was all about before they arrived on site.

Anyway, it would cost money to manufacture the diagrams and to display any other exhibits that could be found, he must take up Marley's offer to examine his finds; perhaps they could be incorporated. The remains of the fire and fish bones should be displayed in-situ but would have to be protected from both the children and the weather. Other small fragments of bones had been found since he had taken Robert down there and these too would have to be identified and preserved; all jobs for the University people, certainly not something he could do.

It was, he realised with some pleasure, entirely possible that if and when they realised what it might cost to mount such a display, they would decide that the whole project should be shelved for lack of funds. He was beginning to hope so. The more he thought about the disturbance his visit with Robert had caused, the more surprised he was that he still had a job. With anything like good luck, the PR department downtown would have forgotten the whole thing by now; he hoped so.

Loretta brought a cup of coffee to his desk. 'I thought I might organise a post-Christmas party this weekend. Who should we invite?'

'This lot here for starters. Look at them! Have you ever seen such a sour faced lot?'

'Why not? Should we invite Bob and Agnes too? They might like to come but they'll have to get baby sitters, it's a strictly no kids party.'

"Definitely no kids. I'm off kids at the moment, I'm trying to make some sort of sense out of this play pit programme.'

'Why don't we hold it here?'

'It has to be here, dolt. The damned pit is here.'

'Not your bloody kids party, our party. We could make it an office party plus guests. There's plenty of parking space so everyone could bring say two guests and at least one bottle. We could call it a spring festival.'

'I think your original idea was better, a post-Christmas-remorse-party.'

'I'll ask the boss if it's OK with him. We could have a ritual burning of Christmas decorations as an outside feature. Everyone must bring their paper chains or whatever as proof of their remorse. No decorations, no entry to the party. How about that?'

'I like it. We could have a big notice put up by the fire saying 'No husbands or wives to be burned'. '

'Sometimes I think you have a nasty little mind.' She disappeared down the stairs to talk first to Mac and then to the Governor if Mac approved, she was sure that the Governor would. She was back in less than ten minutes.

'It's all OK with them as long as they're invited but we have to clear it with Singleton and his guards which means that we have to invite them too. This could get out of hand.'

'What the hell, this is the new world where everything is supposed to be bigger and better than it was in the old country isn't it? Isn't that what you colonials keep telling us poor, ignorant immigrants?'

'When you decide to do something, you don't do it by halves, do you?'

'What have I to lose? When head office work out what this school visits project is going to cost, I'm out of a job anyway.'

'Then, don't tell them. You don't know Canada. We're really quite good at adopting new ideas on a try it and see basis. You should be OK for a while yet.' She turned to the office in general.

'Now, listen up there everybody. We think we should organise a post-Christmas remorse party for next weekend; everyone is invited. Bring up to two guests and a minimum of one bottle and bring some food too. Do we have any takers at that price?'

'And,' Frank interjected, 'you have to bring your old Christmas decorations to be burned as an offering to Bacchus. How about it?'

Paul applauded enthusiastically. 'It's the best idea you've had so far this year but if you invite the Padre, you'd better not mention Bacchus too loudly.'

'With his belly', Loretta laughed, 'he could come as Bacchus. In fact, he could be the man best qualified to bring the wine, I'm sure he waters the stuff he doles out at communion.'

She went off in search of Singleton, to invite his happy band of pilgrims. They would have to be invited or, having let the partygoers in, they might decide that it would be a good joke not to let them out again. The Canadian winter was no time to be locked out in the snowy car park.

The atmosphere in the office seemed miraculously uplifted and, during the afternoon, an occasional joke poked its head above the parapet, the prospect of a party having made everyone feel better.

Frank drafted his memo to the PR Department and put it to one side. He would look at it again tomorrow, just to check. He wouldn't send it unless they contacted him first. He spent most of the afternoon sketching out designs for the information panels they would require for the pit.

What if it rains? How long will the beach display last, exposed to the elements? Not to mention a million children's feet?

I suppose we could box-wall it and glass over the actual beach; that would at least protect that but what about the display panels? How about a giant tepee covering the whole area? He gave in. It was too big a project to be organised by one man with no authority, he would have to leave it to the PR Department, much as he hated that prospect, it was his idea.

He could imagine the kids looking at the remains of the fire, the few bones and fish heads or the like and shrugging their shoulders. Big deal! Saw better than that on the beach last summer! Ah well, that was their teacher's problem. Frank was glad he wasn't to be the guide, he had enough trouble already; why hadn't he kept his big mouth shut? He'd had a nice little number here; quiet, no trouble and he had blown it by showing off to a couple of kids!

Him! Frank Bye. After all those years in the navy, he of all people should have known enough to melt into the background and let others make waves if they wanted to. He had broken the first law of survival in the navy; don't make waves, don't volunteer for anything, keep your head down and your mouth shut.

He, Frank Bye had broken every single guideline! Perhaps his old Chief at Ganges had been right after all. 'Boy', he had told Frank, 'you are an idiot, boy!'

At least it was better than what the other boys had called him until then, Barnardo boy!'

That was the second time today he had found himself thinking of the past. The only way to make a new life was to forget the old. No looking back. He picked up the memo and looked at it again. Yeah, that's OK. Send the damned thing and get it over with. Get the show on the road. He put the envelope in Loretta's out tray, she could decide whether to send it or file it.

'When Head Office see that, they'll want my head on a plate.'

'You're not important enough yet. They'll have to promote you first to make it worthwhile firing you.'

'How far up the ladder do I have to go before it's worth firing me?'

'Far enough to take the flack for someone else's mistake.'

'Then, I'm alright until after the party.'

'I'll file this until they ask for a progress report.'

CHAPTER THIRTY-NINE

The flames reached upwards into the dark of the night, reflected and multiplied in the windows and paintwork of the cars in the car park and again by the glass of the office windows; the party was a success. Everyone had brought so many decorations to be sacrificed that they must have had a street collection. The Padre had declined to attend as Bacchus but was happy to come as Friar Tuck and, judging by the amount of drinking that was going on, Post-Christmas-Depression was going to be succeeded by alcoholic remorse.

'The trouble with Christmas is', a voice explained, 'there's altogether too much good will about. It's unnatural to be that pleasant to everybody for so long. Nature needs a good argument from time to time, just to restore the balance or, as here, a good ritual burning of the symbols of all that good will.'

Bob and Agnes, freed from the children, had been seen enjoying themselves in a manner most unbecoming an old, married couple. They had last been seen in the back of their own car taking no interest in what was going on outside.

Frank decided that, tonight was not a good night to go back to his flat in their basement, tonight was a night they would appreciate a little privacy. The kids, with Grandma, would not be back 'til after school tomorrow and it was a long time since they had had a night to themselves.

Loretta had been feeding Mac's wife with drinks on the basis that he deserved a good night too and she had been careful not to take too many herself; she had also made sure that Frank had kept pace with her. She didn't want him drunk tonight.

There seemed to be fewer people than there had been earlier, some had obviously skipped off home already, Loretta found Frank and pointed to the car.

'I think we can safely escape now. Captain Singleton is asleep in his office and everyone else is busy with someone else.'

Frank held up the partially empty bottle for Loretta's inspection.

'Is this partly full or half empty?'

'Shut up and get into the car.'

'No, it's important. Your answer determines whether you are an optimist or a pessimist.'

'The bottle is partly full, now get into the damned car before I hit you with it.'

'If I take a swig from it, will it make it more partly empty than it was before or less partly full, do you think?'

'You need black coffee not booze. I thought you had stayed sober.'

Frank saluted the guard as they sped through the gate. 'Carry on, Officer of the Guard.' He felt Loretta dig him in the ribs with her elbow but nothing after that.

He knew were he was but was unsure how he had got to be standing in the shower, handcuffed to the tap. The cold water from the showerhead was making speech difficult, every time he tried his mouth filled with water. He opened his eyes again with the same result, was the woman trying to drown him?

Escape was impossible, with his hands handcuffed to the pipe just below the rose, she hit him again with the banjo shaped, long handled wooden back scrubber, using it as a paddle.

'Sober up you bastard!' She was crying, the tears falling into the spray from the shower. 'Sober up, you bastard or I'll do something we'll both be sorry for in the morning.'

He opened his mouth to speak but it filled with water, he turned his head away and tried again.

'OK, OK already! Stop with the drowning Eh?'

'Are you sober yet?'

'The Germans couldn't drown me in the war, I don't see why you should try to do it now!' He tried to escape but the cuffs made it impossible. 'I promise not to run away if you take off the cuffs, Officer. It's cold and wet in here!'

She was still crying. 'Well, you can bloody well stay there in the cold and the wet until I'm good and ready to let you out.'

He could hear her crying in the bedroom as she towelled herself dry; she had got herself almost as wet as he. At least she had undressed him before cuffing him to the shower. She came back into the bathroom with a jar of hand cream.

'You must be sore!'

She dried him, patting gently with the towel, then spread the cold cream on to the burning red marks raised by the brush. He felt himself react.

'Christ, that was quick!'

She unlocked the cuffs and led him into the bedroom, pushing him down on to the bed, falling on to him. 'I want you now. Now!'

Passion spent, she lay beside him. Frank rolled off the bed and staggered to the kitchen to make coffee. He fed the percolator and watered it.

'You want to take these bracelets off me now?' He held up the wrist to which they were still attached.

'I think I may just keep you in them for ever, only letting you out when I want you. How would you like that?'

'Do you want something in this coffee, a reviver?'

'Why not, right now I couldn't lift the cup without assistance.'

Frank could feel the coffee's warmth spreading through his body. The caffeine gently revitalising every part of his body as it coursed through his veins

'I needed that.'

'Me too.'

'I'm hungry.'

'It's your kitchen, help yourself.'

'I feel like being pampered, waited upon.'

'Is there no end to this woman's demands?'

'How are you at making omelettes?'

'Madam, His Majesty's sailors are capable of anything.'

'There are eggs on the side by the stove.'

'Do you want to take this cuff off now? It might get in the way.'

'No. I may just want to sleep handcuffed to you tonight.'

'I'm not sure that the authorities intended this particular application of their equipment when they issued these cuffs to you as an auxiliary constable.'

'How do you know?'

He whisked the eggs in the bowl, adding a little milk, salt and pepper, pouring the mix into the blue smoking fat in the pan; instant omelette.

He turned the edges to the middle and slid it on to a plate, adding a line of grated cheese down the centre as garnish, took the plate into the bedroom and returned to make one for himself.

'You've done this before, 'she called after him.

'Never underestimate a sailor.'

'You're really quite something, you know. Any normal man would have beaten the hell out of me for what I did to you. You, you make me an omelette!'

'It was nothing. When I was a kid beatings were a regular occurrence and they hurt, really hurt. I remember the matron at the Home saying, after about the fifth beating, you must learn to love pain my dear, then nobody can hurt you. What you just did was but a gentle caress between lovers; anyway, we were both drunk at the time so it doesn't count and we both enjoyed it. Forget it.'

'I don't think I want to. I don't know what it did for you but the memory of it makes me feel as randy as hell.'

'Not tonight, Josephine! Once a King always a King but once a Knight is enough for me.'

CHAPTER FORTY

The Public Relations Office in Parliament Buildings down town was, as it happened, just along the corridor from the Veterans' Office in which Frank had had his interview some months previously. The PR man detailed to look after the Reformatory Project examined Frank as he came through the door.

'Frank?'

'Yes.'

'I'm Gerald Thorsen, I'm looking after this little idea of yours. Tell me about it. What are your thoughts on how we should go about it? I understand you are something of an expert on the ice age and glaciation.'

'I'm certainly no expert. At best, a humble seeker after knowledge'

'That's what I like about you English, self effacing to a fault. You'll never get ahead here if you don't push yourself forward.'

'I like to know where ahead is before I start pushing.'

'Yeah, fair enough, I guess that's fair enough. Coffee?'

He led Frank over to the coffee machine and poured two cups. He pointed to a desk across the office. 'Come and sit over there, that's my desk. Right, now, what do we have?'

'What we have is essentially an exposed stretch of post-glaciation beach showing signs of a camp fire and bone debris from at least one and possibly more meals prepared at the site. As it stands, there ain't much to see but, properly exhibited, it could provide the basis for an informative lesson in geology, archaeology and natural history, with an added bonus of providing proof of the existence of pre-Indian habitation at that place at that time. That might please the quote Canadians unquote. They can show that the Indians didn't get here first, someone else did.'

'No shit?'

'No shit.'

'I didn't understand the half of that but if you do, what the hell are you doing working as a clerk in a reformatory?'

'Paying for the groceries.'

'Well, I think we'd better see if we can't get you transferred to this department. If we're going to run with this idea, we'll need someone who understands it.'

'Does it pay better?'

'I'm sure it does.'

'OK, I'm in.'

They ran through what Frank already knew and what he had thought would be necessary in terms of organisation.

'Could we get some more exhibits? We don't seem to have a whole lot.'

'There are more there but, at the moment, the whole site is still covered with snow. We could try the University I suppose, they might have something relevant, even if it's from some other site.'

'OK. What we have now is a snow covered site of a possible exhibition, at least that gives us time to plan the operation; that'll be a nice change, most projects in this department are of the do it yesterday variety.'

'Suppose we invite the University Department of Archaeology to come out for a look see as soon as the snow clears? If they agree, we could ask the Department of Education to act as sponsor for the project and, all this department would have to do is act as co-ordinators. That way, we get the prestige for organising the thing without being responsible for the exhibits or their interpretation; as I said, I'm no expert but they might cough up some of the money too.'

'Frank, I like you. You're thinking like a public relations man already.'

More coffee arrived. Frank smiled at her and thanked the girl.

'I just love that English accent.'

'You'll have to get used to it', Gerald told her, 'I'm hoping Frank here will be able to join us on this project.'

She smiled at Frank. 'Promise me you won't learn to speak like a Canadian. We need someone here with an educated accent.'

Gerald waved her away. 'Push off darling, flirt on your own time.'

He winked at Frank. 'Every office has one, she's ours.'

It was agreed that the best way to display the finds was to, somehow, preserve them in-situ; the University would have to advise on this. Frank suggested a giant tepee over the site.

'How about we get one of those wooden cigar store Indians to stand outside?'

'How about we get a real one?'

'You're kidding.'

'No. I know a real Indian Chief who is also an expert on the exhibits and, he's available.'

'How come?'

'He's a regular inmate at the reformatory. He reckons that, as we built our reformatory on his ancestral homestead, we owe him a home. He comes in every winter.'

'Is he safe?'

'Oh sure. He's a harmless bottom pincher but that's from choice; he's bright enough if you ask the right questions.'

'Does he know about the Indians back then?'

'Don't be ridiculous, nobody does, that's what makes the site interesting.'

'You like this guy!'

'I recognise a character when I see one. We used to have quite a lot at sea, people who got bored with being ordinary so evolved into something a little different. I think the world is a much better place as a result.'

'I think I'm talking to one now.'

'Oh I'm as normal as you are, if you are.'

'Would he do it? I mean, would he be prepared to just stand there and chat to the kids?'

'I don't know. I'll ask him, if you think this department would hire him.'

'You'll have to leave that one with me. I'll have to ask about that one higher up.'

Frank followed the idea, just to see where it would lead. 'Then, there are the other possibilities. We could use him to give lectures on Indian culture and history to the school kid's mothers at the Mothers' Union and Townswomen's Guild groups, they'd be a natural audience. You know, learn about your country's past and meet a real, live but entirely safe Indian at the same time. Absolute safety guaranteed, no chance of rape or pillage though that might be regarded as a disappointment by some.'

Gerald held up his hand. 'Stop! Slow down, at least, I'll do a note to my boss this afternoon and maybe we can all get together for a bull session later in the week. The more I think about this project, the more I like the idea. We might just have a winner and that won't do the department or our careers any harm at all. We're quite a new department, you see and not everyone sort of accepts us yet, they don't understand what PR is all about, where it fits in.'

As Frank took the elevator to the lobby, he was joined by the girl who had brought them coffee.

'I wanted to warn you. Don't let Gerald take all the credit for your ideas, he will, if he can. That's how you get promoted in this business.'

'Now that's a kind gesture', Frank said,' I'll try not to let him make me into a, what is it? A Patsy? Is that right?'

'You take care. Give me a call if you need any inside information; my name's Jesse; extension 2133.'

Outside in the cold, Frank pulled up the collar of the coat Loretta had given him. A bit too woodsman for the city but it was the only heavy coat he had. Anyway, perhaps there was a new job in the offing; more money meant new coats as well as other things. He slammed the car door on the cold wind, let in the clutch and headed out of town.

'I didn't expect to see you again today', Loretta said, 'get the bum's rush?'

'Not exactly. I was asked if I'd go and work there; more money!'

'Take it. If you think it's something you can do and it's more money, take it. You could stay here of course and, in twenty years or so, might be Bursar but exciting it ain't.'

'It's not certain yet, just a suggestion, no specific offer yet. I suspect that what they really want is my knowledge and ideas so that they can claim it all originated in their department.'

'If the offer comes, take it. Its something I think you might be good at, I think you have style and that's wasted clerking in this damned prison.'

'I have to go back for another meeting later this week, don't know yet when, there's to be a bull session with the department's boss. If they decide this is all a good idea, then, perhaps, they'll offer me a job.'

'Well, you watch yourself. Don't let them bleed you of all your ideas then throw you out and claim the credit for themselves.'

'Funny you should say that. I was warned about the fellow I'm dealing with by one of the girls in his own office, said he would do just that if I gave him half a chance.'

'You keep away from girls in offices, or anywhere else for that matter. You've got all the girl you need already and, I'm it!'

'Promises, promises. Can I get you a cup of coffee? '

'Why not, it's been one of those days; Paul has got trouble with Brenda.   Seems she wants to go to Europe for a holiday this spring and he reckons he can't afford it.'

'So, what's his problem?'

'She reckons he can!'

'Perhaps they should talk it over with their bank manager? Give him the casting vote.'

'There, you see, I said you're wasted here as a clerk. You let him tell you his tale of woe and suggest that they talk it over with their bank manager. He'll suggest that to Brenda and, if she refuses, he's off the hook   If she agrees, he's off the hook anyway as the manager will tell her that they can't afford it. Brilliant!'

'What happens if the bank manager says that they can afford it or offers them a loan to cover the trip?'

'Then, lover, you are in the shit up to your neck for suggesting that they should ask him. See?   Being smart ain't necessarily being clever!'

There had been a couple of new entries, Frank looked through the registration forms. Nothing to get excited about, perhaps Loretta was right, exciting it wasn't but he'd been glad enough to get it a few months ago. He wondered what Marley would think of the idea of being a paid lecturer in Indian Affairs?

He completed the new entries' registrations and filed the forms.

'You busy?'

'Hi Paul. What's on your mind?'

'Brenda.   She wants to go to Europe for a month in the spring. We just bought a new car, the house needs some work done on it and I promised her I'd do something with the garden this year. She wants me to plant flowers, would you believe? Flowers!'

'So what's wrong with flowers?'

'She wants them in a rockery! She saw some pictures in a magazine showing a rock garden so, now she wants one. Have you any idea how many rocks I would need to build a rock garden in my back yard? Hundreds! It'll cost a fortune.'

'You don't have to build the height with rocks, you know. You build the different levels with dirt then place the rocks strategically on top. You could probably get a couple of truck loads of dirt from the pit there, they have to dig out great heaps of the stuff to get at the shale underneath. The rocks might be more of a problem but once you've created a couple of hills and a valley in your back yard, the rocks shouldn't cost you the earth; no pun intended; you could take Brenda to Europe to buy seeds for the flowers.'

'Thanks friend! That's all I needed.'

'You could tell her that you can't really do the garden until you've been to Europe to see how they do it. That puts the garden off until next year and, if you're in Europe, you can't be doing the house up, can you?'

'Will I like Europe?'

'Who cares? You'll do as you're told, like the rest of us. Just don't drink the beer in England, you won't like it.'

'I don't know, I just don't know if we can afford it.'

'Why don't you talk it over with your bank manager? Tell Brenda to smile at him.'

'I might just do that, thanks.'

'Anytime.'

CHAPTER FORTY-ONE

Frank's transfer followed shortly after his second meeting with the PR Department. Gerald had introduced him to Michael Stuart who headed up the department and he had moved into his new desk the following week. At the reformatory, Frank's work was returned to Gordon and Paul who had said how sorry they were that he was going 'You're the best thing that's happened around here for a long time. Things seem to happen when you're around; mostly it's dead boring.'

Cherry didn't agree, she whispered into Gordon's ear. 'Paul will soon change his mind when the extra work comes back to his desk. You make good and sure that he doesn't pass most of it on to you just because you're junior. You stick up for yourself. Frank's done alright for himself by pushing, it's about time you pushed yourself forward.'

Gordon nodded. 'Frank's the sort of Englishman who gets us immigrants a bad name here in Canada, pushing himself forward like that; who does he think he is, God's gift to Canada? Don't worry, he'll get his come-uppance downtown at Parliament Buildings, they'll soon spot that he's only got this far because Loretta fancies him. I reckon we're well rid of him, maybe things can now get back to normal, like it was before he poked his nose in.'

'I hope you're right, I never liked him.'

Mac told Frank to keep the car. 'You can use it as a trade-in now you can afford a new one. No one will want it but will get you a discount if you haggle a little. '

At the risk of upsetting Bob and Agnes, he had moved out of his basement apartment. The snow had been above the window line for eight or nine weeks now and constant artificial light made it less attractive, he had dug out the windows two or three times but they always snowed up again.

'Where will you be living?'

'I'm moving in with Loretta, it'll save a lot of travelling!'

Agnes frowned at him. 'I'm not at all sure that I should approve but good luck anyway. I'm sure she's really a nice girl. If she isn't, you come on back here, you hear me?'

It was from his new desk therefore that Frank rang Mac to arrange an interview with Robert Marley to discuss the possibility of his employment by the Department.

'If you can still find your way here, I'll lay it on for three tomorrow afternoon, OK?'

'That's fine, thanks.'

'Pop into my office while you're here, let me know how your project is going and whether I have to do anything, OK?'

'Fine. See you at about half past three tomorrow, then.'

'I thought you might need this. Jesse handed him a cup of coffee, how's it going? Have you found your way around the building yet?'

'I know the way to and from this office and I've found the cafeteria but, as for the rest, it might as well be Outer Mongolia'

'Come with me, I'll give you the grand tour. There's a great view over the lake from the roof, some of us girls go up there in the summer to get an all-over tan. I'll tell the other girls that, from now on it ain't out of bounds, its Outer Mongolia, they'll like that.' Frank made a mental note to misunderstand the implied invitation to visit the roof in the summer; Loretta would kill him.

The tour lasted about an hour. Jesse introduced him to a lot of other girls, with what could only be described as a proprietorial air and some of the other men who might be useful to him.

'In this business,' she told him, 'it's frequently who you know not what you know that counts.'

Andrew Rolls was introduced by Gerald later that afternoon. 'Frank, this is Andrew, he will be doing the artwork for the display panels. I'll leave you two together to sort out what you think is best, just let me have a look at the rough sketches before you get stuck in to the real thing, OK?'

They worked through the afternoon, sketching out the general effect they wanted; the general impression of a forest in the background with more detailed trees and shrubs in the middle and one or two half clear animal shapes amongst the foliage immediately behind the beach. Blue water of the lake at the foot of the picture contrasted with the green-white of the glacier visible at the top, behind the trees.

'What do you think?'

'I think you've done this sort of thing before.'

'I was trained as a book illustrator but nobody reads now!'

'When we've talked to the university, we can rough out some of the side panels with detailed studies of animals, birds, etc. Perhaps, if they still exist, we can get some examples to show.'

'How do we prevent Gerald getting all the credit for this project?'

Andrew gave him an old fashioned look. 'It doesn't matter what Gerald says to get us the funding for this job, he's very good at that. It'll be obvious to everyone that he doesn't understand any of it, and that you do; don't worry about the office politics, you're too recently off the boat. If you get this job right, you'll be OK in this department until you upset Michael. No one upsets Michael and gets away with it.'

Frank recognised the voice of experience, Andrew had obviously seen them come and go.

'OK Andrew, you lead, I'll follow.'

Robert Marley sat, rolling his cigarette between finger and thumb as Frank spoke. 'I'm deadly serious. You told me you were interested in the findings down the pit and I've found a way to combine that interest with a well paid job, he question is, can you stay sober long enough to do it? I'm not joking!'

He looked at Frank. 'Guess I deserved that one. Hell, man, I only drink for amusement and it makes sure that I can come back here every winter. The question is, why should I do it?'

Frank pushed the ashtray towards him, the ash from the cigarette was about to fall on to the table between them.

'When we spoke before, you told me that the Canadians didn't reckon Indians. That you had no chance of getting a decent job so you might as well act the part of the kind of Indian they did believe in, OK? Well, now you've got an offer of a chance to teach the white men's kids what the Indians are really like. Teach them some Canadian history as seen from the other side.'

'We weren't the other side, man. The war was between the English and the French. Neither of them gave a damn for the Indian, he was just a fucking pawn in the game of empire building. Hell, if either of them had really given a damn what happened to us we could have exploited that weakness and neither of you would have colonised my country.'

'The question is, could you work up a lecture along those lines without the F word and, another to follow that and, another to follow that? I don't need an arsehole, I need an assistant.'

'What does it pay?'

'I don't know yet but, its got to be better than working on the municipal garbage dump where you were last time you worked.'

'There's nothing wrong with working for the Cleansing Department, my old man's happy enough. It's honest, respectable and the pay ain't that bad, for an Indian!'

'Does that mean you're in?'

'It means I'm thinking about it. God help you if it ain't on the level.'

'My God is a benevolent God. He looks after children, idiots and drunks, I can't lose.'

'Like I said before, you ain't half bad, for a paleface.'

'Peace?'

'Peace.'

Mac's office looked out over the car park.

'I see you got shot of the old Humber.'

'Yeah, now I drive an old Olds. It's bigger, heavier and hell on gasoline but, at least the steering wheel is on the right side of the car!'

Mac's secretary put a tray of coffee on the table. 'So, how's your big project going?'

Frank told him what had happened at Parliament Buildings and what he had just discussed with Marley. 'Actually. Robert Edward Marley, Chief of the Etobicoke Indians, etc., is almost critically important to the success of the scheme. It would be possible, of course, to manage without him but I think that a genuine Indian Chief explaining the old times to the kids would be a natural, don't you?'

'How come you never got further than Leading Signalman in the navy?'

'Too independent, I probably wouldn't have made that far if the Germans hadn't kept killing off the competition. They had to promote someone and, eventually I guess, I was next in line.'

'Were you any good at it?'

"Actually yes. I had no trouble with the technical side of things, it was the Yes Sir, No Sir that I had trouble with; never could quite get the hang of making it sound sufficiently servile. Respectful I had no trouble with but you know the Andrew, that wasn't what the career officers wanted. As far as they were concerned, the RN was a social club and we were just the servants. The RNVR's were alright though. They were treated like us by the Regular pigs who reckoned that RNVR stood for Really Not Very Reliable so we had a certain sympathy with each other's position. Anyway, they had a proper job to go back to after the war so they weren't too bothered.'

'You'll get on OK over here. We're a Bolshie lot of buggers but it's a great country to be a part of, I couldn't go back'

'I've nothing to go back for.'

'I thought I heard you had a wife and a kid back there. Will you bring them over?'

'Loretta has been speaking out of turn.'

'She only told me when I asked her if you were going to marry her. Don't hurt her boy, she's a friend of mine.'

'She's a friend of mine too.'

They drank their coffee.

'Have you heard the news from Europe?'

Frank looked up from his notes. 'Should I have?'

'The Ruskies are making waves, trying to stop the allied military convoys getting in to Berlin.'

'Ah well, it's none of our business now.'

'I hope not. We don't need another war in Europe before we've paid for the last one. And, I doubt if the US or any of the Commonwealth countries for that matter would want to get involved in Europe again, we lost too many men already!'

'The Yanks would have no choice if the fuss is in Berlin. They're one of the three occupying powers. Still, I doubt if it will come to anything, the Ruskies can't afford another war either.'

'Nope, guess you're right there.'

'I'll come over again in about a week and we can organise whatever is necessary for the University people to come and examine the site. You never know, they might decide it's all a waste of time, then I'm out of a job again.'

Frank dismissed all thoughts of Berlin, the Russians and wars in Europe from his mind, it was none of his business. His business was to organise the reformatory exhibition, make a new life for himself in Canada and to forget all about Europe; Europe had had its share of his life. From here on in, it was look after number one time!

He wondered what would happen to Alice and the child if another war started in Europe; he couldn't just leave them to the tender mercies of an invading Russian army. He knew what invading Russian armies did to women, he had seen the newsreels of Berlin before the division had been accomplished. He swerved to avoid an oncoming car he hadn't seen, cursing himself and telling himself to concentrate on his driving.

He parked the car in the underground park and took the elevator up to his office; he would ring the University in the morning to arrange for an interview with the head of the Archaeological Department. He had written to him already but one thing he had learned in Canada was, no one answered letters. You either phoned them or you went to see them if you wanted something done; you don't write to them!

Jesse said Hi as he sat down. He put his notes into the wallet file on his desk and picked up the phone.

'Can I have a word, Michael? We need to talk about this Indian.'

'I guess we can but I'm not sold on that idea yet. You'll have to convince me we need him. I don't like Indians, they're a bunch of no goods, if you ask me.'

CHAPTER FORTY-TWO

Dr. Arnolds of the Department of Archaeology, agreed to see Frank on the third of March to discuss the finds at the reformatory site. Had Frank ensured that they weren't interfered with?

'Right now, they're under about two feet of snow but I have arranged for the whole area to be roped off until we have been down there.'

'OK, look forward to it. Can't say I've ever been in prison before.'

'Best you don't call it that while you're there, they're a bit touchy about it. It's a reformatory, there's a difference.'

'What difference?'

'Look at it this way', Frank suggested, not eager to get involved in a long discussion about custodial theory. 'It's like Universities; as Red Brick is to Ivy League so reformatory is to penitentiary.'

'Is that right?'

'Not entirely but it's near enough for our purposes.' He put the phone down.

'Why did you tell Mac that I had a wife and child back in England?'

Loretta lay cuddled up to him on the settee, listening to records.

'I couldn't tell him that I had a husband in the funny farm, now could I? He doesn't know about him, nobody does.'

'Just what did you say?'

'I told him that we couldn't marry because you had a wife and kid back in England, that' all.'

'Well, he now thinks I'm a miserable bastard who has run out on his wife and kid and is using that as an excuse for not marrying you! Thanks a bunch.'

'Sorry. I wasn't ready for the question and said the first thing that came into my head.'

'Well, I told him that they were the past and that you were the future .So, now, you're the sort of miserable bastard that would steal another woman's husband, I guess that makes us even.'

'He knew that already, I'm afraid. Our thing lasted about three years.'

She sat quietly for a moment. 'Did you mean that?'

'What?'

'That I'm the future.'

'Only because I'm too lazy to look for anyone else.'

Her elbow forced two of his ribs apart as she dug it into him.

'Hey, that hurts!'

'Well, say it nicely then. Say you're my future, as if you mean it.'

'You're my future because I love you.'

'Do you really?'

'Love you? I'm terrified of you! I was warned when I joined the office that you were a hard case and that I should not, under any circumstances, upset you if I wanted to keep my job.'

'But you don't work for me anymore.'

'Perhaps I've just got used to you.'

She kissed him and stood up. 'You put some more records on that thing while I make some more coffee.'

When she got back from the tiny kitchen, Glenn Miller was playing Yours Is My Heart Alone; not in 3:4 time as any other band would but in 4:4. Muted trombones followed by a tenor sax leading to a chorus of trumpets. Not perhaps, as romantic as the original arrangement but beautiful anyway.

'I like just sitting here, cuddling up with you and listening to music. You won't leave me, will you?'

Frank tightened his hold round her shoulder, drawing her tighter against him. 'No chance.'

'There's something I ought to tell you, if we are going to spend the rest of our lives together. You might want to change your mind.'

'What's that? I already know you're married to someone else, that I'm not your first boyfriend outside wedlock and that you're not sweet sixteen in spite of looking as if you were. What else have you got secreted away with the skeleton in the cupboard?'

'I can't have kids.'

'Kids I have already, well one anyway. That's no problem as far as I'm concerned. If that's the worst thing you have to tell me, we'll get along just fine.'

'You really mean that? That you don't want kids?'

'I mean it.'

'Don't you want to know why?'

'Sweetheart, neither of us is sixteen anymore. If you want me to know, you'll probably tell me; it's none of my business.'

'I want you to know. It was when I was with my husband. He kicked me when I was pregnant. I miscarried and nearly died. Now I can't have any more babies, they took out my womb.'

'Lover, they left your heart and that's the only bit I'm bothered about.'

'The only bit?'

'Now then, this is supposed to be a romantic discussion about our future, not the build-up to another bout of sexual athletics.'

'Can't one develop into the other?'

'Not without some encouragement.'

She placed his hand over her breast, the forefinger and thumb over the top button of her blouse.

'How about we play a little hide and seek?' Her hand dropped to his thigh.

'Thank God that record player has an autodeck I should hate to have to get up every three minutes to change the record.'

'If you could get up every three minutes, that would be a record! Now, take me into the bedroom and explain in detail how much you love me, I need to be convinced and, it may take some time.'

CHAPTER FORTY-THREE

Mac stood at the window in his office watching the dozer bulldoze the new road down in to the pit. The snow had gone and Frank had warned him that he would be bringing three professors from the university to examine the beach level site on Wednesday. He had chosen mid-week he said in the hope that it would cause less hassle.

Standing there, Mac could feel the beginning of a twinge of excitement about the plans for the pit project. The first time he had actually felt excitement about anything for quite a few years. Thinking about it, he realised that he never seemed to make plans nowadays, not even for the summer vacation. Even that had become just something that they did; he and Betty.

He couldn't remember the last time they had sat down together with the map spread out on the dining room table, looking for somewhere different to go, the last time they had packed the picnic gear in the trunk of the car and just drifted, following the country roads through the lakes. I must be a miserable old bugger, he thought.

This summer, I'll take Betty to Europe. The war is over, I'll take Betty to England. I wonder if any of the England I remember is even still there?

More than twenty years! Christ, was it really that long since he got off the boat and started his new life in the new world? It had been fun in those days but they too had been young in those days! He would talk to Betty this evening. They could sit down and plan the trip like they used to when they were first married. The telephone rang.

'Singleton here, Bursar. What are we going to do with these professors? How about security? Do you want anything special laid on?'

'Don't ask me, I'm the Bursar not the Governor. Ask Steve.' Bloody Singleton. Hated approaching the Governor directly in case he made a fool of himself.

The Governor's secretary put his call through. 'Captain Singleton here, Governor. I was just wondering about special security for the professors' visit on Wednesday. Do you think we should lay on some extra guards?'

'Why? We're trying to keep the inmates in not the professors out. Have you heard about a possible breakout?'

'Well, no but I just thought perhaps a few extra guards with guns would impress them. You never know who they might be talking to downtown.'

'If they talk to anybody downtown and tell them we laid on extra guards, downtown will want to know who authorised the overtime payments. No Captain, forget it.'

'If you say so, Governor.'

Governor, Steve Boness put the phone down. That Singleton guy was a pain in the arse, wouldn't take responsibility for anything, always wanted a decision from higher up and that, God help him, meant from him. He had hoped that Singleton would grow into the job, feel comfortable in it after a while but it was three years now and he still asked Steve about everything, unless he asked Mac. He rang Mac.

'What's the score on this professorial visit to the hole in the ground, Mac?'

'We have three of them coming over on Wednesday to examine the beach and remains plus the other bits and pieces that Marley has collected in the past. He has them in his locker, says they're his, finders keepers or something. It's all part of this schools visit thing we discussed last fall.'

'Yeah, I remember. Do you think it might be politic to ask the PR department to let us have a progress report and projection?'

'To be perfectly honest Steve, I've been keeping as far back from the workface on this as I can. Didn't want to involve this department in anything unnecessary. I've kept in touch with Frank Bye though, so that I know what's going on.'

'OK Mac. But keep an eye on it eh? Don't want it getting out of hand.'

Mac gave Frank a call and passed on the message. We're all getting too damned careful he thought, watching our professional backs, taking out professional insurance, making damned sure that, if it all goes wrong, it ain't us that's in the shit!

The three professors arrived. Two were bearded, trying to make themselves look older and more learned but succeeding only in making themselves look like young men with beards. The other was a complete contrast; jeans and mountaineer's boots with a heavy, lumberjack style coat to keep out the cold.

Frank already knew him as Dr Arnolds, the other two were introduced as Dr Anderson and Dr Bathers, zoology and anthropology respectively. Clearly, the heads of their departments were not going to risk tramping all the way out here when there might well be nothing to look at. Since Frank had last been down the pit, a row of white painted posts linked by white rope had been stuck into the ground to fence off the area he wanted them to look at. He led them down to the level showing a blaze of sand and gravel. 'What do you think?'

'Is this it? Is this all you've got?' It was anthropology speaking, bending down and looking carefully at the fireplace. 'How do you know this is old, that some joker hasn't just put it here for a joke?"'

'Because this is a prison, not a university.'

'Someone said you had more.'

'Yes. Until I spotted this and recognised it, no one took any notice of a few bones and blackened sticks except Chief Littlehorse, that is, he knew what they were and collected them.'

'Ah yes, your tame Indian'

'If he was totally tame, he wouldn't be in here and he wouldn't have been able to rescue the finds. Would you like to meet him?'

'I don't think that will be necessary. I doubt we shall be needing his specialist knowledge; he's a drunk isn't he?'

'So was Winston Churchill!'

'Yes, well, shall we look about a bit more?' Dr Bathers turned to the others. 'What do you think?'

Arnolds winked at Frank. 'It looks OK to me, even if there ain't much of it. What do you say Anderson?'

'Well, the bones are primarily fish of a type still common in the lake or, which were common until Toronto discharged too much sewage into it.

Nothing special about them but some of the other bones are not immediately identifiable, I'd have to take them back to the lab for a closer look. We could try and work out their age once we've identified them.' He turned to Frank. 'You say you have more?'

'I don't but the Chief does. I'll have them boxed up and bring them over for you in a day or so if that's OK.'

'Yeah, great.'

'What about the beach level? Should we uncover some more of it?'

'No. I'll send some of my students over to do that', Arnolds was a great believer in setting his students to work in the field. 'At least they'll know what not to do. I'll tell them to keep in touch with you, OK?'

They climbed back up to the old road, the new road was already busy with trucks loading shale. Clearly the Governor was not about to let anyone get the idea that he ran a soft unit.

They walked over to the Governor's office for coffee and biscuits. Captain Singleton watched them go in then knocked and bustled in unnecessarily. 'Everything OK? No problems, I trust?'

If there was going to be any credit arising from this visit, he wanted his share. He introduced himself. 'I'm Singleton, I'm I/C security here.'

Frank took advantage of his entry. 'Ah, Captain Singleton, I wonder could one of your men collect a box of bits and pieces from Marley? ' He explained what he wanted.

'Box of bits and pieces from Marley, yes, er, fine. I'll put someone on to it straight away.' He saluted, turned and left the office, closing the door carefully behind him.

'Where did you find him,' Arnolds asked, 'I thought they only existed in ancient British movies.'

'Don't be unkind', the Governor winked, 'he's good at his job and he can be very useful to you, or not if he chooses.'

'Ah, I understand Governor, thank you.' He picked up a biscuit, 'I'll keep that in mind.'

They all piled into Frank's Oldsmobile. 'I would be grateful for any assistance you can give me on identifying the flora and fauna of the period of the beach and any bright ideas about how to make the information interesting to school kids. As you know, this project is being mounted in association with the Department of Education, that's your Boss, ain't it?' The question was ingenuous and Frank's expression artless.

'Well, not actually our Boss but we do work closely with them on occasion. Are they funding this project?'

'It looks like a joint effort between the Provincial Public Relations Department and the Department of Education. I imagine that between them, they could scare up a few Dollars for research time, that sort of thing. I doubt if they would want to spend a lot though, the school kids don't have votes yet.'

He was still laughing to himself when he got back to his office.

'So what's pleasing you?'

Frank told Andrew what he had done.

'That should get them moving. There's nothing quite so attractive to university departments as jointly funded research projects. They love to play one department off against another; great fun.'

'Yes, they seemed to like the idea.'

'What are you going to tell them when they discover that there is only this department involved and that funding is strictly limited   ?'

'I shall appear just as shocked and surprised as they are. It never occurred to me that Education wouldn't help fund a school kids' exhibition.'

'I'm glad you're on our side.'

'Well, you know how slowly finance departments work. By the time they realise the true position, it will be too late to cancel. Most of the work will have been done.'

'If I were you, I'd get the bones and stuff over to them soonest, before it all goes sour.'

'I'll collect them tomorrow and take them right over to Arnolds. We need to keep their shoulders to the wheel and their noses to the grindstone but not their ears to the ground, eh?'

Loretta thought it was amusing too, when he told her. 'I hope you haven't gone out too far on this limb of yours. Remember, you're expendable should the need arise. Stuart will happily throw you overboard if he needs the only lifebelt.'

'I suppose I could always go back to the Vet's Office and start again.'

'You may have to. Still, if as you say, it's just along the corridor from your present office, perhaps you should stick your head in their door one day and make the time of day. Drink a cup of coffee with them, thank them for all their help, tell them how well you're doing now then, when you do get fired, you have only to walk a few doors down the hall to get rehired.'

'I might just do that small thing. A little bit of personal PR never did any harm. It's like when we were kids, we always wrote long thank you notes for any present we got, in the hope that it would ensure that we got another next Christmas of birthday or whatever. I'm sure it helped.'

'You're a devious bastard but I love you. You didn't have relatives to send you presents.'

'You are beautiful and I love you. Too'

'That's what I mean. I'm not beautiful but you are devious.' She kissed him. 'Shall we drive up to High Park this evening? It's a fine day and I feel like doing a little necking in public, well, in a public car park anyway; it makes me feel less like an old lady.'

'Why not? If all else fails we can always watch the other couples; get a few pointers, perhaps.'

They sat close together in the car, watching the darkening sky over the lake. The radio played softly, the light behind the dashboard dial giving a dim glow inside the car. Their hips touching, Loretta turned to him. 'Are you going to kiss me or do I have to scream for help?'

He kissed her, gently at first then forcing her lips apart, thrusting his tongue between her teeth. She bit it.

'Hey! That hurt.'

'So slow down. We didn't come up here for a quicky, we have lots of time and, when I'm ready, I might let you take me home.'

Her breast felt warm through her dress. Cupping it in his hand, he could feel her heart beating slowly and steadily. His fingers found the nipple and squeezed lightly and he felt it harden, she was not wearing a bra.

She twisted on the car's bench seat and the leather squeaked as she pressed herself against him, giggling. His knee moved gently upwards against hers, pushing her skirt up her thighs, his hand dropped, finding with unerring accuracy the warm flesh above her stocking. She smacked his hand, lifted it and pressed it against the button-through bodice of her dress.

If God had meant people to make love sitting side by side in the front of a car, Frank thought, He'd have given men two right arms. He unfastened the buttons, sliding his hand into the warmth within. Her hand pressed gently on the back of his neck, pushing his mouth down towards the now rock hard nipple. A line from ITMA, the wartime comedy series on English wireless flitted through his mind as he buried his head in her. 'Don't forget the diver, Sir, don't forget the diver.'

He felt the giggle start in his belly, gather force, rise against his ribs and force its way between his lips.

'I'm sorry, just thought of something and couldn't help it.'

She pushed him away. 'Now look what you've done. You'll have to start all over.'

A car pulled in beside them, its lights sweeping across the trees in front of and below them before being switched off. In that short moment, Loretta saw the girl in the blue dress being dragged out of a car parked on the roadway further down the hill, her blonde hair pulled over her face. She reached across Frank and switched on the headlights, flooding the view with their hard, white light. On the road below them, the man looked up towards the light, momentarily loosening his grip on the girl who broke free.

'God, I know her', Frank said, 'her name's Sarah, she's a nurse at St Joseph's.'

He was already out of the car, turning to tell Loretta to keep the lights on and to get the other cars to help illuminate the area below them. 'If any of them have their trousers on, I could use a little help!'

He tripped, rolled and recovered himself before reaching the bottom of the hill and the road where the car was parked. He called out.

'Sarah! Its Frank Bye, come to me, you'll be OK.'

He stood still, letting the light show where he was, hoping that Sarah had heard his call and could see him. In the trees below and to his left, he could hear someone running on the tar macadam path but couldn't tell whether the steps were coming towards him or going away. He stilled his heavy breathing and listened again, the runner had stopped. He shouted again.

'Sarah. Its Frank Bye, come to me!'

Behind him he could hear others coming down the hill. One of them even had a flashlight, swinging it back and forth across the trees in front of them, hoping to catch a glimpse of the girl or the man. He heard Loretta's voice behind him. 'I'll take the number of the car, the Police can trace him from that.'

'What the hell are you doing here lady', one of the searchers asked, 'this guy could be dangerous!'

'He'd only be dangerous to me the once', Frank heard her tell him, 'after that he'd probably be dead.'

'Suit yourself lady.'

They gathered round Frank and the parked car, quiet, listening for some hint of where the quarry was.

'There!' One shouted, pointing to the left where Frank had heard them earlier. 'They're over there.'

He ran off into the trees followed by Frank, Loretta and three others. Ahead of them now, they could hear someone running, crashing through any undergrowth that got in the way. The man was obviously running away now, abandoning his prey and his car. Frank stopped again. Listened and called out. 'Sarah, its Frank Bye. Come to me. You'll be alright now, he's legged it.'

In the bushes to his right Frank heard a sob.

'Sarah?'

He heard another sob. 'Sarah, are you there?'

He pushed through the undergrowth almost falling over Sarah, curled up in the foetal position, sobbing quietly, trying not to attract attention to her hiding place.

'OK Sarah. It's Frank Bye, you remember, we met on the boat. You were with Judy. We got to know each other quite well, didn't we? You remember me, don't you?'

She didn't move but the sobbing got louder as she relaxed. The other searchers had returned.

'No sign of him now, whoever he was.'

'OK and thanks for your help. I'll get Loretta to help her up while I get my car, we'll take her home. Get a doctor to look after her, just in case.'

Loretta pushed her way over to the prostrate girl. 'Come on Sarah', she said, 'we'll get you home, OK?'

Frank heard one of the departing searchers comment that an evening in the park wasn't usually this exciting. Another replied that in another two minutes he would have been in no condition to run after anybody.

Frank brought the car down to where Loretta and the girl were waiting, talking quietly. He pulled up and opened the rear doors.

'You'd better both sit in the back 'til we get Sarah home. Sarah, where's home?'

She told him how to get there, whispering it into Loretta's shoulder. Frank let in the clutch gently rolling the car forward. He drove out of the park and on to the main road, sliding into the traffic stream without pausing and heading east towards the hospital and the nurses hostel.

In the back, he could hear Sarah still sobbing, being cuddled by Loretta. He heard Loretta talking to her quietly, reassuringly; telling her everything was going to be OK that she was alright now.

'I want to go home', he heard her say.

'Yes dear, that's where we're taking you now. We're taking you home.'

'No, I mean home', Sarah sobbed, 'home to England. I hate it here!'

Loretta comforted her as much as she could. 'You'll be alright in a minute, we're almost there.'

At the entrance to the Nurses Hostel, Frank rang the bell long and hard. It took a few minutes but, eventually, Mrs Backlaker appeared, wrapping her dressing gown round her.

'So where's the fire?'

She looked at Frank then, at Sarah and Loretta. Frank explained.

She scooped up Sara into her arms, 'OK my dear, you're home now. I'll look after you.' She carried Sarah into the lounge like a baby, helping her sit down in one of the large, overstuffed, comfortable looking armchairs. She lifted the telephone from its wall cradle and dialled and spoke.

'Hall, this is Mrs Backlaker. I want the duty MO in the Nurses hostel now!' She replaced the instrument without waiting for an answer.

'Right', she said, 'we'd better take her up to her room. You', she turned to Frank,' keep your eyes to yourself if any of the girls' doors are open. I'm not sure you should be in here at all but you claim to be a friend and if Sarah doesn't mind I suppose a friend might be useful just now. I suppose I'd better call the police too.'

CHAPTER FORTY-FOUR

Loretta sat down on the edge of the bed beside Sarah who had, again, curled up trying to make herself as small as she could. She stroked her hair.

'It's alright Sarah, it's alright now. You have a good cry, we won't tell.' She turned to Frank. Have you been in here before?'

'No. I knew they, Sarah and her friend Judy that is, were coming to work here but I haven't seen either of them since we arrived at the station.'

'What a coincidence! If we hadn't been in the park and that car hadn't swung its lights across just when it did, we'd just have read about this in the papers. Uncanny isn't it?'

'Do you reckon the police will be able to catch the man?'

'Shouldn't have too much trouble. We have the car's registration number and he's certain to be local if he's dating nurses from here.'

'Judy's just as bad.' Sarah's voice was tiny but stronger than it had been earlier.

'What do you mean?'

'She's always touching me when we're alone. I told her I don't like it but she keeps doing it. She keeps saying that she'll look after me and that I'll get used to being in Canada but that's not what she means. I'm sure it isn't.'

The sobbing came again, full throated, from the heart now, rushing out pell mell, without any attempt at moderation or restraint; almost as if, at last, someone had broken a dam and released a flood.

Mrs Backlaker came through the door, her eye immediately on Frank to make sure he wasn't touching the girl or looking where he shouldn't.

'The doctor is on his way from Casualty and the police will be here in a few minutes and you'll have to give a statement; who are you, anyway?'

Frank introduced himself and explained who Loretta was. 'I'm Frank Bye, this is Loretta Vetchik We saw her being attacked in High Park. Some guy was pulling her out of his car, trying to pull her into the underbrush. Pure coincidence but I recognised Sarah, we came over on the same boat last Fall, I knew she had been coming here to work. We don't know who the guy was though.'

'Archie, he's a porter in the OR.' Sarah's voice was stronger now. 'We've been out before but he's never done anything like this before.'

Mrs Backlaker's hackles rose almost visibly. 'He'll never do anything like this again, either!'

'He just went crazy. He dragged me out of the car and called me an English prick teaser.'

The doctor looked in through the door. 'OK if I come in?'

Frank took Loretta's hand and made for the door. 'We'd better leave and let him get on with it.'

Mrs Backlaker led them down to the lounge again, pointed to the coffee machine and went back upstairs, leaving them alone. Loretta was obviously upset, now that Sarah couldn't see her. Frank took her in his arms, trying to return to her some of the comfort she had given to Sarah.

'Well, you can't say that life with me is uninteresting!'

'On the whole lover, I think I'd have preferred tonight without the floorshow. All I wanted was a little gentle snogging then back to my place. I think you're trying too hard with the entertainment.'

The policeman was shown into the lounge by Mrs Backlaker. 'You'll want to interview these two first', she said. 'They can tell you what happened. The doctor is with Sarah at the moment.'

'You the couple that found the girl?' He was clearly uninterested, just another boy girl thing.

'No, Frank told him', feeling Loretta stiffen with annoyance beside him, 'I'm the knight on the shining white charger who rescued the damsel in distress. This is Florence Nightingale who dispensed kindness and sympathy!'

The policeman didn't understand a word Frank had said and Loretta took over. She told him who they were and described slowly and with great detail, what had happened. 'I think Frank's the bravest man I've ever met,' she told him.

'That', Frank told her, 'is what the Admiralty thought when they sent me off to war but, you're both wrong, take my word for it.'

The doctor gave Sarah a sedative and ushered Mrs Backlaker out of the room. 'She's alright physically. I'll have another look at her in the morning. She appears to have avoided rape but she's one unhappy little girl, there's obviously something worrying her but I don't think it has anything to do with tonight. It might have brought it to the front of her mind though. I'll have another look at her tomorrow, I might call in a friend for advice.'

They came downstairs. He told the policeman. 'You won't get any sense out of her this evening. I've given her something to make her sleep. She'll be more relaxed in the morning, you can talk to her then.'

'OK. Meanwhile, perhaps we can find this Archie that seems to be responsible for her condition. You say she hasn't been raped?' The doctor nodded. 'Then, he'll probably claim that nothing happened that the girl just panicked when he put his hand on her leg and ran off into the woods where she got scratched and scared in the dark. Doubt if we'll be able to do much but I can try and put the fear of God into him; make him think twice before he tries again.'

It was one in the morning, they had done what they could for Sarah. Frank gunned the engine. 'Let's go home to bed.'

'You're all the same, you men, one track minds!'

'God, not tonight, the mood has left me.'

'Ride off with me, Sir Knight, to your castle and draw up the drawbridge, I don't want us to be disturbed.' Frank drove. 'I mean it, you know, I think you're the bravest man I've ever met. You could have gotten yourself murdered down there in those trees!'

He turned the car into the parking space outside her apartment. 'In that case, you would have called me the silliest man you'd ever met. Now, let's hear no more about it. Let's forget the whole thing, I need a drink.'

He locked the door, pulled the blinds down and led her into the bedroom. 'Should I get you a drink too?'

She didn't answer immediately and he turned to look at her. She had stepped out of the dress that lay at her feet, she stood there naked as the day she was born.

'Christ! You mean you had nothing on under that all evening?'

'If you don't tell that nice policeman, I won't.'

Frank shook his head. 'I definitely need a drink, possibly two.'

Monday morning. Loretta was making a mess in the kitchen assembling breakfast from four slices of toast and some fried eggs and bacon; the radio was on.

'General Lucious D. Clay, the Military Governor of the US Zone in Germany has reported that the Soviet Authority, through who's territory all Berlin bound traffic must pass, has demanded twenty four hours notice of all military and civilian movements and that all personnel should submit to individual documentation and allow all personal belongings to be searched.

'General Clay has refused to conform to this demand. We shall bring you the latest news from Europe as soon as we have it. The US Government has stated that to comply with this demand would render the US army in Germany immobile and that, of course, this is totally unacceptable.

'It is believed that this Soviet demand is the first of an expected series of restrictive measures designed to make the US, British and French joint occupation of Berlin impossible, thus allowing the allied zones in that city to be absorbed into the Soviet sector.

'At home, in Toronto, the temperature is thirty eight degrees and the weather fine. At the University of Toronto, a Professor of archaeology is reported to have discovered a valuable new site of immediately post-glacial colonisation of Ontario by an, as yet, unidentified tribe of pre-Indians. We'll bring you more news about this exciting development as soon as we have it.'

The reporter talked on, but Frank shouted to Loretta. 'Did you hear that? Some Professor from Toronto U has claimed he's discovered a pre-Indian archaeological site. Now I wonder who that could be?'

'Well, what did you expect, your name up in lights?' She put the bacon and eggs in front of him. 'If he is to use his students to excavate the site then, I guess it has to be his site. Anyway, if it all goes wrong now, it ain't your site, it's his!'

'Makes sense, I suppose. So, what do you reckon to this Berlin business?'

'Will it effect you? Will you be called back if it gets nasty?'

'I shouldn't think so. Berlin has to be the army's perks. You can't sail a destroyer up the autobahn.'

'But, are you on some sort of reserve or other? Could they call you back?'

'No. They would have to get me back there first then I would be back on the reserve list. Anyway, there's plenty of ex-sailors there, they don't need me. It's like the song said, it's a wonderful opportunity for someone but it will have to be someone else, not me!'

'If you leave me, I'll kill you.'

'Even if it's just to go to work?'

She kissed him. 'See you this evening Lover. Have a nice day.'

CHAPTER FORTY-FIVE

The artist, Andrew Rolls, was waiting for Frank when he reached the office. He had been, on the Friday afternoon, to see the University people and had had a long session with them designing the artwork for the display.

They had shown him the type of flora that would have been typical at the time and advised on the possibility of finding various types of animals and birds. He had argued that, in a couple of cases, the display would be enhanced by minor inaccuracies in order to give the observer a better view of them and they had accepted his argument that minor inaccuracies were acceptable in order to provide greater clarity for the school children. After all, Professor Arnolds had agreed, the object of the exercise was to get the school kids interested enough to ask questions.

Andrew held up some sketch panels. 'What do you think?'

'Fantastic, have you shown them to Michael yet?'

'No I thought we'd wait until we have some agreed captions, otherwise, it's just a bunch of pictures to him.'

'We need to get something sorted out with Arnolds. I want something from him for a leaflet to be supplied to the teachers too, we have to keep the teachers at least one lesson ahead of the kids.'

'We must show all this to Gerald first. We have to recognise the chain of command, you know.'

'How about Thursday? Should have something by then'

'Fine, say about three?'

Frank marked it in his diary, remembering his talk with Loretta over breakfast. He would see the Professor this afternoon, first he would step down to the Vet's Office, just to make his number. It was Andrew's reference to the chain of command that had reminded him that he was the new boy and, once he had served his purpose, could be fired just as easily as he had been hired and, if this was so, he had best take out a little insurance. He closed the office door behind him.

'Yeah, I remember you. Didn't care what job you got just so long as it paid your hotel bill. How'ya doing?'

Frank filled him in on the developments. 'So, I'm working just down the hall from here. Thought I'd just pop in and pass the time of day and say thanks for your help. I really appreciate it.'

'Glad to have been of help. Its not often anyone comes back and says thanks. '

Back in his own office, Frank phoned the University. Could he pop over to see Arnolds this afternoon? About three, fine. He ate lunch in the cafeteria with Andrew, talking shop.

The Professor shook hands, not something Frank had noticed as common in Canada, perhaps he was conscious that Frank might have heard the news announcement on the radio and might be upset about it. Better be formal until the position became clear. Frank smiled inwardly, nothing much really changes. Canada wasn't that much different.

'Nice to see you again. Hope you didn't mind my announcement to the Press about our little find. I'm afraid one has to do this from time to time. In academic life it ain't what you know that gets you promoted, it's what you have published. When it comes to time for asking for a raise, it pays if they've heard of you.'

'I'm not concerned. Indeed, the more important you can make it sound, the easier it will be to get the funding we need. Everyone wants to be associated with something important.'

'Right. Glad you can take it that way. Now, what can I do for you this afternoon?'

'I was wondering when you would be sending your students down to do their gardening? We need to clear it with security.'

'That's that fellow Singleton, isn't it? I remember him. Won't give us any trouble will he?'

'Just tell your lads to address him as Sir. They'll have him eating out of their hands.'

'I'll have them go over next Monday to lay out the grid and get the feel of the place. We'll take a few pics of the site before we lay out the grid and after then we can do some progress shots during excavation.'

'I'll need a few well chosen words for panel captions and a leaflet I've got to produce for the teachers to crib from. Can you let me have a sentence or two sometime this week? You know the sort of thing, you must have done this sort of thing dozens of times.'

'OK. Meanwhile, could you arrange for the prison people to skim the topsoil off the site after we've done out pre-grid pics? Then we can get the grid lines down and take a few more. It will be one hell of a lot quicker than our team having to skim the whole area by hand.'

'I'll have a word with the Governor, they've got a damned great bulldozer there. I might ask if Chief Littlehorse can supervise the skimming, at least he knows what the desired result is.'

'Great, I'd forgotten him. He might come in quite handy as a site watchman. He knows what we're doing and what we're looking for and, if I understand the situation correctly, he ain't going anywhere for a while.'

'If I were you Professor', Frank emphasised the title, 'I'd approach him with a view to his being the site supervisor rather than the site watchman. Remember, he doesn't need the job.'

'OK, I'll leave that to you. As he's there anyway, he might as well be working for us as anyone else.'

Frank borrowed his phone, rang the reformatory and spoke to the Governor. 'Can you fix it for Marley to be detailed off to supervise the skimming? He knows what's required and it will help keep him onside and, inside the reformatory.'

'Leave it to me', the Governor told him.. 'If the students don't mind being supervised by an Indian, who am I to argue. I just hope you know what you're doing. By the way, while I've got you on the phone, I've had Mac write to your boss Stuart asking for a report on what he intends to do. I imagine you will be getting a call from him pretty soon.'

Frank explained that it didn't work quite like that. 'Gerald Thorsen would get a call from Stuart asking for a report and projections. Gerald will ring me asking for a full report and project plan and I will write a report that, with Stuart's signature on it, will be sent to Mac to pass on to you. That way, we all get to keep our jobs.'

'I'd be grateful if you'd mention that it was the Reformatory that discovered this important site in the first place. Even if, strictly speaking, it was Marley. It won't do us any harm come appropriations time.'

'No problem.'

'By the way. What's with Loretta this morning? She's burning people left right and centre. Seems she arrived in a foul mood this morning and it hasn't got any better.'

'No idea, Chief. She was alright when I left her this morning but, thanks for the warning. I'll throw my hat in through the door when I get home, if she shoots, I'll back off and go to an hotel.'

He said goodbye to the Professor and left the University. It was four o-clock, he rang Loretta.

'Hi, I thought we might go out for a meal this evening, what do you think?'

'OK, where?'

'How about that new restaurant that we saw advertised in the paper at the weekend? It's out towards Oakville but not too far.'

'OK. I'll be ready by the time you get home. We'll have a drink and maybe, stop by the lakeshore for half an hour on our way!'

Frank remembered the last time they had visited the lakeshore but dismissed the thought. She had sounded OK to him. He wondered what Steve had been worried about; she sounded in a good mood.

The students sent out by Arnolds to mark out the site grid had been on site for a couple of hours. The site had been levelled by the dozer to about a foot above the exposed beach, ready for them to put in their pegs and strings.

The ground was still damp from the thaw but, by lying on rubber mats, it was possible for them to scrape away at the top soil with trowel and to brush away the debris into a dustpan for delivery to the site master who would arrange for it to be put through a sieve and, anything even remotely interesting, collected and marked with its grid reference.

From his window, Mac watched them at it. Each one, head down, concentrating on what he or she was doing. Good kids, these students, no skylarking. They were obviously interested in what they were doing.

Captain Singleton was standing, over by the pit top guard, watching what the students were doing with one eye and what the prisoners were doing below them in the pit with the other.

'Make sure there's no contact between the students and the inmates', he told the guard, 'you can't trust students, bunch of anarchists, most of them. Wouldn't trust them not to slip the prisoners a bottle or something if they got the chance.' He glanced at Mack's office window and saw him standing there. 'It's alright for him, it's me that'll get the trouble if anything goes wrong with this little lot. The Governor should never have let him talk him into it.'

One of the students had been watching him watching them. He said something to his partner and they both laughed.

'Bloody students! And, what about his guy Marley? One day he's an inmate and the next he's given special privileges and status on this archaeological site; it ain't right. The cheeky bugger actually smiled at me this morning and wished me good day!'

In town, Michael Stuart had listened to Frank's reasons for wanting the Indian. 'The kids would like it. He's a full-blooded Indian Chief. He knows more about the local history than any of the kids' teachers would and, he's available, cheap. He would give the exercise added status, a real Indian.'

'Give me a few days to think about it.'

Frank wondered whom Michael would have to consult. Would he have to get permission from someone higher up? So much for democracy!

Marley's sentence was up in three weeks and, if they wanted him, they would have to approach him before he pushed off up north for the tourist season. Should he have mentioned that, he wondered? Perhaps not, it wouldn't do to push too hard. Anyway, had Marley not been an Indian, there wouldn't have been a problem. He wandered into Andrew's office. There wasn't much he could do until he got some words from Arnolds. He wondered how Andrew had been getting on with the panels. 'Hi, how's it going?'

'No problems', Andrew stood back from the drawing board. 'What do you think of that?'

'Who's a clever boy then? I think it's fantastic.'

'So, what's bugging you? Why are you in here bothering me instead of sitting outside being creative?'

'I've just been in with Stuart, trying to convince him that we need Marley. I'm not at all sure I succeeded. He said he'd have to think about it some more and, to give him a few days.'

'That's OK. That means, roughly translated, that I'm too important to give you instant decisions. All my decisions are carefully thought through; that's why I'm the Boss and you ain't.'

'Oh, that's alright then. I thought he was against it for some reason.'

'He won't be for or against anything. He relies upon expert advice and, if the expert turns out to be wrong, it's the expert that gets fired.'

'Who's the expert in this field?'

'You are.'

'Shit.'

Jesse stuck her head round the door. 'Michael's on your phone.'

'I've discussed your proposal to employ the Indian on the site and we have a Go on that. Can you arrange for him to be interviewed here? I'd like to meet him before we make a final decision to appoint, after all, it's my Department.'

'I'll have a word with the Governor, I'm sure he can be spared to come over here; I'll get back to you as soon as I've got a yes on this. When would you like to see him?'

'ASAP. We need to keep on top of this project now that the Press are on to it.'

'I'll try for Friday a.m., OK?'

'Yeah but don't sound too keen. We don't want him jacking up the price he wants. He's to be offered the bottom rung of the ladder, you understand?'

'I thought I was on that!'

'Perhaps you'll be one rung up by the end of the week. It's my policy to reward good work and, anyway, we can't have an Indian on the same scale as anyone else in the department, it would look bad higher up.'

Frank hung up the phone and smiled to himself. 'Ah well, a raise is a raise.'

He phoned the Reformatory and spoke with the Governor. It was arranged. He would pick up Marley on Friday morning and take him, in his custody, to the interview and then bring him back.

'No side trips, you understand? No quick visits to a bar to celebrate.'

CHAPTER FORTY-SIX

'What do you interpret from this business with the Ruskies in Berlin?'

Frank sat in the armchair across from the Governor's desk. 'None of my business. I'm not on the reserve as long as I stay here and, anyway, what could the navy do in Berlin?'

'That's not what I mean. What I mean is that, if we get into a war with the Russians, their border is only a few miles from ours, across the strait. If they plan to invade America, we're in the way; Canada's the most direct route.'

'I'll write to Mr Atlee if you write to President Truman. How about that?'

'Very funny. What if they tell you they want you back anyway?'

'I'll get Loretta to write to the Admiralty. No one argues with Loretta.'

Mac, who had sat quietly through this conversation so far chipped in. 'Think about it Governor, if he has to go back, we'll be left with Loretta and she won't be in a good mood.'

'In that case Mac, we'll have to persuade her to go to England with him.'

'Do you two mind remembering that I'm still here. Anyway, I was released from the reserve when I emigrated. I only have to report back to the Admiralty if I return to the UK within five years. And, gentlemen, I have no intention of doing any such thing, Loretta would kill me.'

Marley was brought into the office, interrupting the good humoured but pointless discussion. 'Do you have a coat?' Frank asked him. 'We're going for a ride downtown.'

'If I had a decent coat, I wouldn't have to get myself put in here every winter.'

'Don't push your luck', the Governor told him 'or, next winter we might just be too full to take you and it'd be the Pen at Guelph or the weather.'

They walked out to the car. 'I've pushed this as far as I can', Frank told him, 'if you want the job, this is the moment to forget wisecracks and concentrate on persuading Michael Stuart that you're an expert on Ontario history, Indian affairs and archaeological artefacts. OK?'

'Who's this Michael Stuart?'

'My Boss and yours too if you get the job and remember, he doesn't like Indians.'

'Why does he want an expert?   We're only talking to a bunch of kids.'

'He likes experts, they relieve him of any necessity to know anything about anything.   You'll be working with the Professors from the University and the tour leaders will be schoolteachers who've read up on the subject. OK?'

'OK, so I'm an expert. Did you find out what it pays?'

'Yeah. About two thousand this year, to start.'

'Hell, I can make more than that hustling tourists in the summer and, I don't have to be an expert for that!'

'But you get paid through the winter and through next year and on. If I don't murder you myself, you could make it to pension.'

'Do I get to write the lectures myself?'

'Just so long as they're honest, decent and legal   You got a problem with that?'

'Suppose your Boss doesn't like what I write?   My view of history won't be what he learned at school.'

'As long as you're right, we can probably get the university to back you. They may teach a load of old rubbish at school but that doesn't mean they believe it themselves.'

'OK, take me to your leader.'

The guard Brown sat in the back of the car. As far as he was concerned, this was a trip out on the company's time, nothing for him to do. Frank told him to make himself comfortable.

'Why did Singleton want you to come along?'

'I guess he just wants to have his department represented Frank.   I'm to make sure our friend here doesn't jump you and escape with your vehicle.'

'That guy's a prat!'

Frank elbowed him. 'That may be true Chief but you've got a few weeks to serve yet so button it, OK?'

Brown sat silently in the back, pretending that he hadn't heard the comment. It was none of his business what either the Indian or, for that matter, Frank thought of his Boss. He had his own opinion about Captain Singleton but he would keep his mouth shut and his job safe.

The traffic had, by now thinned out and, as they passed St. Joseph's hospital, Frank wondered how Sarah was coping with her experience in the park. Perhaps she would go back to England as she had said she would.   Who knows, if he did have to go back, they might even meet on the ship again. Loretta would never believe that that was a coincidence. He smiled to himself, wondering if Loretta would come with him.

He nudged the car into its slot in the car park. 'Right, this is the form.' He turned to the guard. 'You may come with us or push off for an hour, as you please. Personally, I would prefer that you didn't come up with us; an escort can't do Marley's case any good at all, but it's up to you.'

'I'll push off.   Do a bit of window shopping, perhaps find a beer.'

'Thanks.   When we're through here, we'll go over to the Ford hotel for coffee and a bun. See you there in about an hour, OK?'

Frank and Marley stepped into the elevator, leaving Brown to find his way out of the car park. 'That was big of you', Marley said.

'Just you remember that both our futures depend on this meeting and play it straight.   You're an educated Indian with a specialist knowledge of history, particularly the history of southern Canada. You're a Chief of the Etobicoke, the local tribe in this area and, thus, you have both a local interest and a specialist knowledge relevant to the job on offer

'You agree with me that the presence of a genuine Indian Chief on this project would give it an extra authority when dealing with school kids. Do I make myself clear Chief?'

'Yes Sir Mr Bye Sir! Though, if I blow this and we both get fired, we could make a good team working the tourist circuit. With me in costume and you doing the spiel, we could separate the tourists from enough money in the season to live comfortably in Florida through the winter.'

'Don't even think like that. If we pull this off, we not only have a good job but, in your case, you become respectable. Your father will be proud of you.'

Michael Stuart was waiting for them. Frank introduced the Chief.

'This is Robert Edward Marley.'

Stuart hesitated for only the barest part of a second before thrusting his hand out towards Marley. 'Glad to meet you Mr Marley, come on in to the office.'

He closed the door behind them, closing out the interested ears and eyes in the outer office.

'Why don't you sit over there Frank', he pointed to an extra chair that had been brought in to the room. 'Why don't you sit here?' He indicated the chair immediately in front of his desk to Marley. Marley moved the chair back a little further from the desk, turning it so that he could see both Michael and Frank without turning his head.

'Thank you.'

The significance of this move was not lost upon Michael who grudgingly awarded him a bonus point even before the interview started.

'Now, Frank. Why don't you talk us into this meeting then we can play it by ear after that I don't like this modern idea of structured meetings where everyone has his part to play, whether he has anything to say or not.'

Amongst the shops and offices of downtown Toronto, Brown felt out of place in his uniform. What the hell was a man in army style uniform with shoulder flashes reading Toronto Reformatory, doing wandering about apparently aimlessly half way through a weekday morning? He hated Singleton for insisting that he be in uniform to escort a man who was within days of discharge and who was being interviewed for a job with the Provincial Government.

What did the prat think Marley was going to do? Start a war? If it had been a little warmer, he could have removed his coat. At least, that way, the Reformatory flashes on his shoulders would be hidden. He turned and retraced his steps towards Parliament Buildings and the Ford Hotel. He could buy a newspaper and sit in the hotel's coffee shop until the others joined him. So close to the Parliament Buildings, his uniform would not appear so out of place.

This guy Bye. He was really something. He'd only been here a few months and he had already got himself a better job and was giving orders instead of taking them. Hell, he was even arranging a good job for a man everyone else had written off as just another drunk Indian and organising a programme of educational visits to what, Brown regarded as a hole in the ground.

What a wonderful country this Canada is. He was certain that nothing like this could happen in Germany and he doubted if it would have been possible anywhere in Europe. Everything was too old and long established in Europe. There was no opportunity for the Frank Bye's or the Brauniger/ Browns to change their lifestyles like that. Only here, in the new world, could a man become whatever he wanted to become. All he had to do was identify his ambition and work for it.

He bought a newspaper, folded neatly and slid it under his arm like an officer's swagger stick. He straightened his back, lifted his chin and strode into the Ford Hotel's coffee shop. He paused just for long enough for the staff to see him then strolled over to a table and sat down. The waitress took his order and called him Sir.

By the time Frank and Marley joined him, he had read the paper thoroughly. What he had read, he didn't like.

In Berlin, the people in the American, British and French sectors were close to starvation; the Russians having made it almost impossible for the allies to transport food across the Russian Zone. They were acting against all the post-war international agreements dividing Berlin between the four victors. Brown felt very German and very annoyed that the Russians were being allowed to make a mockery of the other three occupying powers. He had no faith that the French would do or even say much about it but he felt sure as hell that he wanted the other two to sort it out.

For a moment, he almost considered going back to sort them out himself but recognised that, as a German, he would have no power to do anything at all. In just two years from now, he could apply for Canadian nationality but, until then, he was a nothing and could do nothing.

'You OK?' Frank and Marley sat down.

'Ya ya, alle ist in ordnung.'

'What's bothering you? Your Canadian accent's slipped out of sight.'

The interview with Michael Stuart had been successful and Robert Edward Marley now had a job with the Ontario Government's Department of Public Relations. He started work the Monday after his discharge from the reformatory and he felt the equal of Brown or anyone else. He felt very pleased with himself, with life in general and even one of Captain Singleton's guards couldn't upset him this morning. If he had had any money, he would have bought them all a drink.

'It's this trouble in Germany', Brown indicated the newspaper headline, 'I don't like the look of it. To be beaten by and to surrender to a multi-country military alliance was no disgrace but to be starved to death as a result of a disagreement between the members of that alliance is something altogether different and, there's nothing I can do about it!'

'Do you have family in Berlin?' Frank asked him.

'No, my family lived in Nurnberg, in what's now the US sector. You know, where they held the trials. I don't know whether those guys really did what they were accused of, I was here for most of the war as a prisoner, but what they did can't have been much worse than what the Russians are doing to the Berliners now, can it.'

'They held the trials there because that was where Hitler held his mass rallies, it was symbolic.'

'Are you a reservist?' Brown asked Frank. 'Will you have to go back if called?'

He pointed to an article reporting that both the English and the French were recalling their discharged servicemen from the reserve in case the Russians decided to invade the rest of Europe.

'I'm a reservist only if I go back. I was released from the reserve as an emigrant but anyway, it's unlikely that they'll call back the navy. What can they do in Berlin?'

Brown pointed again to a paragraph in the report stating that the Soviet navy is believed to have almost three hundred submarines that, in the event of a war, could be deployed into the Atlantic to prevent the US resupplying their European armies. The Soviet Black Sea Fleet could break out into the Mediterranean to force the allies to divert troops, ships and aircraft to counter any such move, thus denying these reinforcements to the western European battlefronts.

The British Admiralty is currently reported to be recommissioning warships placed into reserve at the end of hostilities with Germany. The US Government has stated that it has no need to recall discharged servicemen but that it is increasing the number of aircraft based in continental Europe and has transferred warships from its Pacific fleet to ports on the eastern seaboard.

'If Loretta sees this, she'll go absolutely spare!'

Marley thought that this discussion was casting a blight on his good day.

'I'd be happy to perform a war dance, if you think it would help any.'

'Only if you do it on Stalin's grave!'

They finished their coffee in silence, each with his own thoughts.

'Come on, I'll drive you guys back to the reformatory. You'll miss your lunch if we leave it any later.'

The ride back gave Frank an opportunity to brief Marley on what to do when he was discharged.

'You'd better get yourself a room at the Y until you get your first pay cheque.'

Marley winked at him. 'Don't worry Boss, I'm solvent.'

Frank walked up the stairs to the general office and perched himself on the corner of Loretta's desk.

'Any chance of a cup of coffee or anything?'

'All you get here this morning is coffee.'

He told her how Marley had done and that, therefore his own job was now that much more secure with the PR Department.

'Michael will be writing a memo to the Governor informing him that Marley will be joining the department on discharge from here, I suspect that he will also ask Steve to supply full background data. If he asks you to write it, it wouldn't do any harm to be a little selective about what you include. I think the guy deserves this one chance to get ahead, don't you?'

'Why do I get the impression that you're talking about one thing but thinking about another?'

'No, honest Injun. I'm just trying to give the fellow a step up.'

'I don't believe you but if that's what you want. By the way, I've decided to go and visit my husband.'

'Do you want me to come with you?'

'No, this is one I have to do on my own. I thought I'd go up on Saturday.'

'Where is he?'

'Guelph. That's how I came to be in the Prison Service. I got a job at the penitentiary up there when they put him into that home. I thought I should be somewhere close but it was soon obvious that he didn't need me. He didn't even know who I was!

'I moved down here when a vacancy was advertised. It didn't seem to matter to him and I felt better away from there, I could make a new start.'

'And the rest is history, as they say.'

'So? Nobody's perfect.'

When he got home, the radio was on and the reporter was in mid story.

'General Clay has said that the American Army guards on trains and barges passing through the Soviet Zone of Germany into the American sector of Berlin have been instructed to open fire if any Soviet soldier attempts to enter the vehicle. Food supplies to Berlin are reported to be down to just twenty five percent of January loadings but deliveries are expected to return to normal as a result of General Clay's orders.

'In Washington, President Truman has stated that the US has no wish to become involved in a shooting war with the Russians but that vital US interests must be defended with gusto. The State Department has issued instructions to all US Embassies worldwide to draw the attention of overseas Governments to the illegality of the Soviet actions in Germany. Allied Governments involved, the British and the French also have sectors of occupation in Berlin and are said to be standing shoulder to shoulder with the US in this confrontation.'

'What will happen if it turns into a shooting war?'

Loretta was standing beside him, her hand found his and held it.

'It will make the second world war look like a boy scout outing but at least, the Yanks have the atomic bomb now. The Russians wouldn't dare go up against them head to head. It has to be a bluff. You see, they'll call it all off

316

in a few days; just as soon as the politicians can think of a form of words to get them out from under. No one wants another war now.'

'Well, I sure as hell don't! Turn that damned thing off.'

Frank built her a gin and tonic, making a big thing out of getting the ice from the fridge whilst she finished laying the table for dinner but left the radio on.

'Will you be called back?'

'I told you, no.'

'Will you go if you are?'

'The question doesn't arise. Don't worry about it.'

'Answer the question, you bastard.'

'You know the answer. I'm excused as a result of emigration to Canada. It would be far too expensive for them to call me back from here, they would have to transport me, for one thing. No, forget it. By the time they decide that they need little old me, the Yanks will have dropped the atom bomb on Moscow and it will all be over. Take my word for it, it ain't going to happen.'

The next morning, the radio reported the crash of a British Viking transport aircraft in the air corridor between the British zone of Germany and the British Sector of Berlin. 'First reports suggest that it happened as a result of attack by a Russian Yak fighter which itself crashed shortly afterwards.

'The British Military Government in Germany has stated its belief that the crash was the result of a mid-air collision and was therefore an accident. It was understood that the Yak was making attack-like passes at the Viking at the time and miscalculated; a strongly worded complaint has been passed to the Soviet Authorities.'

'Shit. Does this mean that the shooting war is about to start?'

'No. Like I said, its all bluff. If the Yak had wanted to shoot down the unarmed Viking it could have done so from a stand-off position. The fool was showing off and got too close.'

'The Royal Air Force,' the reporter continued 'is reported to have immediately executed a prearranged order for all future air movements through the air corridor to be given fighter escorts. The US Government reports that they have issued a similar order to the USAF. We will bring you the latest, up to the moment news as it comes off the wire.

'I don't want to hear the latest news from Europe. I don't want to hear any news at all. I want to go to bed with you and make love until it's all over. I don't care if it lasts for years!'

'Now there's a challenge.'

'Don't make fun of me. I'm serious. It's all going to go wrong for us, isn't it? I've found the man I want and he's going to go away, aren't you?'

'I'd still be yours wherever I am. I'm your man and you're my woman. Nothing can change that now.'

'You'll go away and you'll get yourself killed and I shall commit suicide.'

'No you won't. I probably won't go anywhere and I certainly shan't get killed, I'm far too long in the tooth for that sort of heroics. Remember, I've done all this nonsense once already, I know the ropes. We shall spend the rest of our lives together and end up in an old folks home hating the sight of one another, bored out of our minds with each other's prattle.'

'I hope you're right. I couldn't go through it all again, the long dark nights without a man. The desperate settling for any man who will say he loves me. I know what the men all say about me at work but they don't understand.'

For just a moment, Frank wondered if he had misunderstood Alice; had he perhaps misjudged the situation.

CHAPTER FORTY-SEVEN

It was early to get up. Loretta had her back to him and, when he turned towards her, their bodies fitted together like two spoons, her bottom nesting on his drawn up knees. He reached round her and cupped one breast in his hand, kissing the back of her neck.

'Don't do that! Unless, of course, you intend to make something of it.'

'I thought you were still asleep.'

'I haven't slept a wink. I've been worrying about you going back to the English navy and getting yourself killed. I don't think I could live without you now.'

'That's very flattering but not very practical. Now, make me a cup of coffee.'

'It's too early for coffee.'

'And bring me a biscuit too.'

The percolator plopped and hissed in the kitchen. She sat on the edge of the bed holding his hand.

'It really is alright, you know, no one is going to call me back to the colours or whatever, not from Canada. The more you look at it the sillier it looks so you're stuck with me for the rest of your life and, if you really want something to worry about, try worrying about that!'

He lifted her hand to his lips and kissed it. 'There's no way you are going to lose me now. It took us both a long time to find each other and now that we have, we can be absolutely selfish. Neither of us need ever again give even a moment's thought to anyone else.'

'What about your daughter?'

'What about her?'

'Will you go and see her if you go back to the UK?'

'Is that what's worrying you?'

'Well, you do have a wife and a daughter over there. It would be natural wouldn't it?'

'So, that's what this is all about. I would only be visiting them, just like you visiting your husband. That's the normal and proper thing to do.'

'I know that even if he got better and came out of that place, you wouldn't go back to him, he's part of a previous life just as my wife is; a life we can't share but that can't come between us either.'

The alarm clock rang before they had finished their coffee, putting all other thoughts out of their minds.

'Another day, another dollar. I'll race you for the bathroom.'

'I'll shower while you shave, you can follow me through while I do my hair.'

Looking into the mirror shaving, he could see her standing naked in the shower, soap bubbles running in rivulets between the cheeks of her bottom.

'God you're a beautiful woman.'

'Keep thinking that and we'll get along just fine.'

They swapped places, she drying herself with the huge bath sheet then whisking the brush through her hair, removing the night tangles. She looked at him through the mirror, standing in the shower just letting the hot water rain over him.

'You're alright yourself. Just take care not to get too fat, old or grey or, at least not until I do.'

'Why are we hurrying, its Saturday?'

'I've arranged to go and see my husband. He won't understand but I feel I had to tell the Sisters, I can't just arrive unannounced.'

'I see.' He turned off the shower and towelled himself dry. 'Don't you let them talk you into anything, you hear!'

'Oh, they know I'm lapsed. They gave up on me years ago.'

'They never give up, that's why you're lapsed instead of ex-'

'Don't worry lover, I'll come back to you.'

CHAPTER FORTY-EIGHT

The door swung closed behind her. The polished floor reminded her of hospitals but why shouldn't it this was a nursing home. The Matron greeted her at the door of her office.

'It's nice to see you again Mrs Parsons it's quite some time since you last came to see Toby. He may not recognise you after so long.'

'He hasn't recognised me for about ten years but I thought I should come up to see him just one more time. I've met someone.'

Sister Amelda frowned. 'It may be better not to tell him that. We can never know just what gets past the mental block he has imposed. Doctor thinks he may sometimes be more aware than he lets on.'

'OK Matron, I'll just pass an hour with him if I may. I promise not to upset him.'

'They're at lunch at the moment. Why don't you go in and have lunch with him? It might be a good way to reintroduce yourself.'

Loretta sat down opposite him. 'Hallo Toby.'

He looked up from his concentration on the food in front of him, his face completely blank. Just for a moment, Loretta thought she had seen recognition in his eyes but dismissed the idea immediately, he hadn't recognised her in years.

'May I join you for lunch?'

Toby made no response but Loretta hadn't expected any. She played with her food, trying to think of something to say to him. Just keep on smiling, she thought, keep on smiling and pretending that there's no problem, no huge gulf of incomprehension separating them. God, she wished she hadn't come. She'd forgotten just how traumatic visiting him could be. The combination of pity, guilt and yes, even fear, made even sitting opposite him difficult.

He lifted a forkful of food to his mouth, his eyes momentarily meeting hers. There it was again, she was sure this time, it had only been for an instant but she was sure of it now. He knew who she was.

'I'm sorry I haven't been to see you for a while', she hoped he wouldn't know how long it had been. 'Been very busy down in Toronto but, I'm here now. Is there anything I can get you? Is there anything you need?'

Toby's fork fell out of his hand on to the floor. He ignored it, picking up a mouthful of food with the knife but spilling it into his lap. Loretta stood up.

'I'll pick it up for you, shall I?'

She bent down beside his chair, reaching for the fork that he had kicked under the table. As she grasped the fork and began to rise, he drove the knife down hard, severing the spinal cord at the base of the neck; she died instantly, still grasping and apparently offering him the dropped fork, the smile still on her lips.

Toby returned to trying to feed himself. It was some moments before anyone realised what had happened. The woman at the next table screamed twice before anyone took any notice of her.

'He's kilt her! He's kilt her!' She continued screaming as one of the nursing sisters led her away from the scene.

Sister Amelda knelt beside Loretta, her fingers pressed lightly against the side of her neck, feeling for a pulse. There was nothing.

'My God, she's dead', she said aloud and the cry was taken up by the diners.

'She's dead, she's dead', the word spread from table to table through the dining room. Another elderly lady screamed then fainted. An old man giggled uncontrollably. 'She's dead by God, she's dead, the old bugger killed her.'

Three nursing sisters had materialised from other parts of the home in response to the emergency bell and were ushering the patients out of the room, hushing and clucking at them like mother hens protecting their chicks from some imagined danger.

There was nothing Sister Amelda could do for Loretta. She helped Toby up from his chair and led him gently back to his room.

'You sit', she told him. 'Just sit there quietly, there's nothing to worry about.' She left him in the room, returning within a matter of moments with some tablets. 'Here Toby, these will make you feel better.'

Toby took the tablets from her outstretched hand, popping them into his mouth without hesitation. For just a moment, just an instant, Sister Amelda was sure; just for an instant his eyes had been clear. In that moment she knew that Loretta's death was not a terrible accident.

'Oh my God!'

Frank read the paper carefully. With Loretta up north, he could read the news about Europe properly, trying to work out if, or worse how, it might affect him. Much as he loved Loretta and safe as he was here in Toronto, unless of course the Canadians decided to get in on the act, he couldn't just ignore the risk to Alice and the child, nor could he let five years of war go to waste; he owed it to all those who had died to ensure that their deaths were not wasted. He had read somewhere that the Royal Navy alone had lost a hundred and forty three destroyers and tens of thousands of the men in them and, that was just in the destroyers; God alone knew what the total butchers bill had been.

He thought of Loretta, up at Guelph, visiting her husband. He wondered why she'd never divorced him then realised, of course she's Catholic. Not practising perhaps but it made no difference really. He thought for a moment about Alice and Virginia, back in England. If he did have to go back, he would have to go and see them but he would explain that he was returning to Canada as soon as he could.

For all he knew, she had already found someone else to help her run her hotel. He wondered if she had found an hotel yet, one she could afford. He had looked forward to after the war and running the hotel with Alice but, that was before he had been told about the others; he would never have known whether she was being faithful to him, would he? Not if they were running an hotel full of travelling salesmen.

It would be dark soon, he poured a cup of coffee. He wondered how Loretta had got on with her visit, she should be on her way back by now.

It still wasn't clear from the news reports whether he could expect the British Government to call reservists like him back. Hell, it wasn't his problem, he was excused party, released from the reserve, it was nothing to do with him. For a moment, he wondered whether he could settle back in the navy as a Leading Signalman. It wouldn't be easy, he'd got used to being his own man.

Forget it. It ain't going to happen. There's no way they'd call me back. I was released and, anyway, I was never that good, they can manage without Leading Signalman Bye. He looked at his watch, almost midnight, Loretta won't be back tonight now he thought, she must have stopped over in Guelph.

Alone in the bed for the first time, he didn't like it much. He missed Loretta's warmth, the smell of her soap and talc after her bath, the feeling of oneness that held them together. Sleep was slow in coming, his mind kept flashing from Loretta to Alice and back. He pictured the child Virginia playing with the doll he had sent her for Christmas. He saw himself standing alone on a ship's bridge, green water breaking over the bow and drenching everything; the north Atlantic in winter! No, he didn't want to go back to that, he'd done his share, it was some other fool's turn. Sleep finally came, the warmth in the bed wrapped and protected him from the wind and the sea in his mind.

The telephone was ringing and ringing. Frank woke, alarmed by the sound in the darkness. He switched on the light, glancing at the clock. Five o-clock. He focused his eyes on the telephone; it was silent.

Had it rung? Had he dreamed it? He lifted the receiver just in case, just the dialling tone. Then it struck him, if she had decided to stop over in Guelph, she would have rung him. Why hadn't she rung him? Had there been an accident? Was that why the telephone had rung? Was she in some hospital somewhere, unconscious?

He looked round, frantically searching for the telephone book, looking for the number of the nursing home. He would ask them what time she had left, did they know if she was staying over?

While the telephone rang in the Matron's office, he looked at his watch. Five fifteen in the morning, they weren't going to be too happy with him for ringing at this time. Hard luck!

'St. Thomas's Nursing Home.'

At last. The night duty staff must have been asleep or, perhaps, doing a round of the home, checking on the patients.

'I'm sorry to ring you at this ungodly hour but I'm trying to trace Mrs Loretta Parsons'; he remembered her married name

The silence on the telephone was almost physical. 'Just one moment Sir, I'll connect you with Matron.'

'Good morning,' the voice was awake, alert. 'I'm Sister Amelda. I understand you were enquiring about Mrs Parsons. May I ask who you are? What is your relationship with Mrs Parsons.'

'I'm Frank Bye', Frank told her. 'Loretta and I are very close. What's happened, why are you asking me such a question?'

'Ah. Mrs Parsons did say that she had met someone else, may I ask if you are he?'

'Yes I am. What's happened? What's the matter? Is Loretta alright?'

He felt the sweat running down his wrist, He was gripping the telephone so tightly that he could feel the muscles of his forearm standing out.

'I'm afraid there has been an accident. I think perhaps, it would be best if you came over, is that possible?' Frank nodded at the telephone, realised what he had done and agreed that it was possible. 'I shall expect you sometime this morning then? There's no reason to hurry, shall we say about mid-day?'

The Matron sounded perfectly calm, as if she were simply passing the time of day with a relative of a patient. Reassuring, that was the word Frank was looking for. What was the woman doing being reassuring at this time in the morning? She should be furious at being woken at five o-clock in the morning! He forced himself to be calm.

'What sort of an accident?'

'There's nothing to worry about, she is in no pain. We can discuss it properly when you arrive. Now, I suggest that you make yourself some breakfast, I'll see you when you arrive.'

'Can I speak to her?' Frank broke in before she could put the receiver down on its cradle.

'I'm afraid that will not be possible. Goodbye Mr Bye.' He heard the click as she broke the connection.

Damn the woman, what did she mean not possible. Was Loretta simply asleep, drugged perhaps in a hospital bed?

There was no point in rushing out to the car now. Guelph was only about a hundred miles away and the roads were clear. It would take him only a little over two hours at most, there was no point in arriving there at the crack of dawn.

He looked at the percolator; he needed coffee. No, he needed a proper drink. He filled a tumbler with whiskey and swung it straight back, Russian style. He caught sight of himself in the mirror, standing there stark naked with a glass of whiskey in one hand and the now dead telephone in the other. He replaced the receiver, walked back into the bedroom and started to dress; unconsciously putting on the clothes he had discarded only a matter of hours before. He'd got as far as his socks and shorts when it struck him. She's dead!

It was the only logical explanation. The Matron had told him that she couldn't come to the telephone, that she was in no pain. He should have realised whilst he still had the Matron on the phone. Loretta was dead!

She couldn't be dead. She mustn't be dead. She was sitting up in some hospital bed swearing at the other driver for the accident. She always drove too fast and always blamed the other driver for any danger. He had told her so. He finished dressing and turned to the percolator, he did want coffee after all.

He made toast, waiting for the coffee. God, these machines took for ever. At sea, they had used Perk Coffee, a liquid to which you added boiling water. It wasn't as good as the pure, freshly ground coffee that Loretta percolated but it was drinkable and, it was quick. He looked at his watch again. Ten past six. Was that all?

He took his clothes off again and stood under the shower, letting the warm water run over him. The combination of the warm water on the outside and the whiskey on the inside relaxed him sufficiently for him to find and dress in clean clothes. He opened the lid of the laundry basket in the bathroom and dropped his dirty clothes in on top of those discarded by Loretta yesterday, was it only yesterday? It seemed like forever.

The toast was cold, he had forgotten it, but the coffee was hot and tasted good. For the first time since he had arrived in Canada, he tuned the radio to the BBC. In England, it was half past eleven at night, he might get the late news.

The cultured tones of the BBC's announcer sounded alien to him after so long listening to the twang of the Toronto accent. At first, he had thought it sounded like a cross between Australian and American but, now, it just sounded normal.

327

'Britain has informed the United States that it shall go to war with Russia if the Russians commit a single act of aggression though, Mr Bevan has stated, the British Government and nation had no desire to do so. The Russians were our valued allies in the late war against Germany and the British nation had no desire to lose a friend of such standing.

'The Russian decision to forbid night flying into Berlin, through the international airspace corridors has made the supply of essential food and fuel to Berlin very much more difficult and, negotiations are being undertaken with the Russians to lift the embargo.

'The RAF state that, under the conditions prevailing, it would be dangerous in the extreme to try flying along the corridors at night without the assistance of the Soviet air traffic controllers. Independent air traffic control facilities were being established in Berlin but this would not be available for some little time.

'The US Government is reported to have been embarrassed by the Russian's selective leaking of confidential discussions that had been intended to solve the problems now effecting Berlin. Leaked selectively, these were being used by the Russians in an attempt to prise a wedge between the allies.

'Their plan seemed to be to separate the British and French, particularly the French who they regarded as the weakest link, from the Americans. The British and Americans are agreed that it is essential for them to preserve their presence in Berlin. The French, the Russians believe, would be prepared to relinquish their sector of Berlin rather than face the embarrassment of being driven out by force.

'The French Government has denied that there is any possibility of their being forced out of Berlin by the Russians and has stated, unequivocally, that the tricolour will continue to fly over the French sector of Berlin, until Paris decides otherwise.

'In Germany, General Lucious D. Clay, the Military Governor of the US Zone is reported to have stated that, in his opinion, war with the Soviet Union could come with dramatic suddenness.   All US military personnel in Germany have been placed at the first degree of readiness. British military sources confirm that the British army in Germany is ready to react at any time to any act of aggression by the Soviet Union.

'In Paris, the French Government, whilst stating that their armed forces are always ready and able to resist aggression from any quarter, do not believe that the Soviet Union intends to escalate the present altercation to the point of physical force and that a mutually satisfactory accommodation will be reached in the conference chamber.

'The threat of a strike by communist-led workers in the London docks remains unresolved and the Ministry of Defence has let it be known that, in the event of a withdrawal of labour coinciding with the need to transport military equipment to the continent, army experts would be directed into the effected docks.'

Frank turned it off. 'Here we go again!'

He tried to remember the name of the communist leader of the London dockers; Jack something. He couldn't remember   the   surname   but   remembered   seeing photographs of him in the papers, leading marchers in some previous dispute with the employers.

It wasn't even six o-clock yet. There was no point in leaving for Guelph and there was not the slightest chance of getting any sleep..

He retuned the radio to one of the twenty-four hours a day music stations and took up the paper he had been reading yesterday. Perhaps there was something interesting that he hadn't read; something, anything, to pass the time until he could reasonably leave for Guelph.

CHAPTER FORTY-NINE

Knickers! I should have brought some clean underwear for her. Why didn't the Matron suggest it? Perhaps Sister Amelda didn't realise just how close we are or, perhaps she was too embarrassed to suggest anything of the sort to a man.

The road stretched out in front of him, as far as the headlights could reach. He was alone, no other traffic was about at this time of morning, too early for commuters, just a few trucks.

I should have brought clean underwear and make up. A girl could manage running repairs with a lipstick and powder in her handbag but, after an accident and a night in a hospital bed, she would need the full kit from the bathroom.

Hell! I can buy whatever she wants in Guelph. Perhaps he should stop off before visiting the nursing home, buy her some flowers. Wait up there, if she had been in an accident, she would be in the local hospital, not the Home. Why didn't that fool of a Matron give me the full strength? Why did she wait until I rang her and then only give me half of the story, forcing me to ask questions?

If Loretta was in the local hospital, not the Home, why did the Matron tell him to come to the Home? She should have told him which hospital Loretta was in and left him to sort out the rest with them. Because she was dead!

He shouted at himself. 'Because she's fucking dead!'

Behind him, the flashing lights of the police car were emphasised by the siren. It took a full few minutes before Frank either heard or saw them. Indeed, the flashing lights were so close that they intermittently lit up the inside of his car before he noticed them. He slowed, pulled over onto the shoulder of the road and stopped; he rolled down the window at the officer's signal.

'OK, where's the fire?'

It took Frank a moment to register what the man had said.

'There's no fire but I suspect there's going to be a funeral.'

'Then, there's no hurry. Let's have your driving licence and your ID.'

Frank passed his little wallet in which he kept his driving licence and Auxiliary Police ID card. The Traffic Policeman handed them back.

'So? What's the hurry, you were doing close on eighty'

'I got this phone call.' Frank simplified the story. 'My wife's had an accident in Guelph and I'm worried sick about her.'

'You'll be worried dead if you drive like that in the dark. If your wife's had an accident then she'll not be in any state to worry about what time you visit her; just so long as you're alive at the time.'

Frank stuck the wallet back into his pocket. 'Didn't realise how fast I was going, sorry Officer. I'll pay more attention from here on.'

'I hope for your wife's sake that you do. Hope she's OK, now you take it easy, I don't want to have to arrest you; I hate paperwork!'

Frank knew that he had had a lucky escape. Traffic police, bored out of their minds after a long night shift with no traffic, had a reputation for arresting anything that moved.

'Thanks, I'll take it easy. I'm much too early anyway. Is there a diner somewhere ahead?'

'Just past Brampton. You can't miss it, it has a neon sign outside.'

'Thanks.'

He rolled up the window. It was cold out there.

He watched the police car pull out and pass him, piling on the power out of sheer boredom. They gave him a short burst of the siren and were gone; two rapidly diminishing red lights fading into the distance.

Frank sat there for a few minutes, surrounded by the dark. He could feel his heartbeat, much too fast! He took his pulse, remembering to breath slowly and evenly while he did it. It was too fast.

He turned on the radio. Country and western music flooded the car. Some girl wanted to hear a good old, thigh smacking, foot tapping, someone's done her wrong song. Someone had done him wrong and he didn't like it one little bit. He rolled the cursor across the bandscale. News? No he didn't want news. More music? Yes, that's better; he left the pointer on the music station.

He started the car and pulled up on to the road again, gently increasing the speed, settling on fifty. He wouldn't put it past the Traffic Cops to have pulled into a side turning or behind some trees up ahead just to see if he had taken their advice. He remembered the chant from his childhood at the Barnardos home in Clapham; 'all coppers is bastards!' Well, perhaps not all but enough for that chant to be almost universal. He must ask Loretta if she knew it.

Loretta. His mind sprang back to Loretta. Of course she wasn't dead. The Matron would have told him if she was dead. At least, she would have taken his name and address and passed it to the Guelph police so that they could contact him. She hadn't and they hadn't so, Loretta can't be dead.

He passed two cars coming towards him, their headlights for a brief moment blinding him. He flashed his mainbeams at them but they had gone before the message could have registered; first of the commuters, perhaps. He looked at his watch, holding his wrist close to the lighted radio band-scale to get the benefit of its light. Seven fifteen. He was running ahead of schedule. He slowed down to forty-five miles per hour.

It'd be light in a little while, forty five was safe enough and fast enough, even for the cops. He'd wind it up a bit after he had had a coffee at the diner ahead.

The Traffic Police car was parked in the lot outside the diner. Frank pulled in beside it. I wonder if they're checking on me?

He ordered coffee and sat in one of the booths from which he could watch the traffic outside. See if anyone went near his car. The Traffic Cop slid on to the seat opposite him.

'Mind if I see that ID again?'

'Problem?'

'Just on the off-chance, I checked with Guelph. There's been no accident reported involving a Mrs Bye. You want to try again?' His attitude was less friendly.

Frank told him the story, Loretta's non-return, his phone call from the Matron suggesting that he visit. He explained that Loretta's name was Parsons; that Mr Parsons was in the nursing home, out of his mind.

'Drink your coffee and stay here, I'll be back.'

He said something to his partner and went out to the car. Frank knew he was being checked out.

'Your story checks out. Here's your ID. Take it easy, there's no hurry, OK?'

The two policemen got back into their car and drove off, back the way they had come. The diner was obviously one end of their patrol. Frank finished his coffee, aware that the girl behind the counter was watching him. She hadn't heard what had been discussed but she was always careful of anyone the police questioned; you just couldn't be too sure on a lonely road at night. She was glad her morning relief would be here soon. Frank left the warmth of the diner and gunned the car up on to the road, spraying loose chippings behind him.

The old fashioned striking clock struck nine as he waited for someone to open the door.

'Sister Amelda wasn't expecting you until lunchtime, I'll take you to her office.'

The smell of fresh floor polish hit him as he entered, something about the smell, mixed with antiseptic reminded him of hospitals.

'Good morning Mr Bye. I'm Sister Amelda, the Matron here. Won't you sit down over here? Rita, bring Mr Bye a cup of coffee. Do you take cream and sugar, Mr Bye?'

The girl disappeared in search of coffee. Sister Amelda busied herself adjusting the bunch of flowers that Rita had just placed in a vase on her desk.

'I understand that you met up with the Traffic Police on your way up here, they rang to check your story. What were you doing to attract their attention?'

'About eighty miles an hour!'

'Ah, yes. They do lack a sense of adventure when it comes to speeding, unless it's them, of course. You were lucky they didn't arrest you, I'm surprised that they didn't.'

He didn't tell her that he, and for that matter Loretta, was an auxiliary police officer. He would hold that in reserve for later, if he needed it.

Rita arrived with two cups. She looked at Frank from under her eyelids, Frank caught her eye and she looked away at once.

'Thank you Rita. I'll ring when you may come back for the tray.'

The Matron sat down, drawing her cup towards her.

'I'm afraid Mrs Parsons is dead.'

Sister Amelda had spent most of the remaining hours of the night trying to devise a simple yet un-hurtful way of imparting this piece of intelligence. She had considered all of the well tried alternatives to the straight forward and decided that simplicity had a great deal to recommend it, particularly when dealing with a man of an age that meant that he must have served during the war.

'I'm not quite clear just what your relationship with Mrs Parsons is, was; perhaps you would explain.'

'Had Loretta not been married to Mr Parsons, we would have been man and wife.'

Frank saw no reason to indulge the Matron with a full background.

'You're English, aren't you?'

'Yes.'

'Protestant?'

'Yes.'

'You know, of course, that Mrs Parsons was Catholic?'

'We hadn't discussed it but I deduced as much from her decision not to divorce Mr Parsons.'

'Divorce would not have been possible.'

'I am aware of that but, as there were no children and as he is in no position to provide them, I imagine the marriage could have been annulled?'

Sister Amelda smiled. 'You've obviously given the matter some thought. Anyway, it is now academic.'

Frank resisted the temptation to respond to this apparent dismissal of his relationship with Loretta. 'How did she die? What happened?'

'It was all a terrible accident. Mr Parsons stuck a knife into her; she died instantly, there was nothing we could do.'

'If she died instantly, he must have known just where to stick the knife. It ain't easy to kill someone with a random thrust with a knife; and, how come he had a knife anyway? I thought he was out of his scull, do you normally allow nutters to run around with knives?'

'I don't think I like your attitude Mr Bye, but for your information, Mr and Mrs Parsons were having lunch. Mr Parsons dropped his fork and Mrs Parsons bent to retrieve it for him. He stabbed her with his dinner knife, severing her spinal cord and killing her instantly. The police have of course been advised and have agreed that, as Mr Parsons is not responsible for his actions, there is nothing to be done. I'm sorry.'

'But the guy has a history of violence. How do you know he wasn't responsible for his actions?'

'Mr Parsons has shown no inclination to violence since he has been in our care.'

Frank looked Sister Amelda directly in the eye. 'Sister, Mr Parsons has a long history of violence. It was his regular and unremitting violence towards Loretta that resulted in his suffering the injury that placed him in your care.'

'Mr Parsons was placed in our care as a result of Mrs Parsons' violence. Criminal violence, almost fatal violence; you are aware of the background, I assume?'

'Yes. I am fully aware of the situation prior to his placement in this establishment.' He remembered the un-started coffee and sipped it, looking at Sister Amelda, waiting for her to break the eye contact. She broke the contact and glanced out of the window.

'How about a funeral?'

'The funeral shall, of course, be held here in our chapel as soon as all relatives have been advised and a date agreed. Mrs Parsons may be buried here in our garden of rest or elsewhere as determined by her family. I understand that Mr Parsons has no family to consult.'

'Neither has Mrs Parsons but I'm sure that all of her many friends and colleagues will wish to attend the service. She is, was, widely known and respected in Toronto. If the arrangements can be finalised this morning, I will ring her office and make what arrangements are necessary for her friends to attend. There will be between forty and fifty of them, I imagine. She worked for the Provincial Government, you know and was also an Auxiliary Police Officer.'

He was happy to see a momentary indication of concern pass behind Sister Amelda's eyes. She picked up the telephone and asked the switchboard to have the Funeral Director call her back.

'Yes, I know today is Sunday. Do as I ask.' She turned to Frank. 'You will need to book in to a hotel. If you will ring me at, shall we say, eleven thirty, I'll be able to give you a date and time for the service. The doctor will be issuing the death certificate this morning so I foresee no delay from that quarter.'

'Thank you. Can you give me the name of the police officer to whom the crime was reported? I would like to have a word with him.'

'His name is Sergeant Pollock but I can assure you Mr Bye that, with Mr Parsons in his non-responsible condition, there is nothing that any number of policemen could do. It was, I assure you just a terrible accident and, in view of your close relationship with Mrs Parsons, I wouldn't like to think that you thought that you yourself were in any way contributive to this situation.'

Frank stood up, placing the coffee cup on her desk with care.

'For me to have been in any way contributive to this killing Matron, Mr Parsons would have had to know of my involvement and his wife's intentions. If, Matron, he was in any way aware of these, then his state of mind cannot be as you would have me believe and, in that case Matron, this was murder.'

Sister Amelda exploded.

'That's preposterous! The very idea! Mr Parsons has been with us for a number of years and has never shown the least awareness of his surroundings or of those about him. I will not even allow you to consider such a possibility. Mrs Parsons' death was a tragic accident, no more. I'm sure that your relationship with her had no relevance.'

Frank turned towards the door. 'Matron. I am not at all convinced of the simplicity of this situation and your attitude suggests to me that you are equally ill at ease with your chosen interpretation of events. However, no useful purpose would be served by taking the matter further. Loretta is dead. I take it there is no possibility of Mr Parsons experiencing a dramatic and sudden recovery from his senses and being allowed to leave this place?'

'None whatsoever!'

'Then Sister, I shall call you in an hour or so and perhaps you will then be able to give me details of Mrs Parsons' funeral service arrangements.'

Sister Amelda rang for Rita.

'Please show Mr Bye out Rita, then you may come back for these cups.' She turned to Frank. 'I shall expect your call. Good day Mr Bye.'

Frank made no attempt to contact the police. Nobody was going to want to challenge Sister Amelda's account of the tragic accident. It was neat, it was tidy and nobody needed to do anything about it. He drove out of the gates and back towards Toronto a mile of two to the motel he had passed on his way in to town.

He ordered more coffee and took it to a table. There was nothing he could do until he had spoken again to the Matron. There would probably be nothing he could do then but he didn't like to just drive away without seeing Loretta just one more time. He would go to the Funeral Director's chapel before driving back to Toronto. His fingers were screwing up a third paper napkin. He looked about him, embarrassed. No one had noticed. He slipped them into his pocket rather than leave them on the table.

His watch had stopped. No it hadn't. It just seemed like it had. The second hand swept round its three hundred and sixty degrees every minute, sweeping away the past and chasing the future. He caught himself stirring his coffee first one way then another; he forced himself to replace the spoon in the saucer and to drink his coffee.

Damn! He couldn't just sit here, nursing an empty cup for a whole hour until it would be time to ring Sister Amelda. He counted the minutes. Twenty minutes guarding his empty cup; the waitress passed by once but he lifted it to his lips and she passed on without comment. He replaced the cup on the saucer and pushed it away from him. He pushed a tip under the saucer for the girl, he had sat there long enough.

In the washroom, he freshened up. Combed his hair and looked at himself in the mirror. God, he looked as if he hadn't slept for a week. He killed another five minutes trying to make himself look better. Not good but better.

The telephone rang several times before it was answered. Yes, Sister Amelda was expecting his call. Would he hold the line please.

'Yes.' She had spoken with the Funeral Director, the funeral service would be held on Wednesday morning, it would take that long to arrange the paperwork and, yes, he could see Loretta at the chapel any time after two o-clock this afternoon. He would be expected to ring the Funeral Director to discuss instructions. Interment or cremation, etc. It could all be arranged on the telephone but he would require a signature against the costs.

Frank thanked her, wrote down the telephone number and address of the Funeral Director and rang off. He was surprised at how normal he felt, almost businesslike. He rang the number he had been given and arranged to drive over at two thirty.

Tomorrow, he would have to explain it all to Fred MacDonald and the others at the reformatory and tell Michael what had happened and that he would not be back for a couple of days. Tomorrow he might feel better able to do so. Right now, he didn't know how he felt; it would be nice just to die with Loretta.

CHAPTER FIFTY

Unaccustomed to the Catholic, or indeed any other civilian form of funeral service, Frank listened with surprised pleasure and gratitude to the Governor's eulogy; composed with great kindness and delivered with genuine affection.

Sitting, eyes closed in silent contemplation, Frank saw again the many many funeral services hurriedly conducted at sea. The simple dignity of the brief burial service spoken by the Captain, conscious of the nearness of death to all those present, aware also of the need to get the ship moving again as quickly as possible. Aware that, but for the grace of God, those attending might at any moment join their shipmates being committed to the deep with so little ceremony

He glanced around him. All her friends were there. He wondered irrelevantly who was manning the office. He searched their faces. What were they thinking? Were they thinking of Loretta as they may have thought her to be as a man eater? Surely, their very presence meant that they remembered Loretta as a friend, with affection.

The Matron was there, more he suspected to avoid adverse comment than out of any genuine regard for the dead girl. In her face Frank saw no regret, no guilt, indeed only, he was sure, a desire to put behind her this funeral of a woman of whom she did not approve.

She's a nun! Where's her compassion, her forgiveness? From some long-buried childhood memory, the words came unbidden into his mind. He that is without sin, let him cast the first stone.

'Damn you God! She didn't deserve to die like that!' He felt his hand taken and pressed gently; there was no one there.

CHAPTER FIFTY-ONE

Four days after the funeral service, Paul knocked on the front door of the apartment Frank had shared with Loretta.

'Let me in Frank, you can't sit in there for ever.'

The blinds were down, throwing the room into shadow even though the afternoon's winter sun shone brightly outside. Paul glanced round, not too much mess.

Frank sat, slumped in an easy chair. Beside him, the radio was still tuned to the BBC, the English accent of the presenter instantly noticeable to Paul. He listened for a moment, it was some programme about farming in Rhodesia; some scheme to grow tobacco and ground nuts. Paul, wondering what a ground nut was, leant over and turned it off.

'Come on Frank, you need company. Brenda insists that you come over for a meal.'

Frank allowed himself to be helped up out of the chair. 'It was murder you know.'

'What was?'

'Loretta. He knew about us. Oh, the Matron denied it of course but she knew, I could see it in her eyes, hear it in her tone of voice. It's not bloody fair! She didn't deserve to be murdered! Did you know she was married?' He held back the tears he could feel welling up again; 'it just ain't fair.'

Paul had no idea what to say. 'Come on. Get yourself sorted out while I ring Brenda and tell her we're on our way.' He told Brenda what Frank had said while Frank shaved and changed.

From the bedroom, Frank said, 'If he ever gets out of there, I'll kill him.'

Looking at himself in the bathroom mirror, razor in hand, Frank saw the redness round his eyes and the whiteness of his face. Christ what a mess!

He splashed cold water against his face until he fell the skin stretch tight across his cheekbones, until he could feel the blood flowing just beneath the surface, ironing out the wrinkles. He towelled his face until it hurt.

The transformation struck Paul. His timing must have been just about right; well, Brenda's timing actually. Frank looked almost civilised. What had Brenda said? Give him enough time to grieve but not enough to mope. Must be her experience working at the YMCA

Brenda kissed Frank. 'Come in, you look half starved. Paul, give the man a drink!' They clinked glasses. 'Here's to life after death. Dinner will be about half an hour.' Brenda left the men together with the bottle.

The food was good and Paul and Brenda kept the conversation general and light hearted. Paul told Frank that Captain Singleton disapproved of the idea of Marley being employed at the reformatory where other prisoners would try to take advantage of their previous association.

'Mark my words,' Paul mimicked Singleton, 'no good will come of it!'

Frank suddenly had a mental image of Michael Stuart parading Marley in front of the Press, dressed in full regalia and looking like a cigar store Indian amongst the suits. 'I think I'd better get back to work.'

Brenda suggested that the two men should move into the lounge whilst she cleared the table. Coffee would be in about five minutes.

'I told Brenda what you said about Loretta's death. She said God would make it fair and that you should concentrate your efforts on making a life for yourself. She's a bit religious at times but she's a good girl at heart and she means well.' They talked on for a while before Paul offered to take him home. Brenda kissed him on the cheek and squeezed his hand. 'You take care now.'

Alone in bed, Frank felt again all the agony of losing Loretta. The loneliness; he wanted her there to hold, he stretched out his arm to cuddle her, feeling the nothingness where she should have been. Under her pillow, his fingers touched her nightdress, he hadn't realised it was still there. He drew it to him, burying his face in its softness, smelling her in it. He sat up, slipping it over his head, feeling the smooth, warm satin fall over his shoulders, enfolding him, comforting him as she had done. He slept.

The alarm clock intruded on his dream, they were together in heaven. He swung his legs out of the bed and stood up, catching a glimpse of himself in the wardrobe mirror. Self-consciously, he let the nightdress fall to the floor at his feet, reaching for his bathrobe.

Shaved and dressed, Frank folded back the bedclothes and opened the window to air the bed, as he had been taught to do at Dr Barnardos. After breakfast, he would remake the bed.

Toast and coffee would do. He had eaten well yesterday and he would have lunch later in the Italian place across from the office. He didn't feel like cooking for one.

Whilst the coffee perked and the toast toasted, Frank tidied up the apartment, placing books back on the shelf and dumping papers in the trashcan, by the time the toaster ejected his breakfast all was more or less in order. He switched on the radio, still tuned to the BBC; listened to the one o-clock news from London and was surprised to hear from that source, that the Canadian Government intended cutting a deep water canal between Lake Ontario and Lake Erie to improve inter-lake shipping and to allow bigger ships up-stream. There was no news about Berlin other than a brief announcement that efforts were continuing in the search for agreement between the Governments concerned. The British Foreign Secretary had assured the House of Commons that he expected very soon to be able to report complete success.

Frank retuned to the local station. The news here was much the same as it was every morning; the weather report, traffic report and local news. Two robberies, police were following up their investigations and a major traffic accident involving a shunt between three private cars and a streetcar on Dundas; it wouldn't affect his drive into town.

He washed his breakfast things and put them in the rack to drain. One thing to be said for a combination of Dr Barnardos and the Navy was that such chores were attended to instinctively and automatically.

In the bedroom, he hung his bathrobe on the hook on the back of the door and made the bed. He picked up Loretta's nightdress from the floor, opened the lid of the laundry basket and re-closed it: he folded the nightdress and replaced it under his pillow.

Driving into town his mind reviewing the remaining requirements of the Reformatory project, his subconscious made the decision he had been avoiding.

Lying alone in the bed, unable to sleep, Loretta had reminded him that he still had a wife and a child and that, whilst she was gone where he couldn't follow, they remained; he should try to rescue what he could from the mess he had left behind in England. Unknowingly he spoke aloud. 'Damn these women. The deader they are the more moral they become! She was perfectly happy to keep me for herself when she was here but, now she was dead, she tells me to go home to my wife!'

He swung the car into the darkness of the car park and slid into his usual slot. By the time he reached his office he was feeling better, he even wished Jesse a good morning.

CHAPTER FIFTY-TWO

Andrew Rolls had quite a lot of artwork prepared for the main display in the tepee. Three large, illustrated storyboards led the visitor through the history of the site from the time that the ice receded to the present day.

The first couple of pictures showed the establishment of the tundra with its mosses and wild flowers, much as the far north of Ontario is today, then the spreading of the pine trees from the south into the now warmer new land; the depressions in the ground forming lakes from melted ice.

Step by step, the pictures and captions led the visitor forward through the initial population of the virgin forest by small animals much like the mice that today's children would recognise and the larger animals, foxes etc., that lived off the mice. The arctic hare probably abounded also and the bears that came later.

As the climate warmed, the storyboards explained, the elk and other grazing animals followed. Man didn't appear until picture eight or nine and, then, only as a fur wearing hunter from the warmer south visiting the area in the short summer and returning with his catch as soon as the days shortened and the snows came. This, the story board suggested, was the period in which the beach fire had been lit, nursed into life and employed to cook the fish of which the bones remained amongst the ashes until the present day.

Such a fire, once established, may have been protected until the site was abandoned; never allowed to go out. Gradually, the story board explained, the ice had receded even further north and man was able to settle along the shores of the southernmost lakes, building houses out of the tree braches formed into cone shaped enclosures, the interspaces filled with mud and mosses to keep out the wind and the weather. Once the snow had fallen, in the winter, the inside of these huts would be as warm and dry as a modern house; a central fire providing warmth and cooking. Later pictures illustrated the arrival of the settling Indians, replacing the hunters and, many centuries later, the first Europeans.

Ontario, which had by then become a heavily forested land abounding in animals and plants and inhabited only by relatively small bands of Indians, was a very attractive prize for the land hungry immigrants from an already over populated Europe.

A picture of a typical European rookery or stew area of the period, with its crowded, narrow streets and poor houses, served to illustrate the conditions from which many of the European immigrants had come. Others, the caption reported, were farm labourers or even poor tenant farmers dispossessed by landlords in Europe and forced to sail westwards to the new world in search of new lands and freedom from oppression.

Soldiers, sent by Governments to secure the new lands for their kings and princes were left unpaid for months, even years and many deserted and carved out homesteads and farms by chopping down trees, burning off the scrub and planting crops. Other pictures showed how many of them lived by hunting, much as the original inhabitants had done but now, armed with firearms, they were much more successful.

In this area, the story continued, England and France vied for control of the new lands, fighting each other for the over-lordship. Armies marched and countermarched within the safety of their forts seldom venturing far from home, unless a set-piece battle had been forced upon them by the other side attacking a town or an important trading post.

More usually the French and English Governors, safe behind the palisaded walls of Quebec or here in Fort York, would send their friendly Indians to attack the other's camp or village. The terminal illustration showed the present position of the ice, in relation to the site and the lakeshore.

Far to the north, photographs showed snow-block igloos of the Eskimos and Eskimos in kiaks hunting seal; the descendants of the original hunters shown in the earlier pictures.

'What do you think?'

Frank stood back and admired Andrew's work. 'I think they're fantastic. You should get an honorary degree for this lot.'

'We've got some new finds too. The students have been working hard over there. The zoology department is doing an identification of the bones they've found.'

'This is going to be a great deal more impressive than I thought it would be. The tepee will have to be as big as Parliament Buildings to house and display this lot properly.'

'Michael's got this idea of mounting a display on the backs of a fleet of trucks so that it can be toured around the schools all over the province.'

'A great man for ideas, our Michael is he not?'

Jesse appeared with coffee. 'I heard about Loretta, I'm sorry.'

Frank took the coffee. 'That's very kind of you, thanks.'

He dialled the University to arrange a meeting with Professor Arnolds for eleven the following morning. Michael came out of the studio and saw him at his desk.

'Nice to see you back. Everything OK?'

'About as OK as its going to get. The funeral was last week as you know; thanks for the flowers, by the way.'

'I thought it only right. You're one of us now. A tragic accident, I understand.'

'Yeah, a tragic accident. Can I have five minutes when you're free?'

Gerald Thorsen came over to say how sorry he was to hear about Loretta and to talk about the project. 'Have you heard, Michael wants to truck-mount the entire show and take it round the country like a bloody travelling circus?'

'Andrew just told me. What do you think?'

'Well, he's the boss but it might lose something if divorced from its surroundings. We'd get more publicity for the Department though so, from our point of view, he might be on to a winner with that idea.'

'I'm inclined to agree with your first point that, divorced from the site, all we have is a few charred sticks, a pile of sand, a fish head and a lot of artwork. Where's the excitement, the attraction for the children? Still, I'm only the new boy here, what do I know?'

'You'll try to talk him out if it then, will you?'

'I'll do my best. I'm going in to see him in a few minutes to discuss progress anyway, I'll allow him to tell me his ideas then.'

CHAPTER FIFTY-THREE

'What do you think, pretty impressive eh?'

'Yeah, I hear they've found some more exhibits. It should make a very impressive display. I wonder if, if it gets much bigger, we should build a permanent cover for it and organise buses to bring the kids from the out of town schools?'

'It's certainly getting too big for just a tepee, however appropriate that idea appeared in the first place. I thought, perhaps, we could mount the entire exhibition on a fleet of flatbed trucks and take it round the Province; easier to move the exhibition than thousands of kids, what?'

'We certainly have to do something impressive with it. Perhaps we could get one of the major commercial companies to sponsor the construction of a permanent hall covering the site. They'd get their two bits worth of publicity and we'd get a free hall, I'm sure you know the right people to talk to.' Frank decided to push his luck, 'perhaps we could get more than one sponsor. I wondered whether the Globe might like to print up the brochures, they could put their name on them somewhere then, they would want to publicise the show to advertise their sponsorship!'

'That might just be a good idea Frank. You're obviously a quick learner, you've been in the department a few weeks and you've picked up the system quick.'

'Well, it's really only an extension of your idea of how to get as much publicity for the scheme as possible and thus, for the Department. I should hate to claim all the credit.'

'You can leave this one with me Frank, we could have a real runner here. I'll get back to you.'

Leaving Michael to rewrite the idea in his own terms, Frank was hailed by Gerald Thorsen. 'How's the idea about flatbeds going?'

'He's had a much bigger idea now. Wants to build a permanent exhibition centre over the site. He's looking for sponsors to cut the costs and get free publicity.'

'Michael's never had an idea in his life but, if you say so, it must be true.' Frank's telephone rang.

'It's Michael, Frank. If we go with this idea of a permanent hall and all that, do we still need your Indian? If we dump the tepee perhaps we should dump your Indian as well?'

'The Indian will get us a lot of publicity Michael, he'll save us a fortune in writing Press Releases. Once the papers get the story that the lectures are to be given by an Indian Chief, they'll have a ball with it, they wont be able to resist a story like that.'

'I suppose you're right but I never did like the Indian.'

'Just let the Press find out that you are a little worried that he'll not keep to the prepared script, depending on whether he agrees with it or not and they'll be down there waiting for him to say something interesting.'

'You just make good and sure that he doesn't say anything too bloody interesting, you hear me? Shit, I'd hoped to get rid of the Indian; untrustworthy the lot of 'em.' Frank went to lunch.

In the cafeteria, Jesse joined him, sliding her tray across from the next table. 'Hi, how's it going?'

Frank looked at his lunch, almost unstarted although he had been sitting there for some time. 'My lunch or my life?'

'Actually, I meant your life. I can see your lunch isn't going at all. You've got to eat you know or you'll waste away and be no use to anybody; and I don't mean Michael.'

'It's a kind offer Jesse but too soon, much too soon.'

'Hell, a girl's got to try. In this life, you don't try, you don't get! That's what my old daddy always told me.'

'Your old daddy was probably right but timing is all, Jesse. Timing.'

'OK. I can wait but don't you leave it too long, you hear. A girl can't hang around forever you know, her knee touched his under the table; and I saw you first.'

'I'll put you at the top of the list Jesse, just as soon as I start my list. OK?'

They talked about the weather, the growing danger of war with Russia, anything but work but neither was really interested; the moment had passed.

Michael buttonholed him as soon as he got back. 'I've spoken to your friend the Governor and he's happy with the idea, just so long as his department doesn't have to pay for it. He says, by the way, that he's had an application for your old job; someone from England, says he knows you! You want to ring him about it? I hope you ain't trying to sell you old job, I don't think the Governor would like that.'

'Hi', Steve said when Frank was put through, 'the funniest thing! We put a notice on the board about a vacancy in the office, yours that is, we haven't decided what to do about Loretta yet. Mac's not sure we need to replace her but the Department has an office manager's job now and it ain't filled. If we don't fill it, we loose it and I'm not sure the Department wants to do that. Anyway, one of the Guards said he had a young nephew over from England looking for a job. Says the lad knows you.'

'What's his name?'

'Peter. Peter Adams. Says he met you on the boat coming over.'

'Don't be ridiculous, the boy's only sixteen or something! You can't let him work in a reformatory at that age, the inmates will have him for breakfast!'

'Well, we could rearrange things a little so he doesn't come into contact with the inmates. He seems a nice enough lad and his uncle's been with us for some time, I'd like to help him out if I can. He told Mac he was eighteen.'

'Well, he's learned to lie a little since I met him, I suppose that's something.'

'If you'll vouch for the lad, I'm inclined to give him a chance. You've got to admit, it takes nerve to emigrate at sixteen, or eighteen for that matter!'

'Give him my regards and tell him I wish him luck.'

'I've had your man Michael whatever on the phone this morning. Is this permanent exhibition hall his real intention or is he just trying it on?'

'It's real enough. His last idea was to dig up half your pit and cart it around Ontario on the back of a fleet of trucks! On the whole, I think this idea is better but I just work here, I'm just the hired help.'

'Call in sometimes Frank, you can see how the lad is getting on. Keep in touch eh?'

Frank put down the telephone. Well, I'll be damned! The kid's got nerve anyway. Must be getting on with his uncle OK or he wouldn't have recommended him, I guess.

Immigration on his mind, Frank wondered whether he should ring the British Embassy in Ottawa about his risk from the Press Gang if he went back to England to see his wife. Tomorrow.

He didn't ring the Embassy, not tomorrow nor on the next tomorrow nor even the next. He made various excuses to himself for this lack of action. He was too busy at the office, he didn't think it likely that they would call him up if he went back just to see his wife, it would all be over by the end of the month.

To himself, he admitted that the truth was that, he was afraid that he might be called back to the colours and he didn't want to go back to the navy and the class-ridden, routine-driven way of life that that represented. He'd gotten used to the freedom of both civilian life and the Canadian form of democracy and he liked it but Loretta still haunted his every night and he had to admit to himself, perhaps she was right.

He must sort out the mess he had left behind. He had wanted God to forgive Loretta her sins, why could he not forgive Alice hers? Who was he to criticise Sister Amelda when he wasn't prepared to do that which he had asked of her? He didn't have to go back to England to sort out the problem, of course, he could write to Alice and tell her where he was and what he intended to do but, that was the problem, he didn't know what he did intend to do. He had no idea. He would have to give it more thought and, meanwhile, he would stay here in Toronto; they could sort out the Berlin problem without his help.

Michael had been busy. The Toronto Globe had agreed to sponsor the provision of printed matter for the exhibition on the condition that they could have their name on it; Michael had of course agreed to this. The province's two major department stores had indicated that they would provide the chairs required for the auditorium, each one to bear the name of the donor organisation.

A local manufacturer of portable buildings, developed from the wartime nissen hut, had indicated that they might be prepared to provide a prefabricated exhibition hall on permanent loan providing their name was clearly displayed both on the hall and in all of the publicity material for the exhibition. You had to hand it to Michael, he obviously did know the right people to talk to and how to approach them. Frank felt secure in his new job and put Europe and the Berlin blockade out of his mind to concentrate on the exhibition.

It was late into June before the news from Europe seriously intruded into Frank's consciousness again. The radio reported, on the eighteenth, that all road, rail and even foot traffic for Berlin was being turned back at Marienborn. The Soviets were insisting that rail and barge traffic would be permitted only under licence of their Soviet Military Authorities.

By the twenty fourth, the Russians had stopped all traffic and cut off the supply of electricity from their sector of Berlin to the other sectors. It was unfortunate that most of the major power stations in the city were in the Russian sector. Western Berlin, it was reported, had food supplies for only thirty six days and power station coal supplies for forty five.

The Soviet Authorities reported that all railway lines into Berlin from the west were closed for technical reasons and would remain closed for an extended period. They were, it was stated, most sorry about this but the technical problems were serious and must be properly dealt with. Berlin was, effectively, blockaded. The Americans and the British instantly instigated a series of supply flights into west Berlin but this was more a show of bravado than a serious attempt to supply Berlin's insatiable demands for food and fuel.

The weekend papers in Toronto reported that, due to post-war selling off of surplus aircraft, the British could, at the moment, supply only six Dakotas each able to lift only two and a half tons of supplies. The Americans could provide just two C54's which, though able to lift ten tons each flight, represented no serious solution to the problem. In the opinion of the writer, the population of Berlin had two choices; submit to the handing over of the whole of west Berlin to the Russians or to remain under the control of the Americans, the British and the French and starve. Why, he asked his readers, should two and half million Berliners prefer starvation under one ex-enemy rather than relatively full bellies under another? Was there, he asked, really a choice?

The Russians were increasing the food supplied to their sector both in quantity and selection in order to encourage the inhabitants of the western sectors to demand that they should be incorporated into the plentifully supplied Soviet Sector.

If the western allies were to hold on to their foothold in Berlin and therefore their credibility, two and a half million Berliners needed to be fed and supplied with food, light and power every day or the whole of west Berlin must inevitably fall into the Russian's hands with an unsupportable loss of face for the three western powers. These western Allies were faced with a problem the solution of which was to everyone clearly impossible. What could the Canadians do to help? Should the Canadians do anything?

On June twenty sixth, Britain's Foreign Secretary issued a Press Statement that, 'Britain stays in Berlin', and, on July first, Canada announced that it had offered to supply dehydrated food for Berlin if the Allies could deliver it. On Monday morning, Frank rang Ottawa.

CHAPTER FIFTY-FOUR

'That was one hell of a relief,' he told Paul and Brenda the following weekend. Frank had fallen into the habit of taking Sunday lunch with them since Loretta's death. He knew he would have to break the habit soon, he couldn't possibly impose upon them for much longer.

'What, exactly, did they say?'

'The Embassy fellow I spoke to said that, as an immigrant I was, as far as they were concerned, now a Canadian and not required to refund any pay I may have received since leaving the service and that I was not required to return to the UK even in the event of a general recall.'

'Do you owe them anything?'

'No. They're bloody awful payers anyway, they stopped everything as soon as I sent them my immigration forms asking for release from the reserve.'

'Doesn't sound unreasonable,' Brenda said, 'then you don't have to go back.'

'No but there's still the other thing. I'm excused party as far as the navy is concerned but Loretta told me to go back and sort out the mess I made with Alice and the child.' He didn't explain that this suggestion had been made since Loretta had died, he wasn't sure that they would understand.

'Will you go back then?'

'Not until I've finished work on the exhibition at the Reformatory. Once that's up and running and Marley is settled in and safe from Michael's desire to dump him, I'll probably shoot back for a week or two, just to square away any lose ends. Who knows, Alice may have found someone else and by now be glad to be rid of me officially.'

Brenda and Paul didn't really approve of divorce but in real life, especially someone else's life, they knew enough not to voice an opinion. It was none of their business.

'You'll have been here a year in a couple of months,' Paul said, 'you could take a month's leave and have time to sort out your other life at your leisure.'

Brenda agreed, 'You should spend some time getting to know your daughter again. Whatever your argument with her mother, the little girl is still your daughter.'

Frank had never explained why he had left Alice nor, indeed, why he had never made any attempt to contact her since his arrival. There was, of course, the question of his relationship with Loretta but they had accepted that without question. After all, both had been friends; you didn't ask friends embarrassing questions. 'Yes, I might do that.'

During the next few weeks, Frank busied himself liaising between the university and the PR department and briefing Marley on the significance of the finds now being made almost daily by the students digging and sifting by the shale pit.

In Berlin, people began to worry seriously about the prospects of survival through the coming winter without sufficient food or heat and, in Chatham, Virginia had another birthday.

Alice Bye, she still used her married name, took up the lease on the Reynolds Hotel in Railway Street, Gillingham and set about making the minor alterations she required to make it attractive to the clientele she wanted to attract. It wasn't the best address in Gillingham but it was convenient for the station. The Royal Engineer's barracks and its electrical school were just at the other end of the High Street, grouped with the NAAFI club and the navy's signal school around the Black Lion field; Prince Arthur Road gave access to the navy dockyard's St. Mary's gate and a sort of back door to the main barracks of HMS Pembroke. The main gate to Pembroke, and to the dockyard, was a short taxi ride away and Alice was satisfied with her choice.

She didn't like the sound of Railway Street but that would have to be endured. Facing the lower exit from the station, the one that saved carrying heavy suitcases up the steps to the main exit and the High Street, was an advantage to the commercial travellers she hoped to attract, at least until they once again had cars as they had before the war.

Ship-borne officers staying or visiting wives staying at the hotel could reach the dockyard via the Gillingham gate at the bottom of the hill, adjacent to Gillingham Pier; itself handy for those joining ships moored in the river.

Unchanged, indeed untouched, since before the war, the hotel was in dire need of redecoration and refurbishment. That, no doubt, was why it had been so cheap. The owners, a first world war Captain from the Royal Engineers and his wife, wanted to retire to the coast and were glad of the sale; Alice recognised the potential of the site and was glad to buy.

The building had been hit by numerous fragments from both German bombs and British anti-aircraft shells returning to earth but the structure was sound and a little paint here and a little plaster there would cover the worst of the sins committed against it. Inside, the decorations were drab and old fashioned.

The French windows of the dining room looked out over the badly overgrown garden. Alice visualised it the way she wanted it. The massively overgrown bushes and three large trees would have to go; she would keep the Rhododendrons, she liked the almost tropical size and colour of their blooms but the majority of the rest would just have to go.

This room would become a lounge with a bar and continental style tables and chairs on a paved area outside the French doors. The high hedge at the end of the garden would ensure sufficient privacy for her guests' comfort. With all these reservists being called back, many bringing their wives down for weekends, it was like it had been during the war, there was business to be had and, there were no air raids!

The position of the hotel, so close to the station, the barracks' and the dockyard was ideal for these clients and, with a little luck and a lot of hard work, she would have her investment back in half the time she had thought originally. She was almost grateful to the Russians who had turned out to be her allies in this project.

Alice had plans for Virginia's education that required money. Virginia was going to have a better start in life than she had had and that had been better than that of many Chatham daughters. Pity about the child's father but that's life. She would have to manage on her own, it had never occurred to her to seek a replacement for Frank. She wondered if he too would be called back but suspected that the navy didn't know where he was either.

She strolled into the other, smaller ground floor rear room. This had been used as a small drawing room. She would keep it as a quiet lounge for guests who liked a little peace and quiet. The main reception rooms of the hotel, and of the private house it had once been, were at the front. The Victorian builders liked to put the best of everything up front, behind large bay windows; she had plans for these too.

The large room to the left of the main entrance would become the restaurant, serving meals to non-residents as well as being the dining room for her guests. It would be difficult with rationing still in force, indeed worse than it had been during the war but a good restaurant and a good hotel, adjacent to the railway station, just had to be a winning combination.

The equally large room opposite she would divide into a large, comfortable reception area, a bit like the lobbies of American hotels she had seen in films, where afternoon tea and an evening drink could be served to residents and non residents alike. Behind the division, in her private office she would be in a position to keep an eye on comings and goings. The basement kitchen needed modernisation and there seemed to be rising damp in the store rooms down there too but that could wait, it was upstairs which excited her most.

The architect responsible for the original conversion from home to hotel had done a good job. The first floor boasted four excellent, large rooms each with an old fashioned but replaceable hand basin and dressing table as well as being fitted with huge wardrobes. All the furniture was big and old fashioned but she would replace it and refurnish these rooms individually, giving each its own style.

The six smaller bedrooms on the second floor were what she considered bread and butter rooms. These were large enough for comfort as singles but useable as rather tight doubles if necessary. She would furnish these with four-foot beds for double, weekend, occupation and as singles for the rest of the week. Most of the guests would be either travelling on their own or company business or serving officers being joined by their wives at the weekends; with luck, she could keep these rooms occupied most of the time.

Clearly, the plumbing arrangements would have to be up-dated but the major pipe work was already there. Initially, it was just a matter of modernising the existing bathroom and toilet; the existing walk-in linen cupboard could be converted into a second toilet without difficulty.

The owner's accommodation was a small flat made by combining what had been the servants' rooms up under the eaves. This was awful! God only knew what the previous owners had been thinking of but that would have to wait. When the builder came tomorrow, she would tell him what she wanted done first. The immediate requirement was the redecoration and refurbishment of the restaurant. This would allow her to earn money whilst the rest of the work went on upstairs. She must find a good chef, ex-navy were best if they hadn't all been called back.

She glanced round the owner's suite again, taking in the full horror of its decoration. That feather bed in the corner had to go! She had no idea what the previous owners had been doing in it since nineteen nineteen but that relic from the first world war would be the first thing removed from the premises.

The thought of war cast a momentary shadow over her outlook. Still, if the present trouble in Berlin developed into a full scale war, the next bomb to fall on Gillingham dockyard would be nuclear and, in that event, she wouldn't have to worry too much about business.

At the moment, the pubs in Chatham and Gillingham were again doing good business with the ever-increasing number of soldiers, sailors and marines being called back from the reserve. Many hated being called back; they had done their share. It was someone else's turn to stand up and be shot at but, as one humorist had pointed out, they were the ones who knew when to duck.

At the Sailors Return, her father offered the same welcome to the lads as he had always done and, in many cases, it was the same lads who had made the Return their local during the war. There were many new faces of course, lads who had joined up after the war as regulars, looking for lots of free travel abroad. They regarded the returning reservists as unfair competition. With all these senior ratings being called back, their chances of promotion were little better than nil.

Alice had often heard this kind of remark in the bar and she remembered Frank telling her what he had been told by an old Chief Yeoman, 'Life ain't fair son, just 'ard!' She told one of the youngsters this. 'Has your old man been called back too then?' He'd never seen any sign of a husband in the bar.

'No, he's in Canada so he's excused party.'

'Lucky bugger. Wish I was somewhere else; even home would be better than this lot.'

Home was Brixton, in south London. He didn't like home much, that was shy he had joined the navy but even

Brixton was better than Chatham and a real possibility of being sent off to war. Peacetime sailoring is what he had joined for, lots of sunny foreign commissions chasing dusky maidens round palm trees. The recruiting posters hadn't mentioned getting killed fighting the bloody Russians in the frozen wastes of the Arctic ocean, that could be uncomfortable!

In a way, the lad reminded Alice of Frank. A nice lad, not like some of the others. A few years ago she thought I might have given him a bosom to cry on but now she was looking at him like a mother. Must be getting old.

She found herself thinking of Frank again, wondering what he was doing. She had let him go too easily, without a fight, she hadn't wanted him to go but much of what he had said was true. She didn't want to spend the rest of her life as her father's barmaid or, as some of her school friends had done, married to some overseas sailor, eking out an existence on a few pounds a week marriage allowance. But, she did regret losing Frank.

In Toronto, Frank helped Marley settle in to the apartment in Bob and Agnes's basement. This convenient arrangement, convenient for all concerned as they needed the rent and he needed a quiet, cheap apartment, had come about as a result of a discussion between Frank and Agnes during a Sunday lunch at Paul and Brenda's.

Bob and Agnes had been invited to lunch, together with Frank as a gesture by Brenda. Frank had said that he couldn't keep on coming over every Sunday and that, grateful as he was, he must start looking after himself. Brenda had decided to make his last Sunday lunch a sort of party. Bob and Agnes were happy to let Marley have the apartment if Frank said it was alright. He was sure he would be OK with the children?

'The kid's will think he's fantastic. He has more stories about the old days than could possibly be true but he tells them well. He'll be perfectly safe with the kids too. He's off the bottle and his only other vice was pinching the bottoms of attractive women or, as he claimed, pinching women's attractive bottoms.'

Bob interjected at this point that the damned Indian had better not pinch Agnes's attractive bottom. He, Bob, had exclusive pinching rights thereto and, in perpetuity, too!

Agnes chose not to become involved in this discussion.

CHAPTER FIFTY-FIVE

The prefabricated exhibition hall was up, the floor covered with green, heavy-duty linoleum contributed by one of the sponsoring department stores. A winding path of equally hardwearing brown linoleum led visitors from the open doors through a series of displays and story boards to the lakeshore 'camp site'.

Here, the finds unearthed by the diggers had been replaced exactly as they had been discovered on a now fully exposed section of beach. Beyond the beach, a lake stocked with real fish extended under the far end wall of the hall. A great deal of care had been taken to ensure that the fish swimming in the lake were the same as the one species still extant from the finds. When required, a hidden projector would throw pictures of approaching canoes on to the wall with a background of the full extent of the lake.

Frank was proud of his association with this highly professional display and, quietly amazed that he had been fortunate enough to be involved with the many professional artists, scientists and public relations specialists responsible for its completion. Every so often, he had to pinch himself to make sure that all of this was quite real.

Just a year ago, or slightly more, he had been an ex-matelot working in the bar of his father in law's pub in Chatham, England; a man who had just discovered that his wife had been unfaithful whilst he had been at sea. A man who's prospects had looked far from rosy, a man who had decided, almost on the spur of the moment to start his life again, to emigrate to a country he knew nothing about and where he would have even less prospects than he had in Chatham. Yet, here he was, largely responsible for all this and, at least to Robert Edward Marley, something of a celebrity.

There was no doubt about it. His old Chief Yeoman at Ganges had been right. 'Bye,' he had said, 'you'll get on. You're too stupid to know it can't be done.' He had been more right than he knew.

He would write to Alice. Ask her if they could meet. Give her a chance to explain. Her couldn't tell her it was Loretta's idea nor that she had been dead at the time, he couldn't tell any one that, they wouldn't understand but once the idea was there, he had realised that Loretta was right. He had to go back. He had to talk to Alice, he would write to her tonight. Loretta would help. She would tell him what to write and how to write it.

He would phone Canadian Pacific this afternoon and book a passage on the first available eastbound sailing; he would pop into their office downtown tomorrow and pay for it. There. The decision was made. He would claim the four weeks holiday he was owed and visit Alice before getting involved in the next project.

'What do you think?' Frank looked round, Michael Stuart was standing behind him, 'what do you reckon? Have we done good or have we done good?'

'We've done extremely good. I had no idea it would turn out as big and grand as this, it's really amazing isn't it!'

Michael drifted off towards a group of workmen putting the finishing touches to one of the exhibits, fussing. In wooded glades, rough timber benches had been placed to accommodate the children whilst their teachers explained the storyboard. On one bench, Frank noticed that someone had scratched 'The Indian was here first', Frank hoped Michael didn't spot it.

Michael had let it be known that Frank had done his part. It now was required that he did no more than stand back and allow Michael to take the credit on behalf of the Department. The Press had been invited in order to provide the politicians with an opportunity to publicise both the exhibition and, more importantly, their own contributions to it. That was the way it was in the real world, Michael had said, politicians control budgets. 'Without budgets, we're all out of a job, OK?'

Frank accepted the truth of what Michael was saying, he knew about the real world, he had just spent five years fighting in it, he wondered idly what Michael had been doing; none of his business, this was the new world not the old. He thought again of Alice. He wondered what she was doing. He wondered if he could persuade her to come to Canada, to make a new life here. Canada was a wonderful country where people were judged and accepted on their merits not their background. A picture of Marley flashed though his mind; unless you're an Indian of course. Indians don't count nor blacks but he hadn't seen more than two of them since he arrived. French speaking Canadians from Quebec were laughed at and disliked here in Ontario and he had, himself, been regarded as a dirty DP, one of the millions of Europe's 'Displaced Persons' when he had first arrived; Canada wasn't perfect but, such inconsistencies notwithstanding, it was a wonderful country, they could do well here.

It was true he realised, he hadn't met a single genuine DP amongst the people he knew. He wondered what happened to them. Had they been absorbed into the Canadian mass or where they still Displaced Persons, transported from the ruins of Europe to a new country that they didn't understand a land into which they didn't fit? Hell, it was none of his business, he had fitted in and Alice, on the other hand, was his business, she and Virginia.

He thought of his childhood in the Dr. Barnardo's home. They had been trained well, given a trade or, like him, apprenticed into the army or the navy as Boys. What more did they expect? Frank had learned more in the year he had been in Canada than he had realised. Not the straight forward things like how to behave, he had learned that years ago, watching his Officers, watching films, keeping his eyes open when ashore, reading, reading and more reading. Since he had been here however, he had learned by unconscious absorption from those around him. They had behaved what they regarded as naturally and Frank had fitted in.

In England he had been brought up to know his place, he couldn't go back to that. If he went back to England, it was England that was going to have to change, not he! In Canada, nobody was anybody so everybody was somebody!

The Press conference and Grand Opening of the exhibition went off without a hitch exactly as he knew it would, Michael would have accepted nothing less. Michael had ensured that everyone thought that they were getting special treatment; that they were someone special, the most important guest there that day.

One of the journalists asked Michael why the exhibition had been mounted backwards, starting at the present time at the door and working back to the fossils found on the beach? Professor Arnolds took the question.

In his experience, it was asking too much of young children to make the mental leap backwards of about ten thousand years in order to start at the beginning of the story. By starting at the present, a time that the children recognised and understood, it was a simple matter to take them back through the ages in a logical series of easily manageable steps.

'We grown ups sometimes forget that our children don't know all the things that we have spent a lifetime learning They are just beginning to learn and, if they are to understand what is presented to them, it has to be fed to them in understandable bites of intelligence; each bite explained and illustrated before the next one is presented. In that way,' he said, 'a firm foundation to learning is laid down upon which they would be able to add other bites until, eventually, they would know everything, like us.'

He gratefully acknowledged the laugh that followed this pronouncement.

'Where's the Indian?'

'Yeah, where's the Indian?'

The first to ask this question represented the leading Toronto newspaper; a man with a reputation as a tough, no nonsense journalist, a man who could be relied upon to ask the questions about Marley's qualifications. Michael had been dreading this possibility; damn the Indian!

'I'm afraid that Chief Littlehorse didn't expect to be required at this function and I imagine that he is busy swotting up at home. If you have any questions of a technical nature, I'm sure that Professor Arnolds can be relied upon to answer them.' Michael looked over to the Professor, hoping that he would take up the proffered baton. Frank whispered in the Professor's ear.

'I'm afraid that, if it's a question of Indian matters or history, I'm totally unqualified to answer you but, I understand that Mr Marley, who is the expert in this field, has now arrived and will be happy to take your questions.'

Dressed in a dark business suit with white shirt and blue and silver striped tie, his steel grey hair brushed back from his high forehead, Marley gave the impression of being a successful businessman or, perhaps, one of Professor Arnolds' associates. 'Perhaps someone would like to pose a specific question?'

'Nah! I just wanted to see the Indian.'

Marley smiled down at him from the podium. 'I am the Indian.'

The silence lasted a very long minute before the man spoke. 'Guess that puts me in my place, eh?'

One or two other journalists made jokes at his expense, about his not being able to recognise an Indian if he wasn't standing outside a cigar store.

Marley introduced himself and apologised for being unable to meet them all before the conference started but, as Mr Stuart had reported, he had had another appointment that could not be postponed. Happily, he had been able to get away earlier than had been expected.

Michael took the microphone and asked if anyone had any questions and, receiving no response, closed the conference and insisted that they should all join in the destruction of the drinks and nibbles laid out in the marquee to the left of the exhibition hall exit. He ushered the dignitaries through the crush, leaving Marley to follow up the rear or, preferably, not to.

CHAPTER FIFTY-SIX

Michael was his usual smiling self. Yesterday's grand opening had passed off very well and his hand had been shaken warmly by all the politicians and dignitaries as they had been escorted to their cars.

In the office, those concerned had congratulated themselves and each other on the success of the event and assured each other that the exhibition would get a very good Press and attract visitors from schools all over the Province. Who knew? Perhaps other Provinces would want to copy the idea and employ Toronto as consultants; that would be a feather in their cap, wouldn't do their careers any harm either.

'I liked the Indian' Jesse told Frank 'but, I should keep him out of Michael's way for a while. He doesn't like being upstaged.'

Marley had gone straight to the hall, rearranging the exhibits disturbed by the Press. Instinct had warned him that this might not be a good morning to be in the office.

Michael poked his head out of his office door. 'Frank. You want to come in when you've finished your coffee?'

Talk had swung over to the news of the morning. The previous day, seven thousand tons of food and fuel had been flown into Berlin by one hundred and forty four British flights and six hundred and fifty American.

'Pretty fantastic, ain't it' someone said 'but apparently still less than half what was shipped in daily before the blockade. What'll happen when winter sets in?'

Everyone turned to Frank, he was the only one who knew anything about Europe.

'I don't know and I don't want to be there to find out.'

'Will we get dragged into another European war?'

Gerald Thorsen drained his coffee noisily. 'I think we should sit this one out for the first couple of years, selling food and equipment to the Yanks. It's their turn to start things off this time.'

Michael's head reappeared through the doorway, Frank saw him. 'On my way, Michael.'

'I'm sure you can understand my position, indeed, the position into which the Department has been put. It could have been extremely embarrassing, had that journalist decided to get upset at your Indian taking the piss like that. W're not accustomed to upity Indians.'

'I am the Indian! Where the hell does he get off talking like that to a man who could, in a single paragraph, render all our efforts worthless. I had told the conference that he wasn't there. You should have made sure he didn't pop up like some damned rabbit out of a hat. It made me look as if I wasn't in control of the event.'

'Public relations Frank is about control, if it's about anything. In a case like this, we exhibit what we want people to see the way we want them to see it. We invite the Press we want, to ask the questions we want asked so that our experts can provide the answers we want printed. We do not, repeat not, want some damn Indian standing up and inviting questions from all and sundry!'

'I'm sure you understand my position. Hell, even the Mayor asked me what the hell the guy was doing there. His job is to lecture the kids, not to shoot his mouth off to the Press and embarrass the Department. And, I can tell you, the Mayor's none too keen on him talking to the kids without an approved script, either. Who knows what crap he'll tell them.'

'I'm sure you understand that I had to assure the Mayor that I would make certain that it couldn't happen again. That, in future, there was no possibility of some junior member of the department embarrassing its sponsors or the Mayor's office.'

Frank knew what was coming. Even before Michael stood up and walked round the desk and perched in a

371

friendly manner, looking down at him, he knew Marley was fired.

Michael looked suitably grave. 'I'm sure you will have no trouble finding a job more suited to your undoubted talents, one in which you are, shall we say, less constrained by the necessity to support and follow the Departmental line.

'I shall, of course, be happy and proud to write you a glowing reference and to assure the head of your next department that you have an original mind, one of great imagination.' He walked back to the other side of his desk and sat down. 'I'm sure that you understand that, sometimes it is necessary to sacrifice the few to save the many. The Mayor agreed that the Indian has to stay if we are to avoid looking pretty stupid but he was your responsibility. I was most specific in telling you to keep him out of the way.'

He shuffled the papers on his desk. Frank's silence, his lack of any response upset him. Frank should have been yelling at him by now, what was with this guy? He was just sitting there, smiling.

'I'm not firing you, you understand, I wouldn't do that to anybody but your function here was to organise the exhibition site. You have done that and my budget cannot stand two supernumeraries; I'm sure you understand that. The Indian has to stay so, Frank, I'm afraid you have to go. I'm sure that Personnel will have no trouble finding you something you will enjoy.

I understand that you were thinking of visiting the UK now that your part in this project is complete? I think perhaps you should. I'll arrange for you to have a couple of weeks study leave added to your holiday entitlement so that you can have a good long rest over there.'

'I've had a word with the Press guys, told them that, now that this project is up and running, you are going back to Europe to check your position as a naval reservist although, as a Canadian resident, you don't need to do so. They liked that, you'll leave a hero.'

Frank had never been fired before but he was in no doubt that he had just watched a bravura performance, the only thing Michael hadn't done was cry. In his third ear, Frank heard his old Chief reminding him again; no one said life has to be fair, son.

He left Michael's office with a half smile on his face at the thought; the old bastard was righter than he knew.

'Michael's just OK'd a few extra weeks leave so I'm going to push off this afternoon, before he thinks of another project for me to do.'

Frank's announcement was greeted with surprised looks from those who knew that the project was barely off the ground and that there would be a great deal more to do before it could safely be put on to the back burner.

'Where'll you go? Florida?'

'What's the hurry? What's wrong with the end of the week?'

'Who'll look after your Indian?'

Frank parried the first two questions and answered the third. 'I reckon the Chief can look after himself from here on in. All he has to do is keep the kids entertained and, hopefully, teach them something. Who knows, he might even give them a whole new slant on Canadian history; from the bottom up!'

In the exhibition hall, Marley had done all that needed to be done and had decided that home offered a better prospect than driving downtown for about an hour and then driving back. He closed up the hall, pocketed the keys and wandered over to the Guardhouse to hand them in.

'How's life on the outside, Chief?'

Like all the guards, Brown had fallen into the habit of calling him Chief now that he was the official Indian.

'Seems like an anti-climax now that all the hard work's been done and all I have to do is try to teach the kids some history. Keep an eye on the hall will you, I should hate to see it burn down before I've had a chance to change the way the kids see my ancestors.' He started to walk towards his car, stopped, changed his mind and returned. 'Can I use your phone? I think I'll drop in on Frank on the way home, I think I've just had a couple of good ideas.'

Frank told him about his meeting with Michael with entirely predictable results.

'Don't be daft,' Frank told him. 'If you resign, Michael will have got away with a clean sweep and all the credit for the project. He didn't dare fire you, you're news. You stay, as a thorn in his side.'

I'll be more than that, I'll be a constant irritation, like a tic under his skin. He can scratch but if he tries to get me out I'll go and have a chat with that guy from the Globe. It could be quite fun. Headline; Popular Indian lecturer fired. The kids would write letters saying they liked the old fellow, he was more fun than school.'

'How do you know the kids are going to like your lectures?'

'Cos, I'm going to make good and damn sure that they do! It's a unique opportunity to rewrite history, to tell it the way it really was.'

'You don't know the way it really was, you ain't old enough.'

'The kids don't know that. To them I'm old, same as you.'

'Well Chief, I wish you luck. I'm off to England for a few weeks leave and to sort out one or two minor problems over there. I'll give you a call when I get back, we can have a drink and a chat.'

'You take care now, you don't want to be over there when the war starts.'

'There isn't going to be a war, providing the Yanks, the Brits and the Frogs stick together. Russia can't afford another major war so soon after the last one. A compromise will be found. Anyway, you've got no problem, Canada won't be involved this time unless you volunteer and I can't see you doing that again so soon.'

'You might be right but you carry your return ticket with you at all times and start running at the first shot!'

The telephone rang; it was Paul. 'I hear you're taking extended leave. If you're still here on Sunday, why don't you come over for a meal. We'll invite some of the others; make it a bit of a going away party.'

'Thanks Paul, sounds like fun.'

'Why don't you bring Marley with you, if he wants to come? He's one of us now that he's no longer one of them.'

'I'll ask him, he's here.'

'Yes, I know. The word has gone round about your meeting with Michael. I rang the exhibition hall to speak to the Chief but the guard said he had gone but was looking in on you on the way home. Thought I could kill two birds with one stone.'

'On the whole, I'd rather you picked another phrase. I've already been killed once today.'

He checked with Marley. 'OK. See you on Sunday and, Marley says thanks.'

'Tell him, he's welcome.'

CHAPTER FIFTY-SEVEN

Brenda was in the kitchen doing things to the lunch and Paul was handing round the drinks.

'What do we call you now? Marley's too formal, you don't look like a Bob and anyway, we have one already.'

'Why don't you call me Chief, I'm used to it and it will save any confusion.'

There were too many of them to sit down for lunch, Brenda had laid on enough beer to keep the party going for some time and almost everybody had brought something in a bottle. Chief had arrived clutching a large bottle of water, clearly marked Medicinal Alcohol; then gone back to his car for a crate of beer that he had acquired somehow without going to a Government Liquor Store where he wouldn't have been served. With his record, he was banned from buying alcohol legally.

'Will you be keeping on Loretta's apartment? I wondered what you would do now that Chief has your old apartment in our basement. I can't throw him out. You never know, he might just save us from being scalped by the next raiding party that comes this way.'

'I'm going back to the UK to sort out one or two minor personal problems over there. I'm sailing on the Empress of Britain next week. I've no idea when I'll be back but I'll keep on the apartment anyway. When I do get back, of course, I'll be looking for a job and I'll need the apartment.' He hadn't meant to bring up the subject of looking for a job for fear of embarrassing his friends but it passed without comment. 'I'll sort something out when I get back.'

The difficult bit of the party was over. Frank's future had been mentioned and the discussion had passed on to other things. Brenda was glad. She had been worrying about it since Paul had thrown out the invitations. She thought Frank was handling it all very well; he must be very annoyed at least and probably very worried. She looked at him, talking to Agnes and Bob, no sign of anything troubling him, his expression was one of simple enjoyment. She wondered how Paul would take it if he got fired. Best not to even think about it.

Compared with Frank, Paul had led a sheltered life. A good home, loving parents, a short spell in the army without leaving the safety of Canada and a good, steady job with the Provincial Government since. Married and settled, that described Paul but then, he had never really been unsettled, had he? Still, she wondered how Frank really felt; it hadn't been a good year.

First there had been the business of coming over from the old country and trying to fit in, then there was Loretta and now this. 'You have to admire his control.'

'Eh?'

She hadn't meant to say it out loud. She turned to Chief who was standing beside her a stick of celery in one hand and a glass in the other.

'I never know what to do with this celery when I'm not actually eating it. '

'You stick it in the breast pocket of your jacket, that's why you should always wear a jacket to a party.'

'You have to admire whose control?'

'Frank's. I was just thinking, it hasn't been a very good year for him has it, yet there he is, chatting and laughing as if he didn't have a problem in the world.'

'Perhaps he thinks like an Indian. Women are allowed to grieve publicly but it's different for a man. The war will have taught him to grieve inside where it won't show and upset other people.'

'But now he's going back to Europe, just when they're about to start another war. Why doesn't he stay here where it's safe and he has friends?'

'I don't know him well enough to answer your question but perhaps he now knows how to solve the problems he left over there and is going back to do that. As his friends, we can only support him in whatever he decides to do. I owe him. Without Frank, I'd still be a drunken Indian trying to get myself rearrested every winter; whatever he decides is OK with me.' He held his glass of water up to the light, looking through it. 'I'm talking too much; better switch to lemonade.'

He wandered off in search of lemonade or, possibly, just away from Brenda. He had talked altogether too much. He was showing his feelings. Damn them, they were making a white man out of him!

Perhaps, when Frank got back from Europe, he would ask him if he'd like to meet his father. The old man would be proud to shake the hand that had been held out in friendship to his wayward son.

'When's the first lecture?'

Paul had seen him standing alone and had come over and been joined by Bob

'Next Monday afternoon. Bob and Agnes's kid's school insisted on being the first group as it was all their idea anyway.'

Bob nodded. 'That's the trouble with life. By this time next month, no one will even remember that Frank was involved.' He noticed that food was low and he went off in search Brenda. It was time to offer coffee too.

He tapped on the side of his glass to attract attention. 'Folks. There's coffee on the table and a few goodies left to be eaten but, before you fall upon them like wolves, I'd like to propose a toast. To Frank, don't stay over there for too long.' The coffee disappeared and, shortly after that, the people.

Frank had paid up the rent on the apartment for three months and arranged for half a dozen boxes of Loretta's things to be collected for charity. Just one item of hers remained unpacked. He would add her nightdress to the box when he left but not before, it was his last, tenuous, connection with her. When he left the apartment, when he left Canada, he would leave that too and return to sleeping naked as he had done for so many years; he knew she would understand.

378

CHAPTER FIFTY-EIGHT

It seemed strange to be doing it again. The urgent, throbbing beat of the ship's engines beneath his feet brought on a well remembered feeling of suppressed, no, controlled excitement.

This time though, it was a bit like playing musical chairs; when the engine's rhythm finally stopped, would there be anywhere for him to sit? Would Alice let him come back into her life?

What did he want of her? He wasn't sure. Did he want her to forget the past and come to Canada with him or did he want her to release him so that he could return to Toronto with a clear conscience?

One way or the other, he had to clear the decks, clear his feeling of guilt at having abandoned Alice and Virginia his daughter. He was sure now that she was his although he knew no more now than he had a year ago. What would Alice say? Would she even speak to him after the way he had simply walked out of her life and that of their daughter?

It had all seemed so simple then, when anger and injured pride had dictated his actions but now, after all this time, he was less sure that he had been right to leave them as he had; worse, to have found another love 'though, God knew, he could not regret one moment of his love for Loretta. It was alright for Loretta, she was dead. She had told him to make his peace with Alice but would Alice make her peace with him?

He stood on the promenade deck alone yet surrounded by people watching the narrow stretch of water between the ship and the shore widen. Though she had been dead for more than two months, Loretta was with him constantly. In the privacy of their bed, he argued with her, told her that to return to England and Alice was not that

379

simple; that it was not just a matter of buying a steamer ticket; he couldn't just walk in on Alice and say guess what, sweetheart, I'm back

He had said too much, she had done too much. She had been unfaithful but, God knew how many wives and sweethearts had been that. Hell, Loretta had said, there was a war on, everyone had done things they might otherwise not have done. He had, himself been instrumental in killing hundreds of young German submariners; Alice, God help her, had shown only kindness. On the whole, Loretta had argued, Alice's was the more Christian act.

He'd been no virgin when they had met and there had been no suggestion that she had been unfaithful to him after they had married so, she had argued, what was his problem? It lacked logic and, she had argued, who was he to judge her? God would judge Alice as she herself had now been judged.

The wind coming off the river was chill, making him shiver. He was on a fool's errand. He was sailing across the Atlantic ocean at the suggestion of a dead mistress to beg forgiveness from a deserted wife! It was insane.

He had loved Alice without limit, without thought of any other future but that of being together until death did them part. Yet, he had denied her his love, withdrawn his recognition of her as his wife and for why?

Because, before she had become his wife, she had given herself to another man, if the stories were true, to other men.

She had broken no vows, she had done nothing that many others had done for far less reason, she had brought him nothing but a little embarrassment whilst others had brought their husbands nameless bastards to support. For that he had cast her out of his life; left her with his child and without support. What sort of man was he?

He glanced at the shore, surprised at how distant it was. The light was fading, the evening chill.

What had Alice told the child? How had she explained his disappearance? He had just walked out of their life, he had deserted a child of two, why should Alice take him back? Why should she even discuss the possibility? She would not. She should not. He glanced about him at the now deserted deck, where was Loretta when he needed her support?

CHAPTER FIFTY-NINE

This time, he was sharing a cabin with just one other, a fellow immigrant going home for a holiday to show off how well he had done. He didn't think he liked the fellow but it didn't matter; he could have shared a cabin with the Devil himself for a few days, it would be luxury compared with the fuggy, damp, for'ard lower messdeck on some old destroyer.

His cabin-mate was sitting at the small dressing table counting money when he arrived. Frank said sorry and made to leave.

'Don't leave on my account, its only money.'

'I didn't mean to barge in on you like that. Clearly you want to be alone. I can come back later, I was only going to change, it can wait.'

'You can do whatever you like mate. You going home on holiday or have you decided that Canada's no place for a civilised Englishman?'

Frank told him that he was going home on holiday. He liked Canada. The other grinned. 'Bloody marvellous place ain't it? You've never seen so many dumb bastards all in one place at one time. Get a good job, did you?'

Frank saw no reason to tell him that he'd been fired. Anyway, the Vets' Office would find him another when he got back. 'Yeah, I got a job I didn't know existed 'til I got it.'

'Where was that?'

'Just outside Toronto.'

'Me, I'm a cop. You wouldn't believe it. They queue up to bribe you here. You only have to look as if you're going to give them a parking ticket or an on the spot fine for jaywalking and they're there with the money in their hands. Now, I'm sure that we can come to some amicable arrangement about this, eh Officer? Am I not right? They practically push the money into your pockets.' He didn't give Frank time to think of a response to this. 'Yeah but the best scam is the domestic call out. You know, when some guy beats up on his wife and she calls the cops.'

'Well, it's only natural ain't it? In a small town like Toronto, the guy doesn't want his name in the paper for giving his wife a duffing up, so he slips you fifty to log it as a malicious call out. You know, like when someone calls the cops to get back at a neighbour who's upset them; happens all the time. So, you pocket the fifty and report a false call; money for old rope!'

Frank wasn't sure that he wanted to hear this. In his mind's eye, he could see the Auxiliary Police card in his wallet. Was this what the real police were like? Not the few he'd met but what did he know?

'I'm going home for a couple of weeks to my old man's funeral but I'll open a bank account while I'm over then I can just send money over to my mum to bank for me instead of trying to hide it in Canada. You never know who's got their eye on you in the police force and, I'd hate to lose it all to some sharp eyed Lieutenant who can get me canned for taking a bribe.'

Frank found himself involved in the story whether he liked it or not. 'But, surely, he would have to hand in any money he found?'

'Don't be half baked! He pockets most of it and hands in just enough to make the charge stick. When you claim that he has ripped you off, the Captain just laughs and makes sure that he gets his cut from the Lieutenant but you end up inside. Very bad for discipline is taking bribes; no choice, have to make an example of you, and all that. But it ain't going to happen to me, I'm too smart for 'em.'

Frank believed him. 'You'd better put that in a safe place like the ship's safe until we get to Liverpool. I don't want anyone thinking I've stolen it if any goes missing on the way over.'

'I ain't letting no one know what I've got here, mate.'

'You don't have to. Just ask the Purser for an envelope, fill it, seal it and hand it back for lodging in the ship's safe. They don't want or need to know what's in it, it's none of their business. And, I'll feel a lot happier if that lot isn't lying around down here for someone to steal.'

'You're sure it'll be safe?'

'Look at it this way mate, either you put that lot in the ship's safe or I go to the Purser and ask for a cabin change because my present cabin-mate has a stash of Dollar bills in the cabin and I don't want to be accused of stealing it.'

'You wouldn't tell them that, would you?'

'You'd better believe it sunshine. The money goes or I do.'

'OK, I'll put it in the fucking safe then.' He slipped a rubber band round the last wad. 'Twenty thousand, not bad for one year eh?'

'I don't want to know, don't tell me.'

They walked together to the Purser's office and Frank watched as the notes were stuffed into the large brown envelope out of the Purser's sight. 'There you go, do I get a receipt for this?'

'Certainly Sir, of course. The Purser handed him a receipt. Will there be anything else, Sir?'

'No ta. Just don't you run off with that little lot, I'll be back for it when we hit The Pool.' The glass shutter slammed shut. 'Touchy bugger ain't he?'

Frank changed for dinner. Evening dress was not normal in tourist but a dark suit or blazer seemed to be in style. Happily, his cabin-mate was not on the same table so he was able to keep out of his way.

For some days, the north Atlantic had been doing its own thing, that which it did best, making everyone uncomfortable. Frank was unsurprised to see that out of something like six hundred passengers, less than half had had the nerve to risk the dining room or any of the other enclosed spaces. Many walked up and down or sat, shivering under rugs, on the promenade deck, unwilling or unable to leave the fresh air of the outdoors for the mugginess of the indoors.

The majority he suspected were tucked up in their bunks waiting, as was his cabin-mate, for the end of the world or the end of the voyage and caring little which came first. It would be alright by the time the Eve of Docking Party started later tonight. By then, they would be well inside the north passage between Ireland and the mainland and the ship would be stable enough for anyone, by the following morning, they would be docked in Liverpool.

Frank was right, almost everyone was back on their feet by the time the party started. From the look of them, now, no one would have known how sick some of them had been. Standing in line to be welcomed by the Captain or the First Officer, they all looked a hundred Dollars.

The First Officer recognised the navy tie Frank was wearing. 'Where did you serve?'

'Around here mainly!'

'This trip will have been a doddle for you then. What ships?'

Frank named a few.

'I remember Comus. We were detached, carrying Canadian soldiers over for D-Day, she was searching for survivors from a torpedoed merchantman. Bloody glad we were to know she was there, trying to help. Nasty things submarines, never did like them, not even ours. There's something essentially dishonest about sneaking about under the water like that.'

'Wasn't over fond of them myself.'

'Well, I hope you've had a good trip over Will you be going back?'

'Oh yes. Just taking a holiday. Sorting out some personal business.'

'Then we may see you on the way back. Good luck.'

His eyes were already on the next passenger in the line. Frank heard her voice trilling.

'So exciting! So thrilled to meet you Captain.'

The poor bloke has to do this every trip, Frank thought. He noticed that he didn't bother to explain that he wasn't the Captain, it would have spoiled her evening.

For this buffet dinner, everyone could select any seat they wished and Frank found himself seated next to a woman of what he had seen described in books as being 'of a certain age'.

'Isn't this just so exciting?' She enveloped Frank in her smile. 'Who'd have guessed that so many people would be seasick on such a big boat. Isn't this arrangement so much more chummy though? I hate being all formal, don't you?'

'Alas Madam,' Frank explained, 'formality is a major part of my life. Under normal circumstances, I am the Verger of St. Christopher's Upper Tooting, that's in London, you know. However, I'm sure you're right, this is much more chummy than the normal arrangements.'

She looked at him, trying to decide whether he was joking. Unsure, she turned to the man seated on her left. 'Isn't this just so much more fun?'

The man's wife lent across him to reply. 'Isn't it just.'

For a moment, Frank almost felt sorry for her. She was only trying to make friends; he half smiled at her. It was a mistake

Her hand rested on his with the slightest of pressure. 'I do so like to have someone to talk to when I'm travelling, you see, it's what I do since my husband died.' The pressure on his hand increased. 'It was so sad, you see, all those years he had worked and worked. All through the war, poor dear and then, almost as soon as it was over, he died. The doctors said it was overwork you know. Still it left me nicely provided for so now I just travel round the world wherever my fancy takes me.'

Frank rescued his hand and reached for the salt. 'I imagine you have to be a little careful who you talk to though. It wouldn't do to get involved with the wrong sort of man, it might not be safe.'

'Oh you little darling. The only men worth talking to are the wrong sort, they're so much more fun than the other kind.' Remembering that Frank had told her he was a Verger, she had the decency to blush. 'Oh but what can you think of me?' Her knee pressed against his. 'I'm sure I shall be quite safe with you, I've never met a Verger before. What exactly does a Verger do?'

Frank had no idea. 'I advise those on the verge of marriage that they might be about to make a terrible mistake.'

'I knew you were the wrong sort the moment I set eyes on you! You're a wicked, wicked man, I can always tell.'

For most of the meal, Frank could feel her knee pressing ever harder against his; twice, her hand slipped beneath the table and gave his thigh a gentle squeeze. 'Isn't this just the most fun you've ever had?'

Frank was tempted to say no but he hadn't the heart. He would escape after dinner and, with luck, breakfast would be served on the formal seating plan used previously and he would be able to avoid her; they would be docking tomorrow morning. He was not at all sure that he wanted to reach England. Her foot pressed down on his toe. 'Do you think anyone would mind if we had just a little more wine?'

Frank caught the eye of a passing steward and nodded towards her glass. The steward grinned at him as he poured wine up to the brim of the glass, ensuring thereby that some of it spilled on to the table.

'So sorry, Sir, Madam. The ship must have rolled just as I poured.'

Frank smiled at him. 'They do, you know, it's the nature of the beast but, don't you worry about it son, you'll get used to it.'

The steward glared at him.

'Oh you shouldn't have been nasty to him, he didn't mean to be rude.'

'Yes he did.'

He had no idea why he had snapped at the steward. So the steward had been trying to be smart, one of the bolshie ones, thought that, as they were almost home, he could be rude to the passengers and get away with it; well, not this time he hadn't.

The dinner was over and they rose from the table together.

'Perhaps I can escort you somewhere?'

'Oh, you naughty man, what a thing to suggest.'

Her arm slid through his as she lurched ever so slightly, suggesting that her control might have been effected by the wine. 'I'm sure that, if I was a good girl, I should go straight to my cabin but, I think I would like to go somewhere else first. What would you suggest?' The disappointment showed on her face for just an instant as Frank led her to the crowded bar and went in search of drinks.

She looked about her but couldn't see him anywhere. A steward placed a large gin and Italian on the table in front of her. 'The gentleman asked me to bring this for you, Madam.'

'But, where is the gentleman?'

'The Gentleman said that he was feeling a little sea sick, madam and asked me to tell you that he had returned to his cabin.'

'Thank you.' She fished in her bag and drew out a shilling tip.

Shit! He had reckoned on at least a Dollar from this one. He smiled at her and expertly slipped the coin into his pocket. Never mind, the gentleman had already given him one.

Monday morning. Liverpool bay looked much as it had always looked to Frank, grey, sullen and not particularly clean. He couldn't actually see it but he had the impression that the shallow water only just covered a hundred years of deposited effluent from Liverpool, Birkenhead and all those towns upstream. Industrial, commercial and domestic, sooner or later, it all found its way out into Liverpool bay. The sky mirrored the greyness of the sea. Low, scudding clouds bringing up sudden, heavy showers of rain; God was trying to wash the bay clean; He was on to a loser. Far astern, the Isle of Man lay only just visible above the horizon. To the south, Anglesey grew larger as the miles between them shortened.

Through his feet, Frank could feel the ship's engines, far down in the bottom of the ship, turning the shaft, driving the ship towards port and her regular destination. Of their destination itself, there was ask yet no sign.

Approached from the north, Liverpool docks are hidden behind Formby point and, from the south, by Birkenhead on the spit of land dividing the Mersey from the Dee; long before Liverpool itself came in site, the Mersey Pilot would be taken onboard.

Frank had never liked Liverpool. To his mind, the indigenous population was a collection of pimps, muggers and dockland thieves who had always regarded jolly Jack as just one more pocket to be picked; one more wallet to be lifted.

This wasn't true, of course. For the vast majority of the population, Liverpool was the second most bombed city in England but, for the villains, Royal navy or merchant marine, it was all the same to them, the war would have been like Christmas every day. Thousands of tired Jacks, happy just to have survived one more crossing of the U-boat pond, delivered to Liverpool's door by a benevolent, if slow witted, Admiralty. Sheep to be shorn! Thank God the war was over.

He had heard on the ship's broadcast of the BBC's World Service that Chatham dockyard was going to refurbish and preserve HMS Cavalier, the last of the general purpose, emergency class destroyers, as a memorial to all the young Jacks that had died in ships like her. He liked the idea, he had known many of them. She would be like Nelson's Victory in Portsmouth Dockyard, a living memorial.

This time, he would be in Liverpool for only a couple of hours. Just long enough to check through customs and immigration then on to the train for London and Chatham. He couldn't get away soon enough, too many memories.

CHAPTER SIXTY

The cold, rain-sodden wind penetrated his coat and, in time, his train of thought. He shook himself, much as a dog might and went below into the warmth of the bar. Even at this time in the morning it was full of people buying each other drinks or just wishing each other good fortune when they got off the ship. He forced his way up to the bar, ordering a large whisky, noticing that the steward had a Scouse accent. Funny, he hadn't noticed it before.

Soon, he would go down to the warmth of the cabin and finish packing his things. Only soap, toothbrush and razor remained unpacked, waiting for just one last attempt at cleanliness before gong ashore. In the cabin, his cabin mate sat at the vanity unit, once more counting Dollar bills. Correct, he returned them to the envelope and looked for somewhere to hide it. Too big to be carried in his pocket, the envelope would have to be hidden, safely within a shirt or some other item of clothing in the suitcase.

Suppose the Customs Officer found it? Would he insist on it being opened? Would he want to know how he had come by so much money? Cash type money! Hell. He opened the envelope again and separated the notes into four piles; one for each of the inside pockets of his jacket and two more for his trouser pockets. So, they bulged a bit? So what?

He left the jacket unfastened; that looked better, no bulges, he would be wearing a raincoat when he left the ship anyway.

Frank was watching this, watching him examining himself in the mirror. 'You look like a pickpocket's dream. That jacket's hanging about you as if you had ton weights in it. Look how the front gapes, must be something stuffed into the inside pockets; its just got to be worth a dip's time to find out what it might be.'

'I've got to hide it somewhere.'

'Why? As you said, it's only money, there's no law says you can't carry as much money about with you as you like, is there? Not coming in to England, anyway. I know you can't take it out with you but this is different.'

'If I put it in this case, won't the Customs man want to know why?'

'Tell him you don't trust banks. He doesn't have to believe you, it's none of his business. Just don't let go of the suitcase for a moment, not in Liverpool!'

'Thanks mate. I thought you didn't approve of me.'

'I don't. I just dislike Liverpool more. I've been rolled here a few times in the past.'

Frank turned to the washbasin and ran the hot water to shave; the water was cold. They were back in England or, at least, under its influence. He had almost forgotten just how bad things were in the UK, he couldn't fathom why this should influence a Canadian Pacific ship but that's life. He knew he had made a terrible mistake coming back, he just knew it. His cabin mate handed him an envelope. 'The steward brought this down for you earlier, I forgot, sorry.'

Even folded, he knew who the cable was from, who it must be from; she was the only person who knew he was aboard. He swallowed, forcing the fear back down to where his stomach muscles could control it. He had known all along that there would be a moment, a split second, between meeting Alice and knowing whether he had done the right thing in coming back. A moment in which, without either of them speaking, they would both know if there was any chance of a joint future for them but, he had never thought of this. He hadn't thought of her sending him a cable to the ship. That was unfair; aboard the ship he couldn't defend himself.

He contracted the stomach muscles and breathed in, unfolding the cable form. His pent up breath exploded, expelling the fear it had been suppressing. The cable was short, just four words.

'WELCOME HOME fullstop ALICE'

For a moment, less than a moment, just for a fraction of a moment, he felt Loretta beside him then she was gone and he knew that she had gone forever.

Lightning Source UK Ltd.
Milton Keynes UK
UKHW010737100522
402764UK00004B/538